NIAGARA ODYSSEY

by Ruth Zavitz

Chronicler
Publishing

Edmonton, Alberta, Canada

ii

Other books by Ruth Zavitz

High on Grass

Flight to the Frontier

Niagara Odyssey is a sequel to **Flight to the Frontier**

E-mail: rzavitz@execulink.com

iii

Chronicler Publishing

For information address:
Chronicler Publishing
402 17150 94A Avenue
Edmonton
Alberta, Canada, T5T 6L7
www.chroniclerpublishing.com

ISBN: 9781928106074

CHAPTER 1

Phoebe Trevlyn shifted on the hard bench as the wagon jolted over the stony trail along the Niagara River. William whimpered and she hugged him close, stroking his cheek to quiet him. Poor little mite, he too was exhausted. They'd left Fort Erie before daybreak, stopped at a tavern above the falls for dinner, but it would be full night before they arrived at Newark at the river's mouth. She looked ahead, hoping to see the houses of the town. She couldn't stand much more of this jolting.

The English government had designated Newark as the capital of the newly created Upper Canada. Her Richard had been transferred from Fort Erie to help prepare Navy Hall and the warehouse for the arrival of John Graves Simcoe, the Lieutenant Governor, and she was on her way to join him.

To distract herself from her fatigue, she surveyed the tiny log cabins in their stump-filled fields as she rode along. The little dwellings seemed overwhelmed by the forest that towered over them. On the other side of the trail, glints of the river showed through the fringe of trees.

What a long road she'd traveled to arrive at last on this frontier trail. Persecuted in the aftermath of the American Revolution, she'd fled with her parents from their home on the Hudson River to the safety of the British colony at Niagara.

The roar of the Falls they were passing interrupted her musing. She couldn't see them through the trees, but they deafened her. She shuddered. It sounded like the thundering river that drowned her parents when the ferry tipped over as they crossed. One of the ferrymen had rescued her, but sometimes, when life became especially hard, she wished he had not been so diligent.

She had hoped Richard would help her move but he said he had to be on duty and hired a carter to bring her to Newark. The carter, Mr. McClaren, appeared to be a man of few words. He hunched over the reins, apparently communing with the horses' tails.

1

Dear Richard. Tall and broad-shouldered, he walked as if he owned the world. She admired that. He kept his long blond hair tied back in a queue, but told her he hadn't grown the sweeping mustache until he joined the army.

When they were married, she thought all her troubles were over. Now she wasn't sure. Richard seemed to have changed from the dashing soldier in the scarlet jacket who'd wooed her so ardently. Sometimes he was attentive and kind, but other times moody and irritable.

She told him she didn't like his drinking.

"I'm in the army. Everyone drinks."

"But I see some of the soldiers reeling about, and one day I saw one lying in the ditch by the road. I'd be embarrassed to see you like that."

"Don't worry, you won't. I can handle it. Stop nagging."

Was she nagging? She hoped not. She must trust that he knew what he was doing, as he said.

She shifted position again and William whimpered.

"Almost there," said Mr. McClaren, as scattered cabins gave way to closer-set dwellings, some log, some frame.

She was relieved to see Richard standing at the door holding a lantern when they drew up in front of a tall stark building. Devoid of paint or any decoration, it sat close to the muddy street. She'd been afraid he wouldn't bother to meet her, and had wondered how she would manage if he didn't.

The house looked anything but handsome. Nevertheless she was so happy to be with him and have a roof overhead, that she ignored the twisted green lumber siding.

Richard enlisted the help of two other tenants to help him and Mr. McClaren carry the Trevlyn belongings upstairs. She held her breath while they maneuvered her walnut chest of drawers up the narrow stairway. She feared disaster to this single relic of her parents' old house.

The next day she set about transforming the single room into a home. A huge task. At Fort Erie they had a loft above for a bedroom, but now the bed had to be crowded in with the table and two chairs, the massive chest, as well as the shipping box that served as a cradle for William.

She looked around the cluttered space and sighed. Her one dream now was to again live in a spacious white clapboard house with wide verandahs like her old home on the Hudson River, now a pile of ashes. Would she ever get it?

The roughly plastered walls were stained from the rain that penetrated the shrunken outer sheathing. The one small-paned window looked as if it hadn't been washed since the house was built. She persuaded Richard to hang out the window to clean the outside of the glass.

He grumbled, "Soldiers shouldn't do this sort of thing," and scowled at the chuckles of passersby.

A fireplace would provide warmth, and wouldn't require her to share cooking space with the downstairs tenants. But the floor was ugly. The more she scoured it, the splinterier it became. Richard said he couldn't afford carpeting, even if any was available.

"But Richard, I can see through the cracks right into the room below."

"That should be fun. You can eavesdrop all you like; it will give you something to do when I'm not here. You might learn something interesting." His face broke into the lopsided grin that always set her heart to fluttering.

She pretended embarrassment. "Richard!"

He guffawed. Then he said. "There's some canvas in the army stores they're going to throw away. It's too rotten for tents. It might do for the floor."

"Oh, see if you can get some. It would be better than the bare boards."

He procured a roll, but it wasn't much better. Dingy gray and water-stained, it smelled moldy, constricting the inside of her nose and causing her to sneeze.

"I don't like it at all."

"Well, it's what you wanted."

He sounded annoyed. How was she to know it would be such worthless, smelly stuff?

Through all this upheaval William cried, upset at his disturbed routine.

Richard scowled at the boy, said he had to return to duty and stamped out, muttering, "What a racket."

What did he expect? Children cried. Richard had been so proud when William was born but didn't seem to realize what a family entailed.

Glad of the peace and quiet, she sat and rocked the baby. She kissed the dark curls on the top of his head and hummed a wordless tune. They were a complete family again. She must be more tolerant of Richard's moods. Family life was a big change for him.

Richard clattered down the stairs. Mrs. McClaren peered out of a door at the bottom and whispered, "Shush. You'll wake my babe."

"Babies, babies. The house is full of babies."

He stamped down the hall and slammed the door behind him, glad to be out of there. Squalling brats had never been part of his plan for marriage to Phoebe. When he saw her living with her aunt and uncle on their farm, he was attracted to this handsome woman, black curly hair and beautiful dark eyes, who turned out to be the brat he knew back in Haventown. He was jubilant when she agreed to marry him and proud to show her off to his mates. But that wore off. Setting up the household was a game, but domestic chores soon got tedious.

It was a great skirmish, taking Phoebe away from her sour aunt who disapproved of her marrying a soldier. But to his disappointment, instead of a dutiful wife, he was saddled with a shrew who nagged him about his drinking and card playing. He was much better off with the doxies who didn't care where he went or what he did. They weren't as expensive, either. He was tempted to leave her at Fort Erie when he was transferred, but she was his wife, after all, and he never gave up anything that belonged to him.

But marriage was a trial. Phoebe continually asked for money for things for William, or herself, or the house. Well, he'd show her who commanded their household.

Tremaine's mongrel dog ran out, barking, as he hurried past. He gave it a vicious kick in its prominent ribs.

"Get out of here, you bitch." The dog yelped and ran, limping, back to the cabin, its tail between its legs.

Black clouds hovered overhead and it began to rain, a dismal drizzle. He'd get wet if he didn't hurry. He headed for the mess hall where he knew a game would be in progress.

CHAPTER 2

All day long, the sound of hammers echoed against the bush as soldiers and carpenters worked feverishly to transform Navy Hall into accommodations suitable for the new governor. Phoebe thought it a terrible place for a head of government to live. A long, gray building with a monotonous row of small-paned windows, damp and moldy inside, it stood on swampy ground near the mouth of the river. Hordes of mosquitoes whined around it, and Mississauga snakes shook their rattles.

The honor guards' practicing interested her more. She neglected her work to run out with William to watch them march up and down, circle and present arms, until they could perform the maneuvers without fault. She wished Richard was a member of the guard. He'd look so handsome in his dress uniform, and she'd be so proud of him.

It was lovely to be reunited with Richard, but their landlord's leering when he came to collect the rent unsettled her. Burly and coarse looking, Sergeant Temple's hair flamed red, but his unruly mustache showed patches of brown. Was that its natural color or tobacco juice stains? Probably the latter. His thin skin was burned and peeling. He walked and stood with his feet apart, his legs at the corners of his rectangular body.

He always came when he knew Richard wasn't home. She couldn't tell Richard she feared the man. He might confront the sergeant with disastrous results to his career. Fort gossips said the sergeant was a bad man to cross. And, anyway, she didn't have anything, really, to complain about except a feeling there was something sinister about the man.

Late in the afternoon of July 26, the schooner Onondaga dropped anchor in the river in front of Navy Hall. Cannon aboard the ship boomed to announce the arrival of the lieutenant governor, and guns at Fort Niagara across the river answered. The guard of honor on this side rushed to form up along the path from the wharf, and everyone ran to the site.

The regular soldiers' red coats gleamed in the sunlight, the green-jacketed militia a suitable foil. A mass of people, astounding for such a new settlement, crowded the area. The soldiers' wives came dressed in linsey, the officers' wives in cotton or silk according to the status of their husbands. Settlers and their families, dressed in butternut-dyed linsey or remnants of old uniforms, were all present. Union Jacks snapped in the breeze off the river and strings of pennants on the ship fluttered. It was the most exciting scene Phoebe had ever witnessed.

A boat, rowed by brawny sailors, put off from the ship and, almost before the band had got themselves in key, the governor and his entourage landed at the wharf. The regimental band played God Save the King to greet his majesty's representative and followed with rousing marches. The civilians crowded forward, jostling for places, to get a glimpse of the dignitaries.

Since no work was being done on the Hall this day, Richard had come with Phoebe and managed to force a passage for them to the front of the throng. That was her Richard. Taking care of her.

The governor and his wife mounted the path from the dock. A maid followed, leading a little girl by the hand and carrying a baby wrapped in a blanket.

Mrs. Simcoe stopped in front of Phoebe, who held William in her arms. "Is your baby a boy?"

"Yes, ma'am. His name is William."

"Ah. How old is he?"

"Nine months."

"He looks healthy." Mrs. Simcoe touched William's cheek with her gloved finger, smiled at Phoebe, and passed on up the path to rejoin her husband.

Phoebe turned to Richard. "What an honor. To be spoken to by her Ladyship. Why did she pick me, I wonder? Or was it William who caught her eye?"

7

"No, it was my beautiful wife," said Richard.

"Oh, Richard." But she was pleased. He seldom paid her compliments since they'd married.

A flurry of comments arose from the crowd.

"The governor is a dear roly-poly man. He looks so jolly."

"Mrs. Simcoe looks very stern. I shouldn't like to cross her."

"She's 'andsome, though. Carries herself like a rale lady."

"How would you know? You never saw a lady in your life."

"Sure an' I was a lady's maid back on the ould sod."

"Sure you were. In the scullery, more like."

Some of the women gathered around Phoebe.

"What did she say to you?"

"Imagine being spoken to by her ladyship."

Phoebe felt herself blush from all the attention. "She said William looked healthy. And he is. She has such a lovely smile."

Imagine! Lady Simcoe had spoken to her. Had singled her out among all these women. Would she have a chance to talk to her again?

Richard, too, was pleased by the vice-regal attention. Perhaps it would lead to something for him. In spite of her aggravating ways, he had to admit his wife was a beautiful woman. If she managed to draw attention to him it would be worth putting up with her nagging. Perhaps when he became a captain, or better yet a major, he could make some changes. But there was the matter of William. He'd have to put up with the mother in order to have control of his son. What a bother.

The Simcoes inspected the shambles of the unfinished Navy Hall and elected to live in tents on the bluff above. Three marquees were erected and the governor, his family and staff took up residence.

When Richard came home after helping with the move, Phoebe said, "I don't understand why the governor should have to live in a tent. Mr. Hamilton has such a fine large house above the escarpment. Couldn't they live there?"

"Navy Hall is to be the capital building. The governor has to live at the capital."

"Then I'd move it. It seems so silly. I think the capital should be wherever the governor lives. It isn't as if it was a large town. There's hardly anything here at all."

"The governor has his reasons. You don't understand politics."

"That's right and I don't care if I never do." She set the plates on the supper table a little harder than necessary. "It seems if there's an awkward way of doing things that's what governments choose."

"They know what they're doing."

"I doubt it." She felt sorry for Mrs. Simcoe, but had enough worries of her own. The governor's wife must look out for herself. She turned to ladle soup out of the kettle in the fireplace.

The next Sunday, all the military not on duty, accompanied by their wives, attended church in a warehouse near Navy Hall. The vice-regal couple received more attention than the sermon. The men were probably considering what sort of ruler this man would be. The women, like herself, examined every ruffle and pleat of Mrs. Simcoe's dress. They'd never have a better chance to see the latest fashion.

Phoebe planned a new gown although she was unlikely to get it. Richard never seemed to have any money. Of course she couldn't copy her ladyship's dress exactly, but she'd like to try that kind of bodice pleat, and she'd never seen sleeves cut that way. She sighed. How she would like to have lovely gowns—but not dark colors like Mrs. Simcoe's.

In the middle of August a violent thunderstorm with high winds swept the region. Phoebe stood at the window of their room watching the lightning zigzagging down the sky. The clouds to the west glowered, almost black, with queer tags hanging down against the sickly, greenish-yellow below. Trees thrashed wildly and the soldiers' tents beside the parade ground collapsed one after another.

But she and William were safe within four solid walls. How were the governor's tents surviving up there on the edge of the escarpment?

Richard had the answer when he returned after the storm. "We had to hold the governor's tent ropes to prevent them pulling loose. I never saw such a storm. I'm drenched. The rain almost suffocated us. For awhile we thought the whole thing would go in the river.

She opened the storage box. "I'll get you some dry clothes. You look like a beaver just out of the water. Are you cold?"

"No, the governor ordered a ration of rum for each of us and thanked us personally. He's a great man."

The rum probably accounted for his praise. He seldom had a good word for anyone in authority. She was sure the army's rum rations were responsible for his taste for alcohol.

He bent to untie his bootlaces. "And that's not all the excitement we had today."

His voice muffled as he pulled his shirt over his head, he continued, "Before the storm the Simcoe's kitchen tent caught fire. The wind I guess. The men rushed to save what they could. The silly buggers threw Mrs. Simcoe's dishes away from the fire instead of carrying them, and broke most of them. She won't be very happy about that. The rain helped put out the fire, though."

"Didn't the soldiers know the dishes would break?"

"Well, they were excited, and I don't think most of them ever saw real china before. The governor wasn't pleased. He didn't give them any rum."

"Better for them."

He frowned. "Now, Phoebe, don't start down that trail. I've had enough for today."

"I'm sorry." She mustn't harp on it.

"I don't know what the Simcoes will do now for proper dishes to serve the prince when he comes."

She stopped rummaging in the chest for dry stockings and sat back on her heels. "Prince? What prince?"

"Didn't I tell you? The Prince of Wales is coming."

"The Prince of Wales? Why is he coming here?"

"To show off his fancy clothes and lord it over us, I guess."

Would Richard like to have such fancy clothes? Well, yes, if it was a fancy uniform she was sure he would. And she'd love to see him in it.

Phoebe and Richard stood outside in the late afternoon enjoying the freshened air. Mr. McClaren joined them, his pipe pouring out blue smoke like a miniature chimney.

He removed it from his mouth, spit in the dirt, and returned it. "They're sayin' a tornado ripped through the Short Hills settlement west of here. Threw down trees in windrows like they were wheat stems. Miner's cabin was blown to bits. Logs scattered all over the clearin'. I helped build that 'un and I know how heavy those logs were. Took some wind to scatter they."

"I know it." Said Richard. I was out in it."

Phoebe was more interested in Mr. McClaren than his story. How could he talk out of one side of his mouth while holding his pipe securely in the other?

Mrs. McClaren came to the door. "Mister McClaren, your supper's on."

"Comin' Missus."

Richard turned to Phoebe. "Where's mine?"

She sighed and turned to the stuffy upstairs room and her housewifely duties.

He shouted after her. "Call me when it's ready. I think I'll just stay out here where it's cooler." He sat down on the step and leaned back against the door-frame.

She was briefly annoyed but then realized he'd been on duty all day and deserved some relaxation. Still she poked up the fire vigorously.

Richard stretched out his legs and sighed. What a day. The rum tasted good afterward. He wished he had another tot. He'd go

11

over to the mess after supper. Phoebe'd complain, but then she always did. He was getting used to it.

He took a deep breath. At least the storm had cleared the air. He considered going in and shouting up the stairs to her to bring supper out here. They could have a picnic. No, she'd grumble about all the extra work going up and down stairs. As if she had anything else to do. Feeling put-upon, he resigned himself to eating in the stuffy, hot upstairs room.

CHAPTER 3

Edward, Prince of Wales, arrived from Kingston on the twenty-first of August. Phoebe could hardly contain her excitement. Imagine! A prince actually coming to Newark. She'd never imagined she'd see a member of the royal family in person.

As for Edward, himself. Well! He fit the picture of what she thought a prince should be. Tall and good looking, with a high-colored complexion, dark hair, and sideburns curving onto his cheeks, he was imposing.

Members of the royal family had visited the troops before in various parts of the world but never in such a small community where it was possible to mingle with them. All the women were in a flutter. Niagara was becoming the center of the world.

Governor Simcoe moved his family into the still unfinished Navy Hall, leaving the marquees to the prince and his staff. Mrs. Simcoe took charge of entertaining His Royal Highness. She gave a ball at Navy Hall in the prince's honor. Since there were such skeleton staffs at this distant outpost of the British Empire, even the non-commissioned officers and their wives were invited.

Other than the linsey or calico ones she wore every day, the only gown Phoebe had was the red velvet she'd worn for her wedding. She took it down from the hook behind the door. It was a little worn at the neck and cuffs. She had a bit of lace that might cover that, but it wasn't a summer dress.

Richard was brushing his uniform, preparing to go over to the mess as usual.

She held up the gown. "Could I have material for a summer gown? My velvet is much too hot."

He laid down the brush and shrugged into his jacket. "You must think I have a shilling-tree back in the bush. If I have, they're not ripe yet," and went out, chuckling.

The velvet gown would have to do.

13

When they arrived at the hall, Phoebe was determined to enjoy herself, even in the heavy gown. Inside, the sweet scent of a few beeswax candles, couldn't compete with the oily pungency of the more numerous tallow ones, and the moldy smell of the room. The mixture of odors was overpowering.

When the prince arrived, the band played God Save the King and everyone stood at attention. The formalities observed, the band swung into a dance tune. The prince led Mrs. Simcoe onto the floor and the guests followed. Richard held out his hand to Phoebe. She placed hers on top, her heart fluttering with excitement, and they joined the promenade around the hall.

Richard was a good dancer and he looked so handsome in his uniform. She wouldn't trade him even for the prince. She didn't lack for partners, but was glad when the bandmaster announced an interlude. August weather was not the best for exertions on a dance floor. She went outside with some of the women.

When music called them back to the hall, she searched the room for Richard, but he was nowhere to be seen. He must be in the card room. He'd forgotten all about her, and here she stood without a partner. And Lancers, too, her favorite dance.

Embarrassed, she stood looking at the floor. A pair of highly polished shoes adorned with silver buckles suddenly appeared. She looked up. The prince. She feared she was going to swoon when he held out his hand. She must be as red as her gown. Taking a deep breath, she let him lead her onto the floor. Though nervous, for once she was pleased Richard had forgotten her.

As they moved through the figures, the prince said, "Your husband was detained."

Detained? How? Where? And how did the prince know? Had he arranged it? Never mind. She'd just enjoy herself.

Each time they met in the dance he smiled at her as if they were alone in the room. Her heart beat so quickly she felt short of breath and by the time the set ended, completely so.

The prince said, "Let us take a stroll outside. You look over warm."

Over warm didn't fit the way she was feeling. Other couples followed them out of the hall and clustered in the pools of light from the windows. But the prince led her down the moonlit path towards the dock. Several men in uniform accompanied them at a distance. They were there to protect the prince, but they made her uneasy.

When they returned to the hall she noticed many of the officers' wives watched her, their eyebrows raised. What was bothering them? Was it her gown? It certainly stood out among the silks and dimities.

The prince lifted her hand and pressed a kiss on it. She shivered with delight and embarrassment. She'd never had her hand kissed before, let alone by a prince. He bowed formally and crossed the room to the vice-regal couple who rose and left the room with him.

Had she done the right thing? Of course she had. She was a married woman.

She found Richard playing cards in the next room and went to stand by him. Engrossed in the game, he didn't even acknowledge her presence. She wondered if the prince had spoken to him, but knew better than to interrupt. The game finished, she noted one of the other officers picked up all the chips. Oh dear, Richard was losing again.

"Richard. We must go home. Mrs. McClaren said she would only keep William until midnight."

Richard pushed back his chair. "Oh, balderdash. Brats are a regular ball and chain."

The other men at the table chuckled and one said, "Amen to that."

Richard turned to Phoebe. "Is the prince still here? We can't leave until he does."

"He left just before I came in here."

"Come on, then." He jerked her arm, causing her to lose her balance and stumble against him.

15

What had she done to upset him this time?

For once Richard appreciated Phoebe's intervention. He had no more money, but couldn't think of an excuse to leave the game. Still, he had to make it look as if he was reluctant to quit. He'd thought his luck was about to change before Phoebe came in. Had she spoiled it? No, that wasn't possible. She couldn't influence him in any way.

She looked beautiful tonight, though. The gown suited her. He liked to see her wear it. It reminded him of their wedding when he thought everything was going his way. Well, it would again. His luck would change. Bound to.

But perhaps he should spend a little more time with her on these social occasions. She was a little too beautiful. And naive, too. With all the vultures around, he'd better guard his property.

Five days after the prince sailed for Kingston, Phoebe found out why the women at the ball had looked at her so strangely. She was preparing for bed when Richard pounded up the stairs. He came in, slammed the door and glowered at her. What was the matter now? William whimpered in his sleep. She turned to go to him, but Richard grabbed her arm and jerked her around to face him.

"Everyone is talking about you. Do you deny having a tête-à-tête with the prince?"

"What's a tête-à-tête?"

"Oh, so innocent. I hear you went walking with him, all alone."

"Not alone. Some of his men were nearby."

"And conveniently turning their backs, I'll warrant. The rumor is all over the camp. I won't be cuckolded, even by a prince. Get out and take the brat with you."

"Richard! How could you think such a thing?"

"I've heard of the prince's taste for pretty women."

He thought she'd been flirting with the prince. She must convince him. "We merely went for a walk down to the dock because I was warm from the dancing. Oh, Richard, I'd never betray you, even with a prince. I love you. Don't you know that?"

"You swear he never even kissed you?"

"My hand, that's all. Richard, you do love me. I wonder, sometimes, when you're playing cards or drinking with your mates, if you wish you'd never married me."

"Don't try to change the subject." He jerked her arm again. "It seems to me you're always flirting with some man or other."

"Oh, no, Richard. I'm just enjoying life here so much. I've been so happy with you—only—I wish I could be with you more. It seems you always have other things to do than be with William and me."

The angry lines in his face were softening, and his grip on her arm relaxed. He believed her.

He pulled her to him, the buttons on his tunic bruising her breasts, and kissed her roughly. "Perhaps I have neglected you." He drew back to look into her face. "Just remember you belong to me. I was furious when I heard the men snickering. No hint of gossip must touch anything of mine."

"Of course, Richard. I don't want anyone talking about me, either. But the prince asked me to walk with him. I had to agree, didn't I? It was the prince."

He looked at her suspiciously. "And if he asked for more you would have given it, too?"

"No, no. Of course not."

"Well, I hope you're telling the truth."

"I am, Richard. I am."

How could he doubt her constancy? He and William were her whole life. She'd been a little jealous of his preference for card games to spending time with her, but after this episode, he came home almost every evening and often appeared unexpectedly during the day. This was the way it should be.

17

At the dances Mrs. Simcoe gave, Phoebe noticed he frowned when she danced with other officers. She must be careful not to appear too friendly. She didn't want another episode like the one over the prince.

If partners offered to bring her tidbits from the supper table when they returned her to him after sets, Richard said, "I can take care of my wife, thank you."

That was rude, but it was because he loved her so much. He wanted to be the only one to care for her.

The autumn frost destroyed the hordes of grasshoppers that stained the women's dresses with green juice whenever they went walking. The trees put on their rich fall colors, cold rains replaced summer sunshine, and winter approached.

Richard returned to his former pursuits. He spent more time away and, when home, was irritable and short-tempered with both Phoebe and William. She made excuses for him: he wasn't used to children crying; he'd lived with men so long he found it hard to adjust to family life. But he didn't seem to be trying very hard. His attention during the summer had been so pleasant she noticed his absences more than ever. Incessant rain kept her and William confined to the single room. Depressing.

Sometimes he came home in good humor, swept her off her feet with bear hugs and kisses and swung William into the air until he chortled with glee. But these intervals became fewer and fewer. More often he returned, staggering and sullen, or, even worse, delivered by his mates.

Some nights he didn't come home at all. The silver goblets he'd given her as a wedding gift disappeared from the top of the bureau. The most beautiful things she owned. But she dare not ask him what happened to them.

One night, braving his wrath, she said, "What's the matter? You seem worried."

"It's nothing."

"Are you losing at cards?"

"Mind your own business."

"But, Richard, it's my business, too. You haven't paid last month's rent. We'll be thrown out."

"Stop nagging, woman!" He grabbed his cap and slammed out.

Oh, dear, she hadn't handled that right. But what other way was there? It would be terrible if that nasty Sergeant Temple made them leave. Where would they go?

She was temporarily relieved when Richard returned that night, spilling coins into her lap. "What are you worrying about? There's the rent money."

Well, that was last month's. Where was this month's, due now? But she was afraid to mention it.

Richard felt hemmed in, his ambitions thwarted. He should keep an eye on Phoebe lest some other officer poach, but the only way he knew to get the money he wanted was to gamble. With no war on the horizon there wasn't a chance of rising further in the army.

He resented paying rent to Sergeant Temple. The man was hauling in money with five families living in the house. If he could just acquire some funds he could buy or build a house to rent out, like the sergeant had. A goose laying gold eggs. But how to do it?

The hope that Mrs. Simcoe's notice of Phoebe and William would have resulted in some attention to himself hadn't materialized. Gambling seemed the only way. His luck hadn't been good lately, and when he did win, Phoebe always wanted the money. However, his luck was bound to change.

In November the last ships left for Kingston. There'd be little contact with the outside world until spring. The weather turned very mild at the end of December and the area around Navy Hall became a quagmire. Phoebe's wooden pattens, strapped to the soles of her shoes, were insufficient to keep her boots and skirts out of the slop. Even a few mosquitoes appeared.

While she relished the warmth, she wished it would get cold enough to freeze the ground. She complained of the mud Richard dragged in on his boots. He retaliated by asking how she'd like to march with half a ton of dirt clinging to her feet.

The community passed the time with frequent social gatherings, dances and sleigh rides. The women indulged in whist parties, a favorite of Mrs. Simcoe. Phoebe enjoyed these and took care not to aggravate Richard. She'd been surprised at his anger and how little he seemed to trust her. He was so different from the swain who'd wooed her so ardently. Didn't he love her any more—or too much? Was he jealous? She must be careful.

CHAPTER 4

At the end of March the ice broke up and drifted out of the river. Flocks of ducks and geese gabbled overhead on their way to northern nesting grounds. The long winter had finally ended. Rumors circulated that the governor planned to hold a levee on the king's birthday in June, concluding with a grand ball at Fort Niagara. Phoebe looked forward to the festivities, especially the ball. But she'd have to cross that terrible river. She still had the occasional nightmare of floundering in its strong current.

When Richard came home with the news that it was a fact, not rumor, she said, "If they're having the levee here, why not the ball, too? It was good enough for the prince." Anything to avoid going out on the river.

"The governor wants to establish that Fort Niagara still belongs to us even though it's on the other side of the river. Besides, the drill hall over there is larger."

"Then why don't they have the levee over there, too?"

"Because Navy Hall is the seat of government."

"It's all very strange."

"That's politics. A woman wouldn't understand."

She decided to brave Richard's wrath. "What I do understand is that I must have money for a new gown for the ball. My red velvet is too shabby, and too warm besides."

Richard said, "Money, money, always money."

"You do want me to look my best don't you? You wouldn't want people to say I was neglected."

"Neglected! You're not neglected." But he threw coins on the table and left.

She counted them. Enough for a muslin—and a bit of lace. He was generous. She just had to ask at the right time. She began to plan her gown.

On the fourth of June the members of the legislature, the army officers, and some officials from York and Fort Detroit met at

Navy Hall. After a formal lunch, the guard fired a fusillade in honor of the king, echoed by ships in the harbor.

At seven in the evening all those lucky enough to be invited, gathered at Fort Niagara. Phoebe knew her new gown became her. Made of white muslin it was sprigged with blue forget-me-nots and trimmed with lace around the hem and neckline. Her waist had returned to its pre-pregnancy slimness, and she had no need of the breath-shortening stays many of the women thought indispensable. But to be in style, she wore the ones Angelique had give her for her wedding,

Candelabra were placed around the assembly room, and chandeliers brought from Navy Hall hung overhead, highlighting the colorful summer gowns and brilliant dress uniforms. The odor of burning candles competed with the perfume emanating from fair bosoms, ringleted hair and men's linen handkerchiefs, but was not so overpowering in this airy drill hall as it had been in Navy Hall. Men outnumbered women more than three to one. No female, be she comely or homely, would sit out dances this night.

Phoebe said, "Isn't it exciting, Richard? I thought the dances at Navy Hall were grand but they were nothing compared to this. Oh, there's Angelique. I have to find out the news from Fort Erie."

She crossed the floor to where Angelique sat on a wooden chair against the wall. "Hello, Angelique. How are you?"

"I survive."

"What is happening up at Fort Erie these days?"

Richard saluted Captain Bryant who stood behind Angelique, then groaned. "There they go gossiping. I'm off to the bar if you'll excuse me, sir."

"Sounds like a good idea. I'll join you."

Angelique waved her fan. "Nothing happens at the fort. It is too boring." She looked critically at Phoebe. "The dress, it is tres chic."

"Thank you. You look beautiful, Angelique."

"Merci. I try." Angelique smoothed her blue and white striped chintz gown and touched the seductive yellow ringlets that cascaded over her shoulders.

Phoebe sat down beside her friend. "What is new with you?"

"The captain keeps threatening to throw me out—but he will not."

"Why would he do that?"

"Eh, you know me. A little excitement I like. He says I lose too much money at cards—and flirt beaucoup." She shrugged. She leaned close to Phoebe. "What is this I hear you had an affair of the heart with the prince?"

"No, I didn't. We only went for a walk."

"Of course, of course. You went for a walk. And then?"

"Nothing. We walked down to the dock and watched the moonlight make a path across the river—until the mosquitoes drove us in."

"Nothing? This I do not believe. With the prince, by the tales, there is always something more. What then?" Angelique folded her fan and crossed her hands in her lap, prepared to hear all the details.

"Well...." Should she tell? She looked around but couldn't see Richard. Good. She leaned close to Angie. "Well, he did ask me...."

"Aha. I knew it." Angelique clapped her gloved hands together. "Tell all."

Phoebe shifted on her chair. She didn't want to talk about it but Angelique would insist. "Well, he asked me if I would come to his rooms if he arranged it, but I said it wouldn't be proper."

"You said which?"

"I said no."

"You said no?" Angelique looked at the ceiling as if she could find some enlightenment there. "Cherie, you do not say no to a prince."

"But I did."

"You refused a prince? He could have you behead." Angelique drew her finger across her throat and clicked her tongue.

"But I'm married."

Angelique tapped her forehead. "Quel innocence. That does not matter if a prince shows you his favor."

"Oh, Angie, don't be silly. He was very kind and said he hoped he hadn't embarrassed me."

"But why did you say no?"

"Angie, I'm married." Why couldn't Angelique understand that?

"Hah! So are many another pretty filly. All sorts of bibelots could follow if the prince is pleased by you."

"But Richard wouldn't like it. He was furious about the gossip, and now he watches whatever I do."

"He would soon get over his pique, Cherie, if the prince gave him advancement in the army. It often happens in such a case."

"Well, it doesn't matter." Phoebe shrugged. "The prince is gone and I couldn't—with someone I didn't love."

"Bah. You do not know what is good for you. I should have been here to look after you. He found someone else, no?"

"I don't know. He left the dance as soon as we came back."

"That does not mean he did not see someone after. These things they can be arrange. You missed your chance."

Then Angelique became more serious. "I have other news. The captain is posted to Oswego and we go next week."

"Oh, no. I'll miss you."

"I'll miss you too, Cherie." She chuckled. "Still, we do not see each other beaucoup, maintenant."

"But I know you are there. Oswego is still farther away."

Angelique shrugged. "It cannot be helped. The army says go, we go."

"But who will look after your tavern?"

"It must run by itself. I have hire a manager but I do not know if he will be good. But I will hope. But Phoebe, attendez. You have a problem. The captain says Richard, he loses too much at the cards."

24

"I thought he must be losing. He is so cross, sometimes. What can I do?"

"For me, I would give him something else to take his time."

"Like what?"

"You said he watched you close after the thing with the prince. A little flirting you could do, I think."

"Oh, Angie, I couldn't."

"Not serious, no. Just bat those long eyelash un peu." Angelique demonstrated. "Every man will follow after. Richard will have no time for the cards. He will be too occupy guarding you."

"Is that what you've been doing? Why the captain is angry with you?"

"Perhaps." Angelique smiled mysteriously.

"Are you really married to the captain? I heard----."

"Non, non, non," Angelique wagged her finger. "You do not ask such things, even from good friends. Everyone must do what they must do."

The regimental band began to play and the two women turned toward them. In their dress uniforms, their horns gleaming in the candlelight, the soldiers were a splendid sight. Richard and Captain Bryant came to claim their wives.

As Angelique rose gracefully from her chair, she said, "Remember, Cherie, when candles are out all cats are gray," and swayed across the room with the captain to join a set.

"What did she say about cats?" asked Richard, as he offered her his arm.

"I've no idea. She's always saying things I don't understand." So Angelique wasn't married. What would happen to her if the captain tired of her? Would she be able to keep the tavern if she didn't have the captain to protect her? Phoebe shivered. What a dangerous world she was living in.

As she stepped through the figures of the second dance with the captain, she compared Richard, partnering Angelique, to the other officers. He certainly was the handsomest. He'd kept the lean

25

hardness from his days on the warpath, and only a slight puffiness under his eyes betrayed his present dissipation. Somehow she had to stop his gambling and drinking.

When the music began for the next dance, she saw Sergeant Temple approaching. Oh, no. He was intending to ask her. She'd tell him she'd promised it to Richard. But Richard was on the other side of the room with his back to her and it didn't look as if he were coming to claim her.

Sergeant Temple bowed. "May I have this dance, Mrs. Trevlyn?"

What could she say? He was the last person in the room she wanted to dance with. But he was their landlord. She dare not refuse him. Housing was much too scarce to risk angering him.

With what grace she could muster she rose, put her hand on his sleeve, and joined the set. There was no avoiding the too-warm clasp of his hand when they met in the figures or the leering looks he gave her.

The dance ended, she returned to her seat. The sergeant, thanking her warmly left, saying he looked forward to a repeat.

Angelique had returned before her. "I think you do not enjoy that dance much."

Phoebe shuddered. "Did it show? He's our landlord so I couldn't say no, but he frightens me."

"That face, it would frighten anyone."

When Richard claimed her for the next dance, Phoebe said, "I wish you'd come for the last one. I had to dance with Sergeant Temple."

"I thought you were still gossiping with Angelique. Anyway, I knew you were safe when I saw you with the sergeant. I didn't think you'd be overcome by his charms."

"Oh, Richard, He's horrible. Please be sure I have a respectable partner, will you?"

Richard chuckled. "That's what I like to hear."

At midnight the band stopped playing, and supper was laid out on the long mess tables. Cold meats: chicken, slices of salt beef, fish and a huge pork pie. Platters were piled with biscuits flavored with ginger or studded with currants, and small iced cakes Angelique called petit fours.

"They are French you know. I think Mr. Hamilton's cook must be helping, no? I do not think the army cooks can make such things."

A huge assortment of cheeses surrounded the many bottles of wine.

"What a feast," said Richard, rubbing his hands together.

The men filled plates for the women and themselves and returned.

Phoebe had been admiring several well-dressed Indians. "Who is the old woman in the brocade gown with braids hanging down her back?"

"That's Miss Molly," said Richard. "She was Sir William Johnson's squaw-wife."

"Squaw she may be, but not much gets decided around here without her opinion being asked," said the captain. "She likes the Indian ways, but she's a match for anyone, man or woman, anywhere."

"Oh, I've heard of her," said Phoebe, "but I never saw her before. She's Captain Brant's sister, isn't she?"

"C'est vrai," said Angelique. "She lives at the Indian reserve on the Grand River most of the time since Sir William died. She probably came tonight to chaperone her daughters, n'est-ce pas? That is Susannah in blue and Mary in the red. The one who wears the striped gown is Doctor Kerr's wife."

Phoebe nodded. "Yes, I met Mrs. Kerr at Navy Hall. Would Miss Molly and the girls have come all the way from the reserve just for a ball?"

"Bien sur," said Angelique. "Miss Molly is determined her daughters will make the white marriages. She brings them to every affair where white men can see them. The banns have already been posted for Susannah and Lieutenant Lemoine."

"I saw the notices but I didn't know who the bride was. It just said Susannah Johnson." Phoebe hoped she'd have the chance to meet the girls and learn about their lives.

Richard glared across the room at the Indian women. He didn't approve of Indians mixing socially with white people. A roll in the hay was all right, but white men marrying squaws revolted him.

Indians were excellent scouts and more than once he'd been grateful for their tracking abilities and warnings of danger, but they should be kept in their place. He never understood why Colonel Butler made Joseph Brant a captain. It rankled, having to take orders from a native. The Indian lorded it over them as if he was smarter than white men. It was insufferable. That was one good thing about the British army. No chance of an Indian getting the upper hand there. He was glad he was able to transfer when Colonel Butler's scouts were disbanded.

All the next day Phoebe danced around their room, humming. What a wonderful evening it had been. Perfect, except for that odious Sergeant Temple. He acted entirely too familiar. She must ask Richard again to be sure to pay him on time so he wouldn't have an excuse to call. Goodness knows what liberties he might try to take now, after she'd danced with him.

CHAPTER 5

I t had been a bad day. The wash line broke and dumped her newly washed clothes on the muddy ground. She had to carry more water from the pump in the square to rewash them.

Mrs. Tremaine was at the pump. "Heard your fancy husband lost all his money at cards again last night."

Well, that accounted for his bad humor when he came home.

"He'll never be able to pay off his debts," Mrs. Tremaine continued. "He owes money to everyone in the place."

Phoebe feared this tirade was at least partially true. Still, she wouldn't give the woman the satisfaction of an answer, and turned her back to watch a carter unloading wood beside a house across the road.

Mrs. Tremaine dropped the pump handle and skirted around to face Phoebe again. "I heard you eloped with him. Two of a kind, I say." She picked up her pail and flounced off across the square.

Phoebe worked the pump handle vigorously as if she was beating the gossipy woman and, her pail filled, returned home, fuming.

She heated the water in her largest iron kettle, scrubbed the muddy clothes and retied the line. While she hung out the washing, William, back in their room, got into the meal bag and slung gritty cornmeal wall to wall. She should have taken him out with her, but it meant two trips up and down the stairs as he still needed help with steps, and she couldn't manage him and the heavy wash basket at the same time. She'd thought he was busy with his blocks and would be safe for a few minutes. By the time she cleaned up the mess, dark clouds loomed overhead, and she had to rush out and rescue the still-damp clothes.

Then Richard upbraided her because supper was late and there were drying clothes draped everywhere. "What have you been doing all day? Can't a man expect his house to be tidy and his meals on time?"

She felt tears well up. She was so tired. "The clothes line broke."

"Well, surely it didn't take you the whole day to fix that."

What was the use of saying more? He never had any sympathy for housekeeping problems.

After they had eaten a scrambled-together supper, she said, "Could you give me some money? I have to ask the cobbler to make William a new pair of shoes. The ones he has are too small." It wasn't the best time to ask, and maybe he didn't have any money as Mrs. Tremaine said, but he was hardly ever home any more. She had to take the chance.

"Money! Money! Always money. William! Stop banging the door!"

William stuck out his lower lip, glared at his father and continued slamming the cupboard door. Richard slapped him on the ear. William emitted a full-throated roar but continued his play.

Phoebe said, "Give him something else to do. It distracts him. Here William, come and play with your blocks."

William shouted, "No," and continued his banging.

Richard scowled. "You baby him. He must learn to do whatever he's told, immediately. Discipline. That's what the army teaches you."

"But, Richard, he's not in the army. He's a baby."

"The sooner he learns to obey orders, the better for him."

He spanked the boy—too hard, she thought—shoved him at her and said, "Here, look after your brat," and stormed out.

She was glad to see him go. They had nothing but arguments these days.

She calmed William, put him to bed, cleared away the supper dishes and sank down by the fire. It seemed the only word William could say these days was "No", which infuriated his father.

No longer was Richard her knight in shining armor, and he seemed equally dissatisfied with her. What had gone wrong? Was it worry about gambling debts that made him so irritable, or was he disappointed in her? She'd been so glad to find him again, and thought they'd be happy together forever.

The crackle of the fire and the click of her knitting needles calmed her, but the problems remained. How could she spend the rest of her life with Richard and his rages? She feared he might really hurt William. But what choice did she have?

If only he'd become again the Richard who'd courted her. It seemed unlikely, by what she saw in him now. She almost wished he wouldn't come back. But then what would become of her? At least he provided a place to live, food and clothes. She should be grateful for that.

She'd better get some sleep before he came home, probably crashing into furniture and swearing in his drunkenness. She folded her knitting into her mother's tapestry bag, smoothing its worn pattern. Would her life have been different if her parents were still alive? Well, no use thinking of that.

Maybe Richard would be in a better mood in the morning and she could ask him again for some money. William's shoes were much too small. He cried when she tried to force his feet into them, so she let him go barefoot as much as she could.

She banked the fire and went to bed. Things would look better in the morning when she wasn't so tired.

CHAPTER 6

A knock on the door woke her. Richard's mates bringing him home drunk again. She grabbed her wrapper. He'd get a piece of her mind tonight! She'd had enough of his carousing. He acted worse than William.

She jerked open the door. Mrs. Tremaine stood on the landing. "Mrs. Trevlyn, your husband has had an accident. I've been sent to get you."

"Accident?" Richard hurt? He said he was going over to the mess. "What happened?"

"You'd better come."

Drat the woman. Mrs. Tremaine had just been put on the earth to bedevil her. How could he get injured playing cards? It couldn't be serious. Still, she'd better go and see.

She stepped back into the room, took off her wrapper and bed gown, heedless of the other woman's presence, and donned her linsey day dress. She pulled her boots over her bare feet, still questioning Mrs. Tremaine who refused to answer. Why wouldn't she? Why such a mystery? Phoebe wrapped William in a blanket and followed the woman down the stairs.

Wakened so abruptly, William howled.

Mrs. McClaren, in her bed gown, braids hanging down her back, opened her door. "What's all the noise?"

"It's Richard," said Phoebe. "Mrs. Tremaine says he's had an accident."

"Bad?"

"Bad," said Mrs. Tremaine. "He's dead."

"Dead?" Phoebe's arms went limp, and Mrs. McClaren reached out for William before he could fall.

Phoebe turned to Mrs. Tremaine, her voice unsteady. "You-you said hurt."

"I didn't want you swooning with no one else around. Come."

Mrs. McClaren said, "Leave William with me. I'll look after him. I'm so sorry."

Phoebe stumbled after Mrs. Tremaine across the parade square. Dead? He couldn't be dead. He'd come through the war unscathed. He was a young man yet. Nothing serious could happen in a mess hall. There was some mistake.

His body lay stretched out on a table, his arm hanging over the side. An officer was questioning a soldier. Other soldiers stood about in small groups excitedly discussing the accident.

She ran to the table. "Richard! Richard. Wake up. Tell me you're all right."

She lifted his hand and squeezed it. The hand remained limp. She slipped her arms under his shoulders and hugged him against her breast. "Richard, dear Richard. Please wake up. You can do whatever you want. I won't complain ever again. Come back. Please."

The hair on the back of his head felt matted and sticky against her arm. She touched it and was horrified to discover blood on her fingers. She knelt and put her ear against his chest. No solid thump, thump that reassured her as it had at happier times when she nestled in his arms. He was dead. Really dead.

Over the next days she drifted in a nightmare. The army officials took care of the funeral. She went where she was told, did what she was told, with only one thought in her mind: her golden-haired knight had vanished from her life forever. How could she survive without his broad shoulders to lean on? She'd thought, when they married, all her troubles were over. What would become of her and William now? The worst of it was, some part of her felt relieved there'd be no more fights. It dismayed her that she should feel so.

She should be planning what she could do to make a living now she no longer had his salary, small as it was, to depend on. But what could it be? Her mind was all in a muddle. She couldn't concentrate on anything. She forced herself out of her depression to feed William, put him to bed and dress him when he woke. The minimum care she gave didn't satisfy him, of course. He alternated between whining and pulling at her skirt, and open defiance at bed and mealtimes.

One day while she sat looking out the window, unable to summon the energy to tackle her housework, William's screams, different from his ordinary tantrums, roused her. He'd ventured too near the fire and burned his hand on an ember that had rolled out onto the hearth. As she smeared grease on the burn and soothed his crying, remorseful at her neglect, she discovered some comfort in the small sturdy body. Poor little orphan. She hadn't lost everything. She still had William—and he looked more like Richard every day. She'd spend her life caring for him.

The details of Richard's death spread through the military community. He'd been accused of cheating at cards, fought with his accuser, fallen and struck his head on the fireplace andiron. The army investigators ruled it death by accident, but a number of soldiers who'd lost money to him said—even within Phoebe's hearing—that he'd got what he deserved. Mrs. Tremaine pointed her sharp nose at the sky and curled her lip every time they met at the water pump. Phoebe ignored her. What did she care what the nasty little woman thought?

Sitting by the fire after one of her encounters with the virago, Phoebe tried to decide what to do now. She knew the rent was paid, so she had a little time. Lethargy overcame her again. Tomorrow she'd make plans.

CHAPTER 7

Sergeant Temple knocked as she was putting William to bed and swaggered in without waiting for her to open the door.

"Good evening, Mrs. Trevlyn. It's a lovely night outside." He strode across the room and sat down on the chair by the hearth, tipping it onto its back legs.

As if he owned the place. Well, he did, but surely she was entitled to some privacy. Why had he come? The rent wasn't due. She felt anxious, alone with him. She considered grabbing William and running down the stairs to Mrs. McClaren. But the sergeant hadn't done anything she could complain of, except coming in without knocking. Hardly a crime in a house he owned. She'd look foolish.

Her heart pounding, she faced him squarely. "What do you want?"

With a nasty smirk, he said, "Mrs. Trevlyn, you will have to leave your quarters at the end of the week. Ensign Trevlyn's replacement is coming from Oswego and I need this room for his family."

"But the rent's paid. I'm entitled to live here."

"Just 'til the end of the week. Then next month's is due. Do you have it?"

"No. I haven't received the pension money, yet."

She shivered at the Sergeant's evil smile. "The pension will have to go to pay his gambling debts. Even then there won't be enough. You're responsible for the rest."

"But I can't pay." She couldn't keep the desperation out of her voice. "Where will I go? I don't have anything."

Once again the evil smile. "Too bad, but that's your problem. Of course, if you'd be friendlier I might arrange for you to stay." He tipped the chair forward and stood up.

Before she realized his intention, he pulled her against him. She gagged, enveloped in fumes of rum and rotten teeth.

"Let go of me or I'll scream."

The sergeant relaxed his grip. She jumped away. Grabbed the heavy iron poker from its place beside the hearth. Waved it in front of her.

The sergeant eyed the poker and snarled, "I'll expect you to be moved out before the first of next week. You'll come to me for help, sooner or later. I can wait. Good-day Mrs. Trevlyn."

He turned and clumped down the stairs.

She sank down on a chair, shaking, and the poker clattered to the floor. What a horrible man. She'd been right to be afraid of him. What could she do now? That fiend after her and no place to live. She'd no money and no family to help her. If the sergeant put her out, what would become of her and William?

CHAPTER 8

Wiilliam in tow, she canvassed all the houses in the village and nearby farms for a place to live. No luck. The settlers' tiny cabins were so overcrowded the inhabitants couldn't make space for her, and the soldiers' wives still regarded her with suspicion. Richard owed many of the men money they would now be unable to collect. They too wanted nothing to do with his wife.

If she were back at Fort Erie, Angelique would help her—if she was still there. It was her only hope. But Fort Erie was far away at the other end of the river. How could she get there? Well, wagons were constantly going up, transshipping goods between Lake Ontario and Lake Erie. Perhaps she could persuade one of the carters to give her a ride.

She bundled her few belongings into a sack. She'd have to leave her bureau for now. Perhaps Mrs. McClaren could keep it for her if she couldn't find a carter to take it. On the following days she and William stood in the road, but the carters shook their heads. Either they were completely loaded, even to the other half of the carter's seat, or they wouldn't take her without pay. William alternately whined and threw tantrums at the boredom of their vigil.

On the second last day before her eviction, she gave up her search for a ride as hopeless and inspected the shanties of some new immigrants. The hovels seemed to be just a limb laid between the crotches of two close-standing trees with brushy branches propped against the crosspiece. Some had a piece of canvas draped over the brush to make it more or less watertight, but some only had overlapping pieces of bark to keep out the rain.

Could she make a shanty? She didn't even have an ax. She did have the canvas from the floor. Rotten as it was, would it be watertight enough as a roof? Could William survive in a shanty? Could she? Perhaps in the summer. She wiped the back of her hand across her sweating forehead. It might even be preferable to the stuffy upstairs room. But the winter.... She returned home in tears, William echoing her sobs.

Mrs. McClaren was just coming out the door. "Oh, Mrs. Trevlyn. 'Tis verra hard for you, I know, losin' yer man, but ye must bear up."

"It—it's not that. The sergeant is turning me out and I—I've no place to go. I can't find anything."

"Oh, no. That skunk." Mrs. McClaren put her arms around Phoebe. "What will ye do?"

"I do-on't know."

Mrs. McClaren wrinkled her brow. "With the five of us in thae one room, we canna make room for ye. I'll try to think of something, and maybe the mister will have an idea. Now I must get a pail of water. The bairns are alone."

Phoebe and William trailed up the stairs to their room. She noticed something missing the minute she walked in the door. Her bureau. The empty space on the west wall seemed huge.

She ran out and shouted to Mrs. McClaren. "Who took my bureau?"

Mrs. McClaren turned from the pump. "Sergeant Temple said he was taking it for Ensign Trevlyn's debts. He said you knew about it."

"I didn't, I didn't. I'd never part with it."

"I'm sorry. I didn't know. But I could do naething, anyhow."

"I'm not blaming you."

William called from the top of the stairs. Phoebe threw a goodbye to Mrs. McClaren and hurried back lest he tumble down.

After their meager supper of cornmeal mush, she put him to bed and sat listlessly in the dark. Now, on top of all her other losses her bureau was gone. It was the last link to her old home and family. It had been a comfort to her. Now there was nothing. She knew there was no use asking the sergeant to give it back. It would just give him another excuse to sneer at her.

But now she couldn't worry about her bureau. She had to find a place to live. A brush shanty was the only solution. She should be gathering up whatever she could carry but couldn't summon the energy.

Someone knocked on the door. Fearful, she grabbed the poker. "Who is it?"

"Mrs. McClaren."

She dropped the poker and opened the door.

Her neighbor stepped over the threshold. "I told the mister about your trouble. He says there's an old shack by the river up above the Falls that nobody's livin' in. He says it's pretty bad but he'll take you there the morn if you like."

"Oh, thank you. I don't have any choice. But does he have room for us? I've been trying to get a ride with the carters but their wagons are all full."

"He's only got a part load of lumber for a settler up that way."

"Oh, could he take me all the way to Fort Erie? I have a friend there who would help me." If Angelique was still there.

"Nay, he's not goin' so far and he has to be back to load for the next day. He says be ready come sun up if you want to go."

"But I can't pay."

"Don't fash yerself. He's goin' anyway. Goodnight."

After Mrs. McClaren left, Phoebe, with renewed energy, repacked her few belongings. They were indeed very few since the contents of her bureau were gone. Mindful of her plan to use the canvas as a shanty roof, she rolled it up. It would be useful. She paid particular attention to every scrap of food, even the tiny bit of cornmeal left in the bag. A place, she had a place to go.

Her spirits fell when she saw the shack. It stood, or leaned, in a weed-covered clearing, separated from the river by a fringe of trees. It was badly settled on one side, the bottom logs rotted almost completely away. The window and door were askew. The glass in the tiny window was broken and the door would scarcely close. Blue sky showed through the roof in several places.

The log walls lacked most of their chinking. But the stone chimney seemed sound, and a small pile of wood leaned against the wall under the eaves behind the cabin.

Not much, but it was better than a brush shelter. It was a wonder someone else hadn't moved into it. Probably its isolation was the reason. New immigrants would tend to stick to the more settled parts until they'd adjusted to their new country.

She swept out the eddies of dead leaves and twigs from the corners of the room and installed all her possessions on the dirt floor on the fireplace side of the cabin. The roof seemed sounder near the chimney. Mr. McClaren spread her bit of canvas over it and weighed it down with rocks.

"I wanted to use some bigger ones," he said, "but I'm feared they'd break through. I hope those 'uns'll hold."

He repaired the cabin door so it would close, and installed a bar on the inside.

"Thank you, sir." She sniffed back tears. Seemed as if she was always crying these days.

"That's all right. You've had a bad time. I must be off, now. Good luck to ye."

Good luck? What was that?

Damp and musty, the cabin seemed more like a root cellar than a home. She found some dry punk in a rotten tree stump and with that, some dry leaves and her flint and steel she soon had a cheerful blaze going on the hearth. The chimney drew well. No smoke in the cabin. Hot as it was outside, a fire made it seem more like home. She heated a bit of stew for their supper. Afterward, she filled their pallets with dry leaves, spread them before the fire, and felt a little cheered.

The next day she climbed on the woodpile, and then to the roof, and covered as many more holes as she could with slabs of bark she tore from dead stumps along the river. She re-chinked the log walls with bits of bark held in place with a mixture of moss and clay, thankful she had some experience at that, helping her aunt and uncle with their cabin. William thought this was great fun and plastered himself with mud from the bucket.

Before her marriage she'd done sewing and mending for the soldiers and settlers. Now she told whomever she met that she was willing to do so again. There were only skeleton staffs at the forts but even the few pennies she made from mending their clothes, or making them new shirts felt like riches. The settlers in the area could only pay with food, but that was what she was most in need of. Perhaps it would be enough.

William kept asking, "Dada? Dada?" which made her heart ache. But over time he forgot that a man in a bright coat was ever part of their family and gave his whole attention to getting his own way. Immersed in her own grief and the day-to-day struggle to survive, she usually gave him whatever he asked for to keep him quiet. On occasions when she tried to discipline him he threw a tantrum, lying down on the floor and kicking his heels until she was desperate what to do with him.

While she'd disapproved of Richard's heavy chastisements, nothing she could do, herself, seemed to have any effect on the boy. She alternately disciplined him severely as his father would have done or, contrite, smothered him with kisses.

Sitting long hours over her mending and sewing, she realized her predicament was her own fault. She'd gone against the wishes of her aunt and uncle who didn't want her to marry a soldier, indulged in dancing, cards and wine. She'd been very wicked. No wonder such evils befell her. It was only right she should suffer for her transgressions. She resigned herself to a life of poverty and toil—if she could survive at all. It would be her penance. But poor little William would suffer for her sins.

No, William mustn't suffer. She must do something before winter. But what?

CHAPTER 9

The leaves fell. Phoebe dreaded the coming winter. Could she and William survive in this miserable shack? Fall storms had already blown away some of the bark pieces she had placed on the roof. She replaced them and weighed them down with rocks. The corners of the canvas flapped in the wind and she piled more rocks on them. But they surely wouldn't withstand winter gales. The woodpile was disappearing and she had no money to buy more. Lacking a ladder, it was the only way to get on the roof for future repairs and there would certainly need to be some.

She'd been gathering fallen branches and driftwood along the river to save the good sticks, but the small bits—all she had the strength to break—would never provide enough heat to warm the cabin in winter. Even now she was burning long branches, too large to break, that she dragged into the cabin. She pushed one end into the fireplace, the rest of the branch protruding into the room. As the end burned off, she shoved the wood farther into the coals. Smoke, and sometimes flames, crept out along the bark. Both she and William were watery-eyed and choking in the fumes.

They'd eaten almost all the vegetables in the abandoned garden patch. Nothing left for winter and no way to obtain more. Even sewing commissions had been less frequent lately.

A woman without family as she was, must have a husband, or money to set up a business, like Angelique with her tavern. Dressmaking might bring in enough to support her, but it required funds for materials and a place to live in Newark or Fort Erie. She didn't even have enough money to get to either place. Perhaps there weren't enough well-to-do wives requiring new gowns anyway.

It looked like a husband was the only solution. She had rebuffed all advances while Richard was alive. How could she reverse that? Her experience with men so far had not led to happiness, but now it was a matter of survival, not bliss.

Something Angelique had said to her at the ball came to mind. How long ago that seemed. "Just bat your eyelashes and you'll have them all at your feet." Could she do that?

She looked at her reflection in the water pail and practiced fluttering her eyelids. Strands of hair straggled around her face, her eyes were sunken, and worry lines creased her forehead. As she turned, she saw the ragged edge of a split shoulder seam. What a mess. How could she have let herself sink so low? She looked like the camp followers. No wonder few women came to her with sewing orders these days. If she wanted to attract a respectable man she'd have to look better than this. She straightened her shoulders. If she must have a man to ensure her and William's survival, then a husband she would get, no matter how distasteful it might be. But a husband for certain. There'd be no camp following for her, or liaisons with disgusting men like the sergeant.

She carried water from the river, washed her hair and gave herself and William baths. William, too, must be presentable. She put on a clean gown she took from the storage box, gathered her still-damp hair into a coil low on her neck and surveyed herself again. She scrubbed her cheeks with the callused heel of her hand and bit her lips to make them red. Not too bad. The dark circles under her eyes and the worry wrinkles would have to wait for security and good food. Then surely they would disappear.

Could she do this? She'd have to be very careful who she selected—assuming she had a choice. It might turn out to be either an unpleasant partner or death by starvation.

She was sewing two lengths of hand-woven linsey together along the long edges to make a bed-cover a settler's wife had commissioned, when someone knocked on the door.

Private Donley stood outside.

She welcomed him in. Her first chance.

He held out a shirt. "C-could you do s-something about these c-cuffs, Mrs. Trevlyn?" His left eye flickered in time with his stutter.

43

Phoebe took the dingy garment and examined the frayed cuffs and the neckband which was full of holes in the inside layer. "I don't have any matching material to replace the neckband, but I could trim off the cuffs and re-hem them. They'll be shorter though."

"I knew you c-could do it." Donley's mouth began to work in unison with the winking eyelid. Then he spat a stream of brown juice onto the dirt floor close to where William was playing.

Her stomach heaved. "Don't do that."

He scraped his boot over the spot. "It'll s-sink r-right in. Ye'll n-never n-notice it."

She pinched her nostrils. Perhaps not the spot, but certainly the smell.

She agreed to mend his shirt and hustled him out the door before he'd be moved to decorate the floor again. Fortunately she saw him coming when he returned for his shirt and completed the transaction on the doorstep.

She crossed him off her list. Even if she were to convince him to stop spitting on the floor, the stutter and perpetual wink would be wearisome.

A few days later Private O'Riley appeared, his arms full of woolen stockings.

"Good eve-evening, Mrs. Trevlyn." He reeled into the cabin and held out the bundle to her. "I bin savin' 'em for ye."

Private O'Riley smelled powerfully of rum, and the stockings smelled powerfully of Private O'Riley.

She indicated the floor. "Put them down there."

O'Riley complied. "Can ye mend 'em fer me?"

She looked at the bundle with disgust. "They'll have to be washed first and I don't have any soap—or yarn to mend them." She did have a little piece of soap but she wasn't going to use it for this.

"I-I'll bring ye some 'morrow night. 'Night."

He staggered out. She watched him go. Would he even remember in the morning where he'd left his stockings.

She gingerly picked up the bundle, took it outside, and hung the stockings over a tree branch to air.

He did return with a square of lye soap and a skein of worsted yarn. It took two kettles of hot soapy water to remove the worst of the smell and grime. As she wove yarn over the huge gaps in the toes and heels she decided Private O'Riley was not husband material, either.

Before she had O'Riley's feet entirely protected from the elements, Ensign Rogers came to the shanty to have his coat mended. Tall and slim, with his dark sideburns cut off square at his earlobes and his mustache neatly trimmed, he was very presentable. His brown eyes looked kind. She knew he was a bachelor. Definitely a prospect. She gave him her brightest smile.

He immediately responded with one of his own. "Isn't it lonely, living here by yourself, Mrs. Trevlyn?"

"Yes, it is lonely." She gave a deep sigh. "It's a big change for me, not having a strong man to take care of me." She briefly closed her eyes, knowing her long lashes lay attractively against her cheeks.

The soldier smiled even more warmly. "My name is David. I hope we can be friends, Mrs. Trevlyn."

"I would like that. Please call me Phoebe."

The soldier stepped nearer. William left his wooden horse lying on the floor and pushed between them.

"Go away, little boy." The ensign shoved him aside. "I want to talk to your mother."

William threw himself down, howled and banged his heels. The soldier stared at him. "What an infernal racket. Can't you make him stop?"

She tried to lift the boy. "William, please stop. William! Please!"

Now that he had their attention, William put on his best display. She couldn't hold onto his rigid little body. He slid out of her arms, kicking out at her and rolling about the floor, screaming.

Ensign Rogers, clearly disgusted, shouted he'd come back in a week for his coat, and left.

As soon as the door closed behind him, William was all smiles again.

"Oh, William, what am I to do with you?" She shook her head at him. "You mustn't be bad when mama has guests. Please be a good boy when people come."

"Don't like him!" said William, his bottom lip protruding.

She sighed. He was so possessive. That was because he felt insecure. If he had a whole family again he'd behave better.

When the ensign came back for his coat, he greeted her cordially.

She smiled at him. "Hello, David. I've finished your coat." She gave it to him and he examined the mend.

"Excellent. I can hardly see where I tore it."

She watched him finger the mend and could almost see his thoughts. He was obviously considering the advantage of having someone with such a talent permanently available. Good.

He put his arm around her shoulders and smiled at her. His hand brushed her breast. She flinched, but didn't move away. She must get used to it. It would be part of the bargain.

But William screamed and pummeled the soldier on the shins with the knob end of his wooden horse.

David let go of her, grabbed William by the shoulders and shook him until his head wobbled.

She sprang to her son's rescue. "Stop! Stop!" She pounded David on the shoulders. "Don't hurt him. What are you doing?"

"I'm trying to teach him to behave himself."

William, who'd been silent with surprise when the soldier shook him, now began to sob.

"Leave my son alone. He's only a little boy."

"Little devil, I say." The ensign picked up his coat and uniform cap, which had fallen to the floor, handed her some coins and stamped out.

Well, he'd seemed a nice man, but she couldn't allow anyone to abuse her son. Good thing she'd found out in time.

The soldiers all seemed coarse and domineering. She'd had enough of the military life anyway. A civilian husband would be a better choice.

She remembered the ferryman who'd saved her from the river when her parents were drowned. She'd been so frightened and lost. He was kind and seemed to like her. What was his name? Oh, yes, Jake. But she had no idea where he was or if he was married. She didn't even know his last name. She'd never seen him again. She hoped he hadn't been involved in another ferry accident.

She tried harder to solicit sewing among the settlers, thankfully taking turnips and cornmeal as pay, and gathered all the walnuts and beechnuts she could find in the woods.

One day a woman gave her a loaf of wheaten bread, just out of the oven. Phoebe held it to her nose and inhaled the aroma as if it were a rare perfume. It had been so long since she had even seen bread. For the next few days she and William savored pieces of it as if they were bonbons.

She managed to knock down some passenger pigeons that roosted in the trees at night. Since she couldn't afford salt to preserve the birds for winter, she and William lived on their flesh almost exclusively until the last of the birds migrated southward.

As the trees stretched their stark branches to the sky, the nights turned frigid. She husbanded her stock of wood as best she could, and the cabin was always cold.

One frosty day Mr. McClaren stopped on his way back from Fort Erie and dumped off a load of wood by her door. She protested that she had no money to pay him.

He said, "It's the least I can do for ye, lass."

Another day he stopped in with a bag of corn meal.

As he set it down on the hearthstone she said, "Could I ask another favor?"

"Sure Missus, if it's anything I can do."

"If I had my pension I'd be able to pay you. Would you ask why I'm not getting it?"

Mr. McClaren looked dubious. "Well, I don't know, Missus. I don't like havin' much truck with them military." He took off his cap and scratched his head while he considered. "All right, Ma'am. I'll ask for ye."

"Thank you."

On his next trip he stopped at the road and she ran out hoping for good news.

He shook his head. "I went to the paymaster where some fellers sent me when I asked directions. He said it was none 'o my business. I said I was askin' fer you but he wouldna say anything. It smelled skunky to me but what could I do?" He lifted his shoulders, and then let them drop. "I'm sorry."

"Well, thank you for trying."

That miserable sergeant had somehow persuaded even the authorities to do his bidding.

With Mr. McClaren's donations and payments in kind for the bits of sewing, they managed to survive the winter, although many times she cowered close to the hearth with William in her arms as gale winds shrieked in the chimney and the rickety cabin shuddered. She often went to bed supperless, saving what little food she had for William. They survived, but barely.

CHAPTER 10

The spring thaw began. The roof leaked in numerous places as the snow melted. Phoebe had to keep moving her belongings from under new drips. Water collected in every depression in the dirt floor. William seemed to think these tiny ponds were for his especial benefit. He splashed in them, laughing with glee, and drenching himself and everything within reach.

He threw a tantrum every time she berated or slapped him, lying down on the muddy floor and kicking his heels until she was desperate what to do with him. She thought if she'd had younger brothers and sisters she might have learned how to handle her son better. He needed a father, and she needed a husband to provide for them. But the candidates who had so far appeared were not alluring.

Perhaps Mrs. Simcoe could help her rescue her pension. Then at least they'd have enough to eat. She'd remind her ladyship of their meeting the day she came to Newark. She decided to go and see her.

Early the next morning Phoebe and William stood in the muddy road hoping to get a ride on a wagon. The sun was beginning to give some warmth, but the north wind was cold. She bent down to do up the top button on his coat.

He struggled against her. "No, no. Too tight." He wrenched at the coat edges until several buttons let go their hold.

She sighed. Even if he felt cold he'd object to anything she wanted, just to be contrary. She tried to persuade him to do up the coat himself, telling him big boys were able to do that.

While they argued, an empty wagon came along returning from Fort Erie to Newark for a load. She waved to the carter and he stopped.

"Could you let us ride to Newark? I'm sorry, I can't pay."

The carter smiled at her and reached down. "Give me the boy and climb up. Glad of the company."

"Thank you."

49

The carter chatted of the goods he'd been transporting as they drove along, uniforms and ammunition for the soldiers at Detroit.

He looked at William. "Better button up your coat, lad. T'isnt spring yet."

Embarrassed at her apparent lack of care for her child, she did up the buttons with no protest from William. That's what he needed. He respected a man.

She scrutinized the carter. Not bad looking, broad shoulders, curly black hair and kind eyes. He could do with more frequent baths, though.

When he made faces at William to make him laugh, she said, "You like children?"

"Should do. Got six of 'em."

"Goodness."

"The missus says she wisht I was home more to help take care of'm. I tell her if I was home more we'd probably have a dozen." He chuckled.

No husband there.

Near noon they reached Newark.

The carter said, "I won't be goin' back 'til the morrow and I don't think I'd have room for ye anyway. Good luck."

What if she couldn't find someone to take her back to the cabin? She'd been so concerned with seeing Mrs. Simcoe once she thought of appealing to her, she hadn't thought of the return journey.

William didn't want to leave the horses and she had to drag him away. "Hurry William."

As they crossed the parade ground she saw Sergeant Temple coming in her direction. She stiffened. The last person she wanted to meet.

"Well, Mrs. Trevlyn. How are you?" The buttons of his coat looked as if they were about to fly off from the strain of his belly.

She said, "Why did you take my bureau?"

"Why, I thought you knew." His eyes widened as if he were surprised. "You were responsible for Ensign Trevlyn's debts and that was the only thing of value you had."

Phoebe's shoulders sagged. Her sole valuable possession, except William. Of course that's why he'd taken it.

He leered at her in a way that made her shiver. "I thought things must be difficult for you. I've been meaning to come and see how you were, but I'm a busy man." He straightened up, his buttons undergoing more strain. His stinking breath struck her as he moved close. She stepped back but he followed. His lips spread in what he obviously thought was a friendly smile. "I'm prepared to forget how you've treated me in the past. Let's start over. I'll make it worth your while."

She shuddered. Could she endure it? No!

She gave him her haughtiest look. "I came to see Mrs. Simcoe," and tried to brush past him.

"She's not here." He sounded pleased.

"I'll see for myself." She took William's hand and strode off toward the headquarters building, head up, her heels striking the packed clay firmly. She wouldn't let the sergeant know she feared him, though her knees shook under her skirts.

The sergeant stood, legs spread, looking after her. "You've nothing to be so high and mighty about. You'll come crawling."

Never. Not even for William's sake could she endure that evil man.

The clerk at headquarters confirmed the Simcoes were in York preparing to move the capital there. No hope from Mrs. Simcoe then. She'd probably never see the vice regal couple again.

Perhaps the clerk could explain why she hadn't received her money.

"I am Mrs. Trevlyn. I haven't received my widow's pension. Perhaps you didn't know where to send it. I'm living in a cabin by the road just above the Falls. Has it been held here for me?"

The clerk rustled through his papers and kept his head down. Why didn't he seem to want to look at her?

Still staring at the papers on his desk, he muttered, "There isn't any record of it here. I'll look into it and let you know. I'm very busy. Good day to you." He turned and went into a back room.

Phoebe turned away, her hopes crushed. That was really strange. Surely the records would be in a drawer somewhere, not all on his desk.

Distraught, and mindful of the carter's advice, she hurried back to the road lest she miss the chance of a ride. She stood there trying to hold back the tears. Between the encounter with Sergeant Temple, finding that Mrs. Simcoe had left Newark, and the clerk's unhelpfulness, she was near to collapse.

Several carters went by, but none had room for her. She started out walking. Could she make it before dark? Could she actually walk so far? And she'd have to carry William most of the way. Perhaps it would be better to stay at Newark. But where?

As she stood undecided, a farmer came along with empty barrels rolling around in the back of his wagon.

He stopped. "Goin' far?"

"Yes. Up to the Falls."

"Well, I'm only going upalong but ye're welcome to ride that far."

"Thank you." A ride even part way would help.

"'Tis a long walk to the Falls."

"Yes."

The settler said nothing more and seemed incurious as to why she was walking so far by herself and with a small child. She thought he was a bit younger than herself. He looked strong and his team and wagon seemed well cared for.

He paid no attention to William but the best opener would be to learn his marital status.

"Do you have any children?"

"Naw."

"Do you like children?"

"Don't know nothin' 'bout 'em."

Probably not married then. Dare she ask him if he was? While she considered how to word her question, the farmer stopped the horses at a neat cabin. A log barn stood behind it, and cleared fields stretched out to each side. How she would love to live here. The farmer cleared his throat and she climbed down, trying to work out how she could prolong the conversation.

A pretty young woman opened the cabin door and called, "You're back in good time. Did you get my churn?"

"No, love. But I got a keg. I think I can make ye one."

Disillusioned, Phoebe thanked him for the ride, took William's hand and started up the road. Still a long way to go.

William's legs soon gave out and she was forced to carry him. Although she'd rejoiced in the way he'd grown, her back began to ache almost immediately, and she wished he weren't quite so heavy. She had to stop part way and sit on a log by the side of the road to rest.

William dug in the rotten bark and crowed when he discovered a large dark brown beetle. He watched it make its way along the log and poked at it with a grass stem. She relaxed and thought of Angelique. She sorely missed her friend. Loneliness was a sharp thorn in her breast. What happy times she'd spent with Angelique. Well, no use looking back. That only made her sadder. Angelique was part of another life.

She stood up. "Come, William."

The beetle had disappeared and, now bored, William willingly took her hand. They continued up the road to the derelict cabin.

CHAPTER 11

The snow retreated into the bush along the river as spring advanced. Phoebe followed it, searching under the trees for nuts the squirrels had missed. The meats of most she found were blue with mold or dried to papery curls, but the few good ones were nourishing. She savored them, but William puckered his lips at the slightly bitter taste of the butternuts.

One evening, William asleep, she slipped out to search again. The days were getting longer. Soon it would be warm. Velvety gray pussy willows were turning into yellow catkins. As she turned over dead leaves, she discovered fuzzy pink buds of hepaticas, just ready to open. Spring was definitely on the way. She drew in a deep breath of the woodsy scent arising from the thawing soil. She'd survived the winter.

Tiny starry clusters of pepper and salt flowers brought a sudden memory of her father digging the roots for her when she was a child. She scrabbled in the dirt, unearthing the tiny finger-like tubers. She ate some, delighted by their spicy crisp taste. Then, wonder of wonders, she found a squirrel's cache of hickory nuts buried in the leaf mold. Even William would like these sweet kernels. She felt no compunction raiding the storehouse. Survival of the fittest.

Intent on her task, other noises masked by the rustle of the leaves she scraped away, she was unaware of the approach of a visitor until he spoke.

"Good evening Mrs. Trevlyn. How are you getting along?"

Sergeant Temple. Feeling like a mouse caught in the glare of a snake, she froze. He grabbed hold of her and tried to draw her to him. She resisted but he was stronger than she thought. She stamped on his foot but his army boots protected him.

He laughed at her. "So you're still being obstinate. I told you I'd make things easier for you if you'd be nice to me. How about it?"

His eyes gleamed and brown spittle leaked from the corners of his mouth.

"You're a beast." She looked around frantically, seeking someone, anyone, to help her. But in the bush there was no one near, no one even close enough to hear her scream.

"Aha! I like a woman with spirit."

She managed to raise her arms high enough to rake her nails down his face from forehead to chin.

He snarled, "You bitch," and pushed her to the ground.

She dug her heels into the soft leaf litter trying to get far enough away to scramble to her feet. "Get away from me!"

"I'll teach you, you hellcat!" He bent down, seized her skirts, threw them over her head and fell on top of her. She screamed and screamed, the sound muffled by her heavy skirts. She flailed blindly, attempting to free herself from the tangled material and exploring hands, but he only pressed down harder on the cloth until she feared she'd suffocate.

Finished with her, he rose, buttoned his trousers, delivered a parting kick, mounted his horse and rode off.

She lay where she'd fallen, sobbing into the folds of her dress. She'd never thought anything so terrible could happen to her. She retched and shuddered.

Not until she heard William calling, "Mama, Mama, where are you?" was she able to pull herself together enough to wipe her face on the hem of her gown and clamber to her feet.

Her throat raw from screaming, she whispered, "Mama's coming. Just a minute," and limped across the field to the cabin.

What else? She thought every calamity that befell her was the worst that could happen, but something even more evil kept following. What vile creatures men were. She renounced the idea of marrying again. She'd stay as far as possible from the monsters. They'd caused her nothing but grief. Goodness knew how she'd live, but no more men. Ever.

Then pure rage took over. She'd show him if he ever came near her again. He'd be dead. Her Quaker mother had taught her never to resort to violence, to turn the other cheek. But there must be a point where this maxim no longer applied. As far as she was concerned, she'd reached it. She picked up the poker and pounded the back of her only chair. That for the sergeant. As the top board splintered, William's terrified screams brought her out of her nightmare.

She looked at the poker and the splintered chair. Had she done that? Taking a deep breath she said, "It's all right, William. Mama's just having a tantrum." She smiled wanly at him. He stopped his screaming and ran into her arms.

"You broke the chair," he said, and giggled. "I didn't break the chair ever."

"No, you didn't, and Mama won't do it again. We have to both be good, isn't that right?"

"You scared me."

She was scared, herself. She examined the damage. She'd never have believed she was capable of such violence.

For weeks afterward, she looked up and down the road to be sure the brute was not in sight before she ventured from the cabin. She kept the iron poker, or a stout stick, always within reach.

As the days went by without her evil visitor, she relaxed her vigil a little. Sergeant or no sergeant, she had to gather roots and dandelion greens, wood for the insatiable fire—and solicit sewing.

A terrible windstorm roared through the area one night. She lay awake, fearful the rickety shanty would collapse on their heads. The cabin withstood the onslaught but many trees in the bush were riven. In the afternoon, while William napped, she ran out to gather the fallen wood. The wind still blew hard. It roared in the cedars along the river, an ominous sound, reminding her of the rushing waters the day her parents drowned.

To distract her mind from her depressing thoughts she rushed about, gathering branches. She saw a large stick and put her

56

foot on it halfway along its length, bending up the end with her hands, trying to break it into a length she could carry. It broke suddenly and she staggered. As she regained her balance, she saw the sergeant driving into the yard. He stopped the horses at the edge of the bush and leisurely tied them to a tree.

How could she have been so careless? It must have been the wind that prevented her hearing the rattle of wagon wheels and the clink of harness. She couldn't escape. He stood between her and the safety of the cabin. She gripped the heavy piece of tree branch in both hands and waited.

"Well, Phoebe." The sergeant swaggered toward her, his jacket unbuttoned, thumbs hooked in his braces. "I guess I can call you Phoebe, now, seeing we're better acquainted. Right?"

"Go away."

"Now, don't get excited." The sergeant held up his hand, palm outward. "I brought some food for you. Your bureau's in the wagon. I thought you'd like to have it again. I've been busy or I would have brought it before."

"Get away from me!"

"Don't be so unfriendly. I'll see you and your little boy are well taken care of. You wouldn't want him to suffer for your stubbornness, would you?"

"He's suffered already."

"So he needn't suffer any more," said the sergeant, reaching for her.

She swung the stick with all her strength. It connected with the sergeant's head with a thud. He went down like a new-axed tree. Dropping the stick, she picked up her skirts and fled to the cabin. She rushed inside, closed and barred the door. Peeking through a crack in the shutter she watched him lurch to his feet. She hadn't killed him then. Was she glad or sorry? It would be terrible to kill another human being. But if anyone deserved to die, he did.

He staggered to the wagon, clutching his head, climbed in the back and rolled her bureau out on the ground. She cringed as the

57

drawers flew out, spilling their meager contents, one drawer collapsing in a mound of loose boards.

He untied the horses, climbed into the seat, and slapped the reins viciously on their backs. She grabbed the poker from the fireplace, holding her breath as he approached the cabin. But he only shook his fist in her direction as he passed, and whipped up the horses. Out on the rutted road he pulled the team down to a walk, and leaned forward holding his head in both hands.

She shook so violently she dropped the poker. She'd done it. She'd saved herself. This time. But what would he do now? Had she scared him away. Or made things worse?

CHAPTER 12

To Phoebe's relief the sergeant didn't return. She had bested him. She felt much more self confident.

When the spring spawning started, she joined the other fishermen along the riverbank, William proudly helping her with his own bent pin and string tied to a stick. One day he caught a fish but it slipped off the barbless hook and fell back into the water.

She grabbed him to prevent his jumping in after it, and stopped the resulting tantrum by saying, "Be quiet. If you scare the fish they'll all swim away and we won't have any supper."

Food, as always, was William's main interest. He conducted further conversations in whispers, though it was obviously a strain to contain his excitement when she successfully landed a large pickerel. Fish became a staple of their diet.

With a broken shovel, left in the cabin by the previous owner and not worth looting, she stirred the small abandoned garden behind the cabin and planted some peas, beans and squash, seeds given to her by a settler in exchange for sewing. William planted his own garden of pebbles in one corner.

She kept a vigilant eye out for the sergeant, and carried a stout stick with her everywhere she went. Of course, William had to have one to match.

One day she set out to deliver some sewing up near Fort Chippewa, William whining at her heels. To distract him, she pointed out a saucy blue jay that was screaming, "Thief! Thief!" at them from a roadside tree. William laughed and tried to imitate the bird. Why hadn't she thought of such things before? Of course the poor boy was bored, following her up and down the roads on his short legs.

She stopped at the rickety Chippewa Bridge and climbed down the bank to the river to show him yellow buttercups in the swampy edges of the creek, and a red-winged blackbird's nest woven between the cattail stems. Over William's crowing she heard the clip-clop of horse's hooves and the rattle of wagon wheels. Was it the sergeant? Where could she hide? Under the bridge looked to be the best place, but the water stretched from one abutment to the other. She couldn't get under there. Surely he wouldn't attack her here on the public road, but her heart beat fast all the same.

"Whoa-up there." The wagon stopped on the bridge and she looked up at the heavy-shouldered man peering down at her. His hair was tied back neatly, but a huge blond beard covered most of his face. He jumped off the wagon and clambered down the bank. What did he want?

Where had she put her stick? She looked around frantically. Oh, no! She'd left it on the road. She couldn't outrun him, especially with William. How could she protect herself?

The man said, "Phoebe?" in a wondering voice. "Is it you, really?" His gray eyes, tiny lines fanning from their outer corners, looked down at her. "Do you remember me? From the ferry accident. It's Jake. Jake Stettl."

"Jake." The riverman who had saved her. She scrutinized him while keeping her distance. His gray eyes were familiar and the blond hair—but not the beard.

"Jah. You remember!" he exclaimed. "Is this your little boy? You are married now, I think so?"

She began to shake. Too many memories crowded back at the sight of him.

"Better you sit down on that stone, there. You don't look so good."

She ignored the invitation. She'd stay on her feet, the better to repel him. He looked at her intently, but not in the lewd way of the soldiers at the fort.

He seemed merely curious, and this was confirmed when he said, "Where were you going?"

A simple question. She relaxed a little. "I have to deliver this sewing to Mrs. Weir, up by the fort."

"Get in the wagon, then. I will take you."

She was immediately alerted. Had she misjudged a man again? What did he have in mind? "Oh, no. You're going the other way."

"You think I don't know how to turn the horses around, maybe?" he asked, grinning.

"No, it's just that it's out of your way." He seemed sympathetic, but....

"I'm in no hurry. Come on, little bit." Before she could intervene, he picked up William and carried him up the bank to the road. He lifted the boy to the wagon seat. William crowed at the horses.

Now he had William, what could she do? Surely he wouldn't attack her in front of William—and she was so tired. She'd just have to watch her chance to get away. She allowed him to help her up over the wheel, wary of groping hands, but he was very respectful. Nothing to complain of, there.

He turned the team and gave William the ends of the reins to hold. William shook them and laughed, shouting at the horses.

When they reached the Weir cabin, she said, "Thank you for the ride, Mr. Stettl. Come, William."

"No! Want to drive horses." William's bottom lip protruded.

Jake chuckled. "Let him stay. We will wait for you."

"Oh, that's too much trouble for you." How could she get William away from him?

He shook his head. "No, it is not, so. I want to talk to you some more."

"I'll hurry, then." If it was just talk he wanted she'd be grateful—but hard to believe. She hurried up the path to the house, anxious at leaving William unprotected.

When she returned, William was sitting in Jake's lap.

Jake said, "Where to, now?"

"I'm going back home, but we can walk now, thank you. Come William."

"You forget I was going that way first," said Jake. "Can you climb up by yourself? I have to hold the horses, already. William's got them all excited." He laughed, a great full-throated sound. She couldn't help smiling. He seemed such a happy man. But you could never tell.

He still had William. She had no choice. She scrambled into the wagon, they once again crossed the dilapidated bridge and the horses broke into a trot. The wagon wheels rattled on the stony road, the harness chains jingled and William laughed with delight.

She didn't want Jake to know where she lived and looked for a likely place to get off the wagon but could not see anything plausible.

Then William pointed at the shanty and shouted, "There my house."

Too late.

Jake reined the horses off the road into the dooryard, jumped down and quickly tied them to a tree. Phoebe railed inwardly at her inability to manage her life. She climbed out of the wagon and reached up for William, but Jake reached over her head and lifted the boy down. Carrying him, he followed her into the cabin. She could think of no way to keep him out. It was considerate of him to give her a ride, and he hadn't said or done anything she could object to. But he probably wanted something in return. She shuddered.

As she thanked him for his kindness, William went into one of his tantrums. Jake watched the performance for a minute. The corners of his mouth twitched and his eyes sparkled. He beckoned her out of the cabin. Good. At least he was going outside. She'd watch for a chance to run back in and bar the door.

He guided her to a stump in the dooryard while she protested, "But William...."

"Leave be," said Jake quietly. "He will all right. Do you have some plan? The cabin is unlivable, I think so."

Phoebe lifted her chin. "We've been living in it."

He shook his head. "I don't know how. Our pigs have better."

Even this expression of concern was too much for her. She covered her face with her hands to hide her tears. He sat down beside her. As she tried to gain control of herself, she became aware of his closeness, jumped up and moved out of reach.

Still, in spite of her mistrust, she answered his questions, telling him of Richard's death and her struggle to make a living—but not of her trouble with the sergeant. No use giving him ideas.

"So, that is how it is, then." Jake nodded, his forehead creased.

The sympathy in his voice upset her again and she wiped away a tear with the back of her hand. "I don't know what to do. I don't have any money and I can't earn enough to keep us properly." Why did she let this man know how vulnerable she was?

William came out of the cabin and sheepishly joined them.

"I can't believe it," she said. "Usually his tantrums go on until he gets his own way. I don't understand why he stopped this time."

Jake chuckled. "That is how my mutti did when we were naughty. She just went away and left us. Such a show is not worth doing if nobody watches." He picked up the boy and set him on his lap. She was surprised William didn't object.

Jake tightened his arm around the boy. "William needs more love, I think—but not when he is being bad."

The nerve of him. Suggesting she didn't love her own son. "I love him. He's all I have."

"But you are all the time worried, no?"

William leaned against the broad chest. His eyelids drooped.

"I'm doing the best I can." Of course she was worried, who wouldn't be? But what business was it of this man's?

"I must go, once, or I will not get home before dark." He set William down and rose. "He is a nice little boy. I will talk to Mutti and see what we can do for a better place for you to live. She always knows what to do."

He carried the sleeping boy into the cabin, laid him on the bunk and covered him with the blanket, tucking it in carefully. She stood by the hearth within reach of the iron poker. What would he do now William was no longer watching?

But he just said, "Do not worry any more. We will think of something. I will again come, soon. Goodbye."

She watched from the door as he gathered up the reins and drove off down the road. Could she trust him—if he came back? He certainly had the opportunity to take advantage of her but he hadn't. He'd been very good to William, but you never could tell what a man was really like. She'd found that out.

Would he come back? Did she want him to? His eyes were certainly kind but who could tell what hid behind that monstrous yellow beard?

CHAPTER 13

All the way home behind the plodding horses, Jake considered the situation. His parents were urging him to marry, but after he'd seen Phoebe on the ferry when she first came to Niagara, he no longer found any of the eager German girls in the settlement attractive. Her dark beauty fascinated him. If he shut his eyes he could still feel the softness of her in his arms as he carried her from the rescue boat into the warehouse. He'd hoped to take her to her uncle's, but the ferryboat captain had refused him leave.

He tried to find her after the boat was back in service. He went to the farm but her aunt said she didn't live there any more and slammed the door in his face. He'd watched for her around the village at Fort Erie, but after he bought his farm he stopped working on the ferry and seldom went to the fort.

This tumbledown shack was not a good place for either her or her little boy. He'd wanted to take her home with him, today. Housework took too much time, to the detriment of his farm. He needed, at the least, a housekeeper. It wouldn't be the right thing to have her in his house without being married, though. He was ready to marry,but of course she wasn't. She hadn't even remembered him. What to do?

He unloaded the lumber in a pile beside Vati's barn and entered the kitchen, fragrant with the aroma of spiced sausage frying in the spider and crusty bread cooling on the table.

His mutti turned from the fireplace, a soup ladle in her hand. A tall, straight-backed woman with laugh lines at the corners of her gray eyes, Hannah was immaculate in her dark dress and huge white apron. How did she keep her aprons so unspotted through all her workday? Anyone could tell what he'd been doing by the state of his clothes.

In her native German she said, "Did you have a good trip? Will you have supper here before you go home?"

"Thank you, I will." Uneasy, he shifted his feet. "You remember the girl I saved from the ferry accident?"

"I remember." She turned and bent over the fire to turn the sausages. "I'm so happy you don't work on the ferry any more. I was always afraid the next one drowned would be you."

Jake shrugged impatiently. "Mutti, I saw her today."

"Did you? How is she?"

"Not too good. She has a little boy. She's living in a tumbledown cabin by the river. And starving, I think so. I wanted to bring her home with me right away. We have to do something for her, quick."

"You could take her some food. I'll make up a basket."

"She can't stay there. It's a terrible place. I thought maybe she could keep house for me."

"No, Jake, that wouldn't do without you were married."

Jake's shoulders sagged. He'd been afraid Mutti would object. What could he do? He must not lose her again.

Then the perfect solution came to him. "Grossmutti needs someone to stay with her on her farm until the doddy house here is finished. She shouldn't be alone now Grossvati is gone. Phoebe could do for her."

"But this girl is an English, you said."

"Does it matter?"

"You know we like to keep separate from other people."

"But she's only a girl. She can't do any harm to us."

"Well, we will see. Maybe Grossmutti won't like it. Does this girl know how to keep the house? Does she speak the German?"

"No, I don't think so." Just when he thought there was a solution. How could they manage?

But he couldn't give up. "I could teach her to speak the German." Could he indeed do so?

Hannah shook her head. "That would take a long time."

"I learned some English pretty quick when I had to, to work on the ferry." He had to persuade Mutti. "I'm sure she could learn. Especially with me to teach her." He smiled.

"You think you are too smart." Hannah shook her finger at him. "You will get your comeuppance."

"Well, I will ask Grossmutti, anyhow."

When he had explained Phoebe's desperate situation to his grandmother, she said, "But an English, Jake. I don't like it."

"But you would like to stay in your house. With Phoebe to do for you, you could. She's a nice quiet girl. And a little boy. You would like a little boy in the house again?"

"Wel-l-l, maybe we could try. I don't like to think of moving to the doddy house." She shook her finger. "But if I don't like her she will go."

Jake relaxed. Grossmutti would like Phoebe as much as he did.

The next day he appeared at the shack accompanied by his mother. He introduced the two women and told Phoebe that his mutti agreed she should come with them.

He said, "My grossmutti needs someone to look after her until the doddy house is finished."

So he didn't expect her to live with him. That was a relief. But would the woman put up with William's tantrums?

Grossmutti? Doddy house? What strange words. Phoebe thought perhaps Grossmutti was another name for grandmother, but doddy house?

"What is a doddy house?"

"Oh it's a little house built against the side of a son's house," said Jake. "For the parents to live in when they can't live by themselves any more. So their children can look after them."

Suddenly Jake's mother raised her hands as if surprised at something, and spoke volubly to Jake.

He looked puzzled and his mother seemed to be explaining something. She sounded excited. What was going on? She didn't look angry, though, so Phoebe hoped she wasn't refusing to take her in.

The problem, whatever it was, apparently solved, Jake turned to Phoebe. "Mutti says you stayed at her house after the ferry accident. I didn't know that."

"I remember I stayed somewhere. Was it at her place? I didn't recognize her. I don't remember much about that time."

"I'm not surprised, and so. It was bad for you."

Hannah smiled at her and said something and, while Phoebe couldn't understand the words, she liked this tall, strong-looking woman. Perhaps it would be all right. But could she trust her own judgment? She'd been fooled before. But most anything would be better than her present circumstances. She decided to take the chance.

"Come then," said Jake. "Pack up your things and I will put them in the wagon, just."

She gathered her few belongings. Then it occurred to her that she wouldn't make a very good impression in her stained linsey dress. While Jake was outside bringing the wagon to the door she took down the red velvet gown hanging behind the door and exchanged it for the threadbare one she was wearing. Why was Hannah frowning? She didn't seem to like the dress. True,it was shabby, but much the best thing she had. She stowed all William's clothes and her own in a sack.

When Jake came in he clucked over the shattered bureau drawer. "Next winter I fix it, maybe, when I'm not so busy."

Next winter! Was it possible she had a permanent home? Dared she hope her troubles were over? All the way down the rutted road she worried. Had she made a mistake? If this didn't work out what could she do then? Go back to the shanty? Never. No matter how distasteful this new life might turn out to be, it was all there was. She had to make it work.

Jake and his mother settled themselves on the wagon seat and Phoebe and William climbed into the wagon bed among their belongings. But this didn't suit William. In spite of Phoebe's remonstrance he climbed over the seat back and pushed between Jake and Hannah.

"Horsies," he said.

Jake chuckled. "You want to drive?"

He gave William the ends of the lines and William happily shook them and cried, "Go!"

Jake seemed to know how to handle children. Did he have some of his own? Was he married?

When they reached Fort Erie, Phoebe considered asking him if they might stop and see if Angelique was still there. If his home was not too far away she might be able to seek refuge with Angelique if her new home became impossible.

As if reading her mind, Jake said, "We should have something a little to eat and drink. It's a long way home yet."

"Jake, you know I won't go in there." Hannah sounded shocked. "What are you thinking, so?"

"I'm thinking a cup of hot coffee would be good. I'm thirsty and I think William is too."

"Thirty, thirty," shouted William.

"See?" said Jake.

"But a tavern."

"There is nowhere else. We don't know anyone here to visit."

Despite Jake's protests that Hannah would freeze, she insisted on staying in the sleigh while they went inside. Angelique wasn't in the tavern, and when Phoebe asked for her, the servant girl said Angelique's husband had been transferred to Oswego and she'd gone with him. No help from Angelique then. When they came out, Jake brought his mother a cup of coffee and a fried cake which she eyed dubiously, but finally nibbled until it was gone.

Refreshed, they turned west and drove along the lake between scattered farms. They were going a long way from Fort Erie.

Phoebe wondered how would she get back if it turned out to be even worse than the shack. She panicked for a moment, but then calmed herself. Whatever happened she would deal with it when it came.

They came to a settlement and Jake said, "This is where we live, so."

Window curtains twitched in some of the houses and she knew they were watched. She nervously twisted her hands in her lap. Of course country people would be curious. But would they like her?

She was a little heartened when Jake reined the team off the road in front of a neat clapboard house. It looked like a mansion. Small-paned windows sparkled, and chimney smoke drifted above a rain-proof roof.

An old lady opened the door at once, as if she'd been watching for them. A little woman, almost as broad as long, in her full skirts and apron, her white hair was pulled severely back under her white cap. Her blue eyes, somewhat faded, seemed kindly, but a little suspicious. This must be Jake's grandmother. Would she like them? Phoebe thought she'd do everything she could to please the grandmother so she and William could live in this lovely house.

The old woman said, "Come in." Then she opened her arms. "Oh, the dear little boy."

Although Phoebe couldn't understand the German words, the meaning seemed to be quite clear. Wrinkles creased the grandmother's whole face, deepening when she smiled at William.

And William, for once, was on his best behavior and clearly captivated the old woman. Phoebe hoped his good conduct would continue.

She and William were soon settled in the big bedroom over the kitchen along with the bureau. Jake had removed the drawers and carried the case and drawers up the stairs in only two trips. Phoebe admired the muscles rippling under his homespun shirt. How strong he was.

She took a deep breath as she contemplated the bright room. It smelled of lye soap and beeswax polish. Bleached towels hung on the rail over the washstand and an intricate patchwork quilt covered the huge bed. The uncurtained windows looked out on stumpless fields. She felt safe. Please God it would continue.

She turned to the old woman. "Thank you for letting us come here."

Jake translated. His grandmother smiled and gestured toward the stairs. It was suppertime and Phoebe had no trouble understanding.

In the spotless kitchen, filled with the aroma of fresh-baked biscuits and frying pork, Jake turned to her. "I take Mutti home. After chores I give you your first lesson in German, or so."

German? Could she learn another language? She'd have to if she were going to communicate with the women in this family. Jake spoke a queer but understandable version of English but his grandmother obviously didn't speak it nor did his mother. Well, she'd try her best. It would be the price to pay to live in this warm, clean house with the lovely old lady. She was so grateful to Jake. For once, a man who didn't abuse her. At least so far.

CHAPTER 14

J ake came every evening and Phoebe soon learned the German names of all the utensils in the house, but there was still confusion when he wasn't there. Sometimes chores had to wait for his visits when Grossmutti couldn't make her understand what she wanted.

"I feel so stupid," Phoebe said. "I don't think I'll ever learn."

"You are doing good." He encouraged her. "It's a hard language, for sure, if you don't start out with it, already."

"But William knows more than I do. He seems to understand what your grandmother says."

"That is what I said, so. It's some easier when you are little? Don't be discouraged."

She was discouraged. Had she made a mistake? But what choice did she have? She did like it here. Jake's grandmother was kind and it was good to, at last, have enough food and a warm, dry place to live. She must try harder to fit in. This was her only chance for a decent life.

Jake's father held a logging bee and Phoebe, Jake's grandmother, and William went across the road to help feed the men. Phoebe was introduced to several women who had also come to help. She liked Esther Martin, a plump motherly woman, but Hannah's sister-in-law, Salome Witmer was stiff-necked and sour-looking, her mouth drawn up like a drawstring pouch. Salome's daughter Rebecca was the opposite, friendly and impetuous and constantly reproved by her mother for her exuberance.

Hannah brought a tiny wooden horse and wagon, and a spinning top carved out of wood, from the attic, and William was enticed to play in the corner of the room, out from under the women's feet. When he became bored, Rebecca knelt to play with him, to Phoebe's relief. As hired help, she should be working. Too much time spent looking after William might jeopardize her position. But it wasn't safe for William to be where they could trip over him.

At dinnertime the men filed in and took their places around a long table while the women waited on them. Jake must get his size from his mother, Phoebe thought. His father, Simon, was small-framed like the grandmother and so was his youngest brother, Peter, although the older brother, Karl, was also a huge young man. Karl was yellow-blond like Jake but Simon and Peter had sandy hair. Only Simon and Jake wore beards. Simon's was a fringe below his jaw-line but Jake's was full below the corners of his mouth and running up around his cheeks to his ears. It was neatly trimmed and made him look very distinguished.

Salome's husband, Amos, a wizened little man, looked as if Salome had sucked all the juice out of him. Daniel Martin, on the other hand, seemed as kindly as his wife, Esther. They all seemed to Phoebe like friendly people—except for Salome, maybe. But she couldn't expect everything to be perfect. It certainly hadn't been in her past. She'd do anything she could to be allowed to stay here.

She noticed Jake watching her as she moved around the room. Was he interested in her as a woman and not just a helper for his grandmother? He hadn't made any suspicious advances. Could she hope he might eventually ask her to marry him? She was sure neither his mother nor his grandmother would allow him any illicit relationship and he certainly couldn't conduct one in this tiny community without them, and everyone else, knowing. The twitching curtains along the trail as they came, were proof of that. After the soldiers she'd considered as husbands, he looked like a prize. Her position as housekeeper was precarious. Married, she'd be safe.

Late in the afternoon Jake escorted her, Grossmutti, and William back across the road.

She said, "Why does Rebecca's mother look so cross?"

"Oh, Aunt Salome. She's a different."

What did he mean by different? He kept saying things that didn't make sense.

Amos Witmer soon noticed that Jake took a special interest in this woman who was not one of themselves. There were rumors of terrible goings-on at the forts and, since she'd lived there, might she have been involved? He'd been a deacon back in Pennsylvania before they came here and he felt it his duty to watch over this little flock in the wilderness even though no church had been established.

He mentioned his worry to Salome, who said, "I saw her going by in the wagon when Jake brought her. In a red dress. Shameful. You must speak to Jake. Tell him to send her away We don't want such an evil influence here for our young people. I was of a mind to bring Rebecca straight home from the bee."

Amos was sorry he'd mentioned it. Now Salome would give him no peace until he acted. The mantle of deacon sat heavy on his shoulders.

Nevertheless as he, Jake, and the other Stettl men worked together in Simon's bush, cutting up the treetops left after the logging, Amos spoke of his worries. "I don't like that girl here, Jake."

"Why not? She needs a place to live and Grossmutti needs someone to look after her."

"But she's an English."

"So? She won't bite, I don't think so."

"This is not for joking. I see you have an interest in her," Amos's nose twitched with a drippy cold. "You wish to marry her?"

Jake stiffened. Aunt Salome was behind this, as always. He thought she laid awake nights thinking up ways to make trouble. He'd wanted the community to know Phoebe before he told her of his love. Well, he might as well tell what he planned. He faced his uncle. "If she will have me. I haven't asked."

"You make a mistake, Jake."

Jake lifted his chin, his beard fluttering. "I don't think so."

Jake noticed that Vati, trimming a nearby branch, was listening.

His father said nothing then, but held a family conference after supper when Amos had gone home to chores.

"You pay too much attention to that girl, Jake."

His mother said, "I thought you just felt sorry for her. I didn't see you were specially interested."

Jake grimaced. "Aunt Salome did, though. She's been at Uncle Amos, for sure. I've been interested ever since I saw her on the ferry, but I didn't know where she went after the accident, already. I looked but couldn't find her."

"So long you remembered her?" said his mother.

"So long." Jake nodded.

"The community wouldn't stand for you marrying an English," boomed Simon.

"I would risk it, for Phoebe," piped up Peter.

Simon frowned at his youngest son. "You don't know what you say. This is not a joke."

"Well, you go too fast, anyhow," said Jake. "I haven't asked her."

"It's time for a family. You should have a wife, soon," said Hannah. "Only not this one, I think." She wrapped her arms in her apron as if for protection.

"This one, or no one." Then he smiled at his mutti. "You like her, so?"

"Yes, but not for you. And not if she causes trouble in the community."

"Aunt Salome is the trouble, not Phoebe. I will make it work. I've searched a long time for her."

He took his hat from the peg by the door and went out to hitch the team to go to his farm for evening chores.

What a hubbub. He hadn't thought his feelings showed. Had Phoebe noticed them, too? What did she think? He didn't want to scare her away.

CHAPTER 15

Phoebe was happy and felt completely safe in the grandmother's home. What a change from her previous environments. She couldn't work hard enough to show her gratitude to Jake and his grandmother. She knew nothing of the family's concern about her being an outsider.

The old lady spent most of her time playing with William and they laughed together over the simple games Grossmutti taught him. Phoebe marveled that William apparently understood everything the old woman said while she was often confused in spite of the German lessons.

She was pleased at William's good behavior. All he needed was a stable home. And of course the fact that the old woman spent most of her time playing with him didn't hurt. He was never averse to attention.

She noticed the old lady nodding her head in approval as her new housekeeper performed all the tasks of a pioneer household. It was wonderful having the tools to work with, to be warm and dry and sure of enough to eat. She and the old woman often went across the road of an afternoon to assist Hannah. Even though as strong as any of her menfolk, with no daughter to help, Hannah was often overwhelmed. Although Grossmutti couldn't walk very well, lamed from the kick of a horse when she was young, she was formidable with a paring knife.

Phoebe became aware of the complicated relationships in the settlement. She went over them in her mind, trying to sort them out. Esther Martin was Simon's sister and Deacon Witmer was Hannah's brother, and his wife, Salome, was Barnabas Sherk's sister as was Gerda Beuhler. It seemed like they were all related. She mentioned this to Jake.

"Well, the old people all came from the same place in Pennsylvania. They wanted to keep together, separate from the outside world. There was no other Mennonite group here for the young ones to marry then, so they married each other. It's not good to marry inside the family all the time, but they couldn't help it."

She felt a chill. What was she doing in this tiny, close-knit community? How could she fit in?

Jake tried not to let his feelings for Phoebe show lest he frighten her. He watched with impatience as she drifted contentedly through the days. He longed to speak of his hopes for their future together but feared she would reject him.

Her quick mastery of his language pleased him, although she said she wasn't satisfied with her progress. She showed impatience at the words she couldn't remember; he marveled at how many she did.

Unable to hold back any longer, he came one Sunday afternoon with the buggy and asked her to go for a ride. William and Grossmutti were absorbed in a game of cat's cradle. The grandmother waved them goodbye, but William was engrossed in weaving his fingers through the strands of string and didn't see them leave.

A southerly breeze drove fleecy clouds across the sky and brought the scent of Grossmutti's daffodils to Jake's nostrils. The fall wheat in Vati's east field was springing up well, as was his own. No winter kill. It would be a good crop, please God. Enough to support a family.

As they jogged down the road, the horse snorting and occasionally breaking wind, he considered how to say what was on his mind.

The gelding slowed on an uphill grade, and Jake turned to her. "Phee, you like us a little, already?"

"Oh, yes everyone has been so kind."

He took a deep breath as if he were preparing to jump into the millpond. "Would you like to stay here always?"

She turned her head quickly to look at him. What was he saying? Was there a chance she couldn't? Her heart began to pound. Was he going to tell her she had to leave?

The doddy house was almost finished and when Grossmutti moved into it, Hannah would be able to look after her. There'd be no need for her. She and William would be homeless again.

He put his arm around her shoulders. She stiffened, involuntarily, and then relaxed. But she must be cautious until she found out where this was leading. What was he thinking? Happy as she was here, she'd settle for nothing less than marriage. She eyed a logging trail leading into a woodlot and gathered herself to leap out of the buggy if he turned into it. There were no houses with trembling curtains to offer a haven right here.

His arm tightened. "I want to marry you, Phoebe. Will you marry me?"

Marry her, not send her away. He wanted to marry her. A fine strong man to take care of her and William. She'd have security in this community. As Jake's wife she would officially be a member. He seemed such a good man, and handsome. William liked him, too, and from what she'd seen already she was sure he'd be a good influence on her son.

She'd better not seem too eager, though. "I d-don't know, Jake. I never thought of such a thing."

"Think some, then, will you, Phee? We could have a good life together, and so." He paused. "I've been planning it this long time. Since I saw you on the ferry, even." His arm tightened and he put his cheek against her hair.

She gritted her teeth to keep from pulling away from him. Why did she always think of the sergeant if anyone touched her? This was not the repulsive sergeant, but a good man who wanted to marry her after meeting her only once before? She couldn't believe it. She'd better grab this chance for security before he changed his mind.

"Yes, Jake, I'll marry you."

He let out such a whoop that the gelding, ambling along at his own pace, was startled into a gallop. Jake had to release her lest the careening buggy upset. He grabbed the reins which he'd wound around the whip stock. Pulling the animal down to a sedate trot he soothed him with soft words interspersed with chuckles. The horse quieted and Jake embraced Phoebe again, while holding the reins in one hand behind her back.

"Just in case the fool decides to run away again," he said, laughing. "I can't blame him, though. I feel like running, myself."

"From me?"

"Just from happy, so."

He kissed her and the great beard tickled her chin, making her giggle. She remembered the passion with which she'd embraced Richard, and wished she could summon those feelings again. If she didn't love Jake, well that couldn't be helped. She could still make a good home for him.

He said, "I'll talk to Uncle Amos right away," and turned the horse toward home, his arm holding her close.

She couldn't believe her good luck. William worshiped him. But after her past experiences she found it difficult to trust anyone. Richard had not been the hero she'd thought him and the sergeant. Well.... Still, Jake was her only choice. Good or bad, he was her hope for survival.

While he watched the road ahead, she studied him: sun-bleached hair tied back with a piece of hemp, broad tanned forehead, craggy nose and the great yellow beard. A strong face, surely one a person could rely on.

She said, "I've wondered why you wear such a big beard, but no mustache. All the soldiers at the fort wore mustaches, some of them huge, but they shaved their chins."

"That's why. We want to look as different from the soldiers as we can."

He smiled at her, white teeth showing through the full lips and tiny wrinkles fanning out from the corners of the gray eyes, now soft with emotion. Surely a man with such eyes could never do her harm. She smiled back and felt her heart begin to beat a little faster. She'd made the right decision. She was sure of it.

Reluctantly leaving her at Grossmutti's, Jake went across the road, bursting with jubilation, to tell his parents the good news.

Apprised of the proposal, Simon said, "Now you see, Hannah. No good I said would come from taking in that girl. Boy, there are lots of nice girls here for you to marry, already."

"But this is the one I want. From the first day I saw her on the boat, even." Then he had an inspiration. Something that would convince his farmer father. "All the girls here are my cousins, close. That's not good, Vati. You know it. We wouldn't breed animals so, close like that."

"Jake!" Hannah's voice revealed her shock. "What are you saying? Animals we are not."

"But an English, Jake," said Simon. "I forbid it."

"Well, I will marry her anyhow. I have said so." Jake picked up his hat and left. He'd marry whoever he chose. Still, it was too bad Mutti and Vati didn't approve.

A very perturbed Hannah and Simon appeared next morning. Hannah noted Phoebe out in the garden. Good.

Simon came right to the point. "You know Jake wants to marry that English?"

Grossmutti smiled. "I thought so."

"You approve?" asked Hannah.

"She is a good girl—for an English. We need some fresh blood."

"That's what Jake said, too." Hannah's voice still held shock. "He says we are animals."

Grossmutti said, "The generations must go on, but healthy. Back home it wouldn't need to be a choice, but healthy children is the best. I think Phoebe will be a good wife."

"I don't like it," said Simon, "but that Jake, he is so stubborn."

"And where does he get that from?" Grossmutti smiled fondly at her son.

Ruth Zavitz

Ignoring the weeds in the cornfield, Jake went over to Uncle Amos's the next morning to ask him to perform the wedding ceremony.

The Deacon was splitting wood in the chip-yard behind the house. No sign of Salome. Good.

"Good morning, Uncle Amos."

"Good morning, Jake."

"I wanted to ask you something."

The kitchen door opened and Salome came out. "Hello, Jake. What did you want to know?"

He might have known she'd be watching. Now he was in for it. After his parents' reaction he knew Uncle Amos, too, might have some doubts, but he was sure he could convince him. Now with Salome it would be a lot harder.

"I wish to talk with Uncle Amos, Aunt Salome. It's private."

"The deacon consults with me on everything, Jake. You might as well tell it now."

Jake was sure Uncle Amos didn't willingly confide in her, but as she said, she knew everything the deacon knew.

Well, she'd find out anyhow. He might as well say it. "Phoebe and I want you to marry us, Uncle Amos."

"Never!" exploded Salome. "An English. Jake! What are you thinking?"

"I'm thinking I love her and she is the one I want for my wife."

"Well..." said Amos,"...I'm not sure...."

"Not sure?" said Salome. "Forbid it!"

"I guess I couldn't do it," said Amos. "I'm not sure I have the authority, anyhow. Back home it's the pastor or the bishop who does the marrying."

"You are the deacon!" said Salome. "You have the authority since we don't have a pastor. But it would be an abomination."

Amos lifted his shoulders then let them drop. "I can't do it, Jake. I'm sorry."

81

"Don't be sorry, Deacon, for doing what's right." Salome pointed a stiff finger at her husband. "You go right away to Grossmutti Stettl's and tell her to turn that girl out before she causes more trouble. The wood splitting can wait 'til afternoon." The finger pointed at a different target. "Jake, repent of your wrongdoing and pick one of our nice girls."

"No, Aunt Salome, Uncle Amos. This girl I will marry. I'll take her to the fort, to the magistrate."

Salome gasped. "Jake. You wouldn't. When the deacon disapproves?"

"I will so. I wouldn't choose it, but since Uncle Amos won't..."

Amos cleared his throat. "Well, Jake, perhaps..."

"Deacon. Don't give in."

Amos dug in the chips with the toe of his boot. "I can't do it, Jake. It wouldn't be right."

Jake turned on his heel without a goodbye and strode off. Drat Aunt Salome. Without her interference he could have persuaded Uncle Amos.

Salome glared at Amos until he set off for the Stettls, and then returned to her window washing, her duty done. He went into the bush on the way to the Stettls' but didn't come out on the other side. Some time later he returned to the chip-yard and took up his ax.

Salome assumed he'd taken care of the problem. He never disobeyed her.

The next Saturday Jake came to Grossmutti's with a pine chest rubbed to a fine glow with beeswax, and decorated with hearts and flowers in bright paint.

"It's beautiful, Jake. Where did you get it?" Phoebe outlined the glowing flowers with her finger.

"I made it, some, in the evenings."

"Must have been late, for sure," said Grossmutti, her eyes twinkling, "since you are here every night, so."

"Thank you, Jake," said Phoebe touching a red heart.

"It's for me, too, you know," he said, grinning at her, his eyes shining.

She opened the chest. The inside was unpainted and the fragrance of fresh-cut pine wood enveloped her. Lovely. What a kind, thoughtful man she was going to marry. She'd do everything she could to please him.

CHAPTER 16

The next Sunday the Stettl family met at Simon's for dinner. Phoebe helped Hannah carry in the bowls of steaming food. Heavy rain fell outside as they gathered around the table.

Simon said the blessing, his deep voice seeming to vibrate in Phoebe's chest. He sounded as if he was talking directly to his God. A good man.

"Amen." Simon picked up the carving knife and began to slice the ham. He laid a thick slab on each of the plates piled in front of him, then passed them down the table to his wife. Hannah added boiled potatoes, and beet greens and distributed the plates.

When everyone was served, bowls of pickles were passed. Hands reached for thick slices of homemade bread and dipped knives into the slab of butter in a saucer in the middle of the table.

Nothing was said while everyone savored the food.

First hunger satisfied, Simon said, "That's a good rain," watching it stream down the windowpane.

"Jah, it will make the weeds grow," said Jake's younger brother, Peter.

"That's my lazy son," said Simon. "I'm glad we hadn't cut any hay yet to get rained on, but we must start as soon as it's dry."

Jake had no interest in the weather, or weeds, right then. Impatient, he brought up the subject of the wedding. "We'll get married as soon as the hay is done. I will go to Fort Erie tomorrow to see the magistrate about it. I think he has to put up a sign saying we want to do it. I've seen signs like that at the mill there, on the door. The hay will be too wet to cut, anyhow."

Simon glared at him. "So. You're going to marry in spite of me."

Phoebe spilled potatoes from her fork. She hadn't thought of the family disapproving. She looked at Jake. Would he defy his father? Perhaps her security was not as settled as she'd thought.

Jake jutted out his chin until his beard cleared his shirtfront. "Yes, I will."

Hannah interrupted, apparently trying to stop the argument from going further. "You're going to the magistrate? Why?"

"Aunt Salome won't let Uncle Amos do the wedding."

Simon growled, "She's right, for once. You're making a big mistake, Jake. I don't think the community will accept an English for a wife. A housekeeper yes, a wife is different."

Jake squared his shoulders. "I will marry Phee whatever happens." He reached for her hand. "I have said so."

She clung to his fingers. He was determined to marry her, but was it right? What would happen to them if she did? Hannah and Grossmutti seemed to have accepted her, but Simon was obviously against it. She hadn't made any friends outside the family. Salome's daughter, Rebecca, had seemed friendly, but her mother certainly wasn't. It would make little difference to her if she was ignored, but what would it mean for Jake?

Hannah sighed. "I hope it will come right."

"I hope so, too," said Simon. He shook his head. "Why the Good Lord gave me such a mulish son I cannot tell."

Even though he obviously disapproved, it sounded as if Simon was beginning to accept the idea. It would work out. It had to. Phoebe's appetite restored, she savored the greens on her plate. Nothing like steamed beet leaves, fresh from the garden, after the winter's boring diet of turnips and carrots.

Hannah took another spoonful of potatoes and passed the bowl to Peter.

"Thanks, Mutti."

She said, "If you are determined to do this, Jake, we must do something about your cabin."

"What's the matter with my cabin? It's good."

"For an old bachelor, maybe, but it's not fit for a woman."

"Who is old, then?" asked Jake.

"Not you, for sure," said Jake's older brother Karl who'd taken no part in the discussion thus far. "You're only a sprout, yet."

"Hah! I have a wife coming. I don't see you with one."

"I have more sense."

They grinned at each other and Phoebe was relieved. She'd feared an argument. The others seemed to have accepted her and she'd do her best to win Simon's approval. Hannah picked up the vegetable bowl and Phoebe followed her, carrying the depleted meat platter.

In the kitchen, Hannah handed her a plump golden pie. "That's the last of the dried apples but I picked a handful of strawberries yesterday so we won't lack for fruit now."

Phoebe sniffed the aroma escaping from the slits in the pie's crust and her mouth watered. She would never take this bounty for granted.

Hannah and Phoebe spent several days at Jake's cabin. They scoured the pine puncheon floor with ashes to a new-wood glow, polished the two small windows and whitewashed the inside of the log walls to a sparkling whiteness. Hannah grumbled at the indifferent housekeeping Jake practiced.

Jake, who had come in to see how they were progressing, said, "What do you think I'm getting married for?" and grinned at Phoebe.

"Hmmph," said Hannah. "You should build some shelves here between the fireplace and the corner. What do you think, Phoebe?"

"Oh, yes. I'd like that."

He measured the space with outstretched arms. "I can do that but it will have to wait for rainy days."

"Just so you don't forget." Hannah frowned at him, then turned to Phoebe. "These men, they always forget if it's something for the house. The barn, it's different."

"Now, Mutti, don't turn her into a nag before we're married, even."

"If you don't forget, there's no reason to nag."

Phoebe enjoyed these exchanges among the Stettl family. It sounded like arguments and then seemed to turn into jokes, but at the same time points were made. When William grew up she hoped she'd have such a relationship with him. But he was so demanding he exhausted her. He seemed always to take and never give. Maybe Jake would be able to change his attitude. She found she depended more and more on him. Surely her troubles were over. Even Simon had spoken kindly to her yesterday when he brought a bundle of kindling for Grossmutti.

As Phoebe and Hannah walked back to their respective homes, Hannah muttered about the previous owner of Jake's farm. "How could a family live in such a poor place? It takes only a little time to put up shelves and make everything neat. For Jake, by himself, it didn't matter. He lived with us most of the time, anyhow, but the poor woman who lived there before must have had lots of trouble. Well, Jake will make it right for you."

Phoebe was certain he would. He'd already given evidence of his concern for her and William's welfare. She would never cease to be grateful.

The wedding day came closer. Every time she thought of it, and of moving into Jake's cabin, she felt apprehensive. He was obviously very much in love with her, but she only felt safe and contented. Perhaps she was being dishonest in marrying him. He'd been so kind she didn't want to disappoint him.

The three women had two large gardens to care for—one at Hannah's and one at Jake's. Grossmutti had planted a small one at the side of Hannah's in anticipation of her move to the doddy house. Her daughter-in-law thought this unnecessary.

"You could help yourself to ours," said Hannah as she and Phoebe opened drills in the loamy soil for beans. "You could eat with us, too. All those pots to cook the same things. It's silly."

Grossmutti paused in her shelling of corn. "I like to grow my way and cook my way. I do it different from you."

"All right, then," said Hannah and began covering the rows of seeds.

Phoebe thought Hannah looked a little angry, and hurt. Even mothers and daughters-in-law who got along as well as Hannah and her mother-in-law, had their differences. Would she and Hannah have disagreements? She couldn't imagine it. No matter what Hannah wanted, she'd do it for the woman who'd agreed to give her a home.

Grossmutti said Phoebe should have a new dress for the wedding. Phoebe thought the white-sprigged blue dress Hannah had given her when she came would do. Hannah agreed. However, the waistband was too tight and Phoebe had to let it out, while the older women chuckled approvingly, their differences forgotten. A Mennonite woman had to carry some weight to stand the hard work.

Jake kept thinking up excuses to take Phoebe to his farm, he said to get her opinion on his various projects, but in reality just to see her in his house. He'd mended her bureau, polished it, and set it against the wall across from the hearth. It was worth the time he spent, when he saw her eyes glow with pleasure at the restoration of her treasure.

"Oh, Jake, it's beautiful. Almost better than new. What a lot of work you've done on it."

"Not so much. It's a nice chest."

He saw unusual warmth in her eyes and reached to put his arms around her but she stepped back. He dropped his arms and turned away with a sigh. However, when they started to walk back to Grossmutti's she put her hand in the crook of his arm and he was heartened. He must give her time.

He thought it was the longest spring he'd ever endured, but at the same time he was filled with boundless energy. At last he was setting up his own family on his own farm, not just dreaming of it.

CHAPTER 17

Phoebe was picking strawberries in the pasture when she experienced something she hadn't felt for four years. Startled, she stood up, putting her hands to her aching back. A killdeer, pattering through the grass, stopped and stared at her with a beady eye, one foot raised. Phoebe raised her arm to wipe the back of her hand across her sweating forehead. The bird scuttled off uttering sharp peeps, its spindly legs revolving like windmill fans.

She squatted down to the berries. Again something in her midsection objected. Her heart hammered and her breath came short. It couldn't be. She stood up and hurried into the shade of the woods.

Leaning against a rough-barked tree trunk she considered the situation. She hadn't had her menses since she moved into the shack by the river, but she'd attributed that to shock and then to the lack of food. She'd been nauseous for several weeks, but thought that, too, was due to the bad food.

It wasn't that. She was pregnant. That horrible sergeant. She counted the time. Almost three months. What could she do? How could she get rid of it? The thought of the seed of that disgusting man growing inside her made her retch.

Would Jake believe she'd been attacked? That she couldn't help it? Such behavior was surely outside his experience. And the family. They'd never accept that it wasn't her fault. Her thoughts went round and round. That's what her life was, a cage. No matter what she did, she couldn't escape. Just one terrible thing after another. And now, when she finally thought she was safe, another disaster.

What could she tell Jake? Even if he believed her, his family and the community would be shocked. One more thing against her. The Stettls had been so good to her; she couldn't face their scorn. But what was she to do? She hugged the tree trunk, sobbing. Angelique was far away and she had no friends here except the

Stettls, and even they wouldn't be compassionate enough to forgive this. Poor Jake. He'd wish he'd never seen her. She must go away.

But what could she do about William? If she took him with her they would surely both die of starvation. Perhaps she should leave him here. Yes, she could do that. Jake and Grossmutti would take care of him. William had done no wrong. It was only her shameful self. She'd just walk away and perish somewhere in the bush and never cause trouble to anyone ever again.

She must plan this carefully. It was hard to do anything here without someone noticing and commenting. She'd have to slip away in the night, and even that would be difficult, for the old lady was a light sleeper. She wiped her eyes and went back to the berries, trying to work out how she could get away.

The small being inside her rebelled at being squeezed, but she deliberately kept on with her picking. Suffer, you little monster, as you're making me suffer. The sergeant was out of reach but this— thing—she could hate.

She returned to the house with her pail of berries to find Grossmutti had taken William over to Hannah's. This was her chance to leave. But men were working in the hay-fields nearby. Someone would see her and report it. If she were caught, she'd have to confess. She must avoid that. Better wait for darkness.

Grossmutti and William returned at suppertime, and she couldn't resist picking him up and hugging him until he squirmed. At bedtime she rocked him, holding him close until he went to sleep. How could she leave him? He was her whole life—but then she had no future life. Jake and Grossmutti would be good to him. William would be all right. She was the only one disgraced.

That night she lay, sleepless, turning restlessly. The room was hot, and her linsey bedgown prickled her sweaty skin. She went over and over her problem, seeking a better solution than running away. But no other remedy presented itself. She looked over the side of the mattress at William, sleeping peacefully on his trundle bed. She'd never see him again. She stifled sobs so as not to wake him. What a mess she'd made of her life. Nothing to do but end it.

When a full moon shone in the window, lighting the room and allowing her to move about without fear of bumping into anything and making a noise, she got out of bed. She donned her clothes, scarcely noticing if they were properly fastened. What did it matter? Kneeling down beside the trundle bed, she kissed William one last time and smoothed the hair away from his forehead. In his sleep he still looked like a baby, not a three-year-old boy. A tear fell on his blanket. How could she leave him? But she must. She got to her feet, wiped at the tears with the back of her hand to clear her vision, and walked away from the only person she loved.

Keeping close to the wall to avoid the creaky step, she went down the stairs and stole out, easing the door latch into place with just the faintest click.

She was only dimly aware of what she did; her body merely followed the plan she'd devised on the previous day. Entering the bush behind the house, she stumbled through the underbrush until she happened on an old deer trail. She followed it mindlessly, tripping over fallen branches, besieged by mosquitoes.

Daylight came and the heat built as the sun rose higher. Perspiration dripped, unheeded, from her chin and the end of her nose and trickled between her breasts. She scrambled through raspberry thickets she could have avoided had she been mindful of her path. Her one thought was to get as far away as possible from the settlement.

Stumbling through the undergrowth, she tripped over a hidden log and lay, exhausted, where she fell. She drifted off into an uneasy sleep. Late in the afternoon she woke and got to her feet, startling a bright-eyed squirrel sitting on a tree branch overhead.

She continued her journey to nowhere. Deer-flies stung her. Swarms of gnats clouded her head, getting into eyes and nostrils. Near dark she came to a stream and waded in. As the water rose to her shoulders, some sense of preservation made her turn and make her way back to the bank. She sank again into sleep, sodden garments clinging.

In the morning, her body's needs prompting her, she mindlessly drank from the stream, ate some berries, plump and juicy from the moisture along the creek bank, and continued along beside the water. A deer raised its head as she passed, stared at her, then darted off. A raccoon sat in the shallows watching her through its bandit mask, a fish held in its tiny hands.

She moved, one foot before the other, her mind blank. In some places the bank was impassable and she waded in the water. She didn't attempt to cross again. What difference did it make which way she went?

Coming upon a dead-fall she tried to force her way through, but was soon entangled in branches and berry vines. At first she stood still. Why go farther? But then the discomfort of piercing thorns and deer-fly bites roused her. She forced her way back, the way she'd come until she was clear of the tangle. Skirting the jumble of fallen trees she continued along the creek bank.

She came suddenly out of the heavy bush and blinked as her eyes adjusted to the blinding light after the dark forest gloom. She realized where she was: Chippawa Bridge.

Her lethargy left her and she shook with rage. There was the river road. She would go to Newark. She'd confront the sergeant and tell everyone what he'd done. Nothing worse could happen to her. She'd tell them what a terrible man he was.

She crossed the bridge and stepped out, briskly. The long road to Newark was as nothing. She could walk it before nightfall. Along the way she detoured into the bush beside the road and picked up a short, thick stick. Testing it, she swung it so hard it whistled. This time he'd stay down forever.

CHAPTER 18

In the morning Grossmutti called up the stairs to Phoebe, and William woke.

"Mutti not here," he said.

Grossmutti went out the kitchen door and called, but there was no answering halloo. She sent William across the road to Hannah's to see if Phoebe was there.

He went into Hannah's house calling, "Grossmutti said breakfast ready. Mutti come."

"She's not here," said Hannah.

"Can't find her," he said. His face crinkled and he began to sniffle.

"It's too early for her to visit the neighbors. Where could she have gone? Surely not into the bush."

"Perhaps she went to see Jake at his farm," said Simon.

"So early—before her breakfast? I don't think so. Peter, go and see if she's there, so."

Worried, Hannah and Simon went across the road. and Jake and Peter came from his farm.

Jake said, "Peter says Phoebe is missing. Where did she go?"

"We don't know, that's why missing," said Hannah.

"She looked pale when she came back from picking berries yesterday," said Grossmutti. "Maybe she got too much sun."

The others nodded. Perhaps that was it. They knew persons who acted strangely with sunstroke, and it had been very hot yesterday.

William kept saying, "Where's Mutti? Where's Mutti?"

Simon said, "If she's out of her senses, she might go anywhere or do anything. We must find her quickly."

Jake and his vati set off along the road on horseback, Simon to the west, Jake to the east. Karl and Peter searched for signs along the edge of the bush and came back, empty-handed.

Simon went to the end of the settlement and returned, shaking his head. "Nobody's seen her, and so."

"Should we call the neighbors to search?" asked Hannah.

"Let's wait until Jake gets back. Maybe he found her," said Simon.

Jake had taken the trail toward Fort Erie because he thought it more likely she would, for whatever reason, return the way she'd come. He stopped at all the cabins along the road and questioned every traveler he met, but no one had seen her. This didn't seem unreasonable, since she had left in the night. Jake spent considerable time at Fort Erie, searching and asking, but could find no trace. She couldn't have gone any farther in such a short time

She must have gone into the bush. He shuddered. If they didn't hurry they might never find her. He tore a branch from a roadside tree and treated the Conestoga to an unaccustomed whip as they galloped back down the road toward home. Clods of dirt spurted from the horse's flying feet.

As he entered the dooryard, he shouted. "Did you find her?"

They all shook their heads.

"Nobody saw her on the road," said Simon.

Peter said, "We found signs, broken branches and trampled ferns along the bush, but who knows if it was her, or some animal."

"Anyhow," said Karl, "It's just here and there, not enough to follow."

"We need help," said Jake.

Simon looked at the western sky where the sun slid behind the trees. "Too late to look more, today."

"But we have to find her," shouted Jake. Desperation crackled in his voice. "Before she wanders too far."

"Well, we will call the neighbors to come at sunup."

Karl and Peter, on horseback, notified the farther neighbors while Simon and Hannah alerted those nearer.

Jake raged through the bush all through the night, shouting her name until he was hoarse.

When the community gathered in the Stettl dooryard in the morning, Caleb Beuhler said, "What did she go in the bush for?"

Simon shook his head. "We don't know. We can't find her. She's just missing and we don't know where else she could be."

"I said it," said Salome. "She's just empty-headed. People with sense know not to go in the bush alone."

They searched, while crops at home stood untended. They all knew they could pass close to her in the dense underbrush without being aware of her unless she made her presence known. Perhaps she was sick and unable to cry out to them. They shivered at the thought she might be lying, unconscious, somewhere near, and redoubled their efforts.

Jake searched through the day and night, though the other searchers told him he could find nothing in the dark. He grabbed the food Hannah pressed on him and ate it while he sought clues.

Amos returned from a visit to the settlement at Twenty-mile Creek on Lake Ontario and was apprised of the calamity. He joined in the search.

As he and Jake poked in thickets and peered into hollow logs, Amos said, "I saw a woman at that old shack this side of the Falls as I came home. She didn't walk like Phoebe. She was staggering a little. But she was about the same size and black curly hair."

Jake's heart jumped. It must be her. She'd gone back to the shack. But why? He crashed out of the bush, Amos following. They caught the horses, saddled them, and set off at a gallop. Amos, although having just returned along this road, followed gamely.

Jake recognized her when he was still some distance away. He clapped heels to his horse's flanks and galloped toward her.

He leaped off the still-moving horse and clasped her to him. "Phoebe, Phee. I've been crazy, looking for you."

Encased still in her nightmare, she fought against him, believing in her trance she was once again in the sergeant's clutches.

"Don't touch me," she screamed, flailing her arms and kicking at him.

"Leave her a little, Jake. She doesn't know what she is doing. Phoebe, it's Jake, and me, Amos Witmer."

She stared at the two men. Was she dreaming? That one couldn't be Jake. She'd left him forever. She touched his sleeve, expecting it to turn into smoke. But it was real, the much-washed linsey soft in her hand. He was real. Where had he come from? She'd left him years ago. She touched his face, puzzled. Dear Jake. But she couldn't stay with him. There was a reason, but she couldn't think what it was.

Jake tried to take her in his arms again, but she shrank away.

"Phee. Phee. It's Jake." He reached for her again and she turned, as if to run. "Come, it's time to go home."

She paused. "Yes, home."

She allowed him to lead her to the horse. Jake mounted, and Amos helped her up behind him. They began a slow return journey.

After a few minutes Amos said, "Keep tight hold of her arms, Jake. She's gone to sleep."

"I will," said Jake. He grasped both her hands, which were clasped around his waist, in his free hand.

When they reached home, the women were too busy rushing to give her some broth and put her to bed to ask questions. The neighbors, who'd come out of the bush when night fell, melted away to their homes, thankful she'd been found.

Phoebe roused a little when William ran crying to her, but Grossmutti told him Mutti needed to sleep, and lured him away to play with his wooden top.

The next morning Phoebe awoke to the sun streaming through the window. In the back of her mind was a hazy memory of a terrible time, but here she was, in her own bed. It must have been a nightmare. The sun was high. She'd overslept. Why hadn't Grossmutti called her? Perhaps the old lady was sick. She leaped out of bed and struggled into her clothes. When she bent over to lace her boots she felt the baby move, and the whole catastrophe burst upon her again.

She sat motionless, and the laces fell from her nerveless hands. It wasn't a bad dream, then, this pregnancy and her sojourn in the bush. She would have to tell the family—and Jake. They'd want to know why she ran away. They would certainly turn against her and drive her out.

Was that Jake's voice she heard downstairs? Dear God, how could she tell him? He thought she was so perfect. Well, it had to be faced. She squared her shoulders and descended the stairs.

It wasn't Jake, but Hannah, in the kitchen. Both women greeted her warmly, but she could see the curiosity mixed with concern in their eyes. Hannah filled a crockery bowl with porridge, bidding her sit down and eat.

William climbed up beside her. "Why did you go away? You didn't take me."

Hannah said, "Let your mutti have her breakfast. She's hungry."

William understood hungry and sat quietly while Phoebe finished the porridge and coffee. She dawdled as much as she could, but she was so famished it was difficult.

Hannah poured her a second cup of coffee and said, "Why did you go into the bush alone and get yourself lost? Were you out of the head from the heat, maybe? Grossmutti said you were picking the berries in the field."

Eyes cast down, picking at the tablecloth with a broken fingernail, Phoebe whispered, "I-I didn't get lost. I went on purpose."

Hannah's face registered shock. "For goodness' sake, why?"

Phoebe took a deep breath, raised her eyes and faced them, determined to tell all and take the consequences.

Diffidently she began. When she said "...and then he grabbed my skirts and threw them over my head," Grossmutti pulled her chair close and put her arms around her. Hannah gasped, her hands covering her mouth, staring.

Grossmutti clucked her tongue. "Some men are beasts."

"...and I can't stay here and marry Jake." Phoebe choked on her tears. "He and everyone else will hate me."

"Well, I don't hate you," said Hannah. "What a terrible thing. I'm so sorry. But it's up to Jake will he marry you. Now go to him and tell him all. He had to go to his farm this morning. One of his cows is having trouble with the calving." Phoebe shuddered at this reminder of birth. "But he's waiting for you, I'm sure."

Phoebe made her way down the road. Men in the fields waved and Caleb shouted, "You are all right?"

She waved and shouted back, "Yes." Well, as all right as she'd ever be.

She hurried on before he could come to the fence to talk to her. She wanted no questions from the neighbors. It was hard enough to admit her disgrace to the Stettls.

How could she tell Jake? It was one thing for the women to understand she had no control over what happened to her. But would he?

He came out of the stable door as she neared the farm. He ran across the field, cleared the roadside snake fence and hugged her, shouting, "Phee! Phee! You are all right, so? You will be careful about the bush, now?"

"I didn't get lost Jake. I went away on purpose."

"On purpose? Why, Phee? You could have died there."

"Too bad I didn't." Her lips curled.

She told her pitiful story again, making it as brief as possible. He leaned back and stared at her.

She'd been right. He hated her. Then he clasped her to him so hard she thought her ribs would crack.

"What a terrible thing. He must be a monster. But why did you run away? It wasn't your fault. You did nothing wrong. I hope the Good God punishes that devil as he deserves."

"But that's not all. I-I'm going to have a baby."

"That man's baby?"

"Yes." This was the end. He must be horrified. "I thought you wouldn't want me any more."

"Want you! Always!" He swung her around until her feet left the ground. "A baby? Now I will have three in my family instead of two. Hurrah! Everybody says I am too late starting but now they'll see...."

"But it's not your baby...."

He looked thoughtful for a minute. Then he said, "Neither is William. We will make a family together. Sometimes a baby comes too soon after a wedding and maybe this one will, too." He grinned at her. "But the sooner born, the sooner big enough to help."

"But the sergeant was such a terrible man. Maybe the baby...."

"So, a baby can't help who its parents are. It will be all right. We will be happy together, all of us." He smiled and kissed her.

He didn't mind. He really didn't mind. Or was he just pretending? If she couldn't accept this horrible thing that had happened to her, how could he? Still, he sounded sincere. She put her arms around his neck and gave him the first spontaneous kiss he'd had from her. He returned it with fervor.

Hannah went home and told her menfolk the news.

"She must have done something to tempt him," growled Simon.

"If she didn't belong to Jake, she'd tempt me without doing anything," said Peter.

Simon scowled at him. "Peter! That's not the way to talk."

Karl, as usual, sat in the corner and kept his own counsel.

"So, where will she go, now?" asked Peter.

"Nowhere, I think," said Hannah. "If I know Jake, he will still marry her."

"More fool, he," said Simon.

Salome prided herself on being a good judge of character. She was sure there was a mystery here. She would find out what it was. Hannah had seemed evasive when Salome questioned her. The others in the community might be satisfied with Hannah's explanation that Phoebe had wandered away, but you couldn't fool Salome. She could always smell something fishy, and there was certainly something smelly here.

She prodded Amos to investigate, but he said, "What could I investigate? She just got lost in the woods."

"But why? Sure she's a scatterbrained little thing but, mark my words, there's more to it than that."

"Leave it, Salome. You're just looking for skunks in the woodpile."

"Don't talk back to me, Amos. There's something wrong here, and I'll find out what it is. Then you'll wish you'd listened to me."

He sighed and went out to chores. Once Salome got an idea in her head she chewed at it like a dog with a bone. He hoped she wouldn't make trouble for Jake but, knowing his wife, he was afraid that was a futile wish.

She tried to rouse the neighbors.

Freda Beuhler said, "Forget it, Salome. You're always looking for trouble."

"Yes, and finding it, too." Then, ominously, "You'll see."

Phoebe marveled at how calm the Stettl family was over her disgrace. She detected a certain reserve in Simon who had just begun to look on her as one of the family. But the others treated her as they always had.

Jake was even more ardent and she warmed toward him. What other man would have taken such a disclosure in stride, as he had?

They were all much more accepting than she was. Every time the baby kicked, horror overcame her again. A baby, conceived in such violence, would surely be malformed, a monster.

She worked hard, trying to forget what was happening to her. Grossmutti cautioned her not to get overheated lest she lose the baby. This prompted her to work harder. That would be a solution. But the baby clung tighter and she resigned herself. Just another thing to endure.

News leaked out, via Salome, that Jake wanted to marry Phoebe. Members of the community were aghast that he would consider such a thing. Not only a foolish girl that got herself lost in the bush, but an English. It was bad enough the Stettls had taken her in to care for Grossmutti, but for Jake to marry her was unthinkable. Prompted by Salome, they demanded that Amos, as deacon, order the Stettls to send her away.

Amos didn't know what to do. He felt besieged—the hostile community on one side, and his sister Hannah who obviously approved of the girl, on the other. Hannah was as formidable, if roused, as all the others together.

He went to Jake's farm to remonstrate with him.

Jake was coiling hay. "I will marry her. I have said so, and I will do it."

"But an English, Jake. Who has ever heard of such a thing?"

"Now you have heard it." He turned his back on his uncle and gathered a forkful of hay.

Amos returned home to face his good wife's wrath. He had done all he could.

CHAPTER 19

Phoebe woke early on another wedding day. No bride's velvet gown and groom's bright uniform this time. Just a modest blue cotton dress and white linen kerchief, and a severe black suit for Jake. Perhaps the difference was a good omen.

Was he as good a man as he appeared to be? Richard hadn't turned out to be the knight in shining armor she'd thought she knew. Jake couldn't have been kinder or more forgiving but would it last?

Well, this was her life. She'd have to live it, good or bad. She heaved a great sigh and William, waking at the sound, climbed into her bed. She hugged him until he squealed. Perhaps she could love the new one as much as William when it came. She'd just have to wait and see. For the present she couldn't muster any emotion but revulsion.

"Come, William, it's time to get up." She got out of bed and dragged him, playfully, off the bed by his ankle. He grabbed her around the knees, prepared for a scuffle.

She tickled his ribs, forcing him to let go and said, "That's enough, now. We must hurry. Mutti's getting married today."

"What's married?"

"You'll see. Now get dressed."

William usually insisted on trying to dress himself while she fumed with impatience, but he seemed intrigued by the strange word and made no objection as she hustled him into his clothes.

Downstairs, Grossmutti greeted them with smiles. "This is a big day for you."

Phoebe smiled back at her, and William rushed for his morning hug.

Grossmutti said, "I will miss William. He makes me young again."

"You've been so kind to us. Thank you for everything you've done. This is a big day for you, too, moving into the doddy house."

"Well, that is life. Nothing stays the same. Always we have changes."

"We won't be far away. We'll come to see you often."

"Perhaps William could stay, sometimes, when you are busy?" Grossmutti sounded wistful.

"I'm not sure about that. You know how contrary he can be."

"We will get along all right, won't we, William?"

William said the one thing that would bring immediate action from the old woman. "I'm hungry."

After a hurried breakfast, Phoebe donned the blue dress. She folded the large white kerchief around her shoulders and tucked the points into her waistband. She presented herself for inspection and had to stand still while the old lady adjusted her kerchief. Grossmutti clucked, and shook her head as she tucked some curly tendrils back under Phoebe's cap.

"Your hair," she said, "it misbehaves like William."

Phoebe threw her arms around the old woman. She was the grandmother Phoebe had never had, and couldn't be a better one.

Grossmutti hugged her and there were tears in her eyes when she drew back. "Be a good wife to our Jake."

"Oh, I will." She'd certainly do her best.

She was washing the remains of William's breakfast from his face and hands when Jake came, and she greeted him with a warm smile. This was her bridegroom. He looked distinguished in his black suit and snowy shirt—the latter probably due to Hannah's ministrations. It would be her job from now on and she welcomed it. Anything she could do to pay the debt she owed him.

"I brought something for you, Phee." He gave her a heavy package.

William pulled at it. "What is it? What is it? Is it sweetmeats?"

"This is for your mutti, not you," said Jake, with mock seriousness.

William's bottom lip protruded, and Jake squatted on his heels and put his arm around the little boy. "This is a special day for your mutti and me—and you. Be a good boy."

William subsided.

Phoebe approved of Jake's evenhanded discipline, so different from the way Richard and the Donley had treated the boy. One stern look from him stopped whatever mischief William might be engaged in.

Jake said. "Open it, then, Phoebe. Don't keep William waiting."

Now included in the proceedings, William jigged impatiently. "Open it, quick, Mutti. I want to see."

The package contained a Bible with a soft brown leather cover.

"It's only a book," said William, turning away.

"A book to write your name in," said Jake. Turning to Phoebe, his eyes sparkled as he said, "This will be our family Bible. See all the plain pages in the back? We will put in there all our family, and start with William." He smiled at the boy who smiled back, obviously mollified. "You think we can fill it, maybe, Phee?"

"Jake," said Grossmutti, while Phoebe blushed, "don't tempt the fates. What comes, comes. The Good Lord decides."

"Where did you get it?" asked Phoebe. She stroked the velvety leather, head down, to hide her embarrassment.

"I admired it when I bought my farm from the Taylors. Mr. Taylor said they could buy another one when they were back in England. They hadn't written in it, yet."

Grossmutti said, "But that was years ago, that you bought the farm."

"Well, I always thought I would have a family some day." He grinned. "It's best to be prepared, you always say."

"This is the first time you listened to me, I think." She looked as if a smile was trying to break through her frown.

"How can you say that?" He hugged her and kissed the top of the gray head. "I always listen to you. I just don't always do what you tell me."

He smiled mischievously, reminding Phoebe of William. Did men ever really grow up?

He held out one arm to her, and kept one around his grandmother. "We'd better go. The magistrate said if we weren't there by dinnertime he would be gone to Chippawa."

Grossmutti said, "Have a safe trip."

Phoebe kissed the old lady. "Thank you so much for being so kind to William and me."

She turned to William. "You be a good boy."

"I want to go, too." William's lip began to protrude.

Oh no, not a tantrum, not now.

"We will make some sweets, you and me," said Grossmutti, "and if Mutti does not come back quick we will eat it all."

William giggled and jigged up and down as Grossmutti went to the cupboard. Over William's head she signaled to Phoebe and Jake to go.

Phoebe wasn't anxious to start out. Now the day was here, her doubts returned again, but Jake hustled her into the buggy. All the way down the road she wavered between hope that now her life would be better, and guilt that she was using Jake. Perspiration began to trickle down between her breasts and she wasn't sure if it was the rising heat of the July morning or nerves.

Near noon they reached Fort Erie. The magistrate was waiting in a dingy paper-strewn office. His wife and his bookkeeper stood by as witnesses.

He gestured Jake and Phoebe to stand before him. Opening an official-looking book and holding it on his outstretched hands, he looked sternly at the bride and groom as if to impress on them the importance of the ceremony. He returned his gaze to the slip of paper lying on the book, then back at Phoebe.

He scowled. "I remember you. I performed a marriage service for you here in this very office some five years ago." Then he thundered. "Where is your husband?"

Phoebe jumped. "He-he's dead."

"And how do I know that? It's a convenient excuse." He glared at Jake. "I'll have you know I perform no bigamous marriages here."

He turned again to Phoebe."Mistress Trevlyn I must have proof that you are indeed a widow."

How could she prove it? The officials at Newark could, but they were at the other end of the river. There would be a delay. Now she'd made the decision to marry Jake she couldn't wait to be Mistress Stettl—and safe.

The magistrate was muttering, "Trevlyn, Trevlyn." Then his face cleared. "I remember now. There was a Corporal Richard Trevlyn killed in a tavern brawl at Newark a year or so ago. That your husband?"

"Yes." would she ever live down the disgrace of Richard's behavior?

The magistrate stared at her, eyes half-closed, then nodded. "Let us proceed."

She let go some of her tension. She wouldn't be sure until the final pronouncement. But it came.

"I now declare you man and wife."

She was safe.

As they came out, Jake smiled at her. "Hello, Mistress Stettl," and kissed her, there, right in the road.

She smiled back. "Hello, Mister Stettl." She was sure her face was bright red. But it was going to be all right. It had to be.

They crossed the road to the tavern.

The slovenly waitress said, "I suppose you want dinner."

Jake said, "Yes, we do, a special dinner. This is my new wife."

The waitress brightened and turned to the other patrons and raised her voice. "We have a bride and groom here."

There were loud shouts of congratulations and a well dressed man said, "Drinks all round. I'll pay."

The waitress hurried to oblige and Phoebe whispered, "Why did you tell her?"

"Because I'm proud of my new wife, and so."

How could he be. She was a disgrace no matter what he said.

The waitress returned to their table with brimming pewter tankards.

Jake held up his hand. "Not for us, thank you, mistress."

"What? You refuse the kind gentleman's offer? You'll offend him."

"We do not drink liquor."

"I never heard of such a thing, especially at a wedding." She flounced off with the slopping tankards. Returning with their meal, she plunked the plates down in front of them and left without a word.

Phoebe surveyed the pork slices swimming in grease and the soggy black potatoes. "This is her special meal?" Angelique would never have allowed such swill to be served when she ran the tavern.

"We offended her, I guess so. But, anyhow she should be happy the man bought all those drinks."

Phoebe couldn't eat. Jake tucked in with a will, finishing the meal with raspberry pie and strong coffee.

When they got up to leave, many patrons wished them well and that flustered her again.

Hannah had planned on having a wedding feast with all the neighbors.

When she went over to invite Freda and Barnabas Sherk, Freda said, "I can't believe you are letting your son marry that hussy. Salome said she wore a red dress when she came. Barnabas and I would certainly not come to celebrate such a travesty, and I'm sure Salome and Amos won't come either, even if he is your brother."

Hannah feared she was right. Were unhappy times ahead for Jake and Phoebe? Why had she ever let Jake bring the girl home? She liked her and would have welcomed her into the family as the daughter she'd never had, but there was sure to be trouble in the community. She gave up the idea of a community dinner and planned a family feast for the newlyweds.

When Jake and Phoebe arrived back at the farm, Hannah and Grossmutti welcomed her warmly and Jake's father and brothers each kissed her, Simon and Karl's just a peck, but Peter's more ardent.

He whispered, "Hello, sister," and winked at her.

"None of that, now. She's mine," said Jake, wagging his finger at his brother.

"Can't I greet my sister-in-marriage?" asked Peter.

"Just so you remember she's my wife," said Jake with emphasis on the last two words.

She relaxed. She'd never known anyone so at home with themselves as this family They were content. Everything would be all right.

"Where were you?" asked William.

"Jake and I went to the fort to get married."

"What's married? You didn't tell me."

Jake knelt down in front of him. "Your mutti and me went to the magistrate and he made us a family."

"Am I a family, too?"

"Of course you are. You are my little boy, now." Jake put his arm around the small shoulders and smiled at him.

"All right," said William, and leaned against him.

Jake cleared his throat, and Phoebe felt her eyes fill with tears. She was so lucky to have found such a kind and clever man to be a father to William.

Jake and Phoebe took the places of honor at the table where enough roast pork, chicken and crusty pigeon pie to feed a harvest bee, gave forth inviting aromas. Tiny potatoes and carrots were piled in crockery bowls. Among the traditional seven sours were piccalilli, corn salad, watermelon pickle, chow-chow and an assortment of pickled fruits. The seven sweets included raspberry, custard, and shoo-fly pie and two kinds of dumplings with strawberry preserves.

Phoebe had never seen so much food. Even if Hannah disapproved of the marriage, she'd done all this for them. Phoebe resolved to do everything in her power to make the family proud of her.

When the bowl of potatoes was passed to her, she said, "New potatoes? Where did you get them, Mutti Stettl? The plants are still green."

Hannah laughed. "I dug in the hills, a little, and stole a few. Some I left to grow big. I do it special for my new daughter."

"Thank you." Phoebe felt her eyes prickle. Hannah had sacrificed part of the crop for them.

When they'd sampled everything, Peter said, "I'm about to burst."

Simon agreed. "You outdid yourself this time, Hannah."

Hannah frowned, "I don't know. Perhaps I should have made some--."

"Enough," said Simon.

"More than enough," said Phoebe. "Thank you all for being so kind to William and me. I know this is difficult for you, but I will do my very best to be a credit to you."

"I'm sure you will," said Grossmutti.

Jake swung William up on his shoulders, put his arm around Phoebe's waist and said, "Well, wife, time to go home."

Wife! Home! What beautiful words. She belonged somewhere again. If only it would last.

CHAPTER 20

Phoebe scarcely had time to consider her marriage, so many things waited to be done. The furnishings of Jake's cabin consisted of a bed, a table and two chairs. He had spent little time there and these few pieces of furniture had been sufficient during his bachelor days. Her hope chest and the bureau were now added, but there was the matter of extra crockery, another kettle, a three-legged spider for frying, a bed and stool for William, curtains for the window and a myriad of other things.

It seemed as soon as her living conditions improved, she was thrust back into basics again. After the comfort of Grossmutti's house this seemed even more primitive. Still, it was her own place, hers and Jake's.

Grossmutti donated a cupboard, a chest and a pair of wooden chairs, not needed in the tiny doddy house.

"They stay in the family then," she said.

Although Jake grumbled at the time lost in trips to Fort Erie for supplies, he seemed quite willing to provide anything she needed,

He brought two more milk cows and a sow from the home farm and installed them in the log barn. Hannah donated six hens and a cock from her flock. The care of these, along with milking the cows, became Phoebe's chore.

One morning she went out to the spring that bubbled from the side of a knoll into a barrel sunk in the ground. The pail of milk, which she'd floated in the barrel to keep cool, had been overturned by some nocturnal animal. The next morning the spring water was again cloudy and the pail empty. She called Jake to come and see.

He stirred the opaque water with his hand and sighed. "I haven't got time, but I must make a spring-house."

He half-buried rocks in a square around the spring and barrel to make a level foundation. William was given the job of gathering little stones to fill the spaces leaving a small opening between two rocks for the overflow water to exit.

"Are you building me a house?" asked William.

"No, this will be a water house," said Jake.

William giggled. "A water house?" He danced around the perimeter. "A water house, a water house. We're making a water house."

Phoebe helped build a tiny log hut on the stone base but William, trying to help, kept getting in the way. She gave him a pail and told him to fill it with mud from the edges of the overflow stream. This would please him, mud being his favorite medium. He dug away, singing to himself, while the adults worked in peace.

The hut was soon finished and the logs chinked with William's contribution of mud. She was surprised at how cool the interior of the miniature cabin became when the elm bark roof was completed.

"The cold water makes it nice, even in summer," said Jake. "We can keep butter and meat in here now the animals can't get to them, already."

"I think I'll just stay in here, too." Phoebe pulled her blouse free from her sweaty breasts.

"So who will cook my dinner, then?"

"The cabin is so hot. I feel like I can't breathe."

"I wish I had time to build you an oven outside." Jake looked with obvious concern at her flushed face. "Then you could let the fire go down. Next year, maybe."

"Don't worry about me, Jake. I'll survive."

"You know I would do everything I could for you."

"I know, Jake. You're very kind."

Jake's lips twisted. Always she said 'kind', never 'I love you'. 'Kind' was not the way he felt.

"So, I am a good husband, then?"

"The best."

He put his arm around her and drew her to him. "I want always to be the best for you, Phee. If I fall down you will tell me, and so?"

Ruth Zavitz

"I don't think it will be necessary, but I will." She leaned against him, her head in the hollow of his shoulder and he thought, it will come. I hurried her too fast. Mutti said not everyone falls in love when they first see somebody, like I did.

William had become very proficient in the German language, to Phoebe's dismay. Unable to communicate in English, except with Jake and William, she'd learned enough German to make herself understood to the family, but made a point of speaking proper English to William. She feared he'd forget his own language.

One morning at breakfast, she asked him if he wanted more toast and he answered her in German.

"William, speak English, please," she scolded.

Jake objected. "German is his language now."

"But sometimes I don't understand what he says; my own son. And I'm afraid he'll forget how to speak English."

"Does it matter? This is the way you both will talk for the rest of your lives. I have to know English, some, to do business, but you won't be seeing outside people."

"Well, William will have to do business, too, when he grows up."

"He has English enough. No need for more."

What had she done? Must she give up her heritage? She had, foolishly it appeared, thought she could remain as she had always been. Now she saw that to retain her own language would forever make her an outsider. She must consider whether her race was more important than the chance to be accepted here.

Salome demanded Amos do something about this foreigner. "As Deacon it's your duty."

"But what can I do? They're married."

"Cast them out. We don't want English blood contaminating us. And now she's having a baby. And pretty soon, I think. She must have tempted Jake to be sure he would marry her. I didn't know he knew her before she came here."

Amos had noted that his sister seemed to have accepted Phoebe. If he ordered Jake and Phoebe to leave, Hannah might take all the Stettls and leave, too. She was capable of it. Their community was small enough. It would be a severe blow to lose that many members.

He dithered.

He liked Phoebe. She'd been raised a Quaker. Not so different except for the language, and now she was speaking the German, a little, she would make a proper, dutiful wife for Jake.

Amos was hoeing corn when Caleb Beuhler stopped his buggy on the road and came across the field.

"Good morning, Caleb."

"Good morning, Amos. I see the weeds are going well."

"Jah, they grow better than the corn." Amos slashed at a vigorous Canada thistle.

"I don't want to stop you from such good work, Amos, but I have something on my mind."

Amos had a good idea what it might be. He sighed and leaned on his hoe. "Yes, Caleb?"

"It's Jake—and Phoebe. That's not good, you know."

"I know," said Amos.

"You're the deacon. What are you going to do?"

Amos explained his fear of losing the whole Stettl family if he expelled Phoebe.

Caleb said, "Jah, Sister Hannah, she has her own mind. But Barnabas and Freda, they're determined Phoebe to go away. It would be bad to lose all the Stettls, though. What to do?"

"I don't know," said Amos and slashed again at the stubborn thistle.

"Well, you had better decide, so. It is your job. This wrangle is not good for the community." Caleb stumped back to his buggy.

Amos sighed. Even thought it was a sin to feel so, he felt proud when he was made a deacon. But it wasn't what he expected. He'd be glad to give it up, now. He didn't like being responsible for others' behavior.

Phoebe was unaware of the turmoil. Pears and plums waited to be preserved in thick syrup. Early apples had to be dried. And always weeds taking over the garden.

In October Hannah and Phoebe dug the root vegetables from the gardens, storing Hannah's in her cellar and Phoebe's in a pit dug in the side of a knoll. They buried carrots and beets in boxes of sand to keep them from drying out and shriveling. Potatoes and turnips were piled in the corners of the pit and cellar along with the pumpkins and squashes. Phoebe gloried in the work. There would be no shortage of food this winter.

She was given the sitting-down task of shredding cabbage while Grossmutti layered it with salt in barrels, for the winter's supply of sauerkraut. When the barrels were full, a large plate was placed upside down on the top of each and weighted with a large stone. Phoebe was surprised to see the salt had extracted enough juice from the cabbage to entirely cover the barrels' contents.

"There must be juice over the top already," said Grossmutti, "or the cabbage will spoil. That is why the stone on top. To squeeze it."

The remaining cabbages were stacked, heads down, in the middle of the gardens and covered with earth and straw to keep out the frost, so they could be dug out in the winter.

When the first sauerkraut barrel was opened after its required month of fermentation, Phoebe was repelled by the smell, but soon relished its sour taste that added flavor to the bland winter diet.

The three women spent days and days, peeling the baskets of apples, coring and slicing them into rings. The men joined them in the evening and on rainy days. They strung the circlets on cords and hung them to dry. Soon the kitchen ceilings of both houses were festooned with loops of drying apples.

Phoebe's body became more and more unwieldy. Her antagonism toward this child continued and kept her despondent. She avoided Jake's caresses, partly out of disgust with her own person and partly because of a lack of feeling, other than gratitude, for Jake, himself.

Although disappointed at her responses, Jake put it down to her condition and looked forward to more intimacy after the baby was born. It was a big change for her, from all the fancy doings at the fort to this plain life. Still, from what she'd told him, her life before the fort had been much like this. She'd soon settle into it. Anyway, he hoped so. He hadn't looked at another woman since the day he'd first seen her on the ferry. But then, she hadn't felt the same way. She hadn't even recognized him at the bridge at first. It would take a little time. He had waited so long, a little longer he could stand.

CHAPTER 21

The wind had raged all through the night. It roared in the bush and whistled down the chimney, sending puffs of smoke into the room. Storm without and storm within, thought Phoebe as she lay in the bed in the corner of the cabin. The storm without was dying down but the storm within was far from over.

She looked with dread at the blanket Hannah worked over, close to the fire. She'd hoped mother love would surface when the baby was born, but all she felt was the same horror that had dogged her all through the pregnancy. Did it look like the sergeant?

Hannah walked across the room, the tiny bundle cradled in her arms. "Here she is. Your beautiful little girl." She laid the baby beside Phoebe.

Phoebe flinched and stared at the log wall across the cabin. "Take it away," she sobbed, and moved to the back of the bed.

"Now, now, you don't mean that. It's your own beautiful baby girl."

Grossmutti, on the settle by the hearth, shook her head. "Get Jake. This is his problem."

He had been pacing between the barn and cabin most of the night. When he saw Mutti come out, he ran to where she stood on the door-stone, hugging her shawl against the harsh wind.

"Is it over? Is Phee all right?" he called before he even reached her.

"The baby is good but Phoebe's upset. Come. She needs you." Hannah turned back into the cabin and he followed.

"What's all this, then?" asked Jake, kneeling beside the bed.

"I can't stand it. Take it away."

"But, Phee, dear, it's our baby. How can you say so?" He smoothed the sweaty hair back from her forehead.

Hannah laid the baby in Jake's arms and he folded the blanket back. "See? We've got a beautiful baby."

She shut her eyes. "You know it's not our baby. I don't see how you can accept it when I can't. It has nothing to do with you, at all."

"So. A baby is a baby. It comes from God. If He sent it, we must look after it. We are caretakers only for His children."

"But I don't love it."

"You will see. Love will come. She is beautiful." He stroked the baby's plump cheek and she squinted her eye. He chuckled.

William scrambled down the ladder from the loft.

Jake said, "Look, William. You have a baby sister. Isn't that nice?"

William looked dubiously at the tiny face in the blanket folds, its lips pushed up in a bow by the plump cheeks, the eyes tight-closed in their rolls of fat. He climbed up on the bed and snuggled close to his mother. She put her arm around him.

"It got red hair," he said, burrowing his hard little head into his mother's armpit.

She shuddered. Red hair!

"We won't keep it, will we?" he asked.

If only we didn't have to. It'd been bad enough, being pregnant with the sergeant's child. Please God why did it have to have red hair? She'd see that terrible man every time she looked at it.

The baby stirred and whimpered.

"She's hungry," said Hannah.

"I-I can't," wailed Phoebe.

"But she has to suckle." Hannah sounded shocked.

"I don't care. Send her to the fort. Let the sergeant look after her." Phoebe broke into a storm of sobs and the two women looked at her, then at each other. William patted her cheek, trying to console her. The baby began to cry.

Jake said, "Phee, remember what I said."

Still reluctant, she nursed her daughter while William looked on. "Can I have some, too?"

Laughing, Hannah scooped him up in her arms. "No. You're a silly boy."

"Why can't I?"

"The baby has no teeth. It can only drink Mutti's milk. You have lots of teeth, so. You can eat bread and meat and fried cakes."

The mention of fried cakes distracted William. "I want breakfast."

After he finished, he went to the stable with Jake. Hannah put the baby to sleep in the large carved cradle that had been Jake's, and his brothers'. When Phoebe dropped off to sleep, the two older women conferred in low voices.

Hannah said, "More trouble. She thinks what she wants to do, not what God wants."

Grossmutti took another nappy from the cane basket at her feet and folded it, adding it to the pile in her lap. "We must be patient."

Hannah laid another log on the fire. "I wouldn't have chosen her for Jake, but she is all he ever wanted from the first day he saw her."

"Such sad things have happened to her. It takes time to forget."

"Maybe it was God's punishment for her worldly ways."

"Maybe. But it is not for us to judge her."

Hannah turned from the fire. "Do you think the neighbors will wonder about that red hair?"

"Well, if anybody asks we will say sometimes red hair comes in yellow-haired families." Grossmutti smiled slyly. "It never did in ours, but we won't say so."

Hannah raised her eyebrows. "But isn't that lying?"

"Mmmm, maybe, but less said soonest mended."

Grossmutti continued, "But Phoebe. What to do? I don't think Amos can help in this case."

"No, that wouldn't be wise. I wouldn't like Salome to know and she would get it out of Amos, for sure.." Hannah looked toward the bed where Phoebe still slept. "I thought when she saw the baby she would love it."

"This is a different thing from a hard birth. For her the pain goes on." Grossmutti sighed. "I hope it comes right for all of them."

Jake, in the barn, sang with joy that her ordeal was over and the baby appeared to be healthy. He hadn't realized how difficult it was to birth a baby. He'd been too young when his brothers were born to remember what suffering God laid on women. Animals didn't have such trouble.

Well, he always noticed he appreciated the things he struggled to get. People treasured their babies more than animals did, and probably that was the reason. Old Sukie, here, had laid on three of her babies and didn't seem to care. He scratched behind her ears as he dropped some corncobs into her pen, and she grunted and smacked her lips as she crunched the hard kernels.

Phoebe felt bad right now, but she would love the baby when she was better. He ran the currycomb through the horses' winter coats while a stately hymn rolled from his heart and the horses nibbled his shoulders with their velvet lips.

The team had been the center of his life until he met Phoebe. But now he had a wife, a son, and a daughter. True, the children didn't have his blood, but they were his. And there would be more, God willing, of his own flesh. His deep voice boomed out and the cockerel, perched up in the shadowy rafters, waked and crowed in protest.

Grossmutti stayed at the cabin to help with the children until Phoebe should be able to cope again. Hannah came every day, also. Jake made sure the water bucket and wood box were filled, but he had his own chores as well as Phoebe's, and was trying to clear more land. Phoebe lay in her bed, taking no interest in anything, nursing the baby when Hannah or Grossmutti brought it to her, but otherwise ignoring it. Jake coaxed, and Grossmutti frowned, but she could not rouse herself.

"What will we name the baby, then?" Jake asked, as he sat on the side of the bed, rubbing her hands.

"I don't care." She made as if to turn her back, but he kept tight hold of her hands, forcing her to face him.

"But she must have a name."

"Whatever you like. It doesn't matter."

He consulted with Mutti and Grossmutti. Choosing a name was a heavy responsibility and the mutti should be involved. A name for life. Maybe when she came out of her depression she wouldn't like their choice. But no matter how they coaxed, she would not consider the problem.

Finally Grossmutti said, "There is a name in our old country that means storm. It seems to me the right thing for this poor babe. Should we call her Hedwig? If ever a baby had a stormy start in life it is this one."

They suggested it to Phoebe and she agreed, but Jake wasn't sure she even heard them. So Hedwig began her unhappy little life.

By the end of the second week, Phoebe had made no effort to take up her responsibilities. Grossmutti took advantage of the absence of Jake and Hannah to speak sternly to her.

"Will you lie here, so, for the rest of your life?"

Phoebe turned her head away to stare at the unadorned log wall behind the bed.

"You've had a bad time, for sure, but now is time to stop the grieving and take up your life again. Come, now, here are your clothes. Out of that bed and dress yourself."

Phoebe put on her clothes, tottered across the cabin and sank down on the settle, staring into the fire.

Grossmutti shook her head. She brought Phoebe the comb and brush, saying, "Put up your hair. You will feel better."

Phoebe pulled out the frowzy braids and brushed the long strands into some semblance of order, then coiled it up on the back of her head in haphazard fashion. Grossmutti brought her a clean white cap from the bureau drawer, and frowned at the half-combed hair.

William and Jake came in from the stable. William saw his mother up and dressed and ran to her. "You're better?"

"Yes, dear." She gave him the ghost of a smile.

Jake grinned. "It's good to see you up. You're all right now, so?"

"I guess so. I just feel weak."

"Jah, so. But you will soon be strong again."

She dutifully rose every morning when Jake did, but accomplished only those things Hannah or Grossmutti prompted her to do.

Hannah lost patience. "What sort of woman has our Jake tied himself to?" she asked, apparently not caring if Phoebe heard.

"The Good Lord alone knows," said Grossmutti. "Bring me some of the dried pine needles from my house. I'll make her a tea and see if that will build up her strength."

Esther Martin and Gerda Beuhler dropped in to see the new baby. Esther brought a bonnet and matching shawl for the new arrival, and Gerda a kettle of stew for the family. They held the baby and admired it, but Hannah saw them raise their eyebrows at the bright fuzz on its head and the new mother's obvious lack of pride in her offspring. Salome Witmer and Freda Sherk were apprized of the early arrival of the red-haired baby in Jake's cabin but did not visit.

Hannah and Grossmutti came to the conclusion the only way to make Phoebe undertake her responsibilities was to leave her to it. They conferred with Jake, who reluctantly agreed. Grossmutti gave Phoebe another stern lecture on her duty to Jake and the children and moved back into the doddy house. Phoebe was left to cope.

Hannah worried about the children, but Jake said, "I keep a close watch. If things go bad I'll tell you. I think it will be all right, though."

Gradually, with promptings from Jake when she forgot, Phoebe tried to make a home for her family again. William's prattling, especially, seemed to rouse her.

Hedwig's needs left her unmoved. Physically she looked after the child well enough, feeding and keeping her dry, but otherwise ignored her. She shuddered every time the wisps of red hair touched her hands.

When he was in the cabin, Jake carried Hedwig about to still her constant whimpering. She didn't bawl as babies usually do, but only uttered a sad wail.

Phoebe was horrified at herself, but couldn't break out of her despondency. She knew the Stettl women disapproved of her behavior and thought she was putting a heavy burden on Jake but she couldn't seem to help it. No matter how much she lectured herself, every chair, the settle, her bed, called to her to sit down, give up. She shut her ears to Hedwig's crying even while she scolded herself for neglecting the child. And Jake; he was so patient with her. How could he love her when she hated herself? Even though the sunshine sparkled on the snow outside, everything looked black and stormy to her.

A few days later Grossmutti asked Jake to take her over to see how Phoebe was getting along.

"How are you feeling?" she asked as she shed her shawl and bonnet.

"I'm all right," said Phoebe. She added another log to the fire and returned to the settle without going near Hedwig, mewling in the cradle.

"What is the matter with Hedwig, then?"

"I don't know. She just cries all the time." Phoebe bent over and hugged herself.

"So. Maybe you would cry, too, if no one cared about you," said Grossmutti.

At the severe tone, Phoebe burst into tears. Life was just too hard. Now even Grossmutti had turned against her.

"Tell me. What's the matter, then?" asked Grossmutti. "You have a beautiful baby, a fine son and a good husband. You should be happy."

"I feel so wicked. I don't like the baby and I can't help it. It looks like that terrible man. Every time I look at it I see h-him." She hiccuped.

"You are thinking too much you do not like it. If it was somebody else's baby you were looking after for them, you would be good to it whether you liked it or not, so."

"But it isn't someone else's baby."

"It's God's baby. Lent to you for awhile."

"That's what Jake said."

"Yah, Jake. You are making him very unhappy, you know."

"Poor Jake. I've been nothing but trouble for him."

"He loves you. But now it's time for you to stop the grieving."

"You're right, I guess." Phoebe straightened her shoulders and tucked a stray strand of hair under her cap. "I've neglected William, too. Would you like some coffee?"

"Jah, that would be good." Grossmutti crossed the cabin and lifted Hedwig from the cradle while Phoebe busied herself making coffee and getting some oatcakes from the stone crock on the shelf.

After Grossmutti left, Phoebe sank down on the settle. What Grossmutti said made some kind of sense. If she could look at Hedwig as just someone else's baby she had to take care of, and not her own, perhaps things would go better.

She got up and lifted the crying baby out of the cradle. Holding her stiffly, she walked about the cabin. Hedwig, however, continued her crying until Phoebe, exasperated, laid her in the cradle again. Well she'd tried, but this misbegotten child was as unlovable as its father.

CHAPTER 22

Early in the new year, Salome Witmer held a quilting bee. Phoebe, busy with the children, and Grossmutti sick with a cold, didn't attend, but Hannah joined the other women. They shed their shawls and gathered around the quilt, exclaiming at the intricacy of the pattern.

Salome, preening, said, "Oh, it's just something I thought of one day."

Esther Martin, said, "It's like the log cabin pattern, but those stars in the middle of the blocks give it a different look."

Hannah thought Salome's imagination exceeded her needlework skill, but tried to ignore the seam corners that didn't quite meet, and the less than pleasing combination of colors. Where had she found that piece of orange with the purple stripes? Surely no one in the community had ever worn such a garish pattern?

The women seated themselves around the quilt on wooden chairs, some borrowed from the neighbors because four of Salome's were supporting the quilting frame on their backs. The quilters threaded needles, and settled thimbles over winter-chafed fingers.

As the needles wove in and out, Freda Sherk said, "Did you ever see such weather? First it snows, then it rains, then it freezes. I fell down good going to the barn yesterday."

"Oh no," said Gerda Beuhler. "Did you hurt yourself?"

"Just my feelings to look so foolish." Freda shook her head. "Skirts flying to show everything."

Salome clucked her disapproval, but Esther Martin laughed. "It's embarrassing, yet. Did it myself last winter."

Esther asked after Phoebe and the new baby. Hannah replied they were both well, but the baby was fretful.

"These colicky babies are a trial," said Gerda.

Hannah pulled a length of thread from the spool and severed it between her teeth. "I'm thankful mine were happy ones. I never realized how draining a constantly crying baby can be."

125

"Well, I think it has a lot to do with the peacefulness of the mutti," said Freda.

Hanna thought she might be right. Certainly Phoebe was not at peace.

When the women had finished quilting as far toward the center as they could reach, everyone rose and stood back while Salome removed the clamps from one side of the wooden frames. Hannah and Gerda began to roll up that side of the finished material.

"Gerda. Roll your end tighter," said Salome. "It's going crooked."

Gerda complied, and she and Hannah replaced the corner clamps while Salome squinted to make sure the corners were square. Then they repeated the procedure on the other side. After Salome had marked quilting lines on the fabric with a little shard of decayed limestone, the women reseated themselves and continued their work.

Salome stuck the point of her needle into the quilt top and took off her thimble, a sign she had something important to say. "Deacon Witmer will be calling on Jake and Phoebe as soon as he finishes hauling wood from the woodlot." She looked knowingly at Hannah.

Hannah shivered, pricking her finger. She sucked the puncture, then replied, "That will be nice." She couldn't resist adding, "It's what Deacons do." It aggravated her that Salome always referred to her husband by his title. Trying to make herself more important.

She regretted the remark when Salome said, "He will have something important to discuss with them," and nodded her head.

"Oh? What?" asked Gerda.

"That is the deacon's business and I can't discuss it." Salome lifted her chin regally. She picked up her thimble, put it on with some ceremony and applied herself to her work, smiling mysteriously.

Would she leave the subject or refer to it again? If Salome asked direct questions about the baby they'd have to be answered honestly, no matter how much Hannah wished to avoid it. She searched for a safe subject but, in her unease, could think of nothing.

Gerda unwittingly came to her rescue. "How is Grossmutti Stettl, Hannah? I hope her cold is better. It's dangerous for the old ones, to get sick in the winter."

"She's no better. I'm worried about her."

The women clucked in sympathy.

Salome shook her head. "You never know when a simple cold will turn to something worse."

The women spoke of cases of sickness they knew of, and Hannah breathed more easily.

The next morning Hannah walked over to Jake's farm. She met him in the yard and warned him of the impending visit of the deacon and that Salome was stirring up trouble.

"Jah, that's Salome. Why Uncle Amos ever married her I cannot tell."

Hannah's mouth twisted. "She was pretty when she was young, and she never showed the men the edge of her tongue, then."

"And Uncle Amos is so soft, she probably told him they were getting married and he agreed without thinking."

Hannah chuckled. "That could be so."

"How did she ever get named Salome?" asked Jake. "I always wondered. Wasn't Salome a dancer?"

"Her mutti was bound to call her that. Some tried to tell her it wasn't right, but she said it was in the Bible so there couldn't be anything wrong with it."

"She doesn't sound as if she was very smart."

Hannah laughed, then sobered. "Look out for yourselves. Salome will try to make trouble, I think."

"I'll stay close to the cabin, then. Phoebe doesn't need more trouble. Will Salome come with him, do you think?"

"Let's hope not."

"Well, I can handle Uncle Amos."

"What can you tell him?" Hannah held up a warning finger. "Remember, Salome will want a full report from him, after."

Jake tipped his head to one side, considering. "I could tell him it's none of his business, maybe?"

"Oh, no, Jake. A deacon, it is his business how his flock keep themselves. It's just not Salome's business."

"I could tell him it wasn't for Salome's ears."

"You could tell him, but she would find out, for sure."

"Well, after all, there's nothing wrong. It is not Phoebe's fault and we told no lie. I never said Hedwig was my baby. It will be all right."

"I hope so. But you know Salome. She always makes mountains out of molehills."

Fully occupied with all the work and her depression, Phoebe was unaware s of this brewing storm.

William, jealous of the new baby, reverted to babyhood, hanging on Phoebe's skirts. The two children seemed to be trying to outdo each other, whining and crying, trying her patience to its limit. She slapped William one day when he tried her patience too far. Of course this didn't help at all for he bawled and Hedwig, frightened by the racket, echoed him.

When Jake came in for his dinner, he found the cabin in an uproar. He picked Hedwig out of the cradle and sat down on the settle, jigging her a little until she quieted. William climbed up on his other knee.

Jake said, "You need help but Mutti can't come. Grossmutti is very sick."

"Oh, no." Phoebe stopped, her hands full of bowls she was taking to the table, appalled at the news. "I thought she just had a cold."

"No. Mutti's afraid she has the lung fever. She doesn't know anything and is talking all the time when she was a little girl back in Pennsylvania."

"Oh, poor Grossmutti." Phoebe set down the bowls and wiped her cheeks with the corner of her apron. "Will she be all right do you think?"

"I don't know. Mutti is pretty worried."

Phoebe considered this new concern. Her own troubles were insignificant compared to this.

Jake set William on the floor, rose and laid Hedwig back in the cradle. He looked at the sleeping baby and clucked his tongue. "Now see what I have done. Dirt on Hedwig's blanket from my clothes. I'm sorry."

"That's all right. At least she's quiet."

He put his arms around Phoebe. "I'll try to help more but," he shook his head, "there's so much else to do."

"I know. If you don't get more land cleared, we'll not have enough grain to feed all of us."

She made no response to his hug and he let his arms drop.

She'd done it again. No matter how often she told herself how good Jake was to her she couldn't help flinching. Carrying a pitcher of milk to the table, she squeezed his shoulder as she passed the settle where he sat. "Don't worry about us. We'll be all right."

"Jah, I hope so."

Phoebe heard the yearning in his voice and resolved to do better. He had enough things to worry about.

With all the domestic commotion, Jake forgot to tell her about Deacon Witmer's impending visit.

Amos kept putting off the visit to Phoebe, but Salome cotinued to prod.

"When are you going to go and order that harlot to leave? Imagine: a red-haired baby," She said at dinner. "I thought it was shame enough that our Jake got the cart before the horse but this can't be his baby at all, so soon it came."

"Well, maybe it is. We don't know when Jake first met her. As for looks, Lena and Ketty don't much look like Barnabas and Freda."

"Nonsense, I know they're Barnabas's daughters. She and Barnabas were married already two years before they were born. Go and look at that baby and see does it look like Jake."

Jake was deep in the bush, swinging his ax heartily, when Deacon Witmer came to call. Phoebe, embarrassed, cleared away the drying nappies festooning the settle. He would have to come when everything was in a muddle.

She said, "Take off your coat and sit here by the fire,"

"Thank you, Sister Phoebe." Amos gave her his coat and hat and sat down, holding out his hands to the fire. "And how are you?"

"I am well, except the children upset me, sometimes, Deacon." Since he'd called her Sister, this was a formal visit. To hide her nervousness, she began to fold the nappies she'd taken from the settle.

Amos nodded. "Children. Jah, they are a burden. But a welcome one."

She didn't want to answer this and changed the subject. "Jake's in the bush."

"Jah. I heard his ax bang."

A long pause followed. Amos seemed to have exhausted all his topics of conversation and shifted on the seat. He seemed as nervous as she felt. Surely he was used to pastoral visits.

To break the silence, she said, "Would you like some tea, Deacon?"

"It's Uncle Amos, isn't it?" He tugged at his bushy, full beard.

Was this a pastoral call, or not?

"Don't trouble yourself," he continued. "I came to see the baby, only."

She lifted Hedwig from the cradle and folded back the blanket. Amos peered at the red little face, the delicate skin on the cheeks chapped from her constant tears, and the wisps of red hair peeping out from under the edges of her bonnet.

"Jah, it's a nice little baby," said Amos.

"Would you like to hold her?"

"No, no, she might cry." Amos put his hands behind his back and edged towards the door. "I will just go out and say hello to Jake." He rose hastily, put his coat over his arm, clapped his hat on his head, said, "Goodbye," and left the cabin.

She stared after him. Didn't church officials offer prayers when they visited? She'd always heard so. And why did he seem so embarrassed?

Amos waded through the deep snow to the bush. He had an idea he might be able to get the information Salome wanted, from Jake. "Good day, Jake."

"Hello, Uncle Amos. It's a fine day, but pretty cold."

"Chopping makes you warm, though, eh Jake? You're getting along good here, it looks like."

"Not as fast as I'd like." Jake took a file from a nearby stump and touched up the edges of his ax.

Amos cleared his throat. "That's a nice baby, there."

Jake caught his breath. He'd forgotten Uncle Amos was coming to visit. Had he upset Phoebe?

"You were at the cabin?"

"Yes, a little while only. Sister Phoebe was busy. Babies make lots of work." Amos settled his hat more firmly on his head and pulled at the cuffs of his hand-knitted mittens. "Ah, Jake, who does the baby look like, already?"

Here it was. Should he discuss the baby's parentage with Uncle Amos? No. Better let sleeping dogs lie.

To give himself time to think, Jake said, "Well, she has Phoebe's nose, I think so."

Amos persisted. "And some thing of you?"

"Not that I can see right now, and that's likely a good thing for a girl. Maybe when she's grown she would have a beard like mine."

Amos realized he wasn't going to get any information from Jake, and that made him suspicious. Maybe Salome was right. Still, he liked Phoebe and didn't want to drive her away. Or cause grief to his nephew who obviously loved the girl. He wouldn't say anything to Salome about his suspicions—if he could help it.

"I must get home. Lots to do, you know."

"That's for sure. There's no end."

"Goodbye, then." Amos turned and trudged off through the snow.

Jake chewed at the inside of his cheek with impatience until Uncle Amos was out of sight. What had he said to Phoebe? Had he upset her again, just when she was beginning to be more cheerful? He hurried to the cabin, apprehensive of what he might find.

As he entered, Phoebe said, "You're back early. Supper isn't ready, yet. Uncle Amos was here. Did you see him?"

"Yes. He came back to the bush. What did he say to you?"

She laughed. "He didn't say much of anything."

Jake relaxed.

"He seemed embarrassed," she continued. "He didn't even have prayers."

What would he tell Aunt Salome, wondered Jake ? Poor Uncle Amos. He was undoubtedly in for a lecture. And poor us. Aunt Salome wasn't accepting Hedwig as his baby. She would make more trouble, he was sure.

CHAPTER 23

Phoebe took the children and went to visit Grossmutti, embarrassed she hadn't gone more often. It seemed there was always too much to do.

Hannah met her at the door of the doddy house and took Hedwig from her. "Come in, come in."

"How is she? Is she better?"

Hannah shook her head. "No, she is worse. She doesn't seem to want to get better. She misses Grossvati—and you."

"I should have come more. Do you think if I took the children in to see her and promised to come oftener it would help?"

"She wouldn't know. She doesn't know anyone, any more. But come in."

The bedroom was oppressive with the smell of fever, rancid goose grease and the tang of mustard from the plasters Hannah had applied to try and loosen the congestion.

Phoebe was dismayed at the loud rasping breathing and the tiny white-faced frame in the big bed. The old woman scarcely made a ripple in the quilts.

She said, "Hello, Grossmutti? How are you?"

There was no response, not even an eyelid flicker.

William whimpered and she hurried him out of the room lest he disturb the sick woman.

"Oh, she is bad," she whispered.

"Yes, bad," Hannah said, following her. "I'm afraid she won't get over this."

There was a hacking sound from the bedroom and Hannah said, "There, she's coughing again. Sometimes if I hold her up she gets rid of the stuff easier."

"Let me help." Phoebe laid Hedwig on the settle, setting a chair against it to keep her from rolling off. She admonished William to watch her, and went back into the bedroom.

Grossmutti was gasping for breath, arching her back in a vain effort to force air into her congested lungs. They lifted her into a sitting position.

Suddenly a great rattling breath came out of her throat, and then no more. They eased her back onto the bed and stared at each other.

Then Hannah gently straightened her mother-in-law's limbs. "It's over, then."

Phoebe began to cry. "I should have spent more time with her. She was so good to me. I neglected her."

"There now," said Hannah. "Don't blame yourself. Everyone, we must do what we must do. You have enough cares of your own. She had a good life and she was to me like a mutti."

"Me, too," sobbed Phoebe.

Just then there was a wail from Hedwig, and they went out to investigate.

Phoebe gathered up the children. "She's hungry and I must go and tell Jake,"

"Don't feel guilty," said Hannah. She opened the door in the front of the tall mantel clock and stopped the pendulum.

"What are you doing?"

"The clock, it will not be started again until after the funeral." Hannah put her arms around Phoebe. "Do not grieve. She is with her man. Where she wanted to be this long time." Then, "I must call Simon from the bush and then go and tell the bees."

"Tell the bees?"

"Yes. We have to tell them about happenings in the family or they'll fly away. Grossvati and Grossmutti brought them all the way from Pennsylvania. They are part of the family."

"But they're in hibernation, now."

"It doesn't matter. They remember until the summer."

This was strange. How could such an intelligent woman as Hannah believe such a thing? And stopping the clock, too. But it did no harm, anyway.

She went home to tell Jake what had happened. He'd be heartbroken. His beloved Grossmutti.

But all he said was, "Jah, I thought so."

She'd thought this would devastate him. Perhaps it was too deep a grief to voice.

Or did he not trust her enough to reveal his feelings since she was always rejecting him? She couldn't understand herself. She felt so tender towards him, but every time he put his arms around her she stiffened. She couldn't help it.

Simon sent word of Grossmutti's passing to relatives at the settlement at 20-mile Creek on Lake Ontario. A large group of relatives and friends who had known her, both here and when they lived in Pennsylvania, came to the funeral. Houses in the little community were strained to accommodate the visitors overnight—and larders seriously depleted. But no one minded, for it was all to honor one of their own.

Amos officiated at the service, held in front of Simon and Hannah's house in spite of the cold, because of the crowd. Then the sad procession made its way down the road. Grossmutti was laid to rest beside her husband in the little graveyard on the bank of the creek. The men of the community had spent two strenuous days shoveling snow and tending fires to melt the frozen ground so they could dig the grave.

People stood around afterward in spite of the cold, reluctant to leave this much loved matriarch.

Amos said, "She was a good woman."

"Jah," said Gerda. "She came a long time to help take care of my mutti when she was so sick."

"We will miss her," said Esther.

And so will I, thought Phoebe.

Jake and Phoebe mourned and, when William asked where Grossmutti was, Phoebe told him she had gone to sleep.

"Why are you crying, then? Is sleeping bad?"

"She isn't ever going to wake up," said Jake.

This apparently alarmed William, for he had several nightmares in the nights that followed and was even more reluctant to go to bed.

Jake told him only really old people went to sleep and didn't wake up.

Phoebe was filled with guilt. Grossmutti was the one person besides Jake who'd accepted her unconditionally, and she'd abandoned the old lady.

Now there was only Jake she could really rely on. She could trust him. He'd take care of her whatever happened in their lives. Dear Jake. How sad he must be at losing his beloved grandmother. She must be especially kind to him now and try her best to accept his caresses.

CHAPTER 24

Amos told Salome that the baby just looked like a baby.
Salome scoffed, "There is always something like: a nose, an eye shape. If you don't see something like Jake, then I am right. This is not Jake's child."

After consulting with Freda, she insisted that Amos confront the couple. Jake must cast off this harlot. In vain did Amos protest it was too soon after the funeral. They should be allowed a mourning period.

"Nonsense! It's never too soon to correct a sin. I shall certainly not speak to Jake or Hannah until this is settled."

With a sigh, Amos considered what he should say to Phoebe. He was embarrassed at the thought of criticizing anyone, let alone talking about the begetting of children. It was all right in the Bible, but about real people.... His ears burned just thinking about it. That was why he had said nothing on his earlier visit. But he knew Salome wouldn't let it go.

Trying to stave off the inevitable, he decided to consult some of the male members of the community. It was easier to talk to men about such things.

He went to see Barnabas. The sound of squealing pigs reached him as he turned in the lane. Barnabas must be in the barn. He was. And Caleb as well. Barnabas wiped a knife on his pant leg as Amos entered, and Caleb dumped a newly castrated piglet back into the pen.

"Well, Amos," said Caleb, "what brings you out on such a frosty day?"

"It's about Jake and his wife," he blurted.

"Jah, it's a bad thing," said Barnabas. "Besides all this business about the baby, she does not look like a proper married woman. All those bits of curly hair by her face."

Caleb put his head on one side and looked at Barnabas from under his bushy eyebrows. "It bothers you, Barnabas, the hair? Gives you impure thoughts?"

"No, no, of course not." Barnabas coughed, turned aside and spat into the pigpen. "I just don't think the way she wears it is right for a modest woman."

"But what should I do?" Amos wanted to get back to his concerns. "I've prayed for guidance but no help came. I can't wait longer. Salome...."

"You're the deacon. It is for you to decide," said Barnabas.

Amos went home, gooseflesh sprinkling his thighs at the task he must perform. He went down on his knees in the pile of hay in the stable to ask for guidance.

The following Sunday afternoon, Salome, with Amos in tow, strode up the lane to Jake and Phoebe's cabin. Amos had said this was his duty, but Salome had insisted on coming.

"You are too soft, Amos. That harlot will just bat her eyes and you will believe anything she says."

Jake opened the door. "Good day, Aunt Salome, Uncle Amos."

Salome acknowledged him frostily, "Hello, Jake."

Amos mumbled something unintelligible.

"Take off your things," said Phoebe, "and come close to the fire."

As she hung their outdoor clothes on the pegs by the door, she glanced at them as they stood before the fire, their backs to her. They were about the same height but there the resemblance ended. Salome looked as if her ample flesh was molded over an iron framework, while lanky Uncle Amos seemed made of more pliable stuff.

"Will you have some tea?" Phoebe asked as she pulled the water kettle over the fire.

"This is not a social call," said Salome. She went over to the cradle and peered in at Hedwig, who for once was sleeping peacefully. She gingerly lifted the blanket, peering in, almost as if she expected something to jump out at her. She nodded as if satisfied and, lips pursed, seated herself regally on the settle next to the hearth, spreading her skirts to take up most of the bench. Amos sat down on the small space at the end and braced his left leg to the side to support himself.

Salome straightened her back, her considerable breasts resettling themselves under her kerchief. "The deacon believes...."

Amos cleared his throat and reset his leg.

"... The deacon believes," Salome repeated, "there has been a transgression here of Bible laws."

"Oh?" said Jake. He turned to Amos. "In what way?"

Amos cleared his throat again.

"Speak up, Deacon," Salome prodded him with her elbow.

"Well...well," stuttered Amos. "Well, ahem, there seems to be some doubt about the baby."

Phoebe suddenly understood the meaning of these visits. How could she have thought everything would be all right?

"Why, it's Phee's baby—and mine," said Jake. Then, with an attempt at levity, "We didn't find her under a cabbage. Phoebe carried it herself, for nine months. You know that."

Salome pursed her mouth, then said, "We know it's Phoebe's baby, all right. Whether it's yours, is the trouble. I can count the months as good as anyone." She gave Amos a dig in the ribs. "Speak up, Deacon. Do your duty."

Amos regained his small share of the settle, swallowed noisily and stuttered, "Ah-ah, I have to ask you straight out, Jake. Is this kinder yours?"

"It's my kinder, sure enough, because Phoebe is my wife, but it's not of my blood."

"I knew it, I knew it," cried Salome. "We've been harboring a woman of loose virtue." She tucked in her double chins and the front of her bodice became even more prominent. "I suppose you knew it all the time. how could you marry a harlot, or did she fool you, too?"

"Now wait a little." He held up his hand. "Wait until you hear Phoebe's story."

"Oh, a story, is it?" sneered Salome. "Another one."

"Tell them, Phoebe." He moved to where she stood facing her inquisitor.

Stumbling in her speech, Phoebe once again lived through her ordeal. Her voice sank almost to a whisper at the sordid details. Uncle Amos looked sympathetic, and very embarrassed, but Aunt Salome's face got even stonier. How could she make her believe?

When she'd finished, Salome said, "Humph! You must have done something to encourage him."

"I didn't, I didn't." She shook so hard she had to lean against Jake. "He...he was a horrible man."

"I believe her," mumbled Amos.

"And I," said Jake, tightening his arm.

"Well, men," scoffed Salome. "They'll believe anyone who has a pretty face. We women are not so easily fooled. Jake, you must put away this harlot."

Jake put his arm around Phoebe, pulling her close, and glared at his aunt. "I will not."

"You defy the deacon?"

"You said it, not Uncle Amos."

"The Deacon and I are one in the sight of God."

"So are Phoebe and me."

Salome stood up. "Come, Deacon. We will have nothing more to do with this godless woman. Jake, my shawl."

He was quick to oblige.

Salome pulled it about her shoulders and sailed out the door. Amos put on his coat, paused to shake hands with Jake and gave it an extra squeeze. He gave Phoebe a sorrowful look before following his wife.

Jake slammed the door after the guests and crossed the room to where Phoebe had collapsed onto the settle.

She saw his face set in grim lines, and said, "Oh, Jake, what will they do?"

"I don't know. We'll just have to wait and see." He sat down and gathered her in his arms. "You are my wife, whatever."

"Well, I don't care if Salome doesn't speak to me. That would be a relief. But it would be too bad if she keeps Uncle Amos away. I really like him, and I think he wants to be friends."

"Jah, Uncle Amos. A sad life he has."

"Do you think she'll turn everyone else against me?"

"I hope not."

Salome spread the word that the new baby wasn't Jake's.

I knew it," said Freda Sherk. "That red hair. But the harlot is an English. What could you expect?"

"We have to do something about this scandal," said Salome.

CHAPTER 25

Warm spring sun and frosty nights started the sap run and everyone was too busy making maple sugar to think of anything else, although Salome carried on her crusade on the rare occasions she met any of her neighbors.

On top of all her other chores, Phoebe had to clarify the maple syrup Jake boiled in the huge iron kettle set up on tripods in the edge of the bush. In the cabin she reheated a smaller kettle of syrup, then added egg whites, which attached to particles in the syrup called sugar sand. The mass floated to the surface to be skimmed off, leaving a clear, golden liquid.

At the end of the syrup season, the Sherks held a sugaring-off party. Phoebe wasn't invited and Jake refused to go without her.

On the way home from the party Hannah said to Simon, "If I knew she wasn't asked I wouldn't have gone, either."

"Now, Hannah." Simon clucked to the team and shook the reins over their backs to speed them. "Barnabas and Freda could ask anyone they liked. It was their party."

She rubbed the worry lines in her forehead with her mittened hand. "What's going to happen? It's terrible to have such unfriendliness."

"I agree."

"It's not her fault. If some lout attacked me would you say it was my fault?"

"For sure. What man in his right mind would look at such an old woman without some eye-blinking by you."

Shocked, she turned on him but noting his twinkling eyes, subsided. "It's no joke, Simon."

He sighed, "Jah, for sure." And shook the reins again. "Get along you, before we freeze altogether."

He grumbled as they prepared for bed. "All this fuss over a woman. You made a mistake, taking her in, already."

"I thought it was the Christian thing to do." She turned to him, her hands full of long strands as she braided her hair for the night. "How could I let that dear little boy live in such a place? I never thought that Jake would marry her."

His head emerged from the neck of his bed gown. "The damage was done, I think, way back when he brought her out from the river."

"Well, damage it is and there's nothing to do, now he's married to her. Much as I like her, I wish he had never seen her." She tied a piece of rag around the end of the thick braid to keep it from unraveling and climbed into bed.

With the rush of spring planting, Phoebe's days were filled with housework, barn chores, gardening, and care of the children. The three cows all had heifer calves and she and Jake rejoiced at the additions to their herd. But now with all the extra milk, she had to add butter and cheese-making to her routine.

Her isolation was brought home to her when she went over to Hannah's. Freda Sherk, who was visiting there, snatched up her shawl and left without speaking to her.

"Oh, did I drive her away?" asked Phoebe as she watched Freda bustle down the lane.

"Well, she was leaving, just." Hannah nervously smoothed her apron.

Freda's leaving so abruptly was suspicious, and Phoebe mentally chastised herself yet again. She was a poison, contaminating everyone who was kind to her. Now Freda had cut short her visit because of her arrival.

After seeding, Barnabas told everyone he was going to put up a new barn. He'd cut logs the year before and spent every spare moment squaring them with his adz. A huge pile of sawn lumber, brought from the mill at Chippewa, lay beside them.

He came over to see Jake who was cleaning manure out of the barn. "Good day, Jake."

143

"Hello, Barnabas. The hay crop looks good, don't it?"

"Yes. I'll need more room to store it—if the Good Lord continues to favor us. The timbers are dry so I'm going to put up my new barn. I'm calling a bee for next Thursday. You can help, some?"

"Sure, Barnabas."

"Uh...there is a thing...uh..." Then with a rush, "Freda says Phoebe not to come." He scraped some loose straw into a pile with his boot and regarded it.

Jake snapped upright and jammed his fork into the manure. He glared at his visitor. "Well, then, Barnabas, I can't help you. I won't go where Phee isn't wanted. You would do the same for Freda, so?"

"Freda would not be guilty of such a sin," said Barnabas, stiffly.

Jake threw up his hands. "Everyone here is deaf and blind, I think. Phoebe hasn't sinned! There's no more to say, Barnabas." He turned his back on his visitor, picked up the fork and threw manure out the barn door, narrowly missing Barnabas who left hastily, his rigid back indicating his outrage.

Tension in the community continued to grow. Esther Martin and Gerda Beuhler were the only ones outside the Stettl family who visited Phoebe. One Sunday afternoon Esther came to visit and she, Jake and Phoebe discussed the situation.

"I thought everyone would soon know what a good woman I married," said Jake.

"Well, it's mostly Salome's doing," said Esther. "If you don't mind my saying so about your aunt, Jake. I fear she is a most unhappy woman."

"So, no need for her to make my wife unhappy, too."

"That is how it works, Jake. Unhappy people like to spread the feeling." Esther smiled, wryly. "As for Freda, some people follow whoever is the strongest—or noisiest."

Jake nodded. "Aunt Salome is noisy, that's for sure. Uncle Amos is pretty much under her thumb, but I don't understand why

Barnabas doesn't say something to Freda. I thought he liked Phoebe."

"Barnabas is very devout and I suspect Salome has convinced him that Phoebe is in the wrong. Salome came to see me but I said her a sermon on Christian forgiveness." Esther chuckled. "I don't think she got the connection. She visited Gerda too, and Gerda showed her the door. Too bad some others wouldn't follow Gerda's example."

Jake rubbed his worry-lined forehead. "What is going to happen, then? It can't go on like this."

He smiled at Phoebe but she thought he looked concerned. Would he come to look at her the way the community did? Their rejection didn't bother her overmuch. She'd been scorned by one group or another all her life: both the loyalists and rebels back in Haventown, and the jealous wives at Newark. But if Jake.... She realized how much his love and support meant to her.

Esther sighed. "I don't know what can be done."

Jake said, "I think we'll have to move away."

Phoebe stared at him. He'd move away and leave his family for her sake? That was too much to ask of anyone. "It's me that should go away and let everyone forget I ever existed," she protested.

"Now, Phee, that's silly. I couldn't get along without you." With an attempt at levity. "Who will patch my pants?"

"How can you make fun, Jake? I just cause trouble wherever I go." She pulled at her hair until her cap fell off, pins flew and tendrils fell over her face. Tears rolled down her cheeks and choking sobs tore at her throat. There was no way out of this mess unless she went away and she'd tried that before and Jake had brought her back. What could she do? "I wish I'd never been born."

"So. That's the Good God's decision," said Esther, taking Phoebe's hand in hers. "We don't know what He is planning. Perhaps something better than you ever thought will come out of this."

"I can't imagine what it could be."

"Just be patient." Esther patted her hand. "It will all work out in His good time."

"And in the meantime, everyone who's been good to me suffers."

"So," said Esther. "That is part of living."

Neither Amos nor Barnabas asked Jake to help bring in their crops as would ordinarily have been the case. So he couldn't ask them to help with his. They wouldn't have come anyway. He and his father and brothers were hard put to harvest all Jake's crops as well as Simon's.

In November, 1795, Noah Beuhler, son of Caleb and Gerda, was married to Lottie Streicher who lived at The Twenty. Almost the entire community went to the bride's home on Lake Ontario for the celebration. Phoebe tried to persuade Jake to go, but he refused.

"But, Jake, you make me feel bad. You're missing all these celebrations on my account."

He waved his hand as if throwing something away. "It makes no mind. I won't go where my wife is not welcome."

He said he didn't mind, but how could he not? These were his people. How much longer would he stand by her?

A few mornings later while they lingered over coffee, planning the day's work, she had to make a dash to the privy, not even stopping for her shawl.

When she returned, white-faced and shaken, he said, "You must have eaten something spoiled."

"I guess so, but I don't know what. Do you feel all right?"

"Yes, and William seems fine."

The next few mornings duplicated the first and a quick calculation verified her suspicions. She didn't need such a complication on top of everything else. But Jake would be pleased.

Jake was indeed pleased. "Now a baby of my own, so. But should you be sick like that? Will it last the whole time?"

"No. Just for a few weeks."

"That's good."

He gingerly put his arms around her and she relaxed against him. No matter how much she'd wished otherwise, heretofore her body had instinctively stiffened whenever he touched her. Whatever had affected her seemed to have gone away. Dear Jake. He was so patient with her. She hoped this lovely feeling would last. She kissed him and his arms tightened, squeezing the breath out of her. But she didn't protest.

The tracks froze and a generous fall of snow made sleighing easy. Chopping and quilting bees and all sorts of gay gatherings filled the days and evenings. But not for the Jake Stettls. Phoebe didn't mind for herself since she felt too ill to take part, the nausea catching her now at any time of day, but she couldn't persuade Jake to go by himself.

Simon held a husking bee and Jake elected to stay home with her. She refused to go for fear everyone would leave when they saw her.

After the bee he went over to his parents' farm to tell them about the baby. Phoebe said she was sure, now.

His mutti upbraided him as soon as he stepped in the door. "You could have come to the bee. It's your home, so."

"Not without Phee, and she wouldn't come for fear Amos and Barnabas would leave when they saw her."

"Things can't go on like this," rumbled Simon from his seat by the fire.

Jake, his shoulders stiff, said, "She is my wife. I will stand by her no matter what anyone says."

Hannah took hold of his arm, peering into his face. "But what will you do, then? You can't live your life shunned by half the community."

"I'm thinking of moving away. Caleb Streicher did that when he disagreed with the way Salome was running things and moved to The Twenty."

"Oh, Jake. So far." Hannah held up her hands in protest.

"No, not to The Twenty. It would be the same there. I'm looking for a farm outside."

"Jake, you don't mean it." Hannah grabbed his arm and shook it as if to instill some sense into this stubborn son. "Leave the settlement? You couldn't do that."

"I can so. I want nothing to do with such heartless people here."

Hannah appealed to her spouse. "Simon, say something. Don't let him go away."

Simon heaved a great sigh. "You're wrong, son. Put her away and come back to your family and your church. I'm sorry you ever saw her."

"I'm not," said Jake, glaring at his vati. "It was the happiest day of my life, and she is still my whole life. Especially now. That's what I came to tell you. She's going to have a baby." He grinned. "And this one is mine, for sure."

"Oh, Jake. Such good news." Hannah hugged him and he smiled, sheepishly.

Simon groaned. He'd been prepared to persuade Jake to put Phoebe from him. But it couldn't be done now she was going to have Jake's baby. He couldn't consider casting off his unborn grandchild. What would be the end of it?

Ruth Zavitz

CHAPTER 26

One day toward the end of February 1796, Jake went to Fort Erie for supplies. When he came home, he shouted for Phoebe while he was still far down the road. "Phee, Phee, I bought a farm. We're moving."

Alarmed at the shouting, Phoebe hurried to the door. He drove into the yard, jumped off the sleigh, threw down the reins and rushed to hug her. "Did you hear what I said, so? We're moving from here. I bought a new place." He whirled her around, her feet flying clear of the ground.

"Jake! Put me down. What are you doing?" He set her back on her feet and she adjusted her skirts, embarrassed. "What's this about a new place?"

He jumped in the air and clicked his heels together. "I just bought a farm. And we can move right away."

He'd bought a farm? It must be outside the settlement. How could he be so happy about moving away from his family and this place he'd worked so hard to improve? In spite of his assurances, he was apparently more worried about the troubles here than he'd let on. Poor Jake. What a trial she was to him. Still, it would be good to escape the scowls and turned backs she encountered whenever she left the farm.

"That's wonderful. Where is this place and why didn't you tell me before you bought it?"

"I didn't know before. I met this man at Fort Erie. He was going back to England and wanted to sell his place. I didn't have time to tell you, so. I thought you'd be pleased to leave here."

"Oh, I am. It would be so good to get away." Dear Jake. Doing everything he could to make her happy. She linked her arm in his. "But you didn't say where it is. Is it near here?"

"Not very close, maybe, but this is the important part." He pointed his finger at her. "It's your uncle's farm at Sugar Loaf."

149

Uncle Edward's farm? The thought of returning there sent shivers up her back. "Oh, no, Jake. I can't go back there." She stepped away.

His shoulders sagged. "What is the matter? I thought you'd be pleased. It's the closest thing to a home you ever had here, isn't it?"

"Not really." Over his shoulder she noticed the team starting to move. "Jake! Get the horses. They're going to catch their harness in the fence."

He ran to rescue the horses—and the fence—and she took the time to consider his news. There wasn't much difference that she could see, between being ostracized here or in her old community.

Seated before the fire in the cabin, after the horses had been tied in the warm stable, Jake held his hands over the flames, rubbing them together.

He turned to her. "Now why don't you want to go back to your uncle's farm?"

She stared at the frost-painted window, remembering. "I was so unhappy there. I felt so bad about father and mother drowning...."

"Jah, I remember." He reached over and took her hand.

"And Aunt Mercy wasn't very kind." Well, that was an understatement.

"I remember your aunt. I went to see how you were, once, and she slammed the door at me."

"She would. Not much mercy in my Aunt Mercy. Did you really go to see me?"

"Jah I couldn't forget you. The first time you looked with those black eyes you wound me round your finger." He gestured with his hands. "No hope for me."

"Oh, Jake. You're soft in the head."

"Jah, so. That's me." He grinned. "But where did your aunt and uncle go?" His forehead wrinkled. "I bought the farm from another man. He didn't know where they were. I asked."

"They died of fever. Angelique told me."

"Oh, that's bad. I remember you said your family was all dead. I thought you meant your vati and mutti. I didn't know, everyone." He put his arms around her. Then he put his finger under her chin and raised her face. "Phee, listen to me. The farm is just a farm. It don't remember bad times."

"I do, though. And I'm sure the Quakers there haven't forgiven me for disobeying my aunt and running away with a soldier. They think fighting is terrible. I'm sure they expelled me from the meeting."

"Will that matter to you, not to be able to go to your church?"

No, I don't think so. It seems to me I never fit in, anyway."

He shrugged. "Well, that makes no mind, and so. You're not Phoebe Carey any more, nor Phoebe Trevlyn even. Just Phoebe Stettl. No one will remember, anyhow."

"I'd rather not go, though, Jake."

"But I bought it. It's a good farm." His arms tightened around her. "Don't worry. It will be all right."

He didn't know what people could do. He probably thought the way she was treated here was unusual. She could tell him it wasn't.

"I can't go, Jake."

All the light left his face. He'd obviously hoped she would be as excited about the move as he. But she couldn't help herself. The thought of going back there made her stomach heave. It was his fault. If he would only tell her what he planned before he did it.

"You will have to find another place."

"But I have two farms, now. I can't afford another one. The new one will be better, Phee."

She heard the pleading in his voice. He was as unhappy as she was. But she couldn't face going back to the Sugar Loaf settlement. It wouldn't be any better than here. Why make the change? All her life, it seemed, she'd let others arrange her life for her. Time she spoke up.

"No, Jake, I won't go."

He got up without a word and went out to the barn.

For several days, the cabin atmosphere was murky. Jake was stubborn, but this time she wouldn't give in.

"You have one farm too many, anyway," she said, one night, as they were having a cup of tea before bed. "They're too far apart to farm together. And how are you going to pay for the new one?"

"Aha. There is a secret." He held up his hand, index finger extended. "Karl wants to marry up with Rebecca and he will buy this one."

Phoebe's cup clattered in its saucer as she set it down, surprised. "I didn't know they were promised. Why didn't you tell me?"

"Well, not exactly promised." He turned his head to look at the fire. "Salome...."

"Of course. Salome." Her lips tightened. "She wouldn't let Rebecca marry him because of me. Oh, I just bring trouble and trouble."

He reached over and took her hand. "Don't worry about it. Rebecca is like her mutti, some." He chuckled. "If she wants something—and she wants our Karl—she'll get her way, Salome or no. They've just been waiting for Karl to buy a farm in the settlement, and now he can."

"But what about your mutti? She won't want you so far away."

"It's not so far. And she can visit without all the noses looking through the curtains."

"No, Jake. I won't go and that's final."

The next afternoon, Hannah came over. Phoebe knew there was a quilting bee at Freda's, to which she hadn't been invited.

"You didn't go to the bee?" Phoebe asked as she pulled the kettle over the fire.

"No." Hannah shifted on the settle as if she were uncomfortable. "I thought I hadn't been to see you for a while, so I come here instead."

That seemed odd. Hannah never missed a community gathering.

Phoebe mentioned to Jake at suppertime that his mother had come over instead of going to the quilting bee. He sighed and said, "Jah. Freda didn't ask her, so."

She stared at him. "Freda is turning against her? You knew?"

"Jah." He reached across the table for a biscuit, broke it open and concentrated on buttering it, his head down.

"Why didn't you tell me?"

Jake shrugged. "What difference if I did?"

"And Mutti Stettl came here the same day just to defy her. Oh Jake. This is terrible. I wouldn't have your mother hurt for anything. What can we do about it?"

"Only one thing, I think, and you will not."

She gave in. She couldn't cause hurt to her mother-in-law, who'd been so kind to her.

Now she was forced to consider the move instead of closing her mind to it, she thought perhaps it wouldn't be so bad. The Quaker community, as she remembered, wasn't a closed one like the Mennonite's. If the Quakers shunned her, there would still be other people living there who might befriend her. She hoped so.

There were mixed reactions to the news among the Stettls. At the regular Sunday dinner at Hannah's they discussed the move.

Karl, of course, was, for him, jubilant. Simon said it was the best solution, although he was sorry Jake was moving away from the community. Hannah became somewhat teary at the thought of losing Jake, but he explained where the farm lay, "Not so far," and that she would be able to visit without antagonizing the community.

"But I'll miss the little ones," she sniffed, reaching into her apron pocket for her handkerchief.

"Well, there will be more here, soon, maybe." He gave Karl a dig in the ribs, which caused that young man to blush furiously.

"There's a lot to do, then, before seeding time," said Simon. "We had better move some hay and grain, first, while there is still sleighing. I don't suppose the settler left any in the barn, there, Jake?"

"I don't know. I haven't been there."

Simon stared at his son. "You bought without seeing? Maybe it's all swamp. There is a lot of swamp over there. I thought you were smarter, boy."

"I have seen it. Just not this year. It's not swamp."

Phoebe shivered. Had he seen it since he came to inquire after her? That must be four or five years ago. A lot could happen to a cabin in that time if it wasn't looked after. It wasn't like him to act so impulsively where money was concerned. It showed how their position here upset him.

"The sooner we're away from here the better I will like it," said Jake. Suddenly looking worried, he turned to her. "Will moving be too much for you? Maybe we should wait until after...."

"No, no, It's all right." Not much choice between staying here where she was ostracized and moving back to where she'd been so unhappy. And Jake seemed excited about the move.

Simon, Jake and Karl went to inspect the farm.

Peter wanted to go, too but Simon said, "No need for everyone . You can finish cleaning out the calves' pen."

Peter sighed. "Always I'm just the chore boy."

Jake asked Phoebe to go, but she said she couldn't leave the children and it was too cold to take them. He said he'd ask Mutti to look after them, but she shook her head.

"Mutti has enough to do." In truth, she wanted to put off going back as long as possible.

When the men returned, Karl said, "Phoebe, you have one lucky man. It's a very good place, I think. If I had bought without seeing, it would have turned out to be all rocks, already."

"The house is in good shape, Phee, and not too dirty," said Jake. "There's some junk in one bedroom but we can clear that out after we move. Maybe something there we can use, and so."

The move began almost immediately. The new barn contained a little hay, but the men took several more loads from Jake's barn using Simon's team. Jake's mare, Jilly, was heavy in foal.

Mares have to be protected, thought Phoebe, as she wrestled stout wooden boxes full of bedding and clothes, and leaned painfully over the edge of barrels packing crockery dishes in straw. For women it's different. She stood up, her hand to her back and chided herself. Stop feeling sorry for yourself. Jake is doing this for you. If you didn't get yourself into such a mess you wouldn't have to move.

The children thought this some sort of new game. Hedwig climbed into a packing box, and while Phoebe was head down in the barrel, William threw straw into the box until Hedwig's frightened cries alerted her.

"William, no."

"I'm packing Hedwig, too. Isn't she going with us?"

"Yes, she is going with us, and if you don't stop being naughty I'll pack *you* in straw."

William giggled. "When?"

"Oh, stop. Please be good. Mutti's busy."

When Jake came in to supper, William greeted him with news. "Mutti's going to pack me in straw." He jumped around the cabin, crowing.

Jake looked inquiringly at her.

"He's been so naughty."

"Why don't I take them over to Mutti's tomorrow. You look worn out."

"Always, it's get Mutti . Don't you think I can do anything without her help?"

"Well... I just thought... you look so tired...."

"I can manage." She was cheered. He was thinking of her. She smiled at him. She shouldn't wallow in self-pity as she had this afternoon.

He said no more, but the next morning Hannah appeared. "I came to help," she said. "It's not good for you, the lifting and bending, when you're having a baby. The baby, it's such good news."

"Well, I guess so, but I would have liked to wait a little. Everything is so upset right now."

Hannah laughed. "The kinder, they don't wait for right times." She sobered. "It's too bad you are going. I'll not see my first grandchild born—well, you know I mean the first blood one," she amended, hugging Hedwig who tugged at her skirt.

Phoebe felt a chill. How would she manage without Hannah's counsel and support? She complained to Jake that he thought she couldn't do anything without Mutti Stettl's help, but she feared it was true. And what kind of reception would she receive when she returned to the community from which she'd fled so abruptly?

"Let me take the children home with me until you get moved, then." said Hannah.

William's quick ears picked up this suggestion. "I want to go to Grossmutti's. I want to go to Grossmutti's," he cried, jigging up and down.

"Of course he does, the happy," laughed Hannah, hugging him.

"Well, I don't know. He's such a handful. And Hedwig whines all the time."

"I can manage. You have to take care of yourself, and my grandchild."

Jake said he thought this was a capital idea and, as the sun lowered, Hannah set off for home in the sleigh, the two children tucked snugly beside her.

Word that Jake was leaving soon spread through the community. Amos mourned the loss of four of his little flock, as well as the loss of his nephew.

Not so Salome, who crowed when she heard the news. "At last we'll be rid of her and her sin-begottten child."

Some members sided with Amos and some with Salome. But the deed was done. Please God, Amos prayed, there would now be peace in the community—and in his house.

CHAPTER 27

Phoebe shivered as they drove down the trail toward her new, yet old, home. In spite of her fear, she noticed many new cabins and cleared fields where unbroken forest had crowded the trail when she lived here. That meant new people. Perhaps she would find friends, after all.

The farm, too, seemed different. The edge of the bush was now much farther away from the cabin. Someone, either Uncle Edward or a subsequent owner, had cleared a great deal more land. That was good. More cropland meant a more secure future.

The cabin looked more weather-beaten, though, and her shoulders sagged as she noticed bits of wood and clay on the snow at the base of the logs. Chinking would have to be done again. There was an ominous sag in the roof line, too. Another log cabin. Would she ever have a proper house of her own?

"Here we are," said Jake as they drove into the dooryard. "Does it look like you remember?"

She gritted her teeth. "The farm looks better, but the cabin is bad."

"Jah, I know. Soon I'll build you a house."

"I hope before the roof caves in on us."

He chuckled. "Like a swayback horse, no?"

"It's not funny."

"I checked. It won't fall in, or leak on us."

It took all her courage to enter the door. Would the ghosts of her aunt and uncle still inhabit the place? No, that was silly. She wasn't superstitious. Like Jake said, it was only a house—well cabin.

She sniffed. The odor of boiling beef was gone. Aunt Mercy thought that was the only way to cook meat and the cabin always reeked of its steamy smell. Now all she could detect was the damp of a fireless cabin. That could soon be rectified.

She must look on the bright side. At least this one had two proper bedrooms. Jake put their bedstead and William's pallet in one bedroom. She opened the door to the other, which had been her own room, and shuddered at the clutter inside. That could wait. She had no inclination to spend time in the room where she'd been so unhappy.

The next day Simon, Karl, and Peter arrived, herding Jake's cattle, with Jake's sow and her hens crated in a wagon. She scurried to unpack enough supplies to make them a meal. As she took the potato peelings out to the hens she was greeted with annoyed crowing from the cock.

She laughed. "You'll have to get used to it, too."

In the pasture, the cows bawled and the sow grunted, all displeased at their change of abode. They'd soon settle in, as she would, she hoped.

Over the next few days she worked hard organizing the household, and was quite pleased with the result. Although some of the outside chinking had fallen, the inside walls were still tight and dry. Except for her initial reaction on seeing the cabin, she felt quite comfortable. Jake was right. It was only a house.

Grossmutti Stettl had always said, "It's a long lane that has no turning." Perhaps no one here would recognize her and she could start a new life. Oh, she hoped so.

She scrubbed the puncheon floor of the main room to a silvery whiteness with ashes, and moved the bureau against the wall opposite the fireplace. With the bright copper pots hung on the fireplace wall, the black iron kettles on the crane in the fireplace and the three-legged spider set on the hearth, she felt more competent to deal with whatever the future might bring.

The rest of the cabin organized, she began on the junk room. Everything the previous owners had no use for had been piled in here. She dragged out several musty straw ticks and set fire to them in the yard, much to William's delight. As she sorted through a pile of discarded clothing, half-grown mice erupted from its depths and disappeared quickly through cracks in the floor. She must ask Mutti for one of the new batch of kittens. She was going to need its services. The pile of rags reeked of mouse so she added it to the bonfire.

When Jake came in for dinner she asked his advice on the utensils and furniture she'd found.

"I think that cracked churn is no good," he said, "but we could save the paddle. I can make a new churn, maybe. I could fix the back on that chair again and make a new leg for the wash stand."

He turned over a pile of staves and hoops of what had been several barrels. "The wood is too rotten but we could ask Caleb to make...." he stopped, mouth open. "I forgot."

He missed his old home already. "Oh, Jake." She threw her arms around his neck. "What have I done to you? You've given up everything for me."

His arms tightened around her. "It makes no mind. I'm contented. It's just sometimes I forget. Well," he continued, giving her a final hug and turning back to the iron hoops, "there's probably someone here who knows how to do new staves. Or I could try it myself."

She wiped her eyes on the corner of her apron. She should show her appreciation more. He was always prepared to make the best of things.

He gathered up the hoops, threading them on his arm. "I'll take these to the barn out of your way and you could burn the boards in the fireplace, so. We shouldn't waste any wood. I don't know if there is much cut. I haven't looked in the bush."

After he'd gone out, she shoved the washstand across the room so she could sweep where it had been. It tilted drunkenly on its broken leg and the little drawer slid out, spilling its contents on the floor: A bone comb with most of the teeth missing, the two halves of a china cup and its chipped saucer, a tiny, jagged piece of mirror and some pieces of cloth. She laid aside the cloth. Whoever had lived here had at least saved patching material—and it didn't reek of rodents.

She held the cup and saucer for a moment, stroking the tiny blue forget-me-nots painted on them. So fragile. Would she ever own such delicate things? These were useless, now. Perhaps not the saucer, though. She carried it out and propped it up on the mantel, the chipped side down, stood back and admired it. Maybe some day....

The cabin neat and tidy, she sat down to catch up on the mending. She'd just taken up one of Jake's socks, the heel sporting a large hole, when someone knocked on the door. Bundling the socks into the sewing basket, she set it on the floor in the corner out of the way, and went to the door.

A woman her own age stood on the doorstep. The visitor was clad in sober Quaker dress and bonnet and carried a towel-covered basket over her arm.

Phoebe's first impulse was to shut the door in the woman's face. She didn't want to see anyone from that group. However, good sense took over. She had to live here and couldn't avoid such encounters.

She said, "Good afternoon."

"I wanted to welcome thee," said the buxom visitor. "I'm Abigail Steadman. I live just down the trail, on the other side of the creek." Holding out the basket, she added, "I brought thee a loaf." She peered at Phoebe. "Why, thee is Phoebe Carey that was."

Jake was wrong. She was recognized. Now it would begin again. They stood staring at each other. Then Phoebe gathered her wits. She must see it through, whatever happened.

She said, "Hello, Abigail. I didn't recognize you," took the basket and peeked under the cover at the golden loaf nestled there. "Thank you. It smells wonderful. I haven't had time to bake bread. We've been living on fried cakes."

"I thought thee would be busy settling in, so I made an extra. Moving is a lot of work."

"Yes it is. But I'm forgetting my manners. Come in." She ushered Abigail into the cabin. "Take off your bonnet and cloak and sit down. I'll just make some tea."

"Don't bother with tea. Sit and rest thyself. I'm sure thee could use a moment."

They settled down on each side of the hearth and Abigail said. "Tell me about thyself. Mercy said thee ran away with a soldier but thy man does not look like a military to me. All that yellow beard." She laughed. "I saw him by the barn as I came in."

How could she avoid this interrogation? She jumped up. "I'll just make some tea. I would like a cup, myself." Abigail sounded friendly, but maybe she was just getting information to use against her.

Phoebe made a big production of making tea and buttering some of the bread Abigail had brought, trying to stave off the inevitable. She'd have to tell her something, though.

Her mind made up to face whatever might come, she sat down at the table across from her visitor, the brown pottery teapot and two of her five crockery mugs between them. "It's a long story. I did run away with a soldier but he died and then I married Jake."

"We thought it so romantic—running away with thy lover." Abigail laughed, a happy tinkling sound.

Romantic? Phoebe felt the hard knot in her stomach begin to relax. "Well, Aunt Mercy said...." She stopped. Should she malign Aunt Mercy now she was no longer here to defend herself?

Abigail nodded. "I can imagine what she said. It seemed to me she begrudged the help she gave thee. And I suppose thee gave her whatever thee made with thy sewing?"

"Of course. She and Uncle Edward gave me a home." Phoebe handed the filled cup across the table.

"And thee is happy? I saw a little boy with thy man."

"Yes, William. And Hedwig is having her nap."

"What an unusual name. Hedwig, is it?"

"It's German. Jake's grandmother chose it. It means storm. It stormed the night she was born." Enough of that. She picked up the sugar bowl. "Will you take sugar and milk in your tea?"

"Just a little sugar, please. And now thee is in the family way again, I think."

"Yes, but I'm so sick with it. I hope it soon settles down. There's so much to do."

"Granny Anselm will help thee with the birth. She is the midwife for all the women here."

Abigail told her all the news of the Quaker community but it didn't mean much to Phoebe. She could scarcely remember any of the people Abigail talked about.

As her visitor drained her cup, Phoebe asked if she would like some more.

"No, I must go and not stop thy work. Please come and visit."

"I'm so glad thee came." Sudden affection for Abigail, and relief, caused her to slip back into the plain language. "I dreaded coming back here. I was afraid everyone would avoid me. Please visit again."

"Thank thee, I will, and do come to meeting on the Sabbath."

As she closed the door after Abigail, Phoebe felt a surge of relief. It wouldn't be so bad, after all.

She told Jake of her visitor and the welcome as they were eating supper.

"I told you it would come out all right. Now you will be happy, so?"

He sounded wistful. What a trial she was to him. "Yes, I will. It's such a comfort to know at least one of them doesn't hate me."

"Jah," said Jake. He smiled and suppressed a sigh.

They went to meeting the following Sunday and were greeted warmly. She reveled in the quiet, so sadly lacking in her recent life, but Jake said it was tedious without singing or preaching. William was vehement in his protests against the inactivity. She insisted on his accompanying them the next week, but he was nowhere to be found when it was time to go. Jake said he'd stay at home and look for him.

He sounded quite happy to do so. What kind of example was he setting for their son?

CHAPTER 28

J ake went home to ask his brothers to help him re-shingle the barn roof that was leaking badly. On his return he said, "Karl and Rebecca got married."

Phoebe was setting the table for supper and a cluster of spoons fell from her hand. She stared at him. "And they didn't tell you? Of course. Salome wouldn't invite you. Oh, Jake, I'm so sorry."

"Oh, well, that's all right. It's only a wedding."

He would say that, but she knew it hurt him to miss his own brother's wedding. How long before he resented the restrictions his marriage to her put on him? Even though she didn't love him the way she had Richard, she must try to make up to him for the sacrifices he made for her. She put her arms around him, startling him with a kiss. "I'm sorry, Jake."

"Phee." His arms closed around her so tightly she could hardly breathe. "You really love me? Sometimes I wonder."

"Yes. You're the best man in the world." He really was. No other man would have put up with her moanings and tears, and all the trouble she'd caused him.

"That's all right, then. I would give up everything for you, you know."

"I know it. You already have." She leaned back in his arms to look in his face. She took one arm from around his neck and ran her index finger along his smooth shaven upper lip and the line where his beard met the smooth cheek. "You're such a good man. How was I ever lucky enough to get you for a husband?"

"I'm the lucky one, so." He rubbed his beard across her face, making her giggle.

She leaned back, smoothing his ruffled hair. Over his shoulder, she noticed William taking the cover off the biscuit crock. "William. No. You've already had two."

Jake chuckled. "With children, there is never a stopping, and so. Well, I must get ready for the shingling. Karl is coming tomorrow.

165

Peter and Vati are going to a bee at the Beuhlers." He kissed Phoebe gently. "Just remember, Phee, I chose you and you are my life forever, entirely."

After he'd gone out, she set William on a stool in the corner for his misbehavior and went into the bedroom to finish the cleanup, leaving the door open so she could keep an eye on both children.

As she worked, tears fell. Tears of happiness. Dear Jake. He was so good to her. She'd been angry that he'd bought this farm without telling her, but it looked like it would turn out all right, after all.

The next morning, as she was forming the bread dough into loaves, the jingle of harness in the yard signaled Karl's arrival. She expected him to go straight to the barn where Jake was finishing chores and was startled when the door opened. A woman called in German, "Anybody in this house?"

Phoebe dropped the loaf she was shaping. "Rebecca. What are you doing here?"

"I'm not welcome, then?"

"Of course you are. Come in, come in." Phoebe wiped her doughy hands on her apron and held them out.

Rebecca laid her shawl on the back of the settle, revealing a willowy figure. She took off her bonnet and smoothed her taffy-colored hair. She faced Phoebe, her blue eyes warm.

Phoebe threw her arms around the younger woman and tears threatened to overflow. "Oh, Rebecca. Come closer to the fire. Your cheeks are like ice. How is married life? Jake said you and Karl are married."

"I am much happy. Karl is a good man." Rebecca spread her hands to the flames. "This is nice, then. Karl wasn't sure you would want to see me after the way my mutti treated you."

At mention of Salome, Phoebe stood still. "Salome let you come?"

Rebecca giggled. "She doesn't know. She went with Vati to Fort Erie today. They left at sunup. It makes no never mind. I would

166

have come, anyway. I'm a married woman now, and can do whatever my man lets me."

"I'm so glad to see you, but I don't want to make trouble between you and your mother."

"Oh, we always have trouble, Mutti and me," Rebecca waved her hand as if brushing something away. "She says I'm bad seed."

"But how about your vati? Won't he mind?"

"No, I don't think so. Your leaving upset him. I don't think he wanted you to go. That was too bad, that. But he can never stand up to Mutti. Anyway, you know, I can wind him around my finger."

Phoebe laughed. It was good to see Rebecca. She was such a happy person.

William pulled at Rebecca's skirts., "Did you bring me something?"

"William!" scolded Phoebe. "I'm sorry, Rebecca. I can't seem to teach him manners."

"Oh, but I did bring him something." Rebecca hugged him, making rude noises on his neck with her lips and tickling him until he squirmed free, giggling. Then she rummaged in her handbag. "Here is your top. Grossmommy sent it. You forgot it."

William shouted with delight and had to be reminded to thank Rebecca. He immediately began to spin it.

Then Rebecca turned to Hedwig, who was hanging onto Phoebe's skirts, her thumb in her mouth. Squatting down, Rebecca said, "Hello, Hedwig, would you like a hug?"

Hedwig let go of her mother and timidly approached Rebecca's outstretched arms.

Phoebe's eyes watered. This woman was kinder to her child than she herself was. Would she ever become reconciled to that flaming hair?

Rebecca stood up with Hedwig in her arms, and said, "But I'm interrupting. You were making the bread. I came to help, not stop." She sat down on the settle and held Hedwig's hands out to the fire. "Now we will let Mutti get on with her work, without a dragging at the skirts," she said, kissing Hedwig's cheek.

William climbed up beside her and Phoebe said, "You're good with the children, Rebecca."

"I hope I have lots. Mutti Stettl says you are going to have another one."

"Yes, and I've been sick with it. If I run out without excusing myself you will know what it is." Phoebe grinned, ruefully.

The sound of hammers indicated the shingling had begun and William grabbed his coat and rushed out the door, shouting, "I'm coming to help."

Hedwig was put down for her morning nap and the two women worked together at the household chores.

Rebecca said, "Don't answer if you'd rather not, but I always wanted to know what really happened, about Hedwig, I mean, and life at the fort. What Mutti believes doesn't sound like you."

"You can't imagine what it was like there. It seemed like every man was trying to get some other man's wife."

"Your man, too?"

Phoebe paused with the paring knife held up in her hand. "Why, I don't know. I never thought about that. I was so much in love, you see." Then, embarrassed. "Well, that was before Jake." Resuming peeling turnips, she reflected. "No, I don't think so. Richard was a gambler and drinker. I didn't know that when I married him. Those were his women, I guess."

Rebecca shivered. "It doesn't sound like a very nice place. No wonder Vati wants us to stay away from there."

"It wasn't all bad. We had a lot of fun, too." She started to say balls and cards, then realized Rebecca would not approve of those pursuits either.

Rebecca pointed to the pork roast hanging on a spit over the fire. "Shall I baste the meat?"

"Yes, please. I can't think where my mind is. Oh, it's good to have company."

Rebecca laughed. "You'll soon tire of me and my questions. Mutti says I never grew up. Tell me where you come from and what it was like there."

The morning passed as they compared backgrounds and the men came in for dinner before they had half covered their past lives.

"Well, how are you getting along, then?" boomed Karl, the noise sending Hedwig screaming to her mother's skirts.

Rebecca laughed. "You will have to learn better than that, my man. Can't have you scaring my babes."

"Your babes? They'll be mine, too."

"Of course, silly, but you'll have to learn not to shout so much."

How nice, thought Phoebe. These two were so happy together, and she and Jake would be the same, now their problems were solved.

"Shhh. I'm sorry, little thing," whispered Karl, squatting down to Hedwig's level.

Peeking out from behind her mother, Hedwig gave him a shy smile.

Jokes and laughter flew around the table during the meal, and Phoebe realized how much she'd missed outside contact. Hannah and Esther Martin had been the only visitors back in the settlement and much as she had appreciated their company, it was good to entertain someone her own age.

When the newlyweds left for home and chores in the late afternoon, Phoebe impressed on Rebecca how much she'd enjoyed her visit and urged her to come again if she could without causing conflict with her mother.

"Oh, Mutti. Though she wouldn't admit it, she enjoys a fight. So do I, so don't worry."

"So long as you don't fight with me," rumbled Karl.

"Why would I fight with you? You let me do whatever I want." Rebecca fluttered her eyelashes at him.

Jake said, "That's how you get along with women. Let them have their own way."

Phoebe stiffened. "Jake! How can you say that?"

He chuckled.

Her anger flared. She was about to turn on him when she realized it wouldn't be proper with others present. She'd almost forgotten how to behave in public. As she calmed, she realized he was mostly right. Except for moving here he'd always put her wishes first. And coming here had been the right thing to do after all.

Their guests on their way, Jake and Phoebe turned back into the cabin. The couple had brought a breath of fresh air into their lives and it seemed to her a lot of the tension had dissolved.

"I think our Karl has done all right by himself," he said, as he laid a fresh log on the fire.

"I think so, too. I like her. She just dives right in."

"Like her mutti, and so?"

"Yes, in a way, but not vindictive."

Jake wrinkled his brow. "Vin.... What is that?"

"Mean, I guess."

"Jah, mean is the word for Salome, all right."

"I hope she doesn't interfere. Rebecca and I could become good friends, I think."

"That is good. You need some."

"How about you. You need friends, too."

"I have my family back home, and you and the babes here. Well, it makes no mind. We will soon make friends."

It might indeed be so. She could already count Abigail as one. She felt happier than she had since, well, how long ago? Please God it would continue.

CHAPTER 29

Phoebe came out of the cabin, carrying a splint basket of newly washed clothes. With luck she could finish hanging them up before Hedwig woke from her morning nap. She set the basket down under the hempen cord strung between the corner of the cabin and the maple tree by the chicken coop.

She'd purchased the basket from a group of Indian women who'd come by the week before, festooned with baskets of all shapes and sizes. This one was made of split willow, cleverly woven with the red bark on the outside and the cream heartwood on the inside. As well as being useful it was a beautiful thing. She'd also bought a smaller basket with a handle for gathering eggs or garden stuff, and a miniature birch bark canoe for William.

Of course he said, "I don't want that. I want a real one," but she noticed he took it down to the creek almost every day.

Would he ever outgrow his contrariness? But she wouldn't let her problems with William spoil such a beautiful day. Dewdrops winked from among the dead brown stems of last year's grass, and she could see the tiny new green sprouts just emerging. A robin in the maple tree informed her this was his territory. She chirped back at him, hoping he'd stay. She inhaled the swampy odor of the thawing garden. Better than perfume. It meant winter was finally over. She sang as she shook out and hung up the clothes with the pegs Jake had carved for her last winter.

Jake heard her singing as he came out of the barn. He hadn't heard her sing since she lived with Grossmutti. That seemed like an age ago. He set down the two pails of corncobs he was taking to the pigs and wiped his sleeve across his eyes. He was getting schmaltzy.

He tiptoed across the yard and put his arms around her.

"Oh," she squealed, dropping the towel she was pegging. She turned within the circle of his arms to face him. "You startled me."

He nuzzled her ear. She hunched her shoulder and shivered. He hugged her tighter. "I haven't heard you sing for a long time."

"I guess I haven't felt like singing for a long time."

"And now you do? That is a good thing."

"That is a very good thing. Oh, Jake, I'm happy at last. Two new friends, our baby, and you've made it all happen." She curled her arms around his neck and kissed him with fervor.

He whispered, "Let's go up into the hayloft."

She drew back. "Jake! In the middle of the morning? What if somebody came?"

"So? We're married."

"I couldn't. The children."

"Jah, I guess so." He expelled a long breath. He kissed her, softly, and let his lips brush across her cheek. "Well, tonight will come—but it's a long time." With a final playful nip on her earlobe, he left her and went back to the neglected pails.

What would it be like, she thought, to make love in broad daylight? Her breasts tingled. She almost wished she'd agreed.

Over the clothesline, she watched him stride down the path to the orchard, swinging the pails so energetically he had to stop and pick up some cobs that spilled out. Dear Jake. He was looking forward to the night. And so was she. She began to sing again and heard him echo her song, his deep bass a perfect foil for her higher voice.

The next morning at breakfast he winked at her, making her blush. He chuckled as he poured milk on his porridge.

William looked up. "Why are you laughing?"

"Just a joke between Mutti and me."

"What joke? Tell me."

What would Jake say? She well knew William wouldn't leave it alone until he got an answer.

"It's a private joke, son."

William's bottom lip showed its inner surface. "Tell me."

"Well..." Jake began and she held her breath. What was he going to say? Surely he wouldn't...?

"I told Mutti I love her, and it made her red all over like a beet." He looked at her and grinned. She felt the blush rise again.

"I didn't hear it."

"I did it with the eyes, so." Jake demonstrated.

"Is that all," said William. "That's not a joke, just silly." He applied himself to his porridge.

She relaxed and smiled at the wicked twinkle in Jake's eyes. This was a cunning man she'd married. He could wiggle his way out of any situation.

As spring progressed, her body became unwieldy. She didn't remember being so bloated and tiring so easily at this stage in her other pregnancies. Hedwig irritated her more, too; probably because she felt so tired all the time. Her ankles were swollen at night, and she was troubled with leg cramps.

One day as she went to the spring for water, a fiendish cramp held her motionless. Luckily, Jake had been within calling distance and helped her back to the cabin.

In the barn that evening, she saw Jake looking at her as she hunched over her swelling abdomen, balancing with difficulty on the one-legged milking stool.

He said, "You look uncomfortable there."

"Well I am. And the baby objects to being squeezed." She laughed and stood up, arching her back.

He took the pail from her. "I will do the milking now. Go back to the cabin."

"But you have so much work of your own."

"That makes no mind. I will do it. It's too hard for you just now."

She liked milking, her head pressed against the warm, vevety flank, and the fragrant milk singing into the pail. But for now she was glad to be free of it. Gratefully, she surrendered the milking stool and returned to the cabin.

William came into the barn to visit the last batch of kittens and, seeing Jake milking, said, "Where's Mutti?"

"Your mutti isn't feeling well and needs our help. I want you to keep the wood box filled for her."

"Do I have to?" William shoved out his bottom lip.

"Yes, you do."

"I don't want to."

"That makes no never mind. You love Mutti, no?"

"I guess so, when she gives me cookies."

Jake came out of the stall, the pail of milk in one hand, the stool in the other. He scowled at William. "Then do what I told you."

"You can't make me. You're not my real vati."

Jake stepped back, stunned. Where had he heard that? Had Phoebe told him? He loved William as if he were his own and thought William loved him, too. "Haven't I treated you like a son?"

"Well, I guess so." Then defiantly, "But you're not my vati."

"Your mutti is your own, for sure. Do it for her, then. Will you?"

"Yes, I guess."

"Good."

Jake told Phoebe of the chore he had assigned William, and she should insist he do it. At six he was quite old enough to contribute. But William was too used to having his own way, and the wood-box, more often than not, was empty. Jake grumbled about William's idle ways, but Phoebe said it was easier to do it herself than continually nag at the boy.

When Jake saw her struggling across the yard, her arms filled with firewood, he hurried to take the sticks from her. "Where's William? He's supposed to do this."

"I haven't seen him all morning. He's probably down at the creek, catching frogs or sailing his canoe."

At Jake's shout, William emerged from the orchard. Jake stormed at him. "Why didn't you fill the wood box this morning? Where have you been?"

Ruth Zavitz

"I was hunting with my slingshot."

"You're supposed to do your chores first."

"I wanted to—"

"Never mind wanted. Get the basket from the barn and gather the eggs for Mutti. Go!"

Dragging his feet, William disappeared into the barn and a short time later returned the basket to its place on the barn wall, a smug grin on his face.

"Did you take the eggs to Mutti?" asked Jake, noting the empty basket.

"Wasn't any."

Suspicious, Jake went to the hens' coop to find the hens savoring the remnants of the smashed eggs that trickled down the wall.

William had always been rebellious and stubborn, but Phoebe was usually able to talk him round, and he'd heretofore been sensitive to Jake's disapproval. His outburst regarding his real vati made Jake realize he no longer had that hold on him.

If he punished him as he deserved, the boy would resent him even more. What to do? Phoebe didn't need anything more to worry her right now. He'd been so busy he hadn't spent much time with William. Maybe if he worked with him....

Thereafter he and William filled the wood box together, and Jake accepted no excuses regarding William's participation. While Jake milked, William was required to shell corn, and Jake gathered the eggs while William spread the kernels for the hens. He couldn't destroy corn. William showed his resentment in his sullen expression but seemed sufficiently afraid of Jake to avoid open rebellion. Only when the chores were done to Jake's satisfaction did he take the slingshot down from a high peg on the stable wall and allow William to follow his own desires.

All this took a great deal of time from the important task of getting the crops into the ground. Although Jake always rose at

175

daybreak and worked until sunset, now he worked even by moonlight.

He spent one whole night in the stable with the mare, Jilly. At breakfast, he said, "Jilly has a beautiful colt, healthy like anything."

William left his breakfast and dashed to the barn despite Phoebe's protests.

"I think I'll call him Tom." Jake rubbed his hands together. "This is the first of my team."

"What do you mean? You already have a team," said Phoebe as she ladled porridge into Hedwig's bowl.

"Vati gave me Joe and Jilly. This is the first of my own. He's black. If I can get another one the same color I will have the best team in the settlement. You will see."

"Oh, Jake. You're silly about your horses."

He ducked his head and shifted his feet. "Jah, I guess I am, just." He poured milk on his porridge and reached for the sugar bowl. He sprinkled sugar, set down the bowl and said, "I want to call a bee next week to take the stumps out of the west field."

"Take out the stumps? Uncle Edward just worked around them. He said it would take years for them to rot."

"He was right. I can't wait so long. I don't like how they look, so. I want things tidy. It will take a lot of food though. Pulling out stumps makes a hungry like anything. Ask Abigail if she'll help you."

Rebecca came to the bee with Karl, and the three women worked amicably together. Since Abigail didn't speak German, Rebecca knew no English and Phoebe's German was uncertain, there was much waving about of paring knives and stirring spoons, and gales of laughter, as they tried to communicate. Phoebe thought she hadn't had so much fun since she was a little girl.

When they had cleaned up after the noon meal, the women went out to watch the stump pulling. Phoebe had seen the hard labor required to build a farm, and participated, but never had she seen such exertions as were now put forth. The men dug around the base of a stump to expose the roots, then chopped through them. They hooked heavy chains around the stump and hitched both Karl and Jake's teams to the chains. Karl shouted at the horses and slapped the reins on their backs to spur them to greater efforts. The other men put their weight on pry poles hooked under the root stubs and the giant was levered out of the ground with loud snappings of still-attached roots.

The men placed their pry poles under the next stump, and William, who'd been watching, set a stick of his own.

Phoebe called, "William. Be careful. You'll get hurt."

Neil McDougall, alerted, said, "Git ye out of there. 'Tis no job for a bairn."

Jake shouted, "William! Stand back."

William ignored the warnings and pried with his stick, forcing Jake to leave the horses and come to him. "It's too dangerous for you, William. You must keep out of the way."

"If it's dangerous why are you doing it?"

"We have to, but we're men. You saw the bruise on Mr. Stedman's arm after we pulled the last one, didn't you?"

"It's only a bruise. That's nothing."

"It may be nothing for him, but you are not so tall. If that root hit you it would have been your head not your arm, and killed you, maybe. Now, go away."

Phoebe called, "William. Come here," but he stalked off into the orchard.

Well, at least he'd be safe there.

In the late afternoon, after the men had gone home, Jake came into the cabin. Phoebe was bustling around preparing supper, while Hedwig reached on tiptoe to set spoons on the table at each place. William sat on the floor by the hearth, building a cabin with the tiny logs Jake had whittled for him.

Jake touched William's shoulder. "Come on, son. The hens are waiting for their supper."

"No." William did not look up.

"What? Come. What's the matter with you, so?"

William still worked at his cabin, ignoring Jake.

Phoebe knelt by her son. "What's wrong, William? Vati is very tired. He needs your help."

"No. He wants me to do things I don't want to. When I want to help he won't let me."

"He's just trying to keep you safe. As soon as you're big enough you'll be able to help with stumping."

"It'll all be done by then."

Jake snorted. "No, it won't. I want to cut down all the trees."

Phoebe continued, "You have to learn to do the little things first. As soon as you can do them right, Jake will let you do bigger things. Isn't that right, Jake?"

Jake nodded. "Of course. That's how it goes. You have to do one thing good before you are allowed to do the next thing. The faster you learn, the faster you get to do more interesting jobs."

This seemed to make sense to William. He got to his feet and put on his coat.

Jake nodded to Phoebe and followed William out the door.

Stumping continued. Looking like ungainly monsters sprouting root tentacles, the stumps were dragged to the edge of the field and interlaced, to form a fence. The men chopped through the remaining roots unearthed by the upheaval, and piled them for burning. They worked for days, returning to their homes at night for chores, while the women turned out mountains of food to satisfy appetites whetted by the backbreaking work.

Neil McDougall remonstrated with Jake. "Mon, why do ye work so hard at it? The weather'll do it for ye, give it time."

"That's the trouble," said Jake. "It takes too much time, and the stumps take up too much land. I want to plant it all, right away."

"Well, I don't mind hard work, but this is daft."

"You've been a big help, Neil. If you're getting tired, we can manage." Jake noticed Karl and Alec Steadman exchange grins.

"Nay, no Dutchman is going to outwork me. If you're bound to do it, I'll stay."

The field finally cleared, men, women and horses were all exhausted. The whole area looked as if a herd of giant hogs had been turned loose in it, and great slabs of limestone protruded through the churned-up earth. Phoebe wondered aloud if it would ever be smooth enough to plant.

"Oh, yes," said Jake. "We'll draw off the stones and drag a log over the ground. That will smooth it out, some, and after two years of crops or so, it will be as smooth as the east field at home."

Jake had said 'home'. Did one ever really make a new start? In spite of all the different places she'd lived, home to her was still Haventown, back on the Hudson River, and home to Jake was obviously the settlement where his parents lived.

CHAPTER 30

The sun crept above the treetops, foretelling a warm day. Jake ran down the forest trail through the morning mist. An early rising jay screamed at him from a branch overhead and cows in Steadman's pasture came lumbering to see what caused the excitement.

Jake neither heard nor saw. Gasping, he hammered on the Anselms' cabin door.

Reinhold Anselm, in his undershirt and pants, braces dangling, cautiously opened it.

Jake, out of breath, could only croak, "It's Phoebe. Help."

Reinhold opened the door wider, "Come in." He pulled his braces over his shoulders. "What's the trouble, Jake? So early in the morning you come."

Jake reached for a breath, gulped, and said, "We—need—your mutti. Phoebe. The baby."

Granny Anselm, a tall raw-boned woman in a wrapper, came from her bedroom, gray hair in a thick braid hanging down her back. "What is it? Phoebe's baby? But she told me July. It's the first of June, only, yet."

"I know. I'm afraid. Please come."

"Of course. Go back to her. I'll come right away, and so." She turned back to her room.

Jake left without saying goodbye and hurried back. He'd been afraid to leave Phoebe alone when she waked him to tell him she thought the baby was coming. But she had to have help. If only Mutti was here. She'd taken over when Hedwig was born, and he'd no idea what he should be doing.

He burst into the cabin. "Phee! Are you all right? Granny's coming."

"Good," groaned Phoebe as another pain struck. When it subsided she said, "You'd better dress Hedwig and take her over to Abigail... and take William with you."

180

"All right." He took clean clothes for Hedwig out of the bureau, glad of something to do. "Do you think Granny can stop it? It's too soon, isn't it?"

Phoebe held her breath for another pain. "Take the children out, quick."

He woke the children and dressed Hedwig. When Granny arrived he took the children to Abigail's. She mirrored his stricken look when he told her what was happening.

Her hand went to her mouth. "Oh, Jake, no." Then her face cleared. "Well, probably she reckoned wrong."

He hoped so.

"Can you keep Hedwig for a little while? We were going to take her to Ma's but it's too late, now."

"Of course. I'll keep them both. Get home with thee. It will be all right."

Reassured, Jake returned. He put his head in the door. "How is Phee? Do you need anything?"

Granny waved him away. "No, do your chores. We're all right."

Still anxious, he kept coming out of the barn, looking toward the cabin, but could see no activity. What was happening in there? The chores finished, he should be starting the day's work in the fields but was reluctant to leave the dooryard.

Finally he picked up his hoe and went to work in the garden to be near by. The regular strokes of the hoe calmed him. Babies were born every day. It was natural.

An inner rumbling reminded him it was dinnertime and he'd had no breakfast. He carried the hoe to the end of the row and set it up against the tree-root fence. He'd go to the cabin and get some bread and a drink of water.

He was halfway there when Granny came out of the cabin and waved. She seemed agitated. His heart thundered in his chest. He ran. Had something gone wrong, after all? Why had he wanted a baby? Phoebe was more precious to him than all the babies in the world. If anything happened to her....

"What? What?" he shouted, as he ran.

"It's all right. Come and see."

"Is Phee all right? Is it a boy or girl?"

"Both."

Both? He followed Granny in to the settle, pulled up close to the fire. Two tiny scraps lay foot-to-foot, turning their heads and mewling like newborn kittens. And not much larger. Two of them! Who would have thought it?

"Are they healthy, Granny?"

"As right as too-soon-born babes can be, and so."

Jake bent over them and tentatively touched one's cheek. "A boy and a girl, you said?"

"Yes."

"And Phee?"

"She is good. She's waiting for you." Granny waved toward the bedroom.

Phoebe greeted him with a smile when he went in. "Can you believe it?"

"You are all right, then?"

"Oh, yes."

"My family grows fast, so." But could anything that small survive? "They're so little. I could carry one on my two hands without any hanging over."

"I know, but Granny says they're strong."

Advised of the double births, Alec Steadman offered to go and tell the Stettl family. Hannah came at once, prepared to stay.

Phoebe and Jake welcomed her, but Phoebe said, "Who will look after Vati Stettl and Peter?"

"Rebecca. She said. She sends her congratulations and wants to know their names."

"I don't know," said Phoebe. "We didn't expect it to happen so soon. I thought if it was a girl I would like to call her Anna."

Jake said, "It would be nice if the names went together. If we called the boy Daniel then we could have Annie and Danny."

Hannah and Granny Anselm agreed, but Phoebe wasn't so sure. She didn't much care for Annie; she thought Anna more dignified. Since no better idea came to her, Annie and Danny they became.

The first day she was out of bed, Jake sheepishly brought Phoebe the Bible that had resided unopened on the mantel since they were married.

"What do you want me to read?"

"Not read. Write." He opened the book to the blank pages at the back. "This is the vati's job, but I don't know how. So." Embarrassed, he pushed the book at her.

Of course. He wanted her to enter the twins' names. He'd bought the book with his first farm and had said, then, it was to record his family.

"But I have no pen, or any ink," she said.

He returned to the mantel and took down a bottle and a long turkey feather from behind the clock. "Abigail lent them to me," he said, a broad grin spreading the beard even wider. "I'm smart, no?"

As she opened the ink bottle and dipped the quill pen, he added, "Put in Hedwig and William, too."

She felt her eyes sting. Even in writing he was prepared to acknowledge her children as his own.

In the fine copperplate writing she'd learned as a girl, although a little shaky from lack of practice, she wrote:

William Trevlyn, born October 14, 1791

Hedwig.... She paused and looked at him.

"Stettl," he said, firmly.

She blinked away her tears and continued.

....Stettl, born December 25, 1794.

Daniel and Anna Stettl, twins, born June 1, 1796.

He called Hannah to approve.

She touched the page under Hedwig's name and looked at him. At his nod she turned back to Phoebe. "That is beautiful writing. Where did you learn it?"

"I went to school in Haventown where I was born. The teacher was very particular about our writing."

"I learned, too, a little, back home in Pennsylvania, but here there is not time to teach the little ones their letters, and no school." Hannah shook her head. "A big galoot like Jake here, can't even write his own name."

"Yes I can," responded Jake with spirit. "But that's all," he added. He ducked his head and traced Phoebe's spidery letters with his index finger. "But it makes no mind," he added, straightening up, "when I have a wife who writes so." He took the book and replaced it on the mantel.

Abigail was ecstatic when she brought the older children home. "Think of it. Twins."

William scowled at the tiny babies, then went out to the barn to see the colt. Hedwig stared in wonder and was enslaved when Daniel closed his tiny fist around her timidly outstretched finger.

Although Hedwig had outgrown the cradle she still, on occasion, climbed into it and huddled there, sucking her thumb. It was her own space. Now she had lost that and all Phoebe's time was taken up with the twins, Jake noticed she looked more doleful than ever.

The twins were so small and delicate the adults were almost afraid to handle them. Granny Anselm fashioned two small pillows. "We will carry the babies on them, so. It will support them until they are bigger."

Phoebe sent Jake to Fort Erie for material for nappies and gowns. The baby clothing she'd made for Hedwig was much too large and there wasn't enough for two, anyway. As he unwrapped the parcel on his return, she wondered how she could find the time to make the tiny garments.

He held up a length of pale green muslin, dotted with white daisies. "That's for you, then," he said. "The woman in the store said it's enough for a gown."

"Oh, it's beautiful," said Phoebe. She picked up a corner of the material and held it to the light, her eyes smarting.

"I liked that fuzzy red dress you had when you came. I looked at some but I didn't have enough money."

"This is much better." It was perfect. She couldn't have chosen better, herself. "Thank you."

"It makes no mind. I would give you anything."

"I know." She held out her arms and he half lifted her from the bed in a massive hug.

When the neighbors heard of the marvel of twins, they rallied round. Afternoon sewing bees outfitted the babies. Phoebe's new dress, complete with lace trim contributed by Meg McDougall, was finished to Jake's satisfaction.

But the neighbors could only spare a limited amount of time from their own work, and the succeeding months were a blur. For Phoebe: hungry babies, nappies and more nappies added to the regular housework. For Jake: all the outside chores she had previously done, as well as the fieldwork. There was no thought of a social life or even attendance at Quaker Meeting.

Hannah had taken Hedwig home with her and that was a relief to Phoebe. She didn't have the patience to put up with the child's hanging on her skirts.

Annie and Danny adapted to life in the outside world and grew quickly. They were as agreeable babies as William and Hedwig had been petulant, greeting everyone who came within their view with smiles and waving fists. Phoebe and Jake gloried in their sunny dispositions.

Hannah kept Hedwig for a month. Then, worried lest she lose contact with her mother, brought her home. Phoebe dreaded having the child whining at her skirts again, but was relieved when

Hedwig's fascination with the new babies kept her glued to the cradle.

Phoebe stopped wearing her Mennonite cap. There was no time to starch and iron the fragile muslin. Most days, her nighttime braids hung down her back or were twisted around her head and covered with an ordinary mobcap. Rebecca came for a day now and then to help, and Karl came with her when he could spare the time.

On a sweltering evening in August, Phoebe sat on the doorstep glad to be out of the heat of the cabin. The twins lay on a blanket on the grass with Hedwig sitting beside them, waving a burdock leaf over them to keep off the flies. William, slingshot in hand, stalked a crow by the corn crib.

Jake came out of the cabin with the Bible and gave it to her.

"What now?" she asked. "There are no more babies to put in it, thank goodness."

Jake chuckled, then sobered. "I thought maybe, would you read a little?"

She took the book and opened it, aware of the great honor he was according her. It was the duty and privilege of the head of the house to read from the Good Book.

Tilting it so the setting sun shone on its pages, she began to read where the book opened. *"As arrows are in the hands of a mighty man; so are the children of the youth. Happy is the man that has his quiver full of them."*

"Jah, it is so," said Jake.

She finished the psalm and they sat silent.

Then he said, "That was good."

She, too, felt comforted. A good man, a healthy family, plenty to eat, a tight roof over her head. She was content.

Somehow the little family made it through the summer. Phoebe sighed with relief when the crops were all harvested and safely stowed away. Jake said the winter would be easier with only chores and cutting wood for the fire . Clearing more land could go for this year.

The twins thrived, and by December had outgrown their joint cradle. Abigail brought hers over.

Seeing the new cradle, Hedwig went to her own and said, "Mine?"

"No, Hedwig," said Phoebe. "One for Annie and one for Danny. You are too big for a cradle."

Hedwig looked at Jake as if seeking his support, then went into the bedroom and climbed into her bed, thumb in mouth.

CHAPTER 31

Jake was confined to the cabin during a four-day blizzard in February. The incessant chatter and crying of the children, the need to step carefully lest he trip over them where they played on the floor, made him realize how crowded the cabin was. As he replaced broken ax handles or whittled ladles and toasting forks for Phoebe, he considered the problem. He wanted to build a real house but did not yet have all the materials he required.

When the weather cleared, he consulted with Alec Steadman who promised to help with the project. Jake spent whatever time was left from chores cutting down some carefully selected trees in the bush. Alec helped him haul the logs up beside the cabin but Jake refused to tell Phoebe what they were for.

She said, "If you're building another barn, I don't want it so close to the house. It draws the flies. Are you?"

"I'm not building anything yet. The logs have to dry first."

He could see Phoebe was fuming but he wanted it to be a surprise. She'd be happy when she saw the result.

On a mild day in March of 1800, Jake pitched manure from the stable onto the stone-boat. He wanted to spread the fertilizer on the hay field before the snow melted, so the stone-boat's runners wouldn't damage the turf. He stopped to take off his coat; it was warm work. As he picked up the pitchfork again he saw the officer in charge of the local militia coming up the lane. Jake knew him by sight but had never talked to him. What could he want? Nothing good, for sure.

"Good day, Mister Stettl." The officer touched his cap.

Jake nodded, wary.

"I came to remind you to report for the training muster on the tenth of June. I'm telling all the settlers. I want to give you plenty of time so there'll be no excuses."

Jake said, "I'm a Mennonite and exempt from military duty."

The officer's manner changed abruptly. Mustache bristling, he spread his legs and glared at Jake. "Oh, it's another one trying to get out of serving his country. There's no Mennonite church in this district and you bloody well know it. You better show up." He stalked off, back rigid.

His instinct had been right, thought Jake. Soldiers always meant trouble. Through the morning he considered his options.

At dinner, he told Phoebe about the soldier's visit. "I won't go and learn to shoot people, anyhow."

"But what will he do to you if you stay away?"

"I don't know."

"Do you think Uncle Amos could do something? You're still his nephew. He wouldn't want you in the army."

"Jah, I will go and see. Maybe he can talk to the army man."

Amos seemed glad to see him, but Salome scowled and said, "So, Jake. At last you see the error of your ways. I suppose you've come to see the deacon about coming back home."

"Not at all. I am happy and Phoebe is, too. My children are healthy like anything. The farm is even better than the one I had here. I'm glad you made us go."

"There is no redemption for some sinners." She flounced out of the room.

"Sit down, Jake." Amos indicated a chair at the kitchen table and pulled out another for himself on the opposite side. "I'm happy for you."

"The only thing...," said Jake. "A militia man came to the farm. He doesn't believe I'm a Mennonite and wants me to go to the muster."

"Well, it's a problem, and so. You never joined the church."

"But Mutti and Vati are members. Doesn't that make me a Mennonite? I don't want to learn to shoot anybody. Can you write something?"

Amos looked dubious, then said, "Jah, I guess I can do that. I think I have some paper and ink in the trunk upstairs. Wait a minute. I look."

He returned with the necessary articles but had to add water to the stone bottle of ink as it had dried up. As he stirred, he muttered aloud the words he intended to write. The ink reconstituted, he sat down and laboriously wrote Jake's credentials. He read it aloud.

"Jake Stettl is the son of Simon and Hannah Stettl, members of the Mennonite settlement at the Ridgeway and is exempt from military service by the laws of Upper Canada.

Deacon Amos Witmer

It's not exactly right, but it isn't wrong either. I hope it works."

"It sounds good, and so," said Jake, relieved. "Thank you, Uncle Amos." He rose to go. He'd give the paper to the officer and the problem would be solved.

Amos put his hand on Jake's shoulder as if to detain him. "I am glad to see you. It's been a long time."

"Jah, it has," said Jake. "I've missed your counsel. Thank you for the paper. Goodbye."

It was good to see Uncle Amos again, and his uncle seemed glad to see him, too. If it wasn't for Aunt Salome he'd still be living in the community. Well, never mind. Except for missing Uncle Amos he was content.

He inquired for the home of the officer and gave him the paper. The officer peered at it, turned it upside down and looked at it again. "What is this scribble? I can't make head nor tail of it."

Of course. Uncle Amos had written in German. Jake repeated what Amos had told him it said, and pointed out Amos's signature at the bottom, the only part he, himself, could recognize.

The officer grunted. "Sure, an' anybody can get a relative or neighbor to write a paper. Who is this Deacon Witmer? Never heard of him. He a relative of yours?"

"Well, yes."

"I thought as much."

"But he's also the deacon of the church."

"Yeah, sure. Show up for muster or you'll be fined."

When Jake returned, home Phoebe said, "Could Uncle Amos help?"

"Jah, he gave me a paper. I gave it to the soldier." He didn't tell her what the officer said. No use worrying her.

He didn't attend the muster and was duly fined.

Parting with the money was a definite hardship, but he paid. Anything was better than training to kill other men.

"Well, that's a poor substitute for doing your duty," said the officer when Jake gave him the money, but Jake noticed how tightly his hands closed around it.

Phoebe only found out about the fine when she mentioned he'd better buy some woolen material for the children's winter clothes next time he went to the fort. "I have so little time to sew, it will take me the rest of the summer, along with all the other work, to make them."

Jake spread his hands. "I don't have any money, Phee. I had to pay a fine for not going to the muster and it took all I had."

"All, Jake?"

"All."

"You said Uncle Amos gave you a paper to exempt you."

"The officer couldn't read it, the German."

There was always something. Just when it seemed security was within her grasp, fate was waiting to take it away. Still, there was nothing to be done but carry on.

How could she manage? Every time she looked, it seemed the children had outgrown their clothes. Too-small clothes of William's and Hedwig's could be refashioned for the twins and she had an old wool dress she could recut for Hedwig, but what about William?

Jake said, "You could cut down my Sunday suit for him.

That's good warm cloth."

"But Jake. That suit is your only good clothes."

"It makes no mind. I don't go anywhere dressed up, anyhow."

She hoped the wheat crop would be good. If so, there would be money for material. But by the time the grain was sold it would be close to winter, leaving little time to make the clothing.

At the end of June, haying finished, Jake prepared for the new building. He worked hard, removing the loosened bark and squaring the logs with his adz. They would fit together better than the round logs of the original cabin and wouldn't require so much chinking.

He set two of the corner stones a few feet from the cabin and Phoebe was furious. "Jake. If you build a barn there I'll never speak to you again."

He only smiled, which did nothing to soften her temper.

After grain harvest, everything ready to his satisfaction, Jake called a bee. Rebecca came to help feed the men. They stood side by side at the table, Phoebe peeling potatoes and Rebecca shelling peas.

Phoebe burst out, "I'm so mad at Jake. I told him I didn't want a barn so close to the house but did he listen? No, of course not. What does he care if the cabin is full of flies?"

Rebecca stared at her. "He didn't tell you? He's building a double cabin. Oh." she clapped her hand over her mouth. "Maybe it was a surprise. I shouldn't have said anything."

"A double cabin? Really? We're going to have more room?" That Jake. Every time she got angry with him for something he did, it turned out he was doing it for her. Why couldn't he explain at the beginning? And now Rebecca knew of their disagreement

. "Jake is always planning things without telling me. He likes to make it a surprise, but I'd much rather know."

"Karl is the same. It must be a Stettl thing. He got a whole bunch of baby chicks from somebody this spring. Just brought them home and dumped them on me. And me with no broody hens to give them to. I had to keep them in the cabin by the fire until it got warm enough to put them outside by themselves. Men. They think we can cope with anything."

Phoebe was a little comforted. It wasn't just Jake, then. She'd have to put up with it, but now she could confide in Rebecca without embarrassment, and they could share their frustrations with their men.

The new building was finished within the week, its door facing the old cabin. Jake cut a door in the original one, directly opposite the new door. He then laid some half logs, split side up, as a walkway between the two cabins and built a roof overhead so they could go from one to the other, somewhat protected from the weather.

"We used to call it a dogtrot," he said, "this between place, but we don't have a dog."

"Why not a breezy way," she suggested, aware it would indeed be breezy in the winter.

"Jah, that sounds good. It will be nice cool place in summer."

That was Jake, looking on the good side, as always.

He suggested the new cabin be sleeping quarters, but Phoebe said the children were too young to be put to bed there before their parents were ready to join them. For the time being, the new cabin was used for storage and even that helped ease the congestion in the main cabin.

And he continued with his plans for a real house.

CHAPTER 32

The twins grew into healthy toddlers. Although intrepid explorers, a single word of reprimand would deter them from inappropriate reconnaissance. Phoebe thought they couldn't be more different from their older brother and sister. In contrast to William's stubbornness and Hedwig's whining, these two were all smiles, no matter what happened. One should love all one's children the same, but she couldn't help responding more to the twins than their older siblings.

Hedwig adored them and entertained them for hours on end. Phoebe wasn't sure who entertained who, but Hedwig's demands on her lessened. William ignored them

In the spring of 1801, Jilly had another colt. Jake was in high spirits. "This one will be black, too, I think so. I will call him Tim."

"Don't you think Tim and Tom sound too much alike? Will the colts be able to tell which one you're talking to?" asked Phoebe.

"Oh, sure. They're smart."

"I think you like your horses more than your children."

"Ah, Phee. That's not so." Then with a grin. "I like them both the same."

"Jake. You don't mean that." But she couldn't help smiling. There was no doubt in her mind how much he cared for his children.

That summer she found herself pregnant again and he held up his hands in mock horror. "Only one this time, please."

She laughed and agreed with him. She wouldn't like to repeat the last five years either.

Benjamin was born in March of 1802 and, although not as sunny in disposition as the twins, gave little trouble. It was William who caused her the most distress. She was still impatient with Hedwig, though, who seemed to always be asking for something, never voicing a question, but always underfoot, trying to help.

Unlike dedicated Hedwig, eleven-year-old William shirked his chores and, when reprimanded, ran away. The first time he didn't appear for supper, Phoebe worried. He loved to eat and, whatever he did otherwise, always turned up for meals. Even though they had three large cleared fields surrounding the house, the heavy bush loomed so close she always feared one of the children might wander in and become hopelessly lost. Even inexperienced adults had suffered that fate.

After supper Jake checked the larder in the second cabin and discovered the empty biscuit crock. He chuckled. "Well, we should have known. William looks out for himself, always."

She sat up late that night, wondering where he might be and if he were all right.

"Well, I go to bed," said Jake, yawning. "Nothing we can do in the dark. I think he's all right, anyhow. I take him often in the woods with me. He knows how it goes in the bush—if that's where he went. Come to bed."

In the middle of the night, he got up and went outside to relieve himself. He came back and beckoned to her, still sitting by the fire. He quietly opened the door to the second cabin and pointed to William, curled up on a buffalo robe in the corner, fast asleep.

"But why didn't he come and tell us he was back?" she asked as they returned to the main cabin.

"He thought we would scold, already."

"And so I would. Scaring us like that."

She did scold the next morning, but he only shrugged.

Jake frowned at him. "You're worrying your mutti. Why did you do it?"

"I wanted to see the soldiers like my vati."

"Of course. It was muster day." Jake sighed. "I'll have to pay the fine, again."

He pointed at the boy, "But you should have told where you were going."

William shrugged. "You would have said, 'Don't go'. I'm going to be a soldier. I want to see how to do it."

"Oh, William, no!" She'd had enough contact with the military to last her all her life. The idea of his becoming involved terrified her.

Jake shook his finger. "You stay away from the soldiers. Your mutti doesn't like it and neither do I."

He ignored their protests. His absences became more prolonged, even overnight, and he refused to say where he went or what he did.

When he was in the mood he would do well, whatever tasks he was assigned, and Jake would take heart. He was coming around. But then, when Jake sent him on an errand to the field or barn, he'd disappear. Jake learned not to send the boy by himself to hoe corn or coil hay for he'd later find the fork or hoe leaning lonely against the fence. He had to keep the boy working by his side.

Jake and Phoebe held long discussions after they went to bed, the only private place in the crowded household.

She stirred restlessly. "I don't know why he's so willful. He used to throw terrible tantrums when he was little if he didn't get his own way."

Jake grinned wryly, "I'm glad I missed that. His sulkiness is bad enough."

"He was much better when we first came to Grossmutti's. I thought he loved you."

"It was a different place and it attracted him for awhile, I think so. He wants more excitement than the farm. But I can't make it so." He sighed. "We just have to hope he grows up some."

"I hope it's soon. He wears me out."

"Jah, and so."

When Benjamin was two and a half years old, a little girl was born.

"I'd like to call her Katrina," said Jake. "After Grossmutti."

Phoebe nodded. "I like that. I never knew what her name was."

"She said, when she was young, her parents called her Katy."

"That's even better." So Katy the new baby became, and her name was added to the Bible under Benjy's.

Even the second cabin was now bursting at the seams. William, Hedwig and the twins were regularly sleeping there. At least Hedwig and the twins were, and William when he was home. He still refused to say where he went on his absences. No matter how carefully Jake watched, he managed to slip away into the bush. Phoebe worried he'd get into trouble, and Jake resented the lack of help.

Hedwig, in contrast, had adopted the babies as they came along; someone to love who loved her in return.

Jake chided William about his lack of assistance and cited Hedwig's usefulness.

William said, "Of course. She's a girl."

Phoebe said, "Boys have to work, too. Your vati needs you."

William squared his shoulders. "My vati's dead. He was a soldier. I'm going to be a soldier, too. Soldiers don't have to work."

"Oh, William, no." Phoebe's hand flew to her mouth. "Soldiers get killed."

"Not if they're smart. And anyway there's no war. Soldiers just wear a uniform and have fun."

How did he know? He was too little to remember when they lived at the fort. She knew he'd been watching the militia train, but none of them had uniforms.

"Where did you see soldiers in uniforms?" she asked.

"Somewhere," said William, and refused to say more.

The mystery was solved when Neil McDougall came over one day. Jake was plowing down wheat stubble in the west field.

After greetings were exchanged, Neil said, "Can I borrow your logging chain, Jake? Broke mine clean in half and I don't want to go to Fort Erie again to the blacksmith so soon. I just got it fixed last week and now it's broke again." He shook his head. "It's clean wore out, I guess. By the way, I seen William at the fort. I offered him a ride home but he wouldn't come."

Jake shuffled his feet in the dirt. He didn't want to admit he hadn't known William's whereabouts, but some response was called for. Having a good opinion of the Scot's judgment, he decided to confide in him.

"I don't know what to do with him. He defies me and Phoebe, refuses to do his chores except when he feels like it and goes where and when he pleases, and so."

"Aye," sighed Neil. "Ye could give him a good thrashing. I doubt it'd do him any good, but it might make you feel better."

"I don't think I could do that. It's against the religion I was brought up in. And, anyway, he doesn't respect my authority since I'm not his real vati." Jake's shoulders slumped and he shook his head.

"Not his real father?"

"No. Phoebe was married before to a soldier. He was killed."

"Oh, I didn't know that. She's had a hard time, then."

You've no idea how hard, thought Jake.

Neil continued. "Real father or not, that's only part of it. Don't fash yourself. I've seen the like before. Not much you can do. The old country ways don't seem to work, here. We'd never have considered disobeying our parents."

I did, though, thought Jake, when I went to work on the ferry. Maybe William is more like me than I thought. Still, I did contribute my wages to the farm.

He decided they'd been too lenient.

When William returned, he confronted him. "I've had enough of this. If you want to eat you will have to work. No more lallygagging around."

William glared at him, then rushed out to the other cabin.

Hearing drawers opening and shutting, Phoebe followed. She knew he was capable of destroying everything there if he took the notion.

He was stuffing his clothes into a grain sack.

"What are you doing?"

"I'm leaving. For good."

"Oh, William, no." She tried to put her arms around him but he shrugged her off.

"Leave me alone. I'm going where I can do what I want to without being scolded all the time."

"But I love you. You're my little boy."

He stamped his foot. "I'm not a little boy! I'm a man. Jake said so. I can go wherever I want and do whatever I want."

He grabbed the gunnysack and bolted out the door before Jake, who was just coming out of the original cabin, could react.

Phoebe ran out after him and grabbed Jake's arm. "Jake, go after him. Don't let him go."

Jake watched the defiant set of the boy's shoulders as he strode down the road, the sack of clothes hanging down his back, and his own shoulders slumped. "It's no use, Phee. He will do what he will do."

"What did I do wrong? I love him. Do you think he'll come back?"

"I don't know."

Preoccupied with worries about William, Phoebe was absent-minded with the other children. Hedwig tried to fill in but she never noticed, except to scold when the girl made a mistake.

She prevailed on Jake to go to the fort to see if he could find William and persuade him to come home. Although he said he doubted it would do any good, he went but could find no trace of the boy. This worried her even more. If he wasn't at the fort, where was he?

On later trips to Fort Erie through the winter, Jake asked everyone he met if they had seen William. They said there were so many young'uns wandering about it was hard to tell which ones had family there and which did not.

After one trip, he told her, "He's probably all right. I suspect he saw me first and hid himself, so."

"But why? Doesn't he love me at all? His own mother."

"Well, we made our own choices and so has he."

"How can he survive the winter?"

"He knows what he wants to do. He will find a way, I think so. I worked on the ferry against my mutti's wishes—and look how that turned out. Without, I would never have seen you."

She emptied the packet of tea he'd brought home, into the tin tea caddy, safe from foraging mice. "And you would be home with your family."

"I'd rather be with you. You know that. If William ever needs help he knows where we are and, if I know William, he won't be slow in coming home if he needs some thing."

All through the winter Phoebe worried about William. Had he found a place to stay? Was he warm? Jake reassured her that the boy knew how to take care of himself. She exhorted both Jake and the neighbors to watch for him when they went to the fort, but no one saw him. She wasn't particularly surprised, as most of them kept as far from the military as they could, and that was where he probably was. Contact between soldiers and male civilians usually led to trouble: nasty remarks about chicken-livered civilians, or roughing up by drunken soldiers.

Then one day in July, Neil reported seeing a boy who looked like William, marching with the soldiers at the fort. "I couldn't be sure, mind. I didn't get a good look at him but I thought t'was him."

She seized on the news. It had to be him. It meant he'd survived the winter and had the army for protection, such as it was. She refused to consider Neil might be mistaken. She couldn't bear it if he were. It would mean her son had disappeared completely and perhaps perished. No, she wouldn't accept that. Much as she hated the army, she hoped it was William that Neil had seen.

CHAPTER 33

The colts were now grown with beautiful coal black coats. They were perfectly matched, both in size and coloring. Jake had spent a considerable amount of time gentling them. He didn't approve of the brutal spirit-breaking methods most men used. Instead, he petted them and gave them carrot treats until they followed him about like pet dogs whenever he was in the pasture. He was inordinately proud of them, and justifiably, Phoebe thought.

He asked the blacksmith to make strings of matched bells for their harness. Phoebe noticed neighbors came out to watch them pass when the jingling bells announced their approach.

The seasons passed in a blur, Jake caring for the crops and pushing back the forest, and Phoebe busy with the children and the livestock. The cattle herd had now increased to the point where she had more milk than the family could use and she began to make cheese to sell. Hannah had taught her the art, and there was a ready market among the neighbors who didn't have that skill. She was happy to contribute to the family's income and make sure there was enough money for the fine, to keep Jake out of jail at mustering time.

He bragged of her talent everywhere he went, and demand for her cheese soon outstripped the supply. He bought another cow, and she felt she was on a carousel. Another cow meant more work that meant more money, probably followed by more cows. Still, it added to their security.

One hot, Saturday afternoon in the fall of 1806 Jake took Phoebe out to the edge of the orchard and showed her the piles of limestone he'd dragged off the fields. Why was he so excited? She already knew of the ugly things and had even helped heave them onto the stone boat.

There they lay, the oldest piles covered with wild raspberry and grape vines. Useless things, the stones, just taking up space that could be growing grain. She sat down on one gray slab and fanned her flushed face with a huge burdock leaf she'd picked as they walked out.

"Why did you bring me to see these good-for-nothing rocks?"

"I'm going to build a house out of them."

She stared at the ungainly slabs. "How can you do that? They're all different sizes."

He laughed. "You'll see. I'll make them all the same size, almost."

She looked with dismay at the misshapen gray stones. "Even if you could, I don't think I'd like that kind of house. Couldn't you build a wooden house?" Visions of her family's Haventown house filled her mind. She waved her hands as she described it. "White-painted clapboard, two stories. Big windows with a porch all around. That's the kind of house I want."

"This will be better. The wind blows right through wood houses, but not stone ones. It will be warm in winter, cool in summer, just right."

No matter how she argued, nothing would sway him from his dream. Why wouldn't he listen to her? Never mind. There was no way he could possibly transform those jagged rocks into walls. He'd have to give up, and then perhaps he'd build the house she wanted.

The next day a huge bonfire erupted over the pile of rocks. What was he doing now? She peered out the window. He was carrying pails of water from the creek and sharp crackling sounds echoed against the barn as he poured the water on the stones.

She went out to investigate.

He pointed at the pile, obviously delighted. "See, the water breaks the hot rocks."

Sure enough, the limestone slabs had split into thinner shale-like pieces and tiny splinters were flying in all directions.

He waved his arm. "Stand back, so. The slivers are sharp."

Every morning after chores, he piled the flakes to one side and built another fire on the stones underneath. The process continued through every bit of spare time during the fall, and piles and piles of the rough slices accumulated.

What a waste of time when he could be cutting timber for her frame house.

After the crops were harvested, he built a small stone chamber in the side of the hill by the creek. What was he doing now? Inside this he piled the smaller fragments of limestone and built a fire. He sealed the chamber, leaving only a small opening to allow the smoke and gases to escape. When he opened it he showed her powdered lime to use as mortar for his proposed building project. He was determined to have his way, no matter what she wanted.

As they dug the turnips, he said, "Where do you think we should put it, the new house?"

There was a pretty knoll overlooking the creek that she had long thought would be a lovely site. Should she tell him? If he started to build a stone house there and it didn't work, the site maybe couldn't be later used for the house she wanted.

When she didn't answer, he asked, "How about that little hill by the creek? That would be a good place, no?"

Reluctantly, she agreed. He seemed dead set against a frame house, so she'd better settle for what she could get. They needed the room.

He suggested she plan the interior to match her old home. On a piece of bark, she marked out a plan for a center hall and stairway. A kitchen and living room on one side and a parlor, with bedroom behind, on the other. The upstairs would be divided into four bedrooms.

He called a bee to dig the cellar and she was embarrassed. He'd be the laughing stock of the neighborhood when his dream failed. The neighbors came with shovels and buckets and the work proceeded, accompanied by laughter and jokes.

"So, Jake. How many bedrooms?" asked Alec Steadman.

"Be sure you make it big enough," Neil McDougall admonished him. "Ye've made a good start on a family but you're a young man, yet."

Jake laughed at their sallies. "You're jealous of my fine family, and so."

With many hands at work, the cellar was dug in a single day. Jake said it was a fine piece of work, and thanked them all as they sat around a trestle table in the yard, polishing off the bowls and platters of food Phoebe and Hedwig had prepared.

"When are you going to start building?" asked Alec Steadman. "Will you be calling a bee? Give us some notice."

"I don't think I'll call a bee."

"You'll do it all yourself?" asked Reinhold Anselm, eyebrows raised in disbelief.

"Have any of you built with stone?" Jake looked around the table.

"Stone?" Alec looked astounded. "You're going to build a house out of stone?"

"That's my plan."

"Can you cut stone?" asked Neil.

"It's cut. Over there." Jake pointed at the huge piles of limestone at the edge of the east field.

"That rubble?" scoffed Neil. "Ye need nice square cut rocks to build with. That's the only kind of stone work I know."

Jake said, "You know we don't have that kind of stone here. This will do."

"Well, you're welcome to it," said Alec. "It's not something I'd try."

The following Monday, Jake, along with his father and brothers began the actual work of building. Phoebe observed that not only Jake, but all of them, seemed to know what they were doing. She despaired. She'd be glad to have more houseroom, but could a house actually be made out of those dreary gray bits?

As they sat at the midday meal on the second day, Simon said, "This is too slow, already. We don't get here until almost dinnertime and then go again in the middle of the afternoon to get home for chores. I think I stay home and do the chores at my place and Karl's, and you two boys stay here if Phoebe can sleep you." He looked at her. "Is that good with you?"

"Of course. I can make up a bed in the other cabin for Peter and Karl. I thought you were looking tired."

"No, no, I'm not tired. I just think it goes better that way."

Karl and Jake exchanged smiles. Vati would never admit he couldn't do as much work as his boys.

She turned to Karl, "Can Rebecca spare you?"

"I'd think she'd be glad to see the back of him for a few days," said Peter. "I would."

Karl blushed. "She will get along all right, I think so."

Phoebe stood in the yard the next day, observing the project.

Peter, who'd been relegated to bring rocks to the site, said, as he unloaded the stone boat, "It's some ugly, no?"

"You think so, too?"

"Jah. I don't remember stone houses from Pennsylvania. I was too little when we came. That's why I'm the rock carrier. I don't know how to build it. I'm just the ox." He laughed. "But I'm supposed to watch and learn so I can build one up some day. But I don't think I ever want to build a house like this, though."

Phoebe heard Annie calling, and turned back to the cabin. Dear Peter. At least someone felt the way she did.

Fascinated neighbors came to watch the construction.

"Seems awful slow," said Alec Steadman. "We could put up a frame one in a couple of days—one if we had enough help."

It was indeed slow. Each slice of stone had to be individually imbedded in mortar. Long narrow slabs were laboriously chipped smooth to form windowsills and headers over doors and windows. Phoebe was called on to doctor fingers, cut on the sharp edges, or bruised when caught between the rocks. Jake assured everyone it would be worth it when it was finished.

The Stettl men completed the walls and closed in the roof before freeze-up and Jake was satisfied. He'd be able to work on the interior during the winter.

Phoebe was far from happy. It was the ugliest building she'd ever seen, even worse than the red brick ones at Albany. The stark gray walls, with irregular stone edges protruding from the darker mortar, repelled her. A door in the middle of the front wall and a corresponding one in the center at the back, flanked by precisely placed, small-paned windows both upstairs and down, added to the monotony. Massive chimneys towered at each end. The glare of the new-cut cedar shingles contrasted unpleasantly with the ancient limestone of the walls.

"When I have time, I will build a stoop around, maybe. You would like that, Phee?"

"That would help." It would never happen. There was a lot of work, yet, to finish the inside. It would take Jake the rest of her life just to make it livable.

With William's absence and the prospect of living in the dreary building, her spirits plummeted. No longer did she sing as she worked.

Jake brought window sashes from the sawmill at Fort Erie and soon had the house closed in. He kept roaring fires on all the hearths to dry out the mortar and warm him while he worked. He had to stop in late winter to cut wood for the next year but by spring he said the house was livable.

She didn't agree. The inside walls were rough mortar and stone, the same as the outside. The log walls of the cabin were not especially pleasing but, whitewashed, better than this.

"I hate the look of the walls."

"Oh, they're not finished, yet. I put plaster on the living room and kitchen first and make it all smooth. Then I do the rest as soon as I have time."

Plaster improved the looks tremendously.

"Oh, that's much better."

He grinned. "Jah, I think so."

How hard he'd worked to build the house. She must make a point of telling him how much she appreciated the work he'd done, and hide how little she liked the result.

At Easter, 1807, they moved into the new house. She had to admit the large rooms and high ceilings were pleasant. The smooth inside walls, now he'd finished plastering them, were handsome and there was no more crowding together of furniture. Indeed, their belongings looked decidedly sparse. The bureau went into its old site in the front hall against the staircase. She gave it a rub with the corner of her apron whenever she went by, delighting in its rich, dark sheen.

If she didn't look at the outside, she could be quite happy in this house. The kitchen cooking fire could be shut off from the rest of the house as well, keeping those other rooms even cooler in summer. The whole house was bright with the many windows, and she could throw them open to the summer breezes. Jake had made the ceilings high and she didn't feel them pressing down on her as the cabin ceilings had.

At first the house seemed huge. How would she ever be able to do all the work? However, without everything crowded together, she found it was easier to keep clean and tidy than the cramped cabins. As she set chairs against the wall she noticed the imprint of a small hand in the wall near the floor.

"Oh, Jake, Katy has stuck her fingers in the wet plaster. It's spoiled, and after you worked so hard to make it smooth."

He laughed. "It makes no mind. Other people will not see it by the floor, and so. And for us it will always remind us of our little Katy." He picked up the child and kissed her soft cheek.

Phoebe smiled. He really loved his family. He loved her, too, and she was beginning to return that love. It seemed as if she'd been frozen for such a long time. She put her arms around both of them, and Jake kissed her over the top of Katy's head.

"What will we do with the old house?" asked Benjy. "Will somebody else come and live there?"

"Yes, but they'll have four legs instead of two," said Jake with a grin.

Benjy looked mystified, but Annie laughed. "I know," she said. "It will be another barn."

"That's right," said Jake. "We can put the calves in the bedroom cabin and the chickens and some more pigs in the other. What do you think?"

Benjy's face creased as he considered the change. "That would be all right. If they're not afraid of fire."

"Afraid of fire?" asked Jake.

"Yes, from the fireplaces."

"Oh, we won't have a fire in there any more. Animals don't need it. They have fur coats."

Benjy nodded. "That's all right, then."

CHAPTER 34

P hoebe sang as she balanced on a stool, hanging curtains at the parlor windows. It was a delight to have so much space, filled with sunshine this bright morning. The farm was prospering and she had this lovely house. She was the most fortunate of women, thanks to Jake. To think she'd only married him for security. How much more he had given her. Dear Jake.

Reaching up to hook another curtain panel, she glimpsed a soldier in a red coat striding down the trail. Just for a moment she thought it was Richard. Her heart faltered. It couldn't be. He was long dead. It was William. She'd never realized how much he looked like his father. He even walked the same—that arrogant stride—as if he owned the world. Seventeen already! A man.

"William's come." She jumped off the stool and rushed to the door to greet him.

"William?" Annie followed her.

He came in, swinging his shoulders "How do you like my uniform?"

She hugged him. He stiffened under her embrace but she was too happy to care. "Oh, William. I'm so glad to see you. Just for a minute I thought it was your vati coming down the road. Isn't that silly?"

"No, it's not. I want to be exactly like him."

Oh no, not exactly. She didn't wish any of his father's gambling and drinking for her son.

"You do look so much like him. Are you on leave? Can you stay awhile?"

"No, I can't stay." He squirmed free of hers arms. "Hello, Annie."

Annie lifted her arms for a hug, but he ignored the gesture.

"I'm important. As you can see." He squared his shoulders and puffed out his chest, straining the jacket buttons.

Katy laid her corn-husk doll on the settee and stroked his red sleeve. "Pretty," she crooned.

"Careful, you'll get it dirty." He pulled away and brushed at the fabric.

Annie took down her bonnet from the peg by the door. "I'll go over to McDougall's and get Hedwig? You'll want to see her."

He shook his head, "Don't bother."

Jake, Danny and Benjy came in from the barn.

Benjy said, "We saw a soldier...."

"Well. William," said Jake. "You look healthy, so."

"Of course. I take care of myself," with some emphasis on the last word. He pointed to a stripe on his sleeve. "I've been promoted to corporal."

"Congratulations," said Danny, holding out his hand.

"Thanks," said William, ignoring the hand.

"Who is he?" asked Benjy, staring at the red jacket.

"That's our brother, William," said Danny,"who went away to be a soldier."

"Oh," said Benjy.

"You wouldn't remember him. You were too little."

"Oh, William, why did you enlist?" asked Phoebe. "They're talking of war again. You could be killed."

He waved his hand in dismissal. "Oh, no. It won't happen. The Yankees won't dare attack us. Too bad, though. It would be exciting."

"It would be that," said Jake. "Maybe more than you want."

William's laugh was scornful. "Not for me. But we're preparing, anyway."

"You'll stay for dinner?" asked Phoebe.

"If it's ready."

She hurried to put the meal on the table, mourning that she didn't have time to prepare something special. Although both Jake and Phoebe talked to him about the new house and happenings on the farm, he ate without comment.

When he'd cleaned his plate, he tilted his chair back and hooked his thumbs in his braces. "I'm in charge of a full squad of men. Of course you don't know what that is, but it's important."

Phoebe did know what a squad was. William was exaggerating.

"I have to drill them every day. They're the best-trained squad on the base. I won't stand for anything less." He banged his fist on the table.

Katy whimpered.

"That's good," said Jake. I'm glad you're successful."

"That's only the beginning. I expect another promotion any day now." He got up, buttoned his jacket and put on his hat. "I must get back. I'm on early duty tomorrow."

Phoebe said, "Take care of yourself, dear."

He waved his hand as if brushing off a fly and swaggered down the road.

Later, in the barn doing chores, the twins and Hedwig discussed the visit.

"I'm sorry I missed seeing him," said Hedwig.

"You didn't miss much," said Danny. "He's a strange one, our brother."

Annie burst out, "He just came to brag. Mutti worries about him, but he's not worth a straw."

Danny nodded. "I guess it's because he was Mutti's first baby. The first one is special."

"How do you know that?" asked Annie, punching him in the ribs.

"Ow, that hurt, you big bully." He returned the punch, lightly.

They laughed, and continued their chores companionably.

In the house, Jake was installing a new cupboard in the kitchen, while Phoebe finished washing the supper dishes.

She said, "He didn't even say goodbye. And he wasn't the least bit interested in us, even the new house. What's wrong with him? Is it my fault? What didn't I do that I should have done? He doesn't seem to care for us at all."

Jake laid down his hammer and put his arms around her. "You were, and are, a good mutti. Don't fret yourself. It's not you. There is something left out of William. He can't help the way he is, and there's nothing to do for it. He can only care about himself."

"If that's so, why did he come?"

Jake chuckled. "To show off his stripe, I think so."

"Only that?"

"Only that."

His words about something left out of her son started Phoebe on a new train of thought. William must have inherited some bad traits from her. Would the other children develop the signs she noticed in him? They all seemed happy and caring now. Would that coldness develop as they grew older?

CHAPTER 35

When work slacked off in the fall, Phoebe began to consider something she'd long wanted: schooling for her children. In most pioneer communities schools were a priority, but for some reason there was none here.

Hedwig and Annie had become very efficient housekeepers and she had more free time. There was nothing she could do about William. He'd chosen his life. But perhaps now she had the time to teach the others their letters. Except for Benjy and Katy, the children were grown. Was it too late? Well, she could teach the two young ones, anyway. But how? Paper and pencils were almost non-existent in the community.

The next time Jake went to the fort she asked him to inquire for writing materials. "See if you can find some slates."

"What is it, slates?"

"You've never seen a slate?"

He looked at the floor and mumbled, "I'm not learned like you."

It was her turn to be embarrassed. "You're learned in all the things that really matter: the important things about living and supporting your family. Book learning maybe makes it a little easier. That's what I want for the children.

"Slates are just thin, smooth pieces of black rock," she continued. "Sometimes with a wood frame around them. You write with a special pencil that makes a white mark on the black. You can wipe it off and use them again, not like paper. Much cheaper."

She reminded him every time he went to Fort Erie, but he either forgot or was unable to find any.

She gave up hope, thinking he didn't want her to start a school. Then one day in the fall, he came home, jubilant, with four slates and a pencil for each.

"The man I got them from didn't even know what they were." He straightened his back. "But I knew. The man said he found them in a house he bought."

After the crops were all stored for winter, she gathered Katy and Benjy by the fire after morning chores and gave them each a slate. Katy made a mark on hers and the pencil squeaked. Phoebe showed her how to hold the stylus so it would only click, but Benjy managed to make his squeal regularly in spite of her protests.

"I can't help it," he said, but his smirk indicated otherwise.

"I'll take the slate away and make you write on birch bark if you don't behave."

Benjy treasured his slate, so subsided.

She taught them the alphabet in spite of Benjy's sighs of boredom. She noticed Annie and Hedwig listening as they did the household chores, so changed the school hours to afternoon so they could participate. Danny also joined in.

After they'd mastered small words, the Bible—the only reading material available—came into regular use, although she was hard put to explain the meaning of many of the words. The girls were avid to learn, and Danny, but Benjy escaped whenever he could.

Jake caught him sneaking away to the bush and brought him in, a firm grasp on the boy's ear. He shoved him down on the settle. "Pay attention to your mutti. She is trying to keep you from growing up a dummkopf already."

When the lessons progressed to numbers, Benjy suddenly became interested. "Can I just learn numbers instead of reading and writing? Then I can count the chickens every night to be sure they're all in the coop? And when I grow up I can go to Fort Erie for Vati and do the business."

Jake said, "You'll need to be able to read then, so the miller or the shop man doesn't cheat you."

This seemed to make sense to pragmatic Benjy and thereafter he paid a little more attention to the reading lessons.

Sometime during that winter Phoebe became aware that Jake always seemed to find some repair work that could be done by the fire during these lessons.

At her questions, he sheepishly admitted a desire to learn. "What I told Benjy is for sure. I'm always afraid I'm being cheated. But after what I said, I'd hate him to know I can't read either. He'd probably balk again. Besides he will think me a dummkopf, and so."

"Jake, you're not a dummy. You just never had the chance to learn."

"Well, I feel it, and so."

"I think you could learn quickly if you really want to."

So Jake swallowed his pride and joined the class.

Annie came in one afternoon carrying a fungus bracket she had torn off a tree trunk. "Look. I can draw pictures on this."

She turned the bracket upside down and made marks on the white underside with a sharp twig.

"I could do that," said Benjy, and over the next few days stripped most of the brackets from the nearby trees.

Phoebe was astonished how lifelike his drawing of a cow turned out, and how accurate his depiction of a grain cradle. She must remember that, although he was averse to books, he too had his talents.

Abigail heard about the lessons and begged to have her four children included. "I can read and write, a little," she said, "but I would never attempt to teach anyone else. We had a school for a year, I guess it was after you left to marry that soldier, but the teacher went back to England and we couldn't find another. Everyone wants to own land, not work for someone else."

Phoebe agreed to take the children, and the slates did double duty, one half of the class writing, while the other took turns reading. Word of Phoebe's little school spread. Other parents begged her to teach their children, but Phoebe said this was all she could handle in the cabin.

The community began to talk seriously of starting a real school. Abigail invited all the parents in the community to a meeting to discuss the project.

They gathered in her parlor on a Sunday afternoon.

Alec started the meeting by welcoming them. "I'm glad to see you are in favor of starting a school again, now we have a teacher." He bowed to Phoebe.

"Oh, no," said Phoebe. "I couldn't teach in a real school."

"Why not?" asked Meg McDougall.

"I don't know enough."

"You know more than the rest of us," said Neil. "It would get the tads started, ye ken."

There was a chorus of, "Please do it, Phoebe."

She really didn't want to. "I don't think I'll have time when the spring work starts."

"The tads'll be needed at home then, anyway," said Neil. "I can only spare mine in the winter."

Well, if it was only for the winter perhaps she could manage. She reluctantly agreed. "But only until we find a real teacher."

"That's settled then," said Alec. "It'll take some work and sacrifice from all of us. I'll start by giving that little field on the west corner of my farm for a schoolhouse."

"I've got some logs I cut last year that'll do for the building," said Neil.

A bee quickly provided a one-room cabin. A collection was taken for funds to buy glass for a window. Parents donated dry wood for the fire and assured Phoebe they'd contribute what they could to her salary though no definite amount was stated.

Later, Jake said, "I don't think it'll be much."

"Well, I said I'd do it and I think it's important."

The older children, and Jake, objected to attending a real school, so she taught the children through the day and the adults in the evenings.

The elder McDougalls and Steadmans joined them but
Reinhold Anselm said, "I have trouble enough just saying the English
without trying to write it, so."

His wife, Hilda said, "I would like to come. I could help my
kinder then."

Hedwig unfortunately was often absent from the lessons. She
was in great demand to lend a hand with sickness or work among the
neighbors and Phoebe felt some stress, trying to run her school and
keep up with the housekeeping with only thirteen-year-old Annie's
assistance.

Archie McDougall squired Hedwig home one night. Jake
winked at Phoebe as the young couple came in.

"What are you winking at?"

"You don't see? " said Jake, grinning.

"Surely not. She's only a child," said Phoebe when Jake
enlightened her after they went to bed.

"So, have you looked at her, lately? She's sixteen. Why did
Archie go all the way to Anselm's to bring her home, else?"

Sixteen. Where had the years gone?

"Well, they'll have red-haired tads, anyway," said Jake. With
Archie sandy and Hedwig red, it couldn't miss." He chuckled and
pulled the blankets up to his chin.

"Jake, It's too soon to think of that."

"I don't think so. Not the way he looks at her."

Hedwig old enough to marry? Surely not. Did all mothers feel
this way when their children struck out on their own? At the same
time she was a little ashamed at a feeling of relief that the red hair
might soon be out of her sight.

Jake seemed determined to make the new house as crowded
as the old. Every trip to the fort provided another piece of furniture.
Bedsteads, cupboards, rugs and couches filled the rooms.

One day he came home from Fort Erie, the wagon stacked with a complete mahogany dining room suite.

"Jake, It's beautiful," said Phoebe, her apron corner in brisk motion over the tabletop. "It must have cost you a great deal of money."

"Not so much. The people were hurrying to go back to England. I don't think the man ever got his hands dirty before he came. I don't know how he thought he was going to live. Must have thought money grows on trees, here."

They set up the suite in the dining room, the old table and chairs now relegated to the summer kitchen. Phoebe polished the new furniture with beeswax until it glowed. She knew Jake wanted an iron plow to replace his wooden one, but he'd spent his money on this, for her. She was so lucky.

CHAPTER 36

The winter passed uneventfully, except for Archie's increasing interest in Hedwig. Phoebe realized the attachment was mutual. Hedwig's conversation was filled with: "Archie says," and "Archie thinks". The fledglings were leaving the nest. First William, and now, apparently, Hedwig. Phoebe felt the years creeping up.

The snow disappeared and the yellowing of the willow trees' bark heralded spring.

School ended. Although Phoebe was satisfied at her pupils' progress, she hoped they could find a real teacher before the fall. She felt she'd reached the limits of her knowledge.

One mild Sunday before spring work took all their time and energy, Phoebe and Jake took the family to visit the elder Stettls.

Rebecca and Karl and their daughter Charity were there, too. After dinner the women sat on straight-backed rush-seated chairs on the porch and the men lounged on the steps. The children bounded around the yard like calves newly let out in the spring. Jake's team, relieved of their harness, dashed about the pasture, manes and tales flying like pennants. Simon's horses stood watching, apparently in disgust at this unseemly behavior. A whiff of new-turned soil wafted from the garden.

Phoebe felt relaxed and content. Everything was going right at last. The children were healthy and she and Jake had become happy together. She looked at him fondly where he lounged on the steps. He noticed her look, winked, and pursed his lips in a silent kiss. She frowned at him in disapproval, but felt a warm glow.

She turned to Hannah, "It's so nice to sit outside, at last, after the winter."

Hannah nodded in agreement and Karl said, "Jah. Just a little break before the real hard work starts."

"Did you have to remind me, then?" asked Peter.

"So, that is my good-for-nothing son," said Simon. He leaned back on his elbows and stretched out his legs.

They sat silent for some time, absorbing the sunshine. The children, tired from their exertions, joined them.

"Look at the team," said Phoebe as the black horses galloped up to the fence then raced away across the pasture. "They think they're colts."

Peter said, "Tim and Tom. Jake can't tell them apart. It gives him an excuse if he speaks to the wrong one. He can say he said the other name. That's the way he named the twins. He can't tell them apart either."

Katy looked at her father, her forehead wrinkled. "But Danny is a boy and Annie is a girl."

Amid the laughter, Jake pulled Katy's braids. "Your Uncle Peter's making dumb jokes, Katy."

Karl said, "Will you take the young sow you wanted, back with you? I'm sure she's in pig."

Jake cleared his throat. "Uh, I guess I won't be wanting her after all. Uh, I don't have the money."

"I thought you were doing good," said Simon.

"Well, I am."

Phoebe thought Jake sounded defensive.

"It's just—right now I have to keep my money for the militia captain."

Oh, dear. She'd forgotten about that. Her annual worry surfaced again. Katy and Benjy, even Anna, went barefoot in the summer, but they'd need new boots for winter, although Annie's might still be big enough. Danny's winter coat-sleeves were already above his wrists and she knew he wouldn't be able to even get into it come fall, the way his shoulders were filling out.

She turned her worried glance on Jake, but he seemed more concerned about increasing his stock than whether his children were shod and clothed. No, that wasn't fair. The one provided for the other, in his eyes.

Ruth Zavitz

Simon pulled in his feet and sat up straight. "Why ever you are giving money to the army?"

"It's a fine I have to pay for not training."

The other men stared at him. Then Simon said, "You're a Mennonite, and so. You don't have to be a soldier. The government says."

"The captain doesn't believe me. I have to pay."

"This is foolish. Ask Amos to send a letter."

"He gave me a letter the first time, but the captain didn't believe it."

"Get Amos to send it to the top man. Go this afternoon, why not?"

Leaving the rest of the family still relaxing on the porch, Jake walked down the road to Uncle Amos's farm. Could he persuade Uncle Amos to write another letter? Would it do any good anyway? Well, nothing to lose, maybe something to gain. Phee would be pleased to save some money.

Fortunately, Salome was visiting at Freda's so Jake didn't have to deal with her.

"Well, I don't know if I should do it," said Amos.

"What is different? You wrote it before."

Amos sighed. "Jah, that is so. I am already wrong."

Once again he retrieved the writing materials from the attic.

"Write it in English, this time, Uncle Amos. The militia man couldn't read the German and the top man probably can't either."

"I don't know can I do that, but I will try."

Between the two of them, with Jake contributing such English words as he knew, the letter was composed and Jake took it home with him. Too bad it was Sunday.

He had to make another trip to the fort to present the letter.

After many inquiries he found a soldier who said he would take care of it. After a long wait, Jake was ushered into an office where an officer with many bars on his sleeve questioned him.

Seeming satisfied, the officer said, "I'll have my adjutant make out an exemption for you."

Another interminable wait. Were they making the paper, too? It would be long after dark before he reached home at this rate.

The sun was setting by the time he reached Simon's. Perhaps he'd better stay the night here. Phoebe would worry but the rest of the trip would be difficult in the dark, this moonless night.

He reined the horse into the yard.

Hannah welcomed him and laid a place at the table where the family were sitting down to supper.

Simon said, "So, you've been to the fort, I think so? Is it settled?"

"Yes, it's all straightened out now. I have to pay a tax but not so much as the captain took."

"Did you get some back?"

"No, the man said he didn't know anything about the fines I paid."

"Didn't you get a paper from the captain?"

"No."

Simon shook his head. "You're not much good at business, boy."

There was no use telling Vati what sort of person the captain was.

Simon said, "I heard at the fort the other day that the Americans are planning another war. Against us, this time. When will people stop fighting?"

When indeed, thought Jake? And Phoebe would be frantic for William if she heard about it. He hoped it was only a rumor.

Through the summer there were discussions regarding hiring a new teacher, but nothing definite was done and Phoebe feared they were expecting her to take the position again. Every time the subject came up she insisted she would not, could not, do it.

Then Neil McDougall came home from Fort Erie one day with the news he'd met a man who was willing to take the job. His name was Jock McGregor. He said he was well educated and Neil said he sounded so. His elder brother had inherited the family estate in Scotland and he'd come out to Canada for the chance to own land of his own. An accident felling trees on his grant had crippled his arm and destroyed that dream. He was looking for employment that didn't involve physical labor.

The community thought that sounded ideal.

Jake, Alec and Neil were appointed a committee to interview the prospect and generally supervise the school in the future. The interview was satisfactory and Abigail offered to board him.

The new teacher took up residence. A tall lanky man with a shock of blond hair falling over his forehead, Phoebe thought he looked quite scholarly. The twisted shoulder and useless arm added to his ascetic appearance.

Buxom Meg said he needed feeding up, but otherwise the community thought they'd acquired a gem.

School opened immediately and Phoebe was pleased to see that the boys—even Benjy—were intimidated by his size and commanding presence.

She was relieved. She'd been afraid the community would prevail on her to take up the school again.

Abigail said he was a model boarder, considerate and appreciative of her efforts to make him welcome. The committee questioned the children—or rather their wives did—about what they were learning. The men concerned themselves with the physical aspects: making sure there was enough dry wood for the fireplace and collecting money from reluctant parents for the teacher's wages.

Everything was satisfactory.

On a blustery day in December Jake was replacing a broken plank in a box stall in the barn when Alec and Neil came to call.

Alec was visibly upset. "Jake, we have a problem."

Jake laid down his hammer. "What?"

"Teacher is a drunkard."

Neil held up his hand. "Now. Alec, I wouldn't say that. Ye havena seen him drunk, have ye?"

"Well, he drinks. Abigail found a whiskey bottle under his mattress when she was turning it. Half empty."

Neil sat down on a keg. "Ah, weel, a wee dram before he goes to sleep doesna hurt anything. Belike it dulls the pain. He moves like his shoulder hurts him."

"We can't have a man of poor morals teaching our children. Better no school than a corrupt teacher—and Abigail refuses to have him in the house."

Jake didn't know what to think. Of course the teacher must set a good example for the children, and he certainly didn't approve of drinking. But if the man was only taking it to ease his pain when he went to bed, it was sort of like medicine, wasn't it?

He said, "Well, if he doesn't drink at school it won't affect the children, will it? We haven't a chance of getting another teacher and Phoebe thinks he's a good one. She says even Benjy is improving." He chuckled. "And that's a miracle, and so."

Neil slapped his knee and got up. "Let's hae a talk with him. See what he has to say for himself."

Alec shook his head. "It's no use. Abigail won't keep him any more."

"I ken Meg won't mind havin' him. We might even be joinin' him in a wee snort happen it's good stuff."

Jake thought Alec looked shocked. He was a little offended himself, but Neil just grinned.

They interviewed Jock, who affirmed that the whiskey was medicine, and he certainly wouldn't allow the children to know. Neil seemed satisfied and Alec was inclined to give him a chance, but Jake thought there was something a little shifty in his eyes.

After some thought as to how to approach the subject, he asked Benjy if the teacher drank tea or coffee with his lunch.

Benjy looked at him as if he thought it was an odd question but said, "I don't think it's tea or coffee, but when he thinks we're not looking he drinks out of a shiny flat bottle he keeps in his pocket. I saw him."

Not only a drinker but a liar, too. Jake's suspicion was confirmed.

The committee gathered again at his request. Two against one decided the teacher's morals were unsatisfactory, and he was fired forthwith in spite of his protests that he'd give up drinking.

Now they faced a dilemma. They'd protected their children against immoral influences. But now they had a school, eager pupils, but no teacher.

They inquired everywhere they went and left word to contact them if anyone suitable appeared.

Jake and Phoebe were preparing for bed one evening in mid January when someone knocked. Who would be calling this late? Jake went to open the door. A young man stood on the doorstep.

"Are you Jacob Stettl?"

"Yes. Why are you asking, so?"

"I heard you needed a teacher. I've walked all the way from Fort Erie to apply for the position."

Hearing this, Phoebe called, "Come in, come in. You must be frozen."

"Yes, Ma'am. Almost."

Jake knelt to stir the fire, banked with ashes for the night, and added wood. Phoebe reached over his head to pull the kettle over the new blaze, then ushered the visitor close to the heat.

"Are you hungry?" she said. He certainly looked it. Gaunt, with dark shadows under his eyes. He also needed a haircut and probably a bath.

"Yes, Ma'am I am."

When he'd eaten his fill of bread and butter and slabs of ham, he cuddled his mug of tea in his long-fingered hands and sighed.

"That's the best meal I've had since I left England. Oh, I should introduce myself. My name is James Greenock. I came out last autumn. I thought I'd find work and save enough to buy some land but people here only want someone to clear the trees and I'm not very good with an ax. When I heard you wanted a teacher, I thought 'that's the ticket'."

"But you're so young," said Phoebe. "Can you really teach?"

"I'm almost seventeen and I've watched my teachers all these years. I'm sure I can do it."

She questioned him about his schooling and it sounded satisfactory, considering how desperate they were. She gave him a bed and the next day the committee gathered.

"I don't know," said Alec. "He seems awful young. Some of the boys are older than him. Do you think they'll mind him?"

"We don't have any choice," said Neil, "Seein' as ye kicked out the other fella."

He's still mad about missing his chance at some free whiskey, thought Jake. "All right. Let's give him a chance, so."

CHAPTER 37

In June of 1812 the United States declared war on the Canadas. The eldest pupils either joined the army or were too busy at home to attend school. The young teacher had no problems with discipline.

When Phoebe heard the news, she cried, "We have to get William out of the army, Jake. He'll be killed."

"Now, Phee. He wants to be a soldier. He's a man; he will do what he thinks. He likes the army. He wouldn't thank you for trying to get him out."

"But he didn't know the war was coming."

"That's the way it goes. Everybody decides what he will do and what happens, happens."

"It's all very well for you. He's not your son."

"Phee! You know I love the boy."

"I'm sorry. I shouldn't have said that. You've put up with a lot from him."

"It's all right. You're upset." He put his arms around her and she rested her head in the hollow of his shoulder. He was a rock she could depend on, whatever happened.

"I love you, you know," he said. "Don't worry about William. He knows how to take care of William." He chuckled. "Probably a general he will be at the end."

His assurance that William was competent to manage his life relieved her a little. After all he'd done so for four years.

The militia captain called the men into camp. Phoebe and Hedwig were picking strawberries and Jake was hoeing corn in the field close by, when Archie came to say goodbye to Hedwig.

He said, "Those Yankees think we want to be part of the United States. We'll show 'em we don't."

Jake and Phoebe told him to take care of himself and not take any chances. Hedwig hung on him, teary-eyed until he pried her loose, kissed her and loped off down the road.

In the fall, the captain, still furious that Jake had escaped his private graft, required him to turn over all his wheat for the men's support. Mindful of Simon's advice, Jake demanded a receipt but the captain just laughed at him.

"Receipt, is it? A turn in jail'd be better. All you yellow-livered Mennonites and Quakers should be sent back to the States where ye came from. Ye're no good for Canada and like as not will help the Yankees if ye git the chance."

Jake refused to turn over the grain until he received an official requisition form. He wasn't going to contribute to the captain's private income, again.

He said, "The man at the fort told me he didn't know anything about the money you took, before. I guess I go right away and tell him if you take the wheat."

"I'll get your stupid paper."

Jake hoped that would be the end of it, but the captain returned with the authorization and a wagon and crew.

He thrust it at Jake. "Here's your fancy paper."

The men loaded the bags of grain on the wagon while Phoebe watched in consternation.

As the wagon disappeared down the road, she wailed, "Jake, what can we do? No wheat to sell, there's not even any for bread."

"Well, the money I can't help. But," he winked at her, "in the haymow some wheat for bread."

She hugged him. "Jake, thank God. You're so smart."

"Jah, so. Just a few bags the captain wouldn't miss." He grimaced. "But there'll be no money for clothes or anything."

It would be a hard winter without the money from the sale of the wheat, no doubt about it. Most of the cows would go dry on winter feed and she'd be unable to make cheese to sell until they freshened in the spring. They'd have to eat more cornmeal mush to stretch out the wheat flour.

Could she lengthen Katy's skirts to last another year? The girl was growing so fast. Well, somehow they'd manage.

Hedwig and Archie had been keeping formal company for some time with the approval of both families. They were planning to marry as soon as Archie had enough money to buy a farm. But now that Archie was leaving for the war front, they decided to marry at once. But how? Settlers here were from so many different backgrounds that no churches had been organized. Consequently there was no minister locally, and who knew when a circuit minister might come, especially now with everything so upset? And it wasn't safe for Hedwig to go to Niagara with the skirmishes along the border.

Phoebe said, "You'll have to wait until the war is over."

"But we want to live together. Archie might-might not come back," wailed Hedwig.

"All the more reason to wait."

"You don't want me to be happy. You never cared about me."

Phoebe cringed. It had been too true, but over the years she'd come to appreciate Hedwig's steadfast devotion although she was unable to return it. "I do care, Hedwig. The community would say nasty things about you. And what if you were left by yourself and maybe a baby?"

"Oh, I hope I have a baby right away."

"You don't know what you're saying."

"Yes, I do."

"No, you don't. When William's vati was killed I had to move out of the room we rented. All I could find to live in was a tumbledown shack and I had no money...."

"Why do you say William's vati? Wasn't he my vati, too? I know I was born too soon after you married my vati."

229

Phoebe wished the floor would open and swallow her up. She'd dreaded this question for years, but Hedwig had never asked before. She'd hoped the girl thought Jake was her father. What should she say? There was no escape. She'd have to tell her.

Hedwig listened, wide-eyed, to the whole tale of the hateful sergeant without uttering a word until Phoebe finished "...and then I found out I was with child—with you."

"Is that why you don't like me?"

"Of course I like you. What makes you think I don't?" Dear God, had Hedwig known all these years that she didn't love her as she did the other children? She thought she'd hidden her feelings successfully.

"I know you don't. And you don't want me to be happy."

The argument raged and ended with Hedwig packing her belongings and moving to the McDougalls'.

"How could she defy me like that?" said Phoebe as she watched Hedwig, accompanied by Archie, disappear down the road. "And William, too. What's wrong with my children, or is it me? Didn't I bring them up right?"

Jake stroked his beard. "Well, William, like I said before there is a feeling left out of him. But Hedwig. That's the other way." He grinned. "That's the sap rising, I think so. I seem to remember hearing about another girl who ran away from her aunt and uncle to marry the man she wanted."

"That was different—and I lived to regret it, bitterly."

"Archie's a good fellow. He'll take care of our Hedwig. They can get married up after the war."

Archie left for the Detroit River with General Brock. Presumably William went, too, although he hadn't visited again and they'd heard nothing more of him. Phoebe lay awake nights. Where was he, and was he safe and well?

The militia captain came, already armed with a paper, and took three of Jake's steers to feed the forces. Jake was more resigned to this as one, or probably two, of their own would benefit.

230

Several weeks later Danny came in from the back field saying he'd seen Archie going down the road towards the McDougalls'. Phoebe immediately went over.

Meg, and an ecstatic Hedwig were plying Archie with food in the McDougalls' kitchen.

"Did you see William? Did he go?" Phoebe asked.

"I didn't see him. Maybe he was there. I don't know which division he's with."

"I don't know, either," said Phoebe. Perhaps he hadn't gone. Perhaps his part of the army was still at the fort, or maybe he had a job at headquarters and wouldn't be required to fight. She clung to the belief he'd never left the fort at Niagara. Otherwise she wouldn't be able to stand the dread.

Archie couldn't stop talking about the boat ride on the lake. "General Brock got enough boats to take all of us and our supplies all the way to Detroit—and bring us back again. That's the way to travel, no mud holes, no corduroy roads, no creeks to wade through."

A few days later William paid his parents a visit.

Phoebe threw her arms around him. "Oh, William. You're all right. I was so afraid."

He suffered her embrace for a moment then pulled away and straightened his jacket. "Of course I'm all right. Those cowardly Yankees couldn't hurt me. You should've seen me. I fired my musket at a general. Hit him right between the eyes. It was a glorious battle. Dead bodies everywhere. That'll teach them to attack us."

Jake questioned Archie later about his experiences and learned the surrender of Detroit was almost bloodless.

"That's just like William," said Jake. "He likes to make things sound big."

Phoebe was offended by this criticism of her son, but had to admit the truth of it.

Rumors of battles fought, and battles planned, flew about the community. Phoebe, to her surprise, missed Hedwig. She vowed to be more affectionate, but when Hedwig came to visit found herself bound by the old reserve.

The talk of battles reminded Phoebe of a time long ago. She hoped the new ones wouldn't have such a sad end. Where would they go if they were driven from their home as she had been after the revolution?

Jake reassured her. "They'll do their fighting along the river. We're safe, here, away from the border."

"I hope so. I don't think I could go through that again."

"Jah," said Jake. He had some sad memories of his own.

"But what about William? He's in danger."

"There's nothing we can do about it, except pray for his safety."

And she did, every night on her knees beside her bed with Jake on the other side. Often through the day she stopped whatever she was doing to wonder where he was, if he were safe, and offer a little prayer for him. It was all she could do.

When word of the battle at Queenston spread throughout the Niagara peninsula in October, everyone rejoiced at the victory, even while they mourned the loss of their gallant General Brock. He'd led his troops straight up the escarpment to recapture the heights previously lost to the Yankees.

On a cold, rainy afternoon a drenched soldier knocked on the door.

Phoebe didn't recognize the man, but said, "Come in. Have you come all the way from Niagara? Your coat is soaked."

The soldier stopped just inside the door and removed his cap, tucking it under his arm. His uniform exuded the smell of wet wool, and a puddle formed at his feet.

"Ma'am...," he began, then stopped, shifting his feet.

She was alerted by his manner. "Is it about my son? William? Is he hurt?"

"Yes, Ma'am, but...."

"Where is he?" She pushed past the soldier and peered out through the rain. "Are they bringing him home?" She turned back to the soldier.

With a rush, he said, "No, Ma'am. He was hurt bad in the attack on Queenston. I'm sorry Ma'am. I was ordered to bring you word. He was buried in the cemetery, there."

"Buried? William? He's dead? Why wasn't I told he was hurt?" She beat at the soldier with her fists. "You should have brought him home. I could have nursed him."

He took hold of her hands. "He was a brave soldier, Ma'am. He fought gallantly. There were so many we couldn't take them home, even the ones who have homes nearby. I'm sorry."

"I must go...." Phoebe looked around distractedly. Annie stood by the hearth, a ladle in her hand and tears streaming down her cheeks. Benjy and Katy stared, wide-eyed.

"No, Ma'am, if you mean go to the cemetery, it's not safe."

She ran to the back door and screamed, "Jake! Jake."

Jake and Danny came running from the barn. Jake called, "What's the matter?" He stopped short in the doorway when he saw the soldier.

"I'm sorry, sir. It's your son. He was killed at Queenston. I was detailed to bring you word."

Phoebe went to the pegs by the door and pulled down her shawl. "Jake, harness the team. I have to go."

"Go where?"

"To Queenston. They buried him there, and they didn't even tell us. We have to go."

Jake gathered her in his arms. "Phee, we can't go. They're fighting there."

"That's what I told her," said the soldier.

"My son is dead and I can't even visit his grave?"

"I'm afraid so, for now," said Jake. He wiped the tears off her cheeks with his thumb, then swiped at his own eyes with the back of his hand.

Over her head, to the soldier, he said, "Thank you for bringing us word."

"It was my duty," said the man. He put his hat back on, bowed, said, "Good day," and hurried back out into the rain.

She couldn't stop crying, not only for William's death but also for the estrangement they'd had for such a long time. Difficult as he'd been, he was her firstborn son. The only thing she had left of her first love.

Jake held her and tried to comfort her. "Phee, William did what he wanted to do, even if it wasn't what we wanted. And he died still doing it. He loved the army. That's where he wanted to be. You're crying for yourself, no?"

He was right. She was mourning what might have been. She had other children besides William and she must consider them. She straightened her shoulders and gave him a tremulous smile.

"That's better," he said.

"And I didn't even offer that soldier anything. Poor man, he was soaked." She looked out the window as if he might still be in sight.

Jake patted her shoulder. "It makes no mind. He knew how upset you were. Anyhow, he was used to being out in the weather."

Annie, and even Katy, outdid themselves helping her, and she fought back tears again. They were concerned for her in the midst of their own grief. Temporarily awed by the grief surrounding them, Benjy and Katy soon revived and Benjy, at least, became his boisterous self again. William had been so long away, the younger ones scarcely remembered him.

CHAPTER 38

Phoebe sat on a log in the sugar grove, reveling in the spring sunshine. It had been a hard winter with deep snow keeping everyone close to home. She hadn't seen any of the neighbor women since Christmas. Hedwig had whispered then, that she was going to have a baby but Phoebe was so angry at her she hadn't asked for any details. Would there be a scandal?

A crow, watching her from a nearby tree, cawed loudly. Another, far away, answered. A cardinal whistled and she puckered her lips and answered him. Through the open bush she could see Jake gathering maple sap. A wooden yoke, with pails hanging at either end, spanned his shoulders, keeping his hands free to lift and empty the sap troughs into the pails.

She rose and laid a few more sticks on the fire. The blaze flared up, sending smoke swirling around her and the large iron kettle hanging on a wooden tripod. The burning wood crackled and the clear sap in the kettle bubbled. Eyes smarting from the smoke, she checked a smaller kettle on its own tripod over a separate fire. The sap in it was boiling up in a yellow cone. She inhaled the fragrant, sweet steam and her mouth watered.

She dipped the edge of the ladle into the liquid and held it up, letting the syrup drip off the edge. The drops fell straight. No, not quite ready. They'd run together and drop as one when the syrup was thick enough. She stirred the fire under the small kettle but didn't add any more wood lest the fire become too hot and scorch the syrup.

Retiring to the log, again, she began planning the spring housecleaning that would follow the end of the syrup season.

Hurried footsteps sounded in the dead leaves behind her and twigs snapped. How could Jake hurry with the heavy pails? She turned around. It wasn't Jake. Archie came running through the bush toward her.

He shouted, "Annie said you were out here."

He seemed excited. She stared at him, alarmed. "What is it, Archie? What's wrong?"

"Not wrong. Right. Hedwig and I, we have a baby daughter." He clapped his hands together.

"Are they all right?"

"Oh, yes, and she's such a bonny bairn." Archie choked, then swiped the back of his hand across his eyes.

"That's good." She couldn't summon any enthusiasm.

When Jake had been told and offered his congratulations, Archie left to gloat over his daughter.

She said, "An illegitimate baby. I'm so embarrassed for her."

Jake laughed. "There's a whole batch of them, then. I could name you a dozen. How about Hedwig, herself?"

She bristled. "That wasn't my doing, Jake. You know that."

"I'm sorry. I shouldn't have said that."

"But that's what you're thinking. I'll never live that down." Maybe Hedwig had inherited something that made her do this. Besides, Phoebe wasn't sure she wanted to be a grandmother, at least not yet.

She couldn't get over her unease concerning Hedwig's waywardness. Still, she supposed she'd better go and see her and the baby, or the McDougalls would wonder why she didn't come.

After dinner she put on her bonnet and shawl and set out, leaving Annie in charge of the sugar making. She stepped out briskly, marveling at the new buildings along the road. The community was prospering.

Nest-building was going on all through the uncleared bush. Robins and jays and cardinals, intent on their construction projects, paid her no heed. Clusters of pink and white and lavender hepaticas winked at her from among last year's dead leaves. Whorls of skunk cabbage leaves, just showing above the muck in every swampy spot, exuded their distinctive odor, competing with the springtime smell of burgeoning earth.

She came out into the open. A settler had girdled the trees on his lot, cutting off a horizontal strip of bark around the trunk of each tree to kill it. She frowned. Didn't he know how dangerous that was? If the trees weren't cut down as soon as they died, they were apt to fall or drop their branches at unforeseen times. A real menace.

Further along the trail, she forced her way through two adjoining clergy reserve lots. They'd been set aside as revenue for the Episcopal Church and everyone wished the church officials would hurry up and sell them so the land could be cleared. Scattered through the country, the blocks of forest separated the settled areas, a constant annoyance.

On the farm next to the McDougalls, a small cabin leaned drunkenly toward the road as if it longed to be on its way. Hedwig had told her the couple who lived there had ten children. Whatever did the woman do with them all in that tiny place? Phoebe felt guilty for the fuss she'd made over the stone house. How much better Jake had looked after her than this settler did his family.

Some of the farmer's children were working with their father in the field behind the cabin but two mites played in the mud in the dooryard. They wore shirts but not a stitch on their backsides. It saved on nappies, she supposed, but they did look cold.

She walked up the path at the McDougalls'. Neil had finished the lean-to kitchen he'd been building against the back of the cabin. Well, they needed the extra room with two families in the house and now a baby.

Meg McDougall welcomed her and ushered her in to where Hedwig lay, with the baby beside her.

Phoebe stood, stunned. Why, Hedwig was beautiful! The flaming hair that she'd closed her eyes to all these years, had turned to a beautiful auburn, the color of chestnuts in the sun. When had that happened? Why hadn't she noticed? Unbound, it shimmered against the white pillowslip. The complexion, which had been mottled and constantly peeling when Hedwig was a child, was now smoothly pink and white.

The baby had no hair at all, but had inherited the other grandmother's button nose. Long fringed eyelashes, like Phoebe's own, lay against the plump cheeks. Phoebe felt an unexpected warmth.

"Oh, Hedwig, she's a darling! Can I hold her?"

Hedwig's face flushed as she held the bundle out to her.

"What are you going to call her?"

"Would you mind—I mean, we'd like to call her after you. Would that be all right? If you don't want to, we'll think of something else, I mean...."

Phoebe's eyes filled, and her heart swelled. "I think that would be lovely, Heddie." How unfair she'd been to this most dutiful daughter. Would she ever stop hurting those closest to her?

Hedwig held up her arms and Phoebe, laying the baby on the bed, gave her a warm hug. "Oh, Heddie. I've wasted so much time."

"It doesn't matter. If it's all right, now. And I like you calling me Heddie. You never did before."

How could she have been so blind? She remembered Hedwig's constant efforts over the years to please her. She'd made the girl suffer for happenings that were in no way her fault. It would take the rest of both their lives to make it up to her. Starting now. She smiled at Hedwig, leaned down and gave her another hug.

Annie had to cook supper, that night, for Phoebe couldn't tear herself away from her new-found daughter and her namesake granddaughter.

CHAPTER 39

In late September, the entire Jake Stettl family engaged in the potato harvest. Jake and Danny dug the potatoes, shaking them so the dirt fell through the fork tines, and dropping them on top of the loose soil like clusters of brown eggs. Phoebe, Katy and Benjy followed behind the men, gathering the harvest into pails which Annie carried to the end of the field and emptied into sacks.

Startled by a booming sound coming from far away, Phoebe stood up. "What's that noise, Jake?"

He paused and listened. "It sounds like guns."

She caught her breath. Her fears were being realized. "Guns? Are the Yankees coming here?"

"No, no, it's far away. We're safe."

He returned to his digging and she to filling her basket, but she jumped every time another boom sounded.

They later heard that the Americans had burned Fort Erie.

"See," said Jake. "I told you it was far away."

"Not so far, Jake, if they're on this side of the river. What can we do?"

"Vati said the Yankee soldiers are staying by the fort, close. It will be all right." The next afternoon, Jake was carrying a bag of potatoes from the field to store in the cellar when he saw Vati turning in the lane. He dropped the sack and ran to where Simon had collapsed on the doorstep.

"Vati. What's the matter? You look tired to death. Are you sick? Why are you walking?" He dropped down and put his arm around his vati's shoulders, an unusual gesture. "What is it? What is wrong?"

Simon rubbed his hand over his head and beard, as if trying to collect his thoughts.

"The Yankees came yesterday," he said.

"Oh, no! Is everyone all right?"

"Jah, except Peter. He's hurt, some."

239

"Hurt? How? Vati! Tell me."

"It's not so bad, now. He was like dead until suppertime and then when he waked up such a terrible ache in the head." Simon clasped his hands to either side of his own head. "And no sense in his talking. Today he's better, and so."

"But what happened? Tell me from the start." Jake tried to curb his impatience.

Simon took a deep breath, then began, "The soldiers came. Marched right in as if they owned the place, just, and chased the cattle and horses into the road. Well, Peter, you know how he jumps in without thinking what he does, ran out shouting to them to stop. A proper Mennonite I don't think he will ever be." Simon shook his head. "One of the soldiers hit him on the head with his gun butt. He fell down right away. I ran to help him. The soldier said, 'Stand back' but I went anyhow. The man lifted his gun. He saw I was going to my boy, not to attack him, already. He went away to help drive the animals." Simon bent low over his knees as if he were feeling faint.

Jake waited impatiently for him to continue. When Simon straightened up again, Jake said, "They took all the cattle?"

"Yah, and the horses. Karl's too. There's nothing left." He spread his hands. "Nothing but two little calves. We will have to butcher them. There's no milk for them any more."

"Why you?"

"Not just us. Everybody. And even over in the Short Hills. All the cattle and horses gone. They even killed some people, there, who tried to stop them."

"Are the soldiers still around?"

"No, they went right away with the cattle and horses. I've got to get back, though, and see if Peter is all right."

"I'll take you home. You can't walk so far again."

"That will help. Thank you."

"Don't thank. You are my vati." Jake harnessed the team, took a ham from the smokehouse and put it in the back of the wagon. "What else do you need?"

Simon rubbed his hand over his beard. "I don't know. I haven't had time to think, yet."

"Come, then."

Jake turned to Danny. "I'll be late, back. Take care of the chores.."

"I will."

Phoebe came home late in the afternoon from the Steadman's where she'd been helping Abigail peel apples for drying.

Benjy met her at the door. "Vati's gone to take Grossvati home."

She looked at Danny. "Why would he have to be taken home?"

Benjy, obviously full of importance at his news, broke in before Danny could answer. "The soldiers came and took all their cows and horses. Grossvati walked all the way here to tell us."

Well, it was bad news, but the same thing had happened here. The militia captain was grabbing everything he could.

"What did he think Jake could do about it? They took cattle from us, too." She was a little irritated. Jake had troubles enough of his own.

"No! No!" said Danny. "It was the Yankees came to Grossvati's. And hit Peter and took the horses, too."

Yankees! They weren't staying by the river as Jake's father had said. How soon would they come here? What could she do? Where could they go? She vividly remembered the rebels coming in the middle of the night and burning her home in Haventown during the revolution. The same thing could happen here. Her heart beat so fast it made her temples ache. She took deep breaths to calm herself. This was no time to go to pieces.

When Jake came home, long after the children were in bed, she voiced her fear.

"It's all right, Phee. The Yankees won't come this far."

"How do you know?" Phoebe twisted her hands in her apron. "Vati said that, too, before."

"Vati said he heard the British are sending more soldiers. The Yankees will soon be forced across the river, back, and we will be safe. They're saying the war will soon be over."

"I wish I could believe that."

"Believe it. That's all we can do.

"Anyhow, we have to help Vati right now," he continued. "I thought we should give them a cow, and the young sow I intended to keep."

"Did they take Mutti's hens? I could give her some."

"Jah, they take everything." He lifted his shoulders and let them fall.

"We could give them Dolly—and her heifer calf. That would start them on a herd again. We must help."

"Jah, so."

Simon remonstrated when they offered the stock, but Phoebe said, "You helped us start. Now we are paying back."

"Bless you, Phoebe," said Simon, his voice breaking. "You are a good daughter."

Her eyes filled at his words. Finally it seemed he approved of her.

A few days later, as they prepared to move the stock to Simon's, they heard the sound of guns to the west, as well as towards Niagara. Were they caught between two American forces? Surely they were in danger. Sharing the stock was a waste of time.

"Well, they need some milk and eggs right now, anyway," said Jake. "We just have to wait and see what happens."

When Archie came home, he said the noise they heard to the west came from a big battle on the lake.

Jake was skeptical. "We could hear it so far away, over the water?"

"That's what they say," replied Archie. "The bad part is the Yankees won, so they own the lake now. I don't know how we'll get provisions to our troops at Amherstburg. We can't go on the lake without being attacked."

CHAPTER 40

Jake drew deep breaths of the crisp air as he worked in the west field. The horses were fresh, and stepping out smartly. The day before, he'd broadcast part of the wheat seed he'd hidden from the grasping captain. Now he was covering it with the harrows, pulled by Tim and Tom.

As he turned the horses at the end of the field, he saw the militia captain standing at the other end. What does he want now? I haven't anything left for him to take.

Cold chills ran up his back at the wheat seeds lying on top of the ground in the unharrowed part of the field. Was that why the captain was here? Had someone told him that he was planting wheat? What would he do? Another fine—or jail—for not giving up all the wheat crop?

The horses pulled strongly and he followed, heart thudding. He stopped at the end of the row. What excuse could he give for keeping the seed grain. Perhaps he could plead the need to provide food for the army.

The captain said, "We're requisitioning all the teams and wagons to take provisions to General Proctor at Amherstburg. You'll be paid two shillings per day for you, your team and wagon. Report to the depot at six o'clock tomorrow morning with enough supplies to keep yourself and your horses for two weeks."

"But I can't leave. Who will look after my farm?"

The captain waved towards Danny who was wheeling manure out of the stable. "Yon lad looks capable."

Leave fourteen-year-old Danny to finish harrowing the wheat seed in, cut the corn and start the fall plowing? Impossible.

"I can't help it if the army needs help. I can't leave."

The captain scowled.

"Well, unfortunately I can't force you to go, but I'm authorized to take your team." He stepped forward and seized Tom's bridle.

Jake thought his heart had stopped beating. Then it gave a great lurch and he took a deep breath. "You can't. You can't take them. How will I get my crop in? If I don't, there won't be any food for the army—or anybody."

"You can keep the old ones." The captain gestured at the other team, peacefully grazing in the nearby pasture.

"They're too old. They don't work any more." Well, they did, but only light work.

The soldier tipped his head in the direction of the pasture. "I see they still walk—and eat. They can do your work well enough. We have to get supplies to General Proctor. He's cut off, now the Yankees control the lake. I'm taking this team."

"Not Tim and Tom. Oh, no, you can't do that." Jake gripped the reins tighter.

"Oh, yes I can." The officer grinned maliciously and jerked Tom's bridle.

Tom stepped sideways, narrowly missing the soldier's foot. The captain jerked the bridle again. "Whoa there."

Jake thought, that's how he would treat them, for sure.

He said, "I won't let you."

"Hah! How will you stop me? You're still a Yankee I'm thinking. You'd like to see the spalpeens win." He looked across the field at the uncovered seed. "I'll let you finish the harrowing, but deliver this team and a wagon to headquarters in the morning or you'll be cooling your heels in the jailhouse. It'd be a pleasure to see you in there. You'd better be at the depot in the morning. Early!"

He swaggered off toward the road, pointing his thumb back over his shoulder toward Tim and Tom, "With them, or it'll be jail for you."

Jake couldn't let the army take his beautiful team. He regretted the show he'd made of them. Mutti had always warned him about the sin of pride, but he hadn't listened. And now see what he'd brought on himself.

When he came in to dinner, Phoebe sensed something wrong. "What's the matter?"

"The militia man wants to take Tim and Tom to haul supplies to Amherstburg. I can't let them go. I don't know what to do."

She was fond of the horses but couldn't see a great problem. As she set a bowl of squash, glistening with butter, on the table in front of him, she squeezed his shoulder. "Horses come and go, Jake. It's not like losing family. My father traded our beautiful Narragansett pacers for the Conestoga team on the way from Haventown. I was sad to lose them, but I got to like the new ones almost as much. You'll survive."

"It's not the same. I raised Tim and Tom from babies. They're like my family."

"I had to let William go." Her eyes filled with tears. "What are horses in comparison to him?"

"It was his choice. It's not the team's."

"I know how much you cherish them, but you can't do anything about it."

He finished harrowing the field and did the chores, worrying the whole time. How could he save his team? Finally he made his decision. The barn work finished, he took a grain sack to the house and began to pack it with clothes and food.

Phoebe came downstairs from saying goodnight to Katy and Benjy and looked into the sack. "Whatever are you doing?"

He took her arm and set her down on the settle. Swinging the slat back chair around, he sat astride the seat facing her, leaning his arms on the chair back,. "Listen to me. I have to go with the horses."

"But why do you need to take clothes and food? It's only a few miles to the depot."

"I mean I have to go to Amherstburg."

"Jake! What are you thinking?" Realizing her mouth was hanging open, she closed it with a click, then said, "You'd leave your family for the sake of two horses? I don't believe it."

"You'll be all right. I have to take care of my horses. It will be only for two weeks, about."

This was a mad idea. "Archie will be going. Can't he watch out for them?"

"No, he'll be with the soldiers. I'll just be taking stuff. I won't have to fight or anything. I'll be in no danger."

"Then neither will the horses."

"You don't understand. Somebody might abuse them. I've seen carters beat horses some terrible."

"How do you know we'll be all right? Jake! What if the Yankees come here? Who'll protect us?"

"The Yankees won't come. Archie says our soldiers are winning here."

"What about the crops? Think what you're doing." She twisted her hands in her apron.

"I won't be long away. Danny can manage for a short while."

"Danny? He can't do the work of both of you. Especially with the harvest not finished."

"He's strong as I am and he knows how. Anyway, I'll be back so quick you won't know I've gone."

"You're determined to do this?"

"I can't help it. I have to look after my horses. And the army will pay me for going, the captain said. Two shillings a day."

She jumped to her feet. "Two shillings! A few coins and a team are worth more to you than your family. If you ever get the shillings. Archie said he hadn't been paid all summer. Well, go then." She stormed into the living room, her heels echoing on the bare floor. "You care more about your horses than us." Abstracted, she poked at the fire.

He followed her. "That's not so, Phee." He put his arm around her but she shrugged him off. "It's only, the horses, they can't take care of themselves."

She dropped the poker, ran into the bedroom and slammed the door. He remained by the fire for some time, trying to find another solution to his problem. Why couldn't she understand? The horses were helpless animals dependent on his care. She and Danny were quite capable of looking after things here. Archie said the British forces were keeping the Yankees close to the river, now, so there was no danger. He didn't want to go but, as he saw it, he had no choice.

Thank goodness the soldier hadn't made a fuss about the wheat seeds. He might now be in jail and the horses gone, anyway—without him.

When he went to bed, Phoebe refused to speak and lay with her back to him throughout the sleepless night.

In the morning he looked so miserable she was tempted to make up their quarrel, but she couldn't agree to his decision to abandon them. The children hung on his neck and cried when they found out he was leaving. Let him go with his precious horses.

"I'll be back, quick, Phee. There's no danger."

Maybe not to you. She didn't share his belief that the Yankees would stay away.

"I just have to go there and come back. It's no different than going to Fort Erie, except a little longer. I wouldn't go if I thought there was any danger to you."

"I wish I believed that."

"Believe it, Phee. I love you." He bent to kiss her, but she turned her head and the kiss landed on her ear.

Rebuffed, he turned toward the children. "Goodbye. I won't be long away. Benjy, Katy, mind what Mutti says. Annie help your mutti. I know you will. Take care of things, Danny—and Mutti."

"I will, Vati." Danny squared his shoulders.

As he disappeared around the bend in the road, the team, minus their bells, trotting along at a good rate, Phoebe was tempted to call him back. She resisted the impulse. He preferred his horses to his family. Let him go.

As the days passed, she found the evenings long and her bed lonely and regretted her treatment of him. She shouldn't have let him go away like that. She hadn't known she would miss him so much. This was the first time they'd been separated for so much as a night. She felt as if she'd lost an arm or something. Somehow, in their almost twenty years together they'd become melded into one person. Well, she'd make it up to him when he came back. Two weeks was not so very long and almost half of it was already past. He was a good man. Taking William, and Hedwig, and treating them like his own. A good father to his own children. Why had she let him go in anger? It seemed like she had to lose something in order to appreciate it.

Danny worked early and late but couldn't keep up with the work. Two more weeks went by and Jake didn't return. The corn ripened and should be cut and shocked but Danny couldn't handle that alone. Should she ask the neighbors for help? She hated to admit that Jake had apparently abandoned her for his horses. While she wondered what to do, Karl and Rebecca came to visit one Sunday afternoon.

Katy met them at the door. Filled with importance she said, "Vati's gone to the war."

"What?" said Karl and Rebecca together.

Phoebe was glad to see them. She invited them in and, when they were settled in the parlor as befitted Sunday visitors, explained Jake's absence.

Karl, obviously exasperated with his brother, said, "What he was thinking of, I don't know. To leave his family for a horse, two even. He is not right in the head, I think so. But we will see to it, the corn."

"But I don't understand why he hasn't come home," said Phoebe with a catch in her voice. "I-I'm afraid something has happened to him."

Rebecca put her arm around her. "I'm sure he's all right."

"I hope so."

Karl, Danny and Benjy went out to see what needed to be done. Rebecca and Phoebe settled down for a chat over cups of tea. Annie and Katy had gone over to visit Hedwig and the baby.

Rebecca picked up her teacup and inhaled the fragrant steam. "Mmmm. That smells good." She sipped, then said, "How long has he been gone?"

"Almost four weeks and he said it would be two. I'm so afraid."

"Well, that's not so much longer than he said. Probably he's delayed or it was farther than he knew. Or maybe they gave him work, there."

"Oh, I hope you're right. If there was a chance to earn some money he wouldn't hesitate to stay. The worst of it is I was so angry at him I didn't give him a proper goodbye." She sniffed, trying to hold back the tears that threatened. "I don't know how I could be so mean."

"You can make it up special when he comes back." Rebecca smiled with a wicked glint in her eyes.

"Rebecca!"

Rebecca chuckled.

That Rebecca. She was irrepressible. "Oh, I feel so much better. Of course it was farther than he knew. He'll be back any day. Well, I'd better start supper."

She felt much relieved after sharing her worries with family, and even managed smiles at the teasing between Danny and Rebecca around the supper table.

As they savored the spicy pumpkin pie made from new harvested pumpkins, she said, "Karl, I don't think there's any need for you to come to cut the corn. Jake will surely be back any day."

Karl helped himself to another slice of pie, "You're a good cook, Phoebe."

Karl was a man of few words and any compliment was to be cherished. She appreciated that.

He continued, "He'll likely be tired, anyhow. It's a long way. We come."

The very next day the Stettl men arrived armed with sickles.

The corn stalks were cut and set up in shocks, the pumpkins stored in the corner of the stable for winter cattle feed as well as pies, and the squash piled in the cellar. Enough turnips and carrots to last them until Christmas were buried in sand in the cellar to keep them from shriveling. Karl dug a pit in the garden and laid a thick layer of straw in the bottom to absorb any moisture that might leak in. The rest of the turnips and carrots were put in and a heavy layer of straw put over the top to keep out the frost.

Phoebe and Annie spent two days chopping cabbages for sauerkraut. The men butchered the pigs and the women cured the shoulders, hams and side meat with maple sugar and salt and pepper, and these were hung in the attic.

Phoebe surveyed these along with the well-filled pickle and jam crocks and felt ready to face the winter.

As he prepared to leave, Simon said, "Peter, you better stay. Danny needs some help."

Peter said, "Jah, I thought so. I brought my clothes."

"So that's what was in the gunny sack," said Karl.

Peter grinned.

Phoebe protested she didn't want to impose on them for her husband's stupidity.

"Stupid it is," said Simon. "He is my son, though, so we help. Peter, you do it good. Not so much joking, please."

"I'm not a child."

"Sometimes you act it, though."

Fall plowing went forward speedily with Peter's help. Thank goodness for Peter. His jokes and cheerfulness lightened the gloomy atmosphere.

Benjy and Katy kept asking where Vati was and why he didn't come home. How could she answer them? What had happened to him? He must be working there as Rebecca had suggested. It had to be that. She wouldn't consider anything else.

As the first flakes of snow drifted down, troops straggled home from Amherstburg with tales of defeat.

One afternoon, as Phoebe came out of the hen-house carrying a basket of eggs, she saw a man coming in the lane riding a black horse and leading another. Jake! Jake was home.

No, it wasn't Jake. It was Archie. What was he doing with Jake's horses? She set down the basket and ran, calling, "Where's Jake?"

Archie, his uniform filthy and he obviously exhausted, slipped off the horse's back and sank down on the doorstep, dropping the horses' reins. They, equally worn out, simply stood, heads low.

Peter and Danny hurried from the field where they'd been plowing.

Danny shouted, "Where's Vati?"

Archie ran his hands over his face as if to gather energy. "I don't know. I seen the horses wandering loose after the battle at Moraviantown and recognized them. I looked everywhere for Jake but no one knew where he was. One man said he hadn't seen him since they left Amherstburg."

Danny said, "Then how did the horses get to Moraviantown?"

"I don't know. I couldn't find anybody who knew how they got there. The carters were all headin' for home."

"Then Jake could be anywhere between Amherstburg and Moraviantown," said Peter.

"If he's still alive," said Archie.

Danny choked, then said. "He wouldn't ever leave Tim and Tom. He must be..."

"No, no, I don't want to think so—my brother," said Peter.

Phoebe couldn't take it in. Here were Jake's horses, apparently sound, but he was...where? It wasn't right. She'd gladly sacrifice the horses for even a word of him. He couldn't be.... She mustn't even think the word. He was lying injured somewhere. Somewhere along that long wilderness road. And with the Yankees in control, she couldn't go looking. She could only hope some settler was caring for him.

Archie, thin and hollow-eyed, was seething. "That General Proctor. What a coward. He wouldn't fight at all. There was an Indian chief there called Tecumseh. If he'd been leading us we would've driven the damn Yankees back across the river in no time. But Proctor kept retreating until Tecumseh persuaded him to fight at Moraviantown. And then Tecumseh got killed, and that was the end of it. Proctor just quit and ran all the way back here." He threw up his arms and let them fall in disgust.

Phoebe clenched her hands. Not only was Jake missing, but now they were in danger themselves. "Are the Yankees coming here?"

Archie shook his head. "Probably not, but who knows? Their supply lines must be pretty thin. They're a long way from Detroit." He brightened a little. "If we had a general who was any good we could drive them back there before they get settled. But not Proctor. He's scared of his own shadow."

"Well, at least you're home safe," said Danny.

"Yes. I must go and tell Hedwig and Ma. I have to go back right away. They only gave me leave to bring the horses home." He got to his feet, stretched, and limped off.

Phoebe called after him. "Thank you for bringing the horses."

He waved without turning and continued down the road.

Danny took hold of the horses' bridles. "Come on. I'll give you some oats and a good currying. Poor boys. You've had a hard time. I wish you could tell us where you've been and what happened to Vati."

He led the horses away, Peter following.

Phoebe agreed. She didn't want to believe she'd never see dear Jake again but why wasn't he with his team ? As Danny said, he'd never leave them. She choked back tears. She had to believe he was still alive somewhere. Her job was to take care of things for him and keep the family's spirits up. She squared her shoulders.

But what if the Yankees came here? How could she protect her family? Could they make a fort of the stone house? No. The big windows she loved would be no barrier to soldiers. She had no weapons but pitchforks and axes. No defense against guns. They were helpless. If the Yankees had beaten the army there was no hope for the settlers, or for Jake.

Ruth Zavitz

CHAPTER 41

Phoebe noticed the concern in Peter's eyes every time he looked at her, and was grateful for his attention. He was as different from Jake as a brother could be, small where Jake was huge, lively where Jake was quiet. Still, it was good to have him here. His antics made them all laugh in spite of their worry. He acted like a child, though. Lovable, but needing to be watched.

One day in the cornfield, waving his arms about wildly as he told the children some long tale, he cut his hand on the sickle he forgot he held. As she bound the cut he said, "Good thing it is my left hand, so, or I wouldn't be able to feed myself."

Another day, coming out of the barnyard, he pulled the gate shut but neglected to throw the loop of rope attached to it, over the fence post to keep it closed. The white-faced cow, always curious, nudged the gate open far enough for the herd to escape and troop down to the cornfield, where they tore apart a number of shocks before Danny noticed and herded them back. Peter promised to be more careful, but soon became his merry joking self again.

While exasperated at his heedless behavior, she couldn't help responding to his good nature. She welcomed a little relief from her heavy responsibilities and worry over Jake.

Days and weeks passed. One Saturday, cleaning their bedroom, she took down Jake's good suit from its peg behind the door intending to shake the dust out of it. A faint essence of Jake rose as she disturbed its folds. She pressed her nose into the material. The rest of her life without Jake? Surely if he'd been wounded he'd recover and return to them. How happy she'd be to have him back. Archie's tales of soldiers buried in unmarked graves in the forest made her feel sick. Had that been Jake's fate?

Was she some kind of evil spirit? All the men important in her life had died: her father, Uncle Edward, Richard, William, and now maybe Jake, but, please, not Jake.

255

A deep fall of snow announced the arrival of winter. Was Jake somewhere warm? If only she knew where he was she could send him some winter clothes. She felt so helpless.

Benjy and Katy were looking forward to Christmas. She couldn't generate any enthusiasm, formerly one of her favorite times of the year. Without Jake it would be too sad. Still, the young people deserved to have it recognized.

Hannah and Simon had always hosted the family gathering, but this year Christmas was more complicated. Hedwig didn't want to make the long trip with the baby in the cold and Archie, of course, wanted to spend the time with his own family.

Now that she had reconciled with Hedwig, Phoebe didn't want to exclude her any more. She gathered all her strength and invited all the clan to the stone house. Perhaps preparing for the feast would take her mind off her worries over Jake. Besides it would be terrible if he came home when they were away at Simon's.

Gingerbread cookies and fruitcakes perfumed the kitchen for days. Dozens and dozens of pfeffernusse nuggets were stored away in stone crocks.

Danny came home from a day-long hunting trip with a pair of wild turkeys. Along with a ham, that should be enough meat.

Of course Peter managed to split his thumb with the hammer while hanging up garlands, and she had to wipe the flour from her hands to bandage it for him.

Finally preparations were complete. Only Jake was missing— and Archie, who hadn't been able to get leave. It would be a sad Christmas.

On Christmas Day they gathered around the massive mahogany dining table, Simon and Hannah, Karl and Rebecca and their daughter Charity, Hedwig and the baby, as well as the home folks.

Phoebe, unable to face Jake's empty chair said, "Vati Stettl will you sit at the head, say the blessing and carve?"

Simon looked at her, bowed and said, "If you wish, Phoebe." He stood behind the chair his gnarled hands on the back and bowed his head. When everyone stood by their chairs he said, for Simon, an eloquent grace asking for God's care of the absent ones. Then he took Jake's place.

Phoebe almost lost her hard-won control and there were sniffles around her. No one looked to see who'd lost their composure, but Hannah blew her nose noisily and Hedwig cleared her throat.

The baby, who'd been given the nickname Phee-Phee to distinguish her from her grossmutti, refused to let go of the corn-husk doll she'd found in her shoe that morning. She alternately chewed it and the food Hedwig fed her, until it turned into a sodden lump.

After the remnants of food were put away and the dishes washed, they gathered in the parlor.

"I did all the decorations myself," bragged Katy.

"Did you now?" said Hannah.

Phoebe was about to reprimand her daughter for boasting, when Phee-Phee spied a straw-filled shoe on the hearth. Recognizing its possibilities from her experience that morning, she squealed. Straw flew everywhere as she unearthed a tight-wound yarn ball that Annie had made for her.

She crawled about the floor, the doll still clutched in one hand, retrieving the ball that the grownups threw for her, until everyone but she was tired of the game. If it hadn't been for the baby it would have been more like a wake than a festival.

In between, the grownups exchanged their own presents: Hand-knitted socks and mittens and toques. Tears threatened Phoebe again when she thought of the sweater, stored away in the chest in their bedroom. She'd spent all her spare time this fall knitting it for Jake. Would he ever wear it?

Danny had made a boot scraper for Peter. This elicited hoots of laughter, for Peter was notorious for forgetting to wipe his boots when he came into the house.

"So," said Simon. "It takes a boy to teach my man-son how to do."

"Don't scold," said Phoebe. "Peter has been a great help."

"I hope so," said Simon, but he frowned.

After an early supper of leftovers, the visitors prepared for home.

Hannah went out to the sleigh and Simon turned to Phoebe standing in the doorway, "Keep your heart up, daughter. Our Jake is a hard man to kill, and so."

Once again she choked back tears. How often had she done that this day? And how kind of taciturn Simon to try and give her hope. Did he really believe it?

She and Annie were alone in the kitchen cleaning up the pots and pans after their guests had left, when Annie suddenly burst into tears.

"It wa—wasn't a real Christmas without Vati. He always made it such fun."

She hugged the girl and they cried together. Jake had been their sun and there would be nothing but cloudy days from now on if he didn't return.

Archie came home again, jubilant, and he and Hedwig came over to the Stettls'.

Archie said, "We captured Fort Niagara back again and then we went across the river at Fort Erie and burned Black Rock and Buffalo. Nothing left there. That'll teach the Yankees to mess with us." Archie exulted, but Phoebe could only think of the lives that had been lost.

"The war will soon be over," said Archie.

Hedwig hooked her arm through his. "Never too soon for me." Phoebe saw the loving look exchanged between them, and her heart ached for her own loss.

Lack of action over the winter seemed to prove Archie's belief, but it was too late for William—and maybe Jake. Evenings around the Stettl hearth were jolly, the children laughing at Peter's jokes and silliness. Phoebe found herself joining in, despite her continued worry over Jake. She wasn't sure just when she first noticed Peter's looks of concern had changed to something warmer. Well, he was just trying to cheer her up.

The winter's snowdrifts melted away in the spring sunshine and still there was no word. Phoebe couldn't muster her usual delight when spring displaced the dreary, frigid winter. Jake had been gone over six months. He'd said two weeks. If he was gone forever could she and the children survive without him?

Still, she took pride in her ability to manage in his absence. All her life she'd looked for someone to take care of her, but now she found that she was capable of taking charge. Except for Peter's lapses, the farm work went on in an orderly fashion. She decided which fields would be sown to oats and corn. She scolded Peter for turning the cattle out before checking the fences and sent him, that very day, to make sure they were livestock-proof.

Seeding finished, the Karl Stettls came on a Sunday visit.

Karl uncharacteristically burst into the house, shouting, "Jake's home? I saw the horses in the pasture. Where is he?"

"You didn't see them when you were here at Christmas?" asked Phoebe. "Archie found them after the battle at Moraviantown."

"No Jake?"

"No Jake, and no sign of him."

"He must have got hurt," said Rebecca. "I hope someone is taking good care of him, wherever he is."

Karl shook his head. "He wouldn't leave his horses if there was any breath in his body. I'm afraid the worst has happened."

He was probably right, but still Phoebe couldn't give up hope.

A bounteous dinner raised their spirits and later around a blazing hearth in the still cool afternoon, conversation turned to farming concerns.

Karl said, "I cut a whole bunch of logs this winter. I've been drawing them up to the yard for a new barn but it's slow work with just the one team. Vati's are too old for such heavy work, though Vati says he's still young enough for it." He chuckled. "I want to build it before haying. It's a big crop this year, I think, and I need the room to store it."

Peter said. "We could lend you Tim and Tom, couldn't we, Phoebe? We don't need them just yet."

"Of course. We can get along with the old team until haying starts."

Later in the afternoon the Karl Stettls set off for home with Tim and Tom tied behind the wagon.

Phoebe felt anxious, seeing the horses go. They were a link with Jake.

CHAPTER 42

Phoebe stood on the doorstep and surveyed her domain. The straight lines of green shoots filling the garden pleased her. Peter and Danny were loading the last of the hay in the west field. They'd better hurry. Sooty clouds were creeping in from the west.

The sound of Benjy's ax echoed from the wood-yard behind the house. The rattle of crockery indicated the girls were busy in the kitchen. Everything was as it should be. Jake would have been proud of her. But would he ever see what she'd accomplished?

She wiped away a tear as she picked up the broom. The children mustn't see her crying. They still believed their vati would return. She swept away the sparrow droppings from under the nest in the rafters—and mud left by the men's boots.

As she swept, she considered the future. Peter now lived with them but this wasn't his home. What if he decided to marry? Or return home? He did go back when a large job required his help, but one of these times he might decide to stay there.

What could she do then? Though willing, she didn't think Danny could manage, alone, the flourishing farm he and Jake had built together. Benjy, though a good worker when he felt like it, was unreliable and hadn't grown into his full strength yet. She stopped sweeping the stoop and stared down the road where Jake had disappeared eight months ago. Then it had been dry and dusty; now it was muddy and rutted.

Jake, where are you? Please come home. We need you. I love you.

But no figure appeared on the empty road. She turned back into the kitchen to check on Annie and Katy who were preparing dinner.

As she was setting the table, Benjy came running in. "Ma, soldiers are coming down the road."

"Soldiers? Would Jake be with them?" She hurried to the door, her heart pounding. They were still far off. But definitely soldiers. Not in formal military formation but walking more or less in step.

Peter drove the hay wagon across the field to the lane fence and tied the horses to the rails. He and Danny joined her and Benjy as they watched the men approach.

A hawk screeched overhead. Danny looked up, shielding his eyes against the sun, then pointed. "Look! There's smoke at Anselm's. See? Over the trees. Too much smoke for a grass fire. Come, Uncle Peter. Their house or barn must be on fire. We'd better go and help."

"No, stay here," said Phoebe.

Something about the soldiers didn't look right. Peter must have thought so, too, or he wouldn't have stopped work. But he hadn't said anything. She looked at him and saw a muscle jumping in his cheek. Fear clamped her stomach.

She stepped out into the yard, Peter and the children clustered around her. As the soldiers came nearer, she shivered. They wore blue jackets, not the militia green or British red. Yankees! She counted. Twenty, and an officer in a different uniform at the front. They were laughing and shouting, even the officer. He didn't seem to be controlling his men. Her hand flew to her throat. What were they doing here?

Two of the soldiers knelt in the lane. Their guns roared. She ducked, pulling Benjy and Katy down, then realized the men were not shooting at her and the children. Horrified, she saw the old team raise their heads, then stumble and fall, thrashing their feet.

Katy screamed, "What are they doing? Why did they shoot our horses?"

Phoebe put her arm around her. "Hush. I don't know. Just keep quiet."

The invaders tramped into the yard. They looked overexcited, some of them even acted crazed, jumping around and waving their guns carelessly. Will they shoot us, too? She felt Annie trembling beside her. Danny stepped toward the men. Phoebe grabbed his arm and pulled him back. She shook her head at Peter who, although white-faced, moved forward.

"Don't antagonize them." It looked as if the soldiers were eager to use their weapons.

Several of the men carried lighted torches. Their faces and uniforms were smeared with something black. Why did they have torches in the daytime? Of course. The smoke she'd seen. They were burning the farms. They'd come to burn hers. How could she stop them?

One man, his full black beard making him appear even more villainous than the others, pointed his gun toward the little group, as if to warn them.

The officer said, "O'Hara, stay here and make sure they don't interfere."

"Yes, sir." Black Beard grinned at them, as evil-looking a man as she'd ever seen.

The rest continued on toward the barn. The torchbearers disappeared in the door. The others stood guard outside. She smelled hay burning. Tendrils of white smoke crept out between the logs and then between the roof shingles. The torchbearers came out, shouting and dancing. The old cabins were set afire in like fashion.

She cried, "Oh, Peter, the calves. They'll burn up."

He started toward the cabins, Danny following, but Black Beard pointed his gun at them and snarled, "Get back, or I'll shoot."

Phoebe clapped hands to her cheeks. "Come back! They mean it. Oh dear, the poor things."

Soon the sickening smell of scorched hair, burning flesh and feathers drifted across the yard. As the confined animals bawled, screeched and squawked, She swallowed and swallowed. She must not be sick in front of the children. She put her arms around the girls. The boys and Peter crowded close. Smoke eddied out the doors, and flames licked at the edges of the shingles. Soon flames burst out everywhere and the soldiers shouted in triumph.

Annie suddenly turned aside and vomited. Phoebe swallowed hard to keep from following her example. Katy's kitten came running out of the barn, meowing piteously, its tail blazing. One of the men clubbed it with his rifle butt, sending its lifeless body sailing into the currant bushes. Katy screamed and hid her face in her mother's skirt. At least the kitten wouldn't suffer more.

The soldiers turned their attention to the cattle in the east field.

"Bet you I can hit that black and white one," shouted one soldier, sighting down his gun barrel.

"Naw, you can't. It's too far."

Bets were laid and the first soldier took aim and fired. Blackie sank to her knees, then rolled over. "See, I told ya. Pay up."

Phoebe gasped. Her best milk cow.

The men rushed into the field pursuing the spooked cattle. All the beasts were slaughtered, some by gunfire, some by bayonets. Molly had run for the bush but, trapped by the snake rail fence, been slaughtered with the rest. When all the cattle lay on the ground, some still, some quivering, the invaders headed back to the house.

Peter stepped forward, apparently intending to bar their way. Phoebe reached out her hand but too late to stop him. Black Beard swung his rifle butt. It thudded against the side of Peter's head. He dropped to the ground without a sound.

"Don't any of the rest of youse move or you'll get the same," growled the soldier. He disappeared through the kitchen door. The rest of the raiders scowled at the little group, waved their weapons menacingly, and followed him into the house.

The clatter of broken crockery and splintering wood mixed with the jubilant yells of the soldiers.

Phoebe knelt beside Peter, calling his name and patting his cheek, flinching at every new crash echoing inside the house. She felt for a pulse and was reassured at its steady beat.

"Annie, bring some water," she said. "Peter's head is bleeding."

Annie had anticipated the request and was already hurrying back from the pump with the overflowing dipper.

Phoebe wetted the corner of her apron and used it to bathe the cut on Peter's head. She kept talking to him. But he didn't respond.

Danny shook his uncle's arm. "Uncle Peter. Uncle Peter. Wake up."

Peter's eyes flickered, and then slowly opened. He groaned.

"He's all right," murmured Annie. "Oh, thank goodness. I was so afraid."

"Ooooh, my head." Peter raised one hand to his forehead. His eyes widened. "I smell smoke. Something's on fire." He stirred as if to rise, then sank back with another groan.

"Lie still," said Phoebe, pressing him to the ground. "The Yankee soldier hit you."

"What's that noise?"

Annie answered, her voice rising. "It's the soldiers. They're in the house. They're breaking everything."

Peter struggled to sit up. "I must stop them."

"No, no, lie still." Phoebe pushed him down. "Listen. I think they're coming out. Keep still. You can't do anything. They'll kill you."

The officer appeared in the doorway, shouting over his shoulder, "Come on, boys. On to the next. We have to get back to the boats before sundown."

The soldiers came out, whooping. Some were wolfing down chunks of her new-baked bread and the biscuits Annie had baked yesterday. They were laughing and joking between bites, except for two who were tussling over a bake pan containing a ham.

"That'll teach you to make war on your neighbors," shouted one of the men as they tramped out to the road in a ragged file.

Make war? What did they mean? They invaded us. Well, it didn't matter. The result was the same.

"Ma! The house is on fire," shouted Danny.

She rushed to the kitchen door and looked inside. The men had piled the broken furniture in the middle of the floor and set it alight.

She turned to the children. "Quick, the milk pails. Annie, pump!"

Annie grabbed the pails from the wash bench by the kitchen wall and ran to the well.

Peter tried to get to his feet. Then his eyes rolled up and he collapsed to the ground again. Torn between going to tend him or putting out the fire, she straightened out the leg that had twisted under him when he fell. He still breathed. She left him and hurried to the well where Annie frantically pumped.

She and Danny carried the filled pails into the house and threw the water on the fire. Benjy carried the empty pails back to Annie for refills.

The acrid smell of smoke and wet wood made them choke, but they persisted. Soon they'd reduced the blaze enough to grab unburned ends of smoldering furniture fragments and drag them out into the yard.

When she was sure the fire was out, she sank down on the door-stone, her legs suddenly unable to support her. Danny leaned against the house wall, apparently in like condition. Annie went to Peter, helping him to sit up, but he made no further attempt to stand. All of them choked and coughed as smoke from the burning barns swirled around them.

Katy cowered beside the fence, sobbing hysterically. Phoebe opened her arms and the little girl ran to her. "It's all over, Katy. There, now. We're all right."

"My-my kitty i—isn't," sobbed Katy.

She hugged her daughter closer. What could she say?

The barn still blazed, smoke rising high into the cloudy sky. Why didn't the neighbors come? Surely they could see the smoke. Neighbors always turned out to fight fires.

She looked up and down the road to see if anyone was hurrying to their aid and saw distant columns of smoke rising above the trees. The whole community was being destroyed.

The hay crop was burning with the barn. There'd be nothing to feed the cattle and horses over winter—or house them. Then she realized no livestock remained to feed or house. What was the matter with her? She couldn't seem to get her thoughts together.

The heavy gray clouds now fulfilled their promise. Rain fell. The cold drops revived her. She got to her feet. "We'd better see if anything is left inside." She stepped through the door. Danny helped Peter to his feet and half carried him into the house, the others following.

The kitchen was a shambles, the air still cloudy and reeking of smoke. A charred ring in the middle of the floor showed where the fire had been. Danny stepped gingerly on the blackened planks, then more firmly. "It seems to be solid, yet," he said.

Shards of broken pottery and utensils, mixed with the cornmeal the men had emptied from its sack, covered the rest of the floor. The flour barrel still stood in its corner, although the cover had been removed. She looked in it and gagged at the brown stinking mess nestled in its white depths. She quickly replaced the lid and turned away. What animals!

In the dining room, the great mahogany table had resisted the soldiers' efforts to destroy it, but showed slashes and scrapes. The chairs were kindling. The china dishes that Jake had brought her so proudly from Fort Erie, were smashed and trodden into the carpet.

Dazed, the little group continued their tour. All the drawers had been removed from the bureau in the hall, the contents strewn about but the drawers mercifully undamaged. Upstairs, in Phoebe's bedroom, the mattress and pillows had been slashed open and drifts of straw and feathers lay about. All her undergarments and her best dress lay among them, patterned with the outlines of dusty, sooty boots. Jake's good suit was missing. She hadn't seen who took it. Her tiny mirror, the only one in the house, lay in shards on the floor beside the upended storage chest.

The other rooms were the same. Someone, or several someones, had jumped on the bed Peter and Danny shared, breaking the sides. The ends leaned drunkenly toward each other.

They surveyed the damage in silence, beyond speech. Phoebe led the way back downstairs and into the cellar. The soldiers had been down here, too. The sharp smell of vinegar cut through the smoky fug that filled their nostrils. Pickle crocks lay in fragments, pickles and brine covering the floor. The soldiers had thrown the preserve pots at the walls and red jam dribbled down, like blood, over the rough stones.

Numb, the family returned to the kitchen. Annie picked up the tin water pail, flattened by someone's heavy boots. She pried it apart as far as she could and started filling it with the broken pottery. This seemed to revive the others and they began to gather up the debris.

Phoebe wandered into the hall, drawn to the bureau, her anchor. Through all the things that had happened to it, and her, there it sat, solid and comforting. She felt like hugging it. She replaced the drawers and picked up the clothing the soldiers had dragged out. Her Sunday bonnet was squashed flat. She tried to straighten it, but the brim was permanently creased. The clothes, like those upstairs, were streaked with mud and soot.

She gathered up the dirty garments and carried them into the kitchen. "Annie, fill the kettles. These things have to be washed. They're filthy."

"Mutti," said Annie, "it's pouring rain outside. And how can you think of doing a washing after what's happened?"

They were all staring at her. Of course. How silly. What was the matter with her? She dumped her armful of clothes in the corner.

Dirty clothes were the least of their problems. She must get hold of herself.

She began to pick up items from the floor, among them the carving knife. She stared at it. The cattle! She looked at the bare mantel, then searched among the debris on the hearth until she found the whetstone that had been swept from its place.

"Danny, come with me," she said, and rushed out the door.

He hurried to keep up. "It's raining. Where are you going?"

"We have to butcher...." She strode down the lane, sharpening the knife as she went, her teeth gritted. Out in the pasture she prowled, stonily, from one slain cattle beast to another, finally stopping by the one with the largest pool of blood around it. Poor Silky. She'd been shot in the neck and it had cut the artery. She would make the best meat, being well bled.

She knelt down and slit the beast's belly from throat to udder, cutting around it and the anus, and dragged out the intestines. She cut out the heart and liver and gave them to a stunned Danny. "Take these to the house, Danny, and bring back the ax." She began to cut the hide loose from the meat, working feverishly, while the rain washed away remaining blood.

Danny returned with the ax, accompanied by Peter, still holding his head but walking more or less steadily.

Peter knelt beside her. "What are you doing?"

"We have to save the meat or we'll have nothing to eat," she gasped, sawing away at the tough membrane.

"Here, give me the knife," he said. "I'll do it."

"No, you cut off the head and feet."

"Oh, that's why you wanted the ax," said Danny. "I....I'll do it...I think." He lifted the ax, then lowered it and handed it to Peter. "Poor Silky."

The sky above soaked them as if with the tears they were too dazed to shed. As they worked at freeing the hide, Peter said, "How will we keep the meat from spoiling? It's not as if it was winter."

"There's part of a barrel of salt in the attic, if the soldiers didn't find it. We can store the meat in brine."

They cut up the carcass and lugged the meat to the house. The girls had meanwhile gathered up the debris and the house had regained some semblance of order. They stored the meat in the cool cellar for the time being, but they must make the brine the first thing next day.

That night at supper they all pushed the fresh fried liver around on their plates and stared unhappily at each other.

"I can't eat Silky," wailed Katy.

Peter said, "It's only meat. Silky' s gone away."

Phoebe's appetite had deserted her, too, after so much destruction. But they should eat while they still had food. She picked up her fork and signaled to the others.

CHAPTER 43

hoebe spent a sleepless night on what was left of the shredded mattress. The other members of the family prowled about from time to time, and she had risen at intervals to peer out the windows, fearful of seeing the soldiers return. Although reason told her they were gone, back across the lake, the fear remained. But everything was quiet. Only the bright coals still winking in the ruins of the burned buildings, and the bitter odor of smoke, indicated the carnage.

The sky lightened, she gave up trying to sleep, dressed and went downstairs. She stepped outside just as the first rays of sunlight illuminated the desolate scene. The barn, the old twin cabins, and the pig sty were heaps of still-smoldering debris. Heat waves shimmered over them and the stink of wet smoke, burnt hair and charred flesh made her stomach heave again.

With the coming of the sun, flocks of turkey buzzards wheeled overhead, and then descended, landing with harsh squawks beside the dead animals in the fields. The birds pecked and tore at the carcasses and she, sickened, turned back toward the house. Jake's stone house. She was grateful for it. A frame house, such as she'd wanted, would now be rubble like the barns.

Inside, she built up the fire and filled the small iron kettle, still hanging there, with water, as she did every morning. Still in a daze, she found part of a sack of oatmeal in a back corner of the cupboard and sifted it over the boiling water. As she stirred the porridge it dawned on her that she'd emptied the bag. Still stirring, she looked at the empty shelves. This was all they had to eat. She shouldn't have cooked it all at once. Well, too late, now. She'd save part of it and fry it for their supper. But what about tomorrow? Even in the heat of the fire, she shivered. What would become of them?

The rest of the family straggled into the kitchen, Danny and Peter from outside where they'd been surveying the damage, the others from their beds. Still numb from yesterday's disaster, they

271

began the meal, although resilient Benjy whined because there was no milk or sugar.

Danny said, "Shut your face," and ten-year-old Benjy subsided, still muttering.

Peter said, "We'll have to bury the stock, quick, before they start to smell."

Annie got up and left the room. The others looked after her curiously.

"What's the matter with her?" asked Benjy.

"I say the wrong thing again," said Peter. "Talking of bad smells, it's not good at eating time."

Phoebe patted his shoulder as she brought the teapot to give him a refill. "You're right, Peter. We must do something about the animals."

After breakfast Peter, Danny and Benjy began to dig a massive hole beside the dead horses. Peter had to sit down every few minutes, holding his head and groaning. Phoebe and Annie came out to help and Phoebe looked at Peter with concern.

Hedwig rushed in the lane. "You're all right? I was so afraid when I saw the smoke." She hugged Phoebe, who returned her embrace.

"Yes, we're all right," said Peter, "except for the lump on my head." He touched it softly. "It's a good thing my head is hard. First a clang at Vati's, now here. That's all I'm good for, already. Just for clanging."

Phoebe said, "Oh, Peter. This is serious."

"Jah. My head says so."

She turned to Hedwig. "Did the soldiers come to your place? Are the McDougalls all right, and the baby? You didn't bring her?" Her voice rose. "Nothing has happened to her?"

"Everyone is all right, except Pa McDougall. He shot at the soldiers and they shot back at him."

"Did he kill some? Oh, I hope so," said Benjy.

Phoebe frowned at him, then turned to Hedwig. "Is he hurt?"

"Yes. They hit him in the leg. But we got it stopped bleeding." Hedwig's voice broke. "And the soldiers killed all our animals."

"Ours too," said Danny.

"And burned all the buildings." Hedwig wiped her eyes with her smudged apron. "The house and everything. I don't know where we're going to live with Pa McDougall hurt and all."

"You must come here. At least we have a roof." Phoebe felt her mind begin to function. "Yes, you must all come here. Oh, but Neil, can he walk?"

"No. He can't."

"We'll go and get him," said Danny. "The burying can wait. We could carry him, couldn't we, Uncle Peter?"

"Jah, sure." Peter nodded. "Two poles, a blanket. Easy. Come on."

But when Peter went with Danny to cut the poles, the exertion caught up with him and his head ached so badly he vomited.

"You can't go," said Phoebe. "Hedwig and Annie and I will go with Danny."

Peter remonstrated. "Neil is a big man, and so. You can't carry him, Phoebe."

"The four of us can, and maybe Meg can help. We'll manage. You stay quiet."

They hurried along the trail through the clergy reserve bush. Everything here looked as usual, birds singing and small animals rustling in last year's dead leaves. Everything peaceful. Birds and animals didn't destroy their own kind. Only humans did that.

On the other side of the woods, the horror all came into focus again. The little cabin, where she'd seen all the children, was a pile of half-burned logs. She'd heard that the family had left during the winter. She hoped that was so.

Approaching the McDougall farm, she stared. The homestead was even more devastated than their own. Not a single structure remained standing. At the edges of what had been their cabin, Meg and daughter Jenny stirred the cooling ashes, evidently searching for anything that might be salvaged. Neil sat with his back against the elm tree in the yard, holding the baby. The women turned to her, their sooty faces streaked with tears.

"Oh, Meg," said Phoebe. She threw her arms around the woman who sagged against her, weeping.

Annie and Jenny McDougall looked at each other, tears flowing, wanting to do the same but too shy.

"Everything's gone," sobbed Meg, "and we worked so hard."

"I know," said Phoebe, "but we still have a house. We came to get you. You carry the baby. We'll manage Neil."

Danny put the litter together and Neil crawled onto it. Phoebe, Danny and Hedwig each took hold of a pole end, Anna and Jenny shared the fourth and they set out. In the bush they had to set the litter down and rest.

Neil protested. "I'm too heavy. If you cut me a forked tree branch, Danny, maybe I can walk."

"No, you mustn't," said Phoebe and Meg together.

"You might start it bleeding again," said Meg. "Here, Phoebe you carry the baby, I'll take your place."

They changed places and continued on.

Arrived at the Stettls, Meg McDougall, seeing a solid building, burst into tears again and Phee-Phee echoed her.

They laid Neil's litter on the floor in the kitchen. He levered himself to a sitting position and said, "Bless you. I dinna ken what we would've done with me hurt and Archie away." Then he added, "The floor. It's all charred, there. They tried to burn your house, too?"

"Yes, but we put it out," said Danny.

Hedwig took Phee-Phee, who was still crying, and sat down on a block of wood in the corner.

Phoebe's hospitable instincts took over. "Have you had breakfast? No of course you haven't. There's only oatmeal but you're welcome." A good thing she had cooked it all. She rubbed her aching shoulders. Neil, indeed, was a heavy man.

As they sat around the table on blocks of wood Danny had brought in, eating from an assortment of wooden bowls and tins that had resisted the devastation, they took stock.

"We've got this house," said Phoebe. "And garden truck, at least as soon as it's grown. There are only greens now,"

"Yes, we have garden, too," answered Meg. "We've got that...but," she swallowed painfully, "no house."

Phoebe reached out and covered Meg's hands with her own. "You must stay here. There's plenty of room."

Neil spoke up. "To think I jeered at Jake spending so much time building this house." He shook his head. "Little did I know."

Phoebe echoed his thought in her mind. Little did they know, indeed.

Hedwig's forehead wrinkled. "Can we live on vegetables alone? What will we do for meat?"

"Oh, I butchered one of the cows they killed," said Phoebe.

Neil looked at her, his eyes wide. "You butchered?"

"Danny helped."

"But will the meat be good, not being bled?" asked Neil.

"I picked one that bled out." She shuddered, remembering her survey of the slaughter.

Neil looked at her, admiration plain on his face. "Ye're a smart lass."

"I thought we could store it in brine. We should do it right away. The weather's too warm for it to keep long." She turned to Danny. "Bring the salt keg down from the attic. It should be all right. I don't think the soldiers went up there."

Danny soon came back to the kitchen with the keg. "Ma, it's almost empty."

She stirred the salt with her finger disclosing the bottom of the keg, then looked at the others. Her shoulders slumped. "We can't do it. There's no way to save the meat with the smokehouse burned. There isn't time to build another, even if we had the lumber."

Meg had seemed to revive under a solid roof once more. "We should cook as much as we can. That will keep it a little longer."

Phoebe agreed and they put the best pieces on the spit and filled the iron kettles. Phoebe looked at the large amount of beef still in the cellar. It would spoil before they could use it. What a waste when they needed it so much.

Neil clapped his hand to his forehead. "I just remembered. I seen smoke over anent Anselm's just before they shot me."

"I saw it, too," said Danny.

"I wonder if they're all right?"

"I'll go and see." Danny headed for the door.

Phoebe called after him, "Be careful. The soldiers may still be about. Check the Steadmans, too, if it seems safe."

Before long, Danny returned with the two families and they added their woes.

The Anselms were totally burnt out and all their animals killed.

The Steadmans said they'd lost their stock, and their barn. "I told them we were Quakers and didn't fight," said Alec. "The man in charge apparently knew Quakers. He called off his men but," he spread his hands, "the barn and stock were already destroyed."

"We do have a roof, though," said Abigail Steadman. "Hilda, thee must come and stay with us."

"It wouldn't be too much?" asked Hilda Anselm. "So many?" She looked at her husband, mother-in-law and her three children, and at the Steadman's four.

Abigail touched the German woman's shoulder. "We'll make do."

Granny Anselm looked at Neil, still sitting on the floor, legs outstretched. "What is the matter, you, then?"

"The soldiers shot me," said Neil, wincing as he pulled up his torn trouser leg.

"Oh, no." Abigail's hand flew to her mouth.

"Let me see," said Granny. Taking Hilda's offered hand, she bent her stiff knees to crouch beside the injured man.

She untied the bandage Meg had cut from the bottom of her apron and inspected the blood encrusted wound. "Ah, a hole both sides. The bullet gone. I think it all right if no fever come. He should have a fresh bandage, though." She stared around the bare kitchen.

"There's not a clean thing in the house," said Phoebe.

"Well, we must just hope it will heal clean, then," said Granny and retied the bloodstained bandage.

Hilda helped her to her feet again and Phoebe shoved one of the blocks of wood toward her. "Sit down, Granny. You must be exhausted."

All the visitors sank down, some on wood blocks, some on the floor. Hilda's children clustered around her, little Bernie holding tight to her skirt as if he feared losing her. Abigail's children also kept near their parents.

Just then one of the kettles boiled over, and Phoebe rushed to pull it a little farther from the fire.

"That smells good," said Granny.

Phoebe turned to stare at the group, her face lighting up. She looked at Meg. "We won't have to waste the meat," she said. "We'll share it with the Steadmans and Anselms."

"That's good," replied Meg. "Och, I hated to see it spoil after all your work skinning it out."

The story of the meat was repeated for the newcomers. Then Reinhold Anselm turned to his wife and said, "The black cow was not with the others killed. I wonder...?"

"She was ready to calve, and so," said Hilda. "She broke from the fence again, already, and went to the bush?"

"Maybe."

Neil broke in. "I don't know where my head is. My pigs are in the bush. If the soldiers didn't find them we'll have meat." He chuckled wryly. "Even if they did find them, I think the old boar would discourage them. He's an ugly beast."

The four families pulled themselves together. The McDougalls stayed at the Stettls' and the Anselms went to the Steadmans'. Phoebe and Anna did huge washings and the Anselms and McDougalls were outfitted with a change of clothes The men buried carcasses in shallow graves.

The Anselms discovered their root cellar intact and the four families shared the last year's few remaining turnips, potatoes and carrots. Reinhold's cow returned with a wobbly-legged heifer calf and Alec said he thought he saw one of Neil's shoats in the edge of the bush.

Silky had not been a young cow and Phoebe found, to her dismay, that no amount of cooking would make the meat tender. They were reduced to cutting it into tiny pieces and using it in stews. Still, it nourished them and even Katy mastered her repugnance when hunger took hold.

CHAPTER 44

Contact with more distant neighbors revealed the Stettls and their friends were not alone in their losses. The raiders had cut a swath of destruction from Lake Erie to just north of the Anselms' homestead. Other families were doubling up and sharing what they had.

In a few days, Neil McDougall was able to hobble around with a forked tree branch for a crutch. One night at supper he voiced his worry about shelter for his family. "I dinna want to keep bothrin' ye, stayin' here."

"You're welcome to stay as long as need be," said Phoebe. "You're not imposing at all."

"I've a slew of logs cut where I was clearin' land, but I dinna ken how tae get them out to rebuild the cabin with no horses, not even an ox, to drag them there."

Danny had been sitting, quietly, his brow wrinkled. Now he said, "Do you have to build where the other cabin was?"

"Well, no, beside it, like. What did ye have in mind?"

"If we built your cabin where the logs are, we could roll them that little ways."

"Och, it's such a mess, there, with all the brush."

Meg spoke up. "We can't be choosy, Neil. We must hae a home."

He sighed, "Aye, you're right, as always." He gave his wife a wintry smile.

Reinhold and Alec were asked to help and willingly agreed.

Anselm said, "I, also, have logs cut. I help with yours, then we build mine, and so."

"Aye, that will be grand." Neil turned to his wife. "It won't be a hoose ye ken. Only a shanty forninst the winter. Not even a loft. Without horses or oxen we can't lift the logs so high."

The very next day the men gathered in Neil's woodlot to begin the building. It was backbreaking work, even for five men, rolling the green logs with pry poles to the site, then levering them into place. They were forced to choose the lightest, smallest logs, poles really, compared to the general run of twelve to eighteen inch diameter timbers they'd rather have used. Shingles being unavailable, they covered the roof with slabs of bark held down by poles lashed to the end logs by grapevines.

Peter still complained of headaches and had to frequently sit down when nausea overtook him.

Neil's leg was still too painful for him to help move or raise the logs, but he cut all the mortises that held the logs together at the corners. He declared the walls were high enough when he could no longer see over them.

Reinhold said, "You're lucky to be a little man, so. Mine I have to make bigger, or I can't stand up inside."

Phoebe and Meg brought lunch for the men. Phoebe surveyed the completed walls. "It's so small," she exclaimed.

Meg peered in the open doorway. "Aye, but we have nothing to put in it but oorselves."

"And not even a window."

"I know," said Neil, "but there's none nearer than the fort. It's too dangerous to go there with the fighting, and there probably aren't any, anyhow."

"That bark you put on the roof won't keep out the rain very well." Phoebe knew that from experience.

Neil shrugged. "We don't have any choice. If I had a draw-knife I could probably make enough shingles to cover the roof before winter."

"What's a draw-knife?" asked Danny.

"A long blade with handles at both ends. It's for shaving wood."

Danny straightened. "There's one of those in our attic. I never knew what it was for."

"That's great. Then all I need is some blocks of cedar about as long as I can reach, and split into layers. I could probably make enough shingles over the winter for both our house and Reinhold's. That's if it's a good knife."

The knife only needed sharpening. Danny spent every evening splitting the blocks into thin layers and Neil shaved one edge of the slices so they would lie snugly over.

With the windowless cabin finished, Phoebe shared what utensils and food she could spare and the McDougalls moved back to their farm. In order to lessen the congestion in the tiny shanty, Phoebe invited Hedwig and the baby to stay with her.

Waving to the departing McDougalls, baby Phoebe in her arms, Hedwig called, "Be sure to tell me if you hear any news of Archie."

"We will," shouted Meg.

Neil's cabin finished, all the men and women took a break from construction to hoe the corn. They needed an extra good crop this year.

Danny said, "I always thought hoeing corn was hard work. This time it seems like a holiday after what we've been doing."

"Jah," said Reinhold. "It's all in the comparing, so."

The cornfields weedless, and the wheat not quite ripe enough to cut, the men decided to at least start on Reinhold's cabin.

The day they began, Simon, Hannah, and Karl arrived at Phoebe's, having belatedly heard of the raid. Hannah kept asking, "You're all right? You're all right? The kinder? The soldiers didn't hurt them?"

"No, just Peter," said Phoebe, "but he's all right, now."

"Peter? My son? He's hurt again?"

"He's all right," Phoebe hastened to assure her. "The soldier hit him with his gun handle. He had a headache for awhile but he's better, now." It wasn't quite true. He was better, not cured. But she didn't want her mother-in-law to worry.

"Where is he?" asked Simon.

"Over at Reinhold's. The men are building the Anselms a cabin. They were completely burnt out. At least we still have the house."

"Jah, for us they left the house, too, when they came before," said Hannah.

"Well, they tried to burn ours," said Phoebe, pointing at the charred floor, "but we put it out."

Hannah's hands flew to her mouth. "So close. It's terrible."

"We go and help the cabin," said Simon, and he and Karl left.

With the two extra hands, and the team, Tim and Tom, that Simon and Karl had brought back, the men soon finished the Anselm's cabin, except for chinking between the logs.

Hannah worried about milk for the children. "We should give you back the cow you gave us when we were raided." she said.

"Benjy and Katy are old enough to get along without milk," said Phoebe, "and Reinholds have a fresh cow for their little ones. Don't worry."

As soon as the wheat ripened, all hands turned out to cut and thresh it. "My mouth waters all the time for bread, already," said Peter, chewing a mouthful of kernels. "Garden stuff is all right but it doesn't stick to the ribs so good."

Fortunately the soldiers had left the grain sacks stored in the attic, and they were soon filled with the golden kernels and stored up there again.

Although still suffering from occasional headaches, Peter assured Phoebe he felt fine. He set off for the mill with the horses, each with a gunny sack of wheat draped over its back, and he perched on top of the sack on Tom.

"I just hope it's still there, the mill," he said. "If the Yankees burned it, we'll have to grind some in a hollow tree stump like Vati did when we first came. Not very good stuff, and so." He wrinkled his nose.

He didn't return until sunset of the next day.

"Good news," he shouted, as he came in the lane. "The Yankees didn't come there. Is there something to eat, maybe?"

"Annie, give him some stew," said Phoebe, untying the flour sack. "I'll make some fried cakes."

That night they gorged on the cakes, savoring them even though they lacked butter or jam.

Peter, revived, reported on his trip. "The miller is going to send a team and wagon for the rest of the wheat. He says he will buy all we have."

"That's good news," said Phoebe.

He grinned, self-consciously, and reached for another cake.

"Where did you sleep?" asked Benjy.

"Upstairs in the mill. The miller lets men sleep there if they've come a long way. The floor was pretty hard." He rolled his shoulders and grimaced. "And I like to sneeze my head off from the dust.

"Oh, I saw a man, there, I forget his name but the miller will remember. From west of the mill, somewhere. He has a cow to sell. Maybe there will be enough wheat to pay for it."

Just like Peter, thought Phoebe, to forget the name of someone so important to them.

"I just hope the militia captain doesn't come here before we get the wheat to the mill," she said. "We'll just hope he's away with the army. You've done well." She patted his shoulder as she brought him another helping of fried cakes.

He seized her hand, holding it against his cheek. "I'd do anything for you,Phee, you know it."

That's what Jake always said. She jerked her hand loose and moved away. Peter shouldn't be touching her in such a familiar way. And she wished he wouldn't use Jake's pet name for her. Jake wouldn't like it.

Jake. With all the work and decision-making here, she hadn't thought of him for several days. How could she have forgotten him, even for a moment? What would he think of the destruction of his farm? He'd be very angry, of course. But he never wasted time, fussing, when things went wrong; just got up and went on with the job. She crouched down on a block of wood, staring into the coals. Common sense told her he was dead, but she kept thinking and acting as if he were on his way home.

She must stop that. He was gone. Forever. Time to make plans for the future. Caught up in day-to-day problems, she hadn't considered what her life would be like, permanently without him. Just like the present, she guessed, for loneliness.

She shouldn't keep Peter here. He should be home helping his father. Could she and Danny manage the farm? At eighteen, Danny was strong and willing but didn't have the experience. Still, as soon as they could manage by themselves, she'd send Peter back home. But there was so much to do.

The grasping militia captain didn't appear. The wheat sold for a good price and they acquired a fresh cow from the man Peter had heard of. Then came the problem of feed and shelter for the animals. Peter and Danny built a pole lean-to against the south side of the house and filled one corner with straw, and some ripe hay cut from the pasture field. Not as nourishing as fodder cut at the right time but it should help the animals survive the winter. The two men, with Benjy's help, cut and shocked the corn, then hauled enough wood from the bush to last the winter.

Phoebe fretted whether the stock would be warm enough in the lean-to. While she considered what they could do to make the shelter better, a distant neighbor came, offering to put up a barn for them.

"We heard you had the trouble," said a man who introduced himself as Israel Miner.

"Oh, you're the man Peter bought the cow and ox from," said Phoebe.

"That's right. He told us what a terrible time you had. We thought we would help out if you would like. They missed us, those devils, thank the Good Lord."

She gratefully accepted the offer, and Israel promised to return with his crew the next day.

She appreciated the men's offer of help but they'd have to be fed. She had an abundance of garden truck and the bag of flour, but what could she feed them for meat? Men needed solid food to work. However, the men came equipped with a hindquarter of beef.

"Thought you might be short," said Israel.

Tears smarted. "How can I ever repay you?"

"Oh, that's all right," they chorused. "We have to help each other over the rough times."

A log barn speedily rose on the stone foundation of the old, and when the visitors found out about the other families' losses they promised to come back after harvest and help build barns for everyone.

With a good house, tight barn, a nest egg from the wheat sale, and a good crop of corn now tasseling, Phoebe felt secure for the winter.

Several days later she was milking the cow in the oppressive heat of an August evening. As she stripped the teats, she pondered her future. Simon looked more bent recently, and the joints of his fingers swollen. He surely needed Peter at home to help him. Should she bring up the subject? It was better to know where she stood.

Finished milking, she picked up the pail and stool and stepped out behind the cow. She set down the stool and wiped her forearm across her perspiring forehead. Turning to Peter who was husking corn for a sow Karl had given them, she said, "I've noticed Vati is looking frail. I think you're needed at home."

He stopped stripping the kernels from the cob and stared at her. Why did he look so dismayed. Hadn't he noticed? "We can get along for the winter. I don't know how we'll manage in the spring but we'll have to find a way. Vati comes first."

"But Phee...."

She did wish he wouldn't call her that.

He laid down the corncob and rubbed his hand across his beard. "Don't you want me here any more? Don't I do a job good enough?"

"Of course you do. It's not that. I've been selfish to keep you here so long."

"I wanted to stay. Vati is still strong like ox. Anyhow, he has Karl to help, close. You need me."

He sounded as if he didn't want to go home. "I have to know what to plan for. You must ask him if he needs you."

He picked up the corncob again and mumbled something in reply which she took for an affirmative.

He stayed.

CHAPTER 45

L ittle Phee-Phee was a delight to the whole family. The grown-
up Phoebe marveled at how quickly her granddaughter
learned new skills: from tentative walking to running, from
messing in her food with her fingers, to mastery of a curved-handled
spoon.

Phoebe had been so overworked when her own children were
little, she hadn't appreciated them as she should have. Now with
Anna and Katy able to do a major part of the housework she had
time to enjoy her granddaughter.

Neil had added a lean-to to his cabin, and Hedwig returned
home to help her mother-in-law. Phoebe made excuses to visit the
McDougalls and often brought the child back with her.

The war seemed to be coming to a close and the rapacious
militia captain no longer visited any of the settlers. With the income
from the abundant harvest, Phoebe bought another cow.

Archie came home after New Years, a civilian again, with the
news that peace had been declared. Well, at least Archie was now
safe. Hedwig was ecstatic to have him home permanently.

Returning soldiers provided an abundance of help and the
homesteads soon were rebuilt. Archie diligently looked for a farm to
buy, and Phoebe feared he would take his family far away, as nearby
land was all taken up.

She also had another concern. The thought of William's
lonely grave had never left her. She asked Peter if he would take her
to Queenston.

"It's too far, Phoebe, and too cold."

"I have to see where William is buried. Please. It's all I have
left of my son."

"Ya, I guess I like to see, too," he said.

"And me," echoed the twins.

"I know what to do," said Peter, his face clearing. "We will
stop at Mutti's for the night on the way. But first, Danny and I have

to finish the wood. Then we go quick before the sap starts to run, already."

When Hedwig heard of the projected trip, she said, "Archie and I will come and look after the place. That way you won't have to hurry back."

So it was arranged. Archie and Hedwig and baby Phoebe, now an energetic toddler, with huge pale blue eyes and hair so fair it looked like silver threads, came to stay.

Phoebe hugged her namesake and delighted in her unintelligible chatter. "What is she saying?"

"I have no idea," said Hedwig. "I think it's cat talk. Her kitten seems to understand her all right." She looked around. "It will be nice to be by ourselves. Archie's family could not be nicer to me but it's—so close all the time."

"Well, Archie will soon find a place."

But Phoebe's interest in Hedwig's problems, and her grandchild, were fleeting. She had more important things to deal with right now.

Peter filled the sleigh box with straw and buried several large stones, heated on the hearth, in the straw to keep the travelers' feet warm. Danny piled all the spare blankets and the buffalo robe into the sleigh and the family set out.

By the time they reached Simon's, Katy and Benjy had had quite enough of this slow mode of travel and elected to stay there. Hannah made them all welcome and bustled around, preparing food and making up beds.

The stones were reheated and early the next morning, Phoebe, Peter and the twins set out again. Phoebe had thought she understood the reports of destruction along the river but had not realized the scope of it. Formerly imposing Fort Erie was a pile of rubble and all the houses round about laid waste. Along the river, blackened chimneys were all that remained of what had been prosperous farms. There was an occasional shanty or shored-up cabin, but most of the farms looked abandoned and desolate. What had happened to the settlers who'd lived there? To lose everything after all their hard work. Well, she could relate to their despair, but considering everything, she'd been fortunate.

A rickety temporary bridge had been recently built over Chippawa Creek. She held her breath until they were safely across. She shuddered as they passed the spot where her old shanty had stood, remembering her struggles to survive there. But nothing remained of it.

Annie and Danny were mesmerized by the mighty Falls. They scrambled out of the sleigh to look at the flow of translucent green water and the huge ice chunks piled along the river banks below. Annie exclaimed at the trees, coated with ice from the constant spray. They gleamed in the sunshine like silver.

Phoebe had difficulty tearing the twins away from the sight, but she was even more anxious to continue now she was so near. They asked a man they met on the road where the cemetery was, and followed his directions to a spot on the edge of the escarpment.

They stared, appalled, at the rows and rows of wooden crosses.

"These are all dead soldiers?" asked Danny, his voice hushed.

"How awful," said Annie.

Phoebe looked over the rows of markers: like a field of corn hills. But corn stalks held promise, these crosses only signified loss.

She rubbed her hand across her brimming eyes. "How will we ever find William's grave. So many."

Her legs were rubbery. Could she even walk to look? She must. She'd come so far for this. She gritted her teeth and started down the first row.

Peter said, "I think the best way we each take a row. That way it goes faster, already."

So they did. Reading the names on each of the crosses. Row after row. Name after name. Phoebe's eyes blurred. They all looked the same. Would she miss the right one? Even if they had to go over them all again, she wouldn't leave until she found it.

The name leaped out at her as if it were written in fire. "Cpl. William Trevlyn", and a number.

She cried, "I found him," and dropped to her knees, sobbing, in the snow.

The others rushed to her, Danny tripping over a cross in his hurry. He murmured an apology and touched the marker as he got to his feet.

They knelt in front of the cross, around the snow-covered mound that covered William's mortal remains. She wept as if she'd never cried before. The twins furtively wiped away their own tears. Peter's flowed into his beard, unchecked.

After some time Peter's hand on her shoulder roused her. "Phoebe, it's time to go."

She took a deep breath and reached out her hand for him to help her to her feet. She was chilled clear through.

"Yes, we must go," she said, her voice husky. Reluctantly, she walked out of the cemetery, stopping every few steps to look back. She must leave William here, too far away for her to even care for his grave. She turned to go back to the grave, she couldn't leave him. But Peter caught her arm and urged her on.

The team had stood, untied, glad of the chance to rest. Now chilled, they stamped their feet ready to move again. The travelers shook off the snow that had clung to them as they knelt around the grave and climbed into the sleigh, pulling the blankets and robe close. The stones in the straw still felt vaguely warm but they'd all be chilled to the bone before they reached the Stettls again.

As the horses plodded along the snow covered road, she remembered there had been other groups of people, as well as solitary women, staring at crosses in various parts of the cemetery, mourning their dead. She'd been so immersed in her own grief she'd scarcely noticed them at the time. What a load of sadness. Her heart went out to her fellow mourners. But she no longer felt the despair that had fueled her crying before. She began to understand what Jake had said. She would never cease to mourn William's loss. But he'd done what he wanted with his short life and now was surrounded by his mates. It comforted her a little.

The moon had long risen before they entered the Stettls' yard.

Simon came out. "Go inside. I take care of the horses."

Hannah hustled them in, clucking, "You must be frozen, already. Come to the fire."

"Th...thank you," Phoebe's teeth chattered with the cold—and her emotional exhaustion.

"Did you find it then, the grave?"

"There were hundreds and hundreds," said Annie, "but we found it."

"So sad. All those young men." Hannah shook her head, her face sober.

Simon came in and they sat down to bowls of hot soup. Phoebe revived and her shuddering lessened.

Annie kept talking about the number of graves.

"Jah, and that is just some," said Simon. "More at Fort Erie and at Lundy's Lane and everywhere. Such a loss." He clucked his tongue.

Back home again, Hedwig said, "So you found it, then? And now you are more content?"

"Yes, no. Oh, Hedwig there's no one there of family to look after it. And so far away." Phoebe felt dazed from the long trip in the rocking sleigh. She rose from the table and went to the hearth, holding out her hands to the warmth and rubbing them together. "I don't know when I've been so cold. I must be getting old."

Hedwig got up and put her arms around her. "You will soon be all right. It's the strong feeling as well as the cold."

Phoebe felt her throat close up and tears start again. She stiffened her back and, to get her mind off her grief, said, "And everything is all right, here?"

"Oh, yes." Hedwig nodded her head. "And Archie and I loved having a place to ourselves, didn't we, Archie."

"Aye," said Archie. "But now I won't get no peace until I find a farm." He gave a mock sigh.

Hedwig frowned at him. "You know I never nag."

"No, you never nag. You just keep asking and asking until you get what you want." He grinned at her to take the sting from his words, and everyone chuckled as the tension lessened.

Archie and Hedwig and little Phee-Phee returned to the McDougalls, and the Stettls settled back into the familiar routine. But Phoebe kept seeing the image of that stark cross everywhere she looked.

Did Jake's grave have a cross? And where was it? How could she find out? She must finally accept that he'd perished. What a lot of time she'd wasted before she realized what a wonderful man she'd married. She'd give anything to have that time back again. But that was foolish. No use sighing over might-have-beens.

CHAPTER 46

Phoebe and Peter sat beside the kitchen fire, Phoebe busy with the never ending mending and Peter repairing harness, the children away visiting at the McDougall's. The couple's shadows climbed the white walls and then retreated in the flickering light. The wood snapped and crackled and the kettle sang its own tune. So peaceful. The house was never quiet when the children were home.

She looked at him and voiced a thought she'd often pondered. "Why have you never married? You're almost forty. Most people marry as soon as they're adults."

He stopped his work, shifted on his stool, looked at the floor and then raised his eyes to hers. "I couldn't see any other girl after Jake brought you home."

"Me? You wished you were married to me?"

"Jah, so." He bent low over his work, hiding his face.

How sad. All these years, yearning after her. So typical of impractical Peter.

He laid down the awl with which he'd been punching holes in a trace. "Phee, it's been over a year. Jake isn't coming back, you know it."

Tears sprang to her eyes. "Yes, I know."

He put his hand over hers. "I didn't mean to make you sad."

"I know. If I could only find out what happened to him."

"Jah." He shook his head and let out a gusty sigh. "But we have to go on, already."

He took both of her hands in his, but she immediately withdrew them. What was he thinking?

He leaned toward her, but kept his hands clasped together. "Let's marry up? I've loved you all my life, I think so."

"Oh, no, Peter. I'm still married to Jake."

"No, Phee. You mustn't think so, any more. Please marry me."

293

"I don't know what I would have done without you here, but I couldn't marry you."

Peter's face sagged. "if Jake was alive he'd try by hook or by crook to come back to you. He loved you like anything."

"Yes, I know."

"He isn't coming back. You know it. Marry me."

"I don't know. I'll have to think about it."

She did. Peter was willing and he worked tirelessly for them, but she'd have to be the one in charge. Peter could not be depended upon to make decisions or even keep track of the day-to-day work. Still, they needed his help and if he went back home what would they do? She'd married Jake because she needed him. Should she do the same thing again? Peter had certainly been loyal. All these years he'd loved her. She hadn't known it, or paid any attention to him except to laugh at his jokes. She argued back and forth in her mind but could come to no decision. And every day Peter looked at her with longing.

She thought of the men she'd been involved with. None of the relationships had been long lasting, not like the marriages of her parents or her aunt and uncle. Why did she have such bad luck? All she wanted was a home and a peaceful life and it seemed unattainable. Could Peter fulfill her desires? He was so happy-go-lucky.

But she couldn't forget Jake. Though he'd been gone for so long, she still felt married to him. What should she do?

Now that the war had ended, people returned to civilian pursuits, not the least of which was gossiping about their neighbors.

Abigail confirmed this one day in February as she and Phoebe walked to Meg McDougall's to a quilting bee. "Thee knows that people are talking about Peter and thee?"

"But he's my brother-in-law. He's part of the family."

"Well, thee knows how people are. Always ready to believe the worst."

She knew. "But what can I do? It's too far for him to go home at night, and Danny can't manage the work by himself."

"Maybe thee should marry."

"But I am married."

"Does thee really think Jake is still alive?" Abigail's hand flew to cover her mouth. "Oh, I'm sorry, Phoebe, I shouldn't have said that."

Phoebe squeezed her friend's arm. "It's all right. That's the problem; I don't know. I was angry at him for abandoning us, but I miss him so much. I wish I knew what happened to him. I don't know where I am without him."

"I can understand that." Abigail nodded. "It's the uncertainty. Almost better to know the worst. Well, don't worry about the gossips. I just thought thee should know. They can't do thee any real harm."

Phoebe was not so sure. Her past experience led her to believe otherwise.

She'd seen the place where William was buried, but where was Jake's grave? Or did he have one? She shuddered at the thought that perhaps his bones were lying on the ground somewhere in the forest where bears and cougars could gnaw on them.

Every time they were alone, Peter said, "Phee?" But she shook her head. She had no answer for him.

One night they sat up late in the sugar bush, boiling the day's sap in order to have room in the kettles for the next day's run.

The spring peepers were in full chorus. The earthy exhalation of the thawing swamp vied with the sweet fragrance of boiling sap. A full moon lit the clearing and highlighted the swirling steam.

Phoebe, seated on a log by the fire, sighed, her hands clasped loosely in her lap. It was so peaceful here.

Peter re-stoked the fires under the kettles and came to sit beside her. He picked up her hand and stroked it. "Have you decided yet?"

She pulled back. "I don't know what to do. I'm very fond of you but it doesn't seem right, somehow."

"You know the neighbors are talking?"

"Yes, Abigail told me."

"You have to look at it straight. You know Jake is gone forever. You have to make a new life."

He was right. Jake had perished and Peter was a fine man. It felt good to laugh again, and Peter was always ready with a joke. The children loved him, too. She must let go of the past life and start anew.

"All right, Peter. I'lll marry you."

For the first time, then, although the neighbors wouldn't have believed it, he hugged her and planted kisses all over her face.

"Peter, stop," She giggled, even while she relaxed in his arms. She'd been holding herself so tight, ever since Jake left, it felt so nice to be in comforting arms again. And Peter made her feel young.

The next morning at breakfast, Peter, grinning widely, announced to the children that he and their mutti were going to marry. She looked at each child in turn to gauge their reaction to this news. Katy and Benjy seemed unmoved. After all, she supposed, they wouldn't think it much different from the present family circle. Danny nodded his head.

Annie became teary, though. "You don't think Vati is ever coming home, then?"

Phoebe got up from the table and hugged her daughter, then cupped the girl's wet cheek in her hand, turning her face up. "Annie. It's been so long. I know how you feel. Peter asked me a long time ago but I kept hoping." She took a deep breath. "It's time to move on." She turned to the others. "Peter will be a good vati to you all."

"No," said Peter.

Phoebe looked at him in surprise. "No? You've changed your mind?"

"For sure we will be married but—but their vati I will not be. Jake is their vati. The uncle I am still to them."

Annie and Danny nodded.

She relaxed. She hadn't thought Peter would be so sensitive to the children's feelings. A good man she was marrying. Dear Peter. She wanted to hug him right then but they'd better go slowly. It would take the children time to get used to the new order of things.

"So you think it all right, I should marry your mutti?"

Danny spoke up. "I think it's for the best, but we will never forget Vati."

Annie's tears sprang again and Phoebe's followed, as they hugged.

When Hedwig was told, she reacted more strongly. "You are forgetting Vati, I mean Jake, already? How could you?"

"Hedwig, he's gone forever. I have to get on with my life."

Hedwig subsided. "Maybe it's all right, then. I know about the gossip, and I know you need Uncle Peter's help but," defiantly, "I'll never forget Vati-Jake."

"Nor will I, Hedwig." Phoebe kissed her daughter. "We will remember him in our hearts, and Peter won't begrudge us that."

That evening, in the barn, Peter came to the stall where she was milking and squatted down to her level. "Phee. Can I come to your bed tonight when the kinder are asleep?"

"Certainly not. What are you thinking?"

"I'm thinking I want to be with you, already."

"Not until we're married."

But as with Hedwig, deciding to be married was the easy part.

"We could just say we're married, like Hedwig and Archie," said Peter when she voiced her concerns.

"No, Peter."

"Well I heard there is a Methodist minister traveling the country. If he comes this way would that be all right?"

"Yes, I guess so. I don't know anything about the Methodists, but a minister is a minister."

"Be ready, then. We'll get married quick if he comes."

For better or worse, she'd made her decision. Please God it was the right one.

"We will go on Sunday and tell the folks," said Peter.

She was uncertain again. Was she doing the right thing? Would Hannah think she'd abandoned Jake? She still felt as if she were doing so.

Hannah welcomed them with open arms when they drove in the yard at the Stettls'. "So. I cooked a big ham. I must have known you were coming. Karl and Rebecca and Charity are here, too."

"We brought a roast chicken," said Annie.

"And two pies," piped up Katy.

Hannah hugged her granddaughter. "We will have a feast for sure."

The men retired to the porch while the women put the finishing touches on the meal. Phoebe was so nervous she almost dropped one of the pies she was unpacking.

To her relief, Karl's daughter, Charity, took Katy off to the haymow to see the latest batch of kittens. Phoebe feared Katy would blurt out the news before she decided how to tell Jake's parents.

Out on the porch, Karl looked quizzically at Peter. "You look like a cat that's been in the cream. What are you up to, now?"

Peter, obviously bursting with his news, puffed out his chest and said, "Phoebe and I are going to marry up."

The front legs of Simon's chair hit the floor with a thump. "What?" he turned his head toward the door. "Hannah, come out here, so." His deep voice sent echoes bouncing off the barn.

The women hurried out, Hannah saying, "What is it, Simon? What's wrong?"

Peter looked sheepishly at Phoebe, "I'm sorry, Phee, I couldn't wait."

Hannah repeated, "What is it, Simon?"

"Tell her," said Simon, gesturing between Hannah and Peter.

"Phoebe and I want to marry."

Phoebe held her breath.

"Jake isn't coming back, for sure," continued Peter, "and Phoebe needs somebody."

Hannah burst into tears and Rebecca put her arms around her, while Phoebe stood frozen. She'd made a mistake—again. They thought she was being unfaithful to Jake's memory. Why had she said yes? She wouldn't have hurt Hannah and Simon for anything. Why hadn't she thought how it would affect them?

Simon cleared his throat, noisily. "Well...well...."

"Mutti," said Karl, going to her and taking her hand in his. "Jake is gone. We have to face it, so. It's time for Phoebe to go on, and Pete has loved her this long time, I think so." He looked at his brother.

"For sure," said Peter. Phoebe thought he looked upset at this storm he'd caused.

Simon said, "Well," again, and once more cleared his throat. "You're right, Karl, but it is a hard thing to swallow. Yes, this is probably best." He reached over and clapped Peter on the shoulder. "Good luck to you."

Hannah wiped her eyes on her apron and went to Phoebe. "I'm sorry I cried, so. I don't think it is a bad thing, marrying, you and Peter. It is just hard to accept that Jake is gone."

"I know, Mutti Stettl," said Phoebe, hugging her mother-in-law. "Me, too."

"We will not forget Jake, anyway," said Peter standing free of the porch post he had been squatting against, and putting his arms around both women.

"Of course not," said Phoebe, swallowing her own tears of relief.

There was silence for a moment while they all remembered the absent member, then Karl said, "Now for food. A real celebration. Rebecca, put the dinner on the table. What am I keeping you for?"

Rebecca stuck her tongue out at him as she went into the house.

He turned to Benjy. "Go and call the girls from the barn."

Benjy, obviously glad to be away from the tension on the porch, ran off at once.

Simon got up and went to Hannah, Peter and Phoebe, still standing, arms entwined. "Well, it's for the best, so," he said, clearing his throat again. "Let's go in."

The family gathered around the laden board and Simon, his voice still husky, gave the blessing, including the absent member in his prayer while Phoebe felt the tears start again, whether from grief for Jake, or relief, she could not have said.

CHAPTER 47

On a sunny morning in May, housecleaning was in full swing at Jake Stettl's farm. Annie washed curtains in a tub of sudsy water in the back yard. Dust swirled where Katy swung the broom against the parlor rug thrown over the clothesline. Benjy reluctantly pulled weeds in the vegetable garden, throwing them over his shoulder, careless of where they landed. Peter and Danny strode across the far field, abreast, scattering oat seed from the sacks under their left arms.

As she polished the bureau with beeswax, Phoebe contemplated its nicks and scratches. Poor old bureau, it had had a hard life. She ran her fingers over a deep groove in the top. A rock or something in the river had done that. The chip broken off the corner post happened when the sergeant dumped it out of his wagon. One of the carved drawer pulls was missing, lost in the debris after the Yankees' raid. This old thing mirrored her own life. She had a gouge to match every one in the bureau. But please God there'd be no more. Both she and her bureau deserved an uneventful future. With Peter at her side, and her children almost grown, it could happen. Peter wasn't as ambitious as Jake had been and wouldn't always be looking to something new or grander.

The bureau polished to a warm glow, she washed the windows, singing as she worked. She must have the house shining, ready for the weddings. Hedwig and Archie were going to be married with her and Peter. She smiled to herself. Imagine having a double wedding with your own daughter. Now that spring had come, the minister might appear any day. Peter had heard he was up near Burlington a couple of weeks ago and heading this way.

The two couples planned to be married in front of the hearth in Phoebe's parlor. All the neighbors were invited and promised to come, no matter how short the notice, and to let her know immediately if they heard news of the minister.

She and Annie, with Katy's dubious help, had filled the cellar shelves with all sorts of good things. Peter and Danny had earmarked a steer for slaughter the moment they knew the minister was nearing. Hedwig and Meg had also been busy baking. Hedwig had found a patch of wild grapevines in the corner of their woodlot she said she was going to use to decorate the mantel. Meg had offered lilacs from her prized bush if they opened in time.

Peter had made a secret visit to Fort Erie (he said he was going to visit his folks) and bought her a gold wedding band. It was beautiful. Dear Peter. He was such fun, always had a joke. It was good to laugh again. He was sometimes thoughtless, but he'd worked hard for them. Yes, time to let go of the past and start a new life.

As she dug the winter's dirt out of the corners of the tiny panes, some unusual movement outside caught her eye. A man was weaving down the road from the west. As she watched, he fell, then slowly raised himself and continued his staggering progress.

A drunk. Should she call the men? No, no need. He would keep on to wherever he was going or he'd have stopped at the McDougalls. There was no danger. As he came closer, she stopped her work, the washcloth against the pane, her heart thumping painfully. Was it? It couldn't be. It must be a trick of the wavy glass. She crossed the room and stepped out onto the stoop for a clearer look. The set of his shoulders was familiar. The man staggered across the bridge and fell again. This time he lay where he fell, face down in the dirt. She dropped the washcloth, hitched her skirts up to her knees and ran.

Katy turned from the clothesline and called, "Where are you going, Ma?"

She didn't answer but raced onto the road. Seeing her destination, Katy shouted, "There's a man lying in the road by the bridge." She dashed after her mother, followed by Annie and Benjy.

They reached the bundle of rags together. Phoebe stared for a moment at the long matted hair covering the man's shoulders and an equally matted beard showing on each side of the down-turned face.

One arm was crumpled under him. The other hand, which still clasped the tree branch he'd been using as a cane, was coated with ground-in dirt and cracked at the knuckles. Was it? She was afraid to look.

Benjy turned the stranger over onto his back. Phoebe gasped and reached out to Annie to steady herself. She must not faint, she must not.

"It's Vati, it's Vati," screamed Annie, throwing herself on him. Phoebe, losing her balance, sank down beside her.

Jake. He was home. He wasn't dead. Taking a deep breath, she got to her feet again. "Come. Help me."

They half carried half dragged him to the house and laid him on the settle in the parlor. She put a pillow under his head, tears so obscuring her sight she could hardly tell where to place it.

Annie knelt on the floor, holding his hand as though she would never let it go. Katy hung back, as if unsure about this shaggy being.

She wrinkled her nose "He smells bad."

"He can't help it," said Phoebe.

Benjy rushed out, shouting, "I'll tell Danny and Uncle Peter."

Phoebe knelt beside Annie. "Oh, Jake, you did come home to us. Wake up, Jake. You are home, now." She kissed his eyelids and the tip of his nose, the only skin free of hair. Her fastidious Jake. Never had he missed his Saturday night bath but it looked like he hadn't had one in a long, long time.

At her touch, his eyes opened, then widened. "Phee-e-e," on a long sigh. "I'm home," he said. "I'm home," smiled, and closed his eyes again.

As she knelt there, her arm across his chest, her cheek against his, Peter and Danny hurried in.

Peter said, "Benjy said Jake's come home."

He stared at the bundle of rags, then at Phoebe. She saw his conflict plain on his face, joy that his brother was alive, grief that his hopes were ended. He started forward, then turned and rushed out the door.

Danny leaned over the back of the settle. "Is he dead?" It was more a breath than words.

"No," she whispered, touching Jake's cheek.

"Poor Vati." Danny picked up his father's hand. He squeezed it, watching his father's face closely for any response.

Peter came back in as abruptly as he'd left and peered at the sleeping figure, then at her. "Is he all right?"

"I don't know. He spoke to me, then went to sleep—or unconscious." She stroked the matted hair.

"He looks like he's had a terrible time." Peter watched the regular rise and fall of the rags over Jake's chest. "I guess he's just worn out. Let him sleep." He turned away, then back, gave her a mournful look and went out again.

She brushed aside the matted hair and kissed Jake's weathered forehead, then turned to Annie, who stood by, tears still creeping down her cheeks. "Annie. Put some water on to heat. We have to clean him up. I'll get his clothes."

She kissed Jake, and went up to the chest in their bedroom, followed by Katy who obviously didn't like being left alone with that strange, dirty man who was supposed to be her vati. Phoebe lifted out her winter clothes to get at Jake's, stored in the bottom. She'd considered giving them to Peter but had held back and now she knew why.

Holding his old sun-bleached shirt against her breast, she took a deep breath. What if he hadn't come home until after she and Peter were married? She shuddered. What a disaster that would have been. While she sorted through the clothes, she compared the two men. Except for his horses, all Jake's thought had been of her and the children. Would Peter have been so selfless? She closed the chest and gathered up the clothes she'd sorted out. Maybe Jake had awakened.

She came downstairs to the kitchen and tested the water that Annie had put on to heat. Just nicely warm. She ladled some into the washbasin and carried it into the parlor. Generously soaping a scrap of soft, worn linsey, she wiped the grime from Jake's face while Danny looked on. Jake sighed, turning his face into the warm cloth, but didn't waken.

His face clean again, although chapped and sore looking, she said, "Annie, bring some of that goose grease Meg gave us."

When she'd dabbed the oil on the sores, she turned her attention to his beard. It was knotted with dirt and filled with burrs. There was no way it could be cleaned. She got her sewing scissors and clipped close to the skin. Jake might not like it, he'd always been proud of his luxuriant beard, but there was nothing else to do. Finished, she gave a wry smile. It was an improvement but she certainly couldn't be a barber. Well, when it was washed, it would be easier to neaten it. Even close to the skin it was matted with dirt.

His hair was in the same condition. She lifted a tangled lock and immediately dropped it, horrified.

"What's the matter? What is it?" asked Danny.

She lifted the lock of hair again. "His ear!" gasped Danny. "The top is gone."

Just above the ear there was a hairless groove almost wide enough for her to lay her little finger in. She touched it gingerly. This close he had been to not coming home. What must he have suffered?

Annie, at the kitchen hearth, unaware of her discovery, called, "Benjy, call Peter for dinner. It's almost ready."

Benjy went out but returned almost immediately. "He's gone."

"Gone? Gone where?" asked Phoebe, rocking back on her heels.

"Home, I expect. He just jumped on King and galloped off. He'd want to tell Grossmutti and Grossvati."

"He could have waited for his dinner," said Annie. "He'll be awful hungry before he gets home."

"He was excited and didn't think," said Phoebe, knowing full well that wasn't what had driven him away. Poor Peter. He'd worked so hard for them. She should have sent him home long ago and never have agreed to marry him. Now there was nothing for him but to take care of his parents. She hoped that would be enough.

Jake roused once during her ministrations, smiled slightly, murmured, "Mmmm, that feels good," and lapsed into sleep again.

She didn't want to disturb him further, so when she'd finished cutting the snarled hair on the sides of his head, she sat on her heels, watching him sleep. What terrible things had happened to him? Dear Jake. He'd used the last of his strength to come back to her. Her heart swelled until she could hardly breathe. She leaned forward and kissed the chapped lips. A smile flitted across his face.

He opened his eyes and whispered, "I love you Phee, you know it?"

Sobbing, she threw herself across his chest hugging him fiercely. "And I love you, too. Where have you been, all this time?"

"Something hurt my head there, where we were unloading the wagon. A settler took care of me. A long time. I couldn't walk at first. I came as soon as I could a little."

"I'm so glad you're home. Please God we will never be parted again."

"Yah, so." Jake sighed and lapsed into sleep again.

Out in the pasture, Tom whickered and Tim answered. All was now right in the Jake Stettl world.

CPSIA information can be obtained at www.ICGtesting.com
Printed in the USA
LVOW08s1629250316

480783LV00001B/71/P